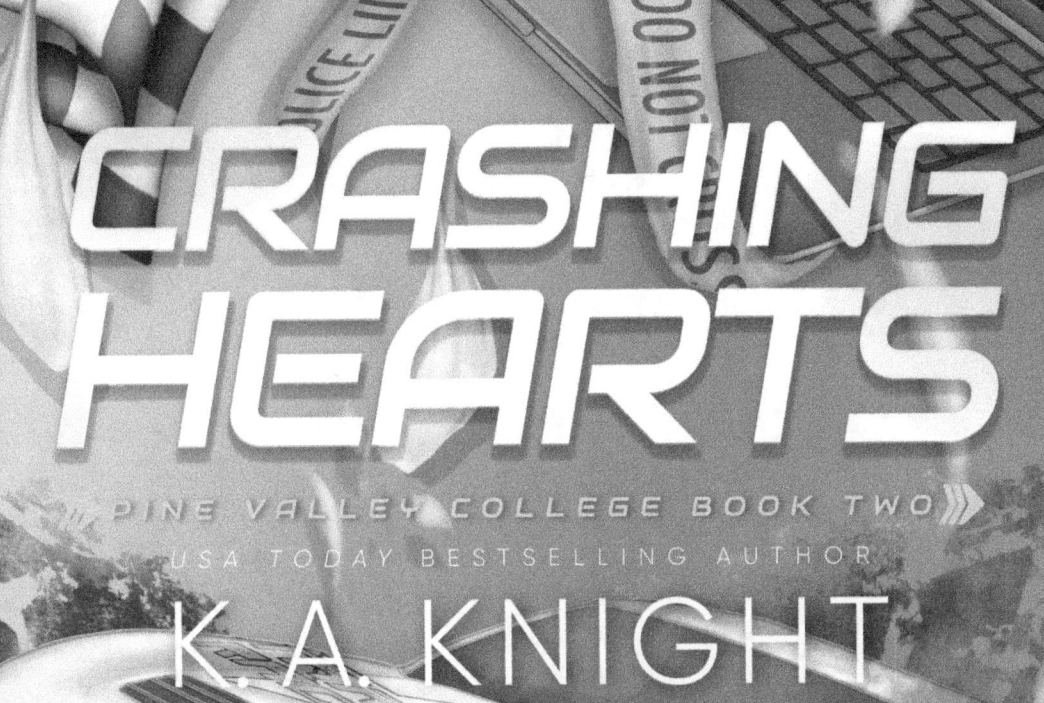

CRASHING HEARTS

PINE VALLEY COLLEGE BOOK TWO

USA TODAY BESTSELLING AUTHOR

K.A. KNIGHT

READER CONSIDERATIONS

This is a dark book not meant for anybody under the ages of 18.
Content includes: explicit sex, explicit violence, stalking, murder,
torture, sexual assault, dubious consent, depression.

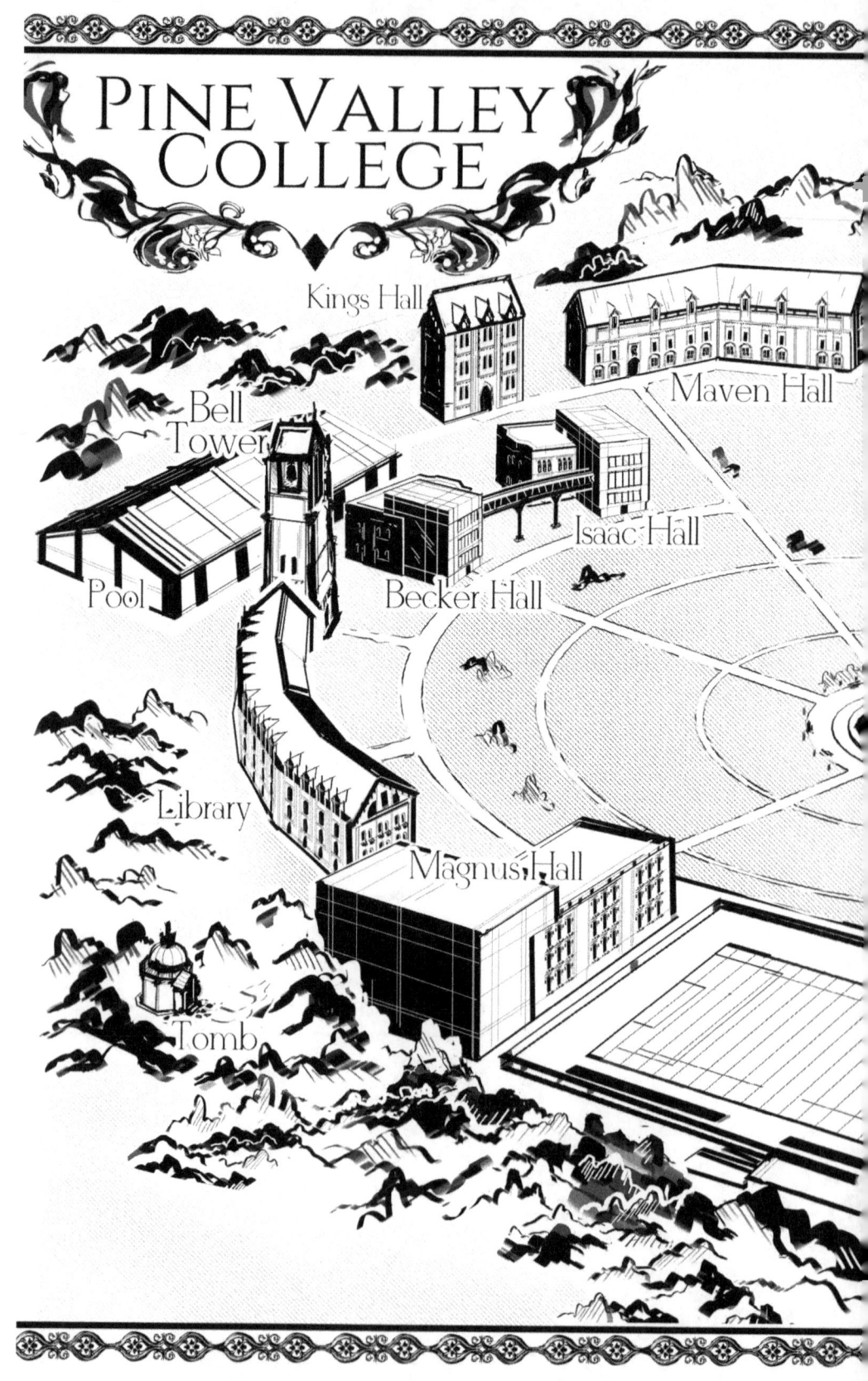

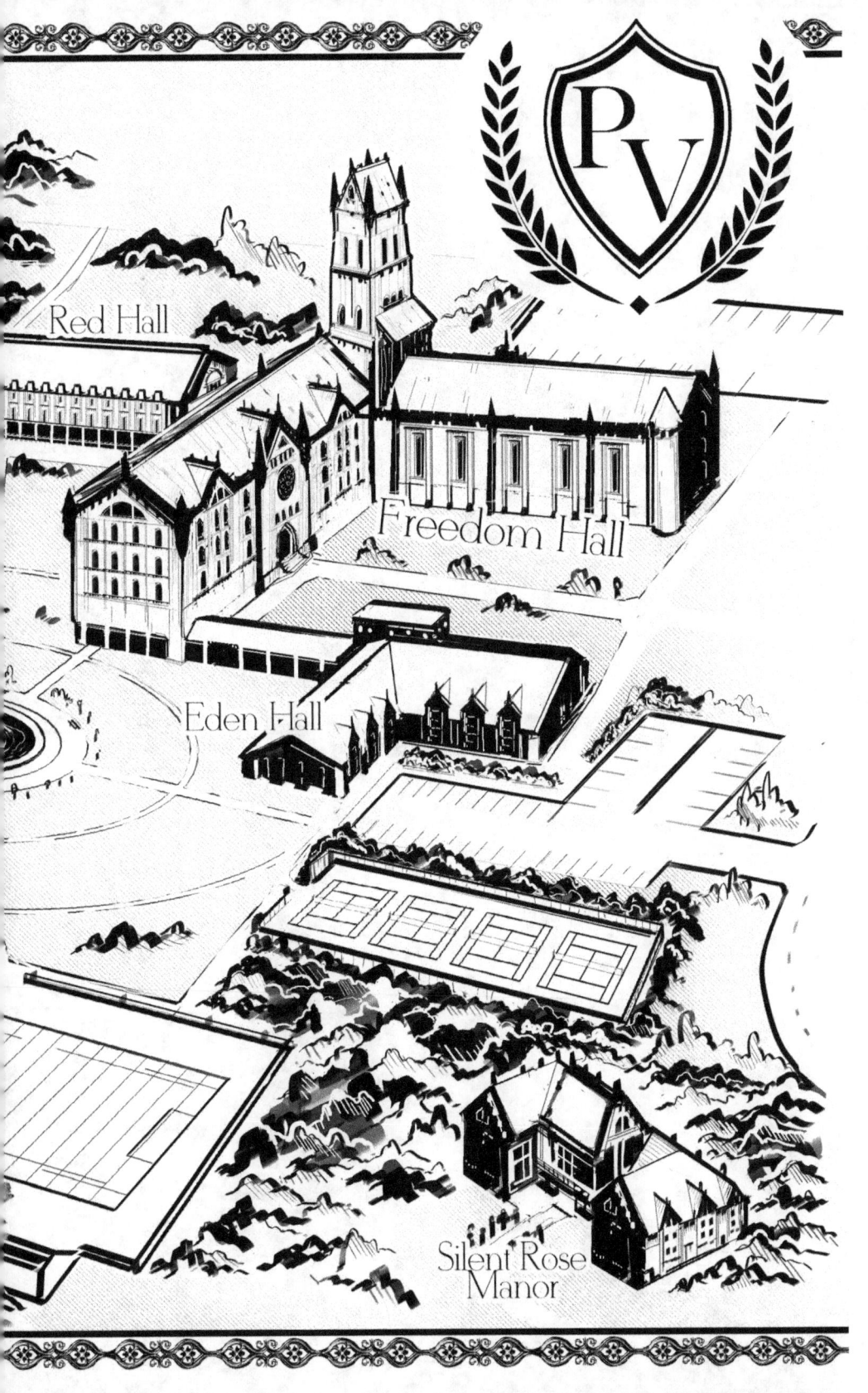

CHAPTER 1
SKYLAR

As I stomp down the steps after an annoyed Bones, I can't help but grin. I pull a pack of cigarettes from my striped racing jacket, then I light one up and blow smoke as he turns. Striding over, he covers the distance between us, and like normal, my heart begins to pound when he's close. He's just a few inches below my six-foot-five frame and covered head to toe in tattoos. Ink crawls across his exposed hands and neck, and I ache to move closer and explore them. His bright amber eyes narrow on mine and his cheeks tighten. I know he hides two dimples there, and they drive me crazy. The sides of his hair were recently faded, giving him a dangerous look while also showcasing the ink there, with the rest of his brown hair swept artfully back. Bones is a fucking masterpiece, and he knows it. He carries himself with power, his cold expression warning everyone away. It's not my fault that turns me on rather than scares me like he wants.

Grabbing the cig I'm holding, he slams it to the ground and grinds it under his expensive leather shoes, all while glaring at me. "You have some damsel in distress syndrome in a delinquent body. Stop getting arrested," he warns me, pointing an inked finger at me. I have the insane urge to lean forward and suck it, but he would probably punch me.

I'd like it, but I don't think he would.

I lean in and drop my voice, watching his eyes narrow further. I can never quite tell if he hates me or wants me, but I don't think he even knows. "Why? It's the only time I see you."

He pushes me back, annoyance contorting his usually calm face. Maybe that's why I do it. I love riling him up and cracking his careful control.

"I won't show up next time," he says as he turns and starts to walk away.

"Yes, you will!" I call, both of us knowing he's a liar. He might not want to see me, but Bones won't ever let anyone down, and he's friends with both Alek and Evan, so he won't let me rot inside. He'll come and get me out, which is why I keep getting arrested.

Hell, maybe he really does like me.

I can live in that delusion.

He flips me off over his shoulder, his perfectly manicured nails glistening in the light. I still don't know how he's going to be a lawyer. He's a walking conundrum, one I want to pick apart and understand.

He's different and exciting, and I want him.

Despite his insistence and ability to avoid me, since we saw each other last at Alek's, I haven't given up. I know what I want, and it's him for a night or two.

Bones will be mine.

I'm going to unravel his careful control and reveal the animal that lives underneath.

I watch him walk away, my smirk only growing. He will be my boy—he just doesn't know it yet.

My phone rings, and I glance down. "Sanjay," I greet even as my eyes find Bones again, tracking his movements like the predator I am.

"Yo, are you coming for a drink?"

"Yeah, I'll be there in ten." I turn away from Bones's retreating form and head toward where I'm needed and wanted.

"I'm just so bored," I complain for the hundredth time to Sanjay and the people around us. They aren't exactly on the right side of the law, which is ironic since I'm still thinking of that lawyer boy. Dim lights flash around us, and the music is fast and thumping. Everybody is partying like dawn will never come. "I've raced everybody on the streets. It's not even a challenge anymore. There's nothing else for me to do except—"

"Drink." Sanjay smirks. "And drink you have been."

He isn't wrong. I've been out every night. Alek said I'm wasting my life, even though he seemed worried. I told him not to be. I'm just enjoying my youth, something he should understand. Hell, we almost died a few months ago, so I think I'm allowed to spend some time celebrating being alive, right?

I stare down at my empty glass and wonder what the fuck I'm doing.

"Another?" a husky voice whispers in my ear. I barely remember his name, and I'll forget his face tomorrow.

He's not the one I want, but he'll do for tonight. I force my head up and see a flirty smile on his face, but I feel exhausted.

"Sure thing." I hand over my glass and let him ply me with alcohol until I'm numb and don't feel dread and hopelessness.

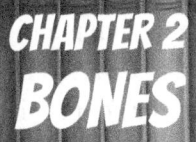

CHAPTER 2
BONES

My professor drones on, and I know I should be listening because this three-hour lecture is important. Everyone around me is busy taking notes, preparing for the quiz at the end of the week, but me?

I'm staring at my phone, fighting my irritation as I stare at Skylar Warren's smirking face on my screen. It's my own fault for going to his social media. I don't even know why I did it. Hell, I don't know why I keep bailing him out when he gets into trouble. I'm not even a lawyer yet. To be fair, it's usually a cut-and-dried case of a misdemeanor, so he really doesn't need me, but he uses it as an excuse every time, and every time, I fucking fall for it.

Why?

I tell myself and everyone else it's because I'm friends with Evan and Alek and they would be annoyed if I let their friend suffer. The true reason? I don't have a fucking clue why I can't say no to him.

Skylar is an impatient, crude, rough delinquent bordering on stalking with no hopes or dreams for his future, just his obsession with illegal races.

I can't seem to stop him from invading my life.

Annoyingly, I scroll through his page, looking at photo after photo.

Most are of cars or him with cars. There are some with bikes and a few with him and Alek, where it looks like Alek wants to kill him, and my lips twitch. As soon as I realize that, I slam my phone down on my desk, making the guy next to me jump and stare.

Most people would apologize, but I simply narrow my eyes, and he quickly looks at the front of the room, his face turning red, including his ears.

Why isn't it that easy to get rid of Skylar? Everyone else takes one look at me and runs the opposite way, or they keep me at arm's length. Not him. He is determined to worm his way into my life. Why? It can't be just sex, or I would give in to him in hopes he would leave me the fuck alone. Skylar is like a feral dog with a bone, and if you throw him the barest hint of attention, he will latch on and never let go.

My phone buzzes, and I foolishly pick it up, ignoring the sharp sting of disappointment when I realize it's not that pesky guy.

> Evan: Did you bail Sky out again?

> Evan: You have to stop or he'll never learn.

> Evan: These racer boys are like kids. You have to be firm with them.

>> Bones: Like you are with Alek? I saw you following him around like a puppy this morning after he sulked when you said no.

> Evan: Yes, but I'm firm with him elsewhere ;)

> Evan: Maybe that's it! You need to fuck the brat out of him, and then he'll leave you alone.

Desire hammers through me, and an image slides through my head before I push it away.

>> Bones: Please stop using the words "fuck" and "brat" in the same sentence as his name.

> Evan: Why? You like it.

I hate that he knows that. Evan really does see too much. I'd hate him if I could, but his bright personality makes it impossible. He has this aura around him that drags people close without realizing it. It's probably why he got that big, grumpy bastard to fall in love with him. It's easy for Evan. Everyone loves him; even Sky dotes on him. Me? I'm used to being hated and feared, but I like it. It keeps people at a safe distance so I won't get hurt again.

Evan: I'm right, aren't I? Do you like Skylar?

Bones: Don't even joke like that. He's a petulant, annoying child I seem to have adopted because of you and your boyfriend.

Evan: Want me to get Alek to kick his ass? I would offer, but it's hotter watching him do it.

Bones: You two are like humping bunnies, you know that, right?

Evan: Very true, but can you blame me? He's so pretty.

I switch over to another chat as a message comes through.

Alek: Did you bail Sky out again?

I roll my eyes with a deep sigh. These two are so in sync, it's unreal, but the difference between Alek and Evan is very obvious.

Bones: Unfortunately.

Alek: Okay. Don't next time.

That's it, nothing else. How does a guy like Evan match with a guy like this? I don't know, but they work.

Putting down my phone and ignoring the notifications, I focus on my laptop in front of me and the blank document. Instead of taking notes, I list reasons to stay away from Skylar Warren.

He's annoying.
He doesn't take no for an answer.
He is a bit of a slut.
He's clearly into illegal shit that won't do well for me in the future.
He doesn't take anything seriously.
He's dangerous and crazy.
As I continue listing reasons, I keep coming back to one fact . . . .
Why can't I stop thinking about him?
My groan is loud as I let my head smash into the desk. I feel every eye turn to me, but I ignore them like I wish I could ignore him.

CHAPTER 3
SKYLAR

The constant buzzing of my phone wakes me up. I reach out and smack around to find it, finally connecting with the metal device. I lift it and answer without looking as someone sighs and drapes themselves over my back.

"Skylar?" Alek's deep voice asks. He's way too loud this early . . . or late. Either way, I'm too hungover for it right now.

Shit, am I in trouble again?

"I didn't vomit in your bushes. That was Evan." It's a safe bet. When I open my eyes, though, I realize I'm not at their place like normal when I crash. I'm in a hotel room, an upscale one at that. The blinds are open, showing Pine Valley's skyline beyond, the bed I'm lying across has silk sheets, and there's a desk and a table somewhere off to my left.

The person whose warmth is draped over my back groans, burying their face into my skin, and I glance over my shoulder to see a blond head. His bare back and ass are on full display. It's a nice ass. No wonder I took him to a hotel.

"Are you hungover? Never mind. I have an opportunity for you. Starfire needs a racer. Do you want in?" I blink a few times to clear the post-alcohol fog and nausea rolling through my sticky and overheated

9

body. His words try to pierce through it all, but they feel jumbled and wrong, and when they finally click, my mouth hangs open.

Alek works for Team Starfire. Is this for real?

Is he offering me a job? He knows how badly I wanted to race for them before, but I knew I wasn't good enough. Who would take a street racer like me? They want actual professionals. They want champions . . . .

"Are you fucking with me?" I finally ask, trying to quash the hope in my chest as I sit up, ignoring the whine from the guy next to me who rolls over and promptly goes back to sleep.

"Nope. You get one shot. Don't fuck it up. Give it your all and be here tomorrow."

The phone goes dead, and I tug it away from my ear, staring at it in shock.

He's not fucking with me. Even Alek isn't that cruel, which means... I have a chance to be an actual racer like I've always wanted. Wasn't I just saying how everything felt boring and predictable?

Starfire is anything but that.

It's my chance to get off the streets.

A text comes through, and I huddle around my phone like it's the Holy Grail.

> Alek: Tomorrow, 10 AM. Don't be late or hungover. You know the address.

I gawk at the text when another comes through.

> Alek: You've got this, Sky. Show them what us street racers are made of.

Hope and excitement bloom in my chest, and I scramble from the bed before wincing. My back is cut up to shit. I glance over my shoulder and spare the guy in the bed a look, debating waking the hellcat for round two. It was obviously fun, but I have more important things now. As quickly as I can, I locate my clothes, all but my boxers, which I leave behind. After scribbling a note, I prop the card on the desk.

Room is paid for. Thanks for a good night—S

I hightail it out of there, stopping at reception to take care of the bill, and then I'm in my car, shooting into the city before my companion even wakes. There's a wide grin on my lips, and all signs of my hangover are gone, replaced by the adrenaline of what I know is coming—the excitement of the race.

There is only one person I want to tell, but I resist. He probably won't care. Hell, I don't even know why I want to tell him so badly. Aren't I just playing with him and having fun to occupy my time?

Why is he the first person I think of after getting this news?

CHAPTER 4
BONES

I rub the towel along my face and neck, then let it hang over my shoulders as I arch my brow at Alek and Evan. They turned up halfway through self-defense class, and now that everyone is gone, they stand before me, holding hands and looking way too loved up.

It almost makes me sick.

"What?" I snap.

"Someone is grumpy today." Alek grins. "Can't we see our friend?"

"You're weird when you're in love," I retort. "I think the cool distance we had was great."

Evan rolls his eyes. "What dumbass here is trying to ask is, do you want to come out for some food?"

"With whom and why?" I ask, smelling a trap but not sure why.

"Just us." Evan shrugs, seeming to deflate a bit. "Lally is busy all the time, and so are Alice and Tommy—" He stops, forcing himself to brighten up. "No Skylar, I promise. He's busy anyway."

"So I'm your last resort?" I arch a brow and hold back from voicing the question I want to ask: why is he busy?

I don't want them to think I care. They seem to be team Skylar and keep pushing us together.

"You're our friend." Evan sighs. "Please? Don't leave me with grumpy all night."

Alek frowns and looks at me. "And he's less grumpy? He's a total prick."

He isn't wrong. I really am. There's a good reason for that, but Evan never cared, nor did Alek. They don't care how much I push them away. They just keep coming back. They forced themselves into my life and became my friends. It's times like this when I wonder why they show up time and time again, but I find myself nodding.

"Okay, but you're paying."

"Awesome!" Evan slings his arm around me before wrinkling his nose and stepping back. "You need to shower first. You're all sweaty."

"You don't complain when I'm all sweaty." Alek smirks, looking him over.

I roll my eyes. "None of this flirty shit all night or I'll leave," I warn as I head to the showers.

"Why couldn't Skylar come?" I finally ask. There, I held off for two hours while we ate and drank. It shouldn't cause any suspicion, and it's not like I care. I'm just curious.

Evan snorts and hands some bills to Alek, making me frown. "We bet on how long you would resist asking." My nostrils flare and I go to stand, but he leans in like he's sharing gossip with me. "He started a new job."

"I was not aware Skylar had any prospects or dreams other than being a delinquent," I remark as I sip my beer, frowning at the cheap taste.

Alek snorts out a laugh as Evan sighs. "Nah, he just acts that way," Alek says. "He's wanted to be a professional racer since he was a kid, but he grew up poor, so he started street racing to earn money so he didn't live on the streets. It's how we became friends. A job came up at my garage and they wanted him. He's really excited." He eyes me. "Be nice about it. Sky acts all tough, but he's been down lately, and this is good for him."

That's also news to me, and I digest it. Skylar has been in more trouble than normal recently. Is it an act, or is he looking for attention? I never knew he grew up so poor, and it makes more sense considering his behavior. I guess I just assumed he was the spoiled, racing playboy I see everywhere—always drunk and fucking around.

I act like I don't care, leaning back with my beer dangling from my fingers. "At least it means he will be out of my hair."

"You're prickly when it comes to him." Alek sips his beer, one arm slung possessively over Evan's shoulders. Evan's hand is on his thigh for everyone to see. As if anyone needed more signs that they were both off-limits. They practically have "married" written across their foreheads.

I shrug. "He annoys me."

Evan grins like he knows something I don't. "I think it's good for him. He'll be great at it. I saw him race, and no offense, baby, but he might even be better than you."

Alek's eyes narrow in defiance, and I smirk, but Evan ignores him. He's the only person who could ever get away with saying shit like that to Alek. The boy has him on a leash and he knows it. "I guess he will be busy now."

A stab of sadness fills me.

He won't bother me anymore, so it means I won't have to spend all my time at the police station. I'm impressed that he's finally taking life seriously. It's clear he has too much potential to waste it the way he does. I saw the intelligence in his eyes the night of the attack. He's smart; he just masks it behind arrogance and playboy flare.

"Why do you look sad?" Evan grins evilly as he sits back. "Do you want to know something, Bones? The harder you hate someone, the harder you fall." He glances at Alek. "Trust me. Hate is awfully close to love."

I snort. "You're both insane. The day I love Skylar Warren is the day when hell freezes over." Leaning in, I point at them. "I will never care for that stupid boy."

The grins they wear tell me what they think about that.

They think I'm a liar.

The worst part is that I think I'm a liar as well.

Later that night, I stare out at Pine Valley's skyline from my penthouse. My hand is wrapped around a crystal tumbler holding aged whiskey imported from the UK. The wind whips around me, cooling me, but I refuse to head inside. I lean onto the glass barrier and peer down at the city spread below me. My mind wanders, and I wonder where he is.

Skylar . . . I shouldn't, but I'm curious.

I can count on one hand how many things I know about him. He likes to race and watch horror movies, he's sarcastic and impulsive, and apparently, he grew up poor. That's it. That's all I know. He's no closer to me than anyone else, yet here I am, thinking of him. It has to be because of Alek's and Evan's teasing.

They are wrong, though. I will never fall for him or anyone.

I won't let anyone close, not again. I can't, not with my past still hanging over my head, and Skylar would be trouble with a capital T. No, it's better this way.

I need my solitude.

It's safe, which is what I need for now.

Turning around, I down my drink and head back inside the modern penthouse my father funded. It's another form of his control, and I allow it for now so I can get what I want. After all, he taught me to play the game and play it well.

Once I learn the truth, I can finally be free of this fucking agony.

My mother once told me I was too much like my father, and maybe she's right. Walking through my bedroom, I head toward the bathroom, and with a press of a button, low lighting flickers on and the walk-in shower turns on. Dropping the glass to the counter, I step into the cubicle and tip my head back, letting the burning water chase away my past until I feel nothing.

A smirking smile pops into my head—his smile, daring me to love him.

Doesn't he know I'm not capable of that?

Not anymore.

There is nothing left of me to give to another.

CHAPTER 5
SKYLAR

I'm early for once, and I see Alek's shock as he pulls up, coffee in hand. I push from my car and head his way, plucking the cup from his grip and sipping it. "Thanks, bro."

He frowns. "Evan made that for me."

"For me? Such a sweetheart on my first day." I grin, slinging my arm around him. "Come on, show the new kid around."

He grabs his bag, hauls it over his shoulder, and pushes me away. "He did make you lunch," he admits as he digs out a box with a Post-it note on top.

I flip it up and smirk.

GOOD LUCK, SKY.
EVAN <3

"Are you sure your boy doesn't want me?" I wiggle my brows then dodge the fist heading for me with a laugh and back away. "Just joking. Don't worry, I have a victim in mind."

"I know." He smirks, pulling off his shades as he stretches. "I saw your boy last night."

I perk up. "Bones? Was he missing me?"

"Not even a little." He grins, running his eyes down my form as I slump. "But you're getting to him. You get under his skin."

"I knew it." I bounce at his side as we head to the garage. "He'll be mine. I'm like a virus you can't get rid of."

"How attractive. I'd bet a month's wage it would be sexually transmitted," he deadpans.

"Alek, it still freaks me out when you make jokes," I tease as I stop at the entrance of the garage, peering around in awe. I try to hide my excitement, but when my eyes land on Alek, he's smiling.

"Welcome to Starfire"—he sweeps his hand out—"your new home. Come on, let's go meet Noah."

I nod, craning my neck to look around as we walk. I try to appear cool and mysterious, but it's impossible. I've been dreaming of racing for a garage like this since I was old enough to know what a car was. Now is my chance, my opportunity, and with Alek as my mechanic, nobody stands a chance. I'm going to be the best fucking racer they have ever seen.

"It's nice to finally meet you." Noah holds out his hand, and I shake it as he gestures for me to sit. "Alek has told me a lot about you."

"Only terrible things, I hope," I joke before I realize what I'm doing.

His eyebrow rises as he laughs. "Good to know you have a sense of humor. You'll need it."

Alek leaves us, and I sit. He observes me. I know he needs me, and I try not to act too eager. I don't want to come off as green, even if I am.

"You're a street racer, right?" I nod, and he grins. "Good, at least you know the basics. It's no less cutthroat here, but there are different rules. First, no more street racing. If you get arrested, we'll drop you. Got it?"

I swallow but nod. I can handle it.

"You don't party nights before races, and you will meet the minimum hours for practice and exercise—I will check. You will study the cars in your free time, and you will be signed into promotional contracts you must commit to. No fighting other racers and nothing illegal. Got it?"

"Got it." I knew this was coming. Looks like I'll have to settle down.

"Don't worry, you can still have fun. I'm not a total asshole. Party, fuck, do whatever you want, just don't get caught." He smirks. "We're a team here, a family, and we have each other's backs, but you racers are our heart. Don't let us down. If one of us fails, we all fail."

Panic winds through me as I begin to feel the pressure. I just wanted to race. I never considered how it would work within a team. I'm not really a team player, but I'm going to have to be.

"Look . . ." He spreads his hands. "We are going to get on just fine, Skylar. You're an extroverted attention whore who craves the adrenaline of racing. You only feel alive there, right? It's your home and the reason you do everything. You struggle to maintain relationships, and you probably have family issues." I gape, and he grins. "I know because I was a racer. We all have our own issues. I'm a narcissistic perfectionist still chasing a trophy I never got to win due to the accident I had. What do you think? Can we work?"

"We can," I murmur, hating how quickly he understood me.

"Don't worry, I'm just good at reading people." He winks. "You're not that obvious. Come on, I'll introduce you to Mackie, who will be your racing partner, and the rest of the team. We are throwing you in the deep end with the first qualifying race next week, so until then, you'll live, eat, sleep, and breathe racing here to get you prepared."

"I can do that." I look at him before we leave the office. "Noah, thank you for taking a chance on me. I know there were plenty of others who wanted this spot, so why me? I'm a street kid, a nobody."

"A nobody who loves racing just as much as we do. It doesn't matter where you came from, Skylar. It matters where you're going." Slinging his arm around me, he steers me from his office. "Like I said, family, and family always has your back." He whistles, and the sounds of the garage quiet down. "Guys, come meet our new racer, Skylar Warren. You better remember his name because he's going to be a champion."

Noah wasn't kidding. I have already been measured for suits and helmets, given a locker, had my picture taken for promos and websites, and signed more contracts than I can even count, and I haven't even seen my car yet.

It's obvious they are all ramping up for qualifications, and they expect me to catch up. Luckily for them, I can.

I finally escape and wander the garage, and Mackie steps into my path. I met him briefly earlier, but we eye each other now. We will be teammates, working as a unit to dominate the track and earn trophies. It's hard to build that kind of familiarity and bond in just a week, but we need to.

He finally smiles at me. "Want to see your car?"

"Hell yeah." I follow him into one of the bays, and my mouth drops open at the beauty.

"Alek just finished painting it yesterday. It's all yours."

I eye the incredible blue paintwork. He added his own twist, and there's a blue sky over the back half, making me grin. He expects me to stay, and for some reason, that makes me happy. Mackie watches me the whole time, both of us trying to feel each other out. He's younger than I am, but he has a shit ton of experience, just no medals as of yet. He's never been fast enough or had a good enough partner. If he's not careful, it could be his last championship. He needs this win, and I can work with that kind of determination.

I do not like to lose.

I check the engine before climbing in, getting used to the inside and the seat.

He watches me as I sit in it, and I arch my brow. "Problem?"

"Not at all, just wondering if you can hack it," he admits. "I need someone I can rely on, someone who can keep up and get us where we want to go. If you're here to fuck around, leave now because that championship is ours. So, are you going to help us get there or not?"

Sliding from the driver's seat, I stand toe to toe with him. "Help? I'll win it for us."

The smile he gives me makes my own grow. "Good, then let's see what you've got." He steps back with a grin. "Guys, we're heading to practice. Get the gear and cars ready."

The whole garage is out here waiting. It's evident they want to see what the new racer can do, but it won't be a wasted show. I'll be the best they've ever seen.

I borrowed a suit for now. They weren't joking about rules—we have to suit up every time. It's a little snug, but I make it work. My helmet is waiting on the roof with my gloves.

"Think you can keep up, pretty boy?" Mackie teases as he reaches my side. I almost snort, since he's probably the prettiest man I have ever seen in my life. He's not my type, that's for sure, but even I can appreciate his looks. After sliding his gloves on with practiced ease, he arches a brow at me.

Leaning into my car, I smirk at him. "Keep up? The only thing you'll see are my taillights."

He laughs, knocking my helmet as he heads to his own car. "Then show us what you've got, newbie."

I struggle into my gloves, and Alek walks my way, helping me into my helmet.

"Show them what street racers are capable of." He pats my shoulder and steps back. "And do not crash my car."

"Alright, boys!" Noah calls. "Five laps. Fastest time wins, loser buys dinner. Give it your all. We can work on your team the rest of the week. Today, show each other what you've got, then we can focus on weaknesses."

Nodding in understanding, I climb into the car and fasten my belts. I grip the wheel and slide my hands along it.

Mackie pulls up alongside me, tapping his window as I nod. Glancing back at the track I have seen a million times, I take a deep breath. My heart begins to race as the usual adrenaline before a race fills me.

This time, though, there is a lot more depending on it. When I lose on the streets, I lose some cash, but here, I'll lose my chance. I'm good under pressure. If I didn't win, I went hungry. I always win.

I'm not about to start losing now.

The flag drops, and we take off at the same time, speeding down the stretch, but at the first corner, I'm slower and he's not. He swings in front, his taillights ahead of me.

It's different than what I'm used to. The helmet is getting in my way and the gloves are slowing my movements, and it's the only reason Mackie slips past, but I'm a hunter. I follow behind him, watching his moves and learning them, and then I perfect them, using them against him.

I tail him for the first lap, making it look like I'm simply fumbling, but on the second stretch, I swing from behind at the first corner, overtaking him like he did me, and then I accelerate, moving faster around the S-bend until I shoot out onto the stretch. He's farther back in my mirror, and I smirk, but I don't let up. I put as much distance between us as I can, but during the third lap, he starts to catch up. I block him every time he tries to make his move, and when we pull over the line on the final lap, he's behind me.

Climbing from the car, I tug off my helmet and grin as Alek gives me a proud smirk. Noah whoops as the mechanics clap, and I grin, but when a door slams, I turn to see Mackie.

I expect his annoyance as he heads my way, since it was a dirty trick, but he grins and lifts his fist, and I bump it with mine. "The championship is ours if you race like that, killer."

"Then let's get that trophy," I murmur.

CHAPTER 6
SKYLAR

I spend days racing like my life depends on it. Noah breaks us down inch by inch, showcasing our weaknesses to each other so we can build around them to create an impenetrable barrier. It's the way to win this, and we not only spend hours practicing on the track, but also doing teamwork exercises, until we are in sync. I know it will take a while to get even closer, but we are doing well. Even Noah thinks so. Both of us know what is at stake, and that creates a bond, a partnership, we agree can work. We are brothers now, united by the dial and squeal of tires.

When Noah lets us out early, there is only one place I head. I haven't seen him in far too long, and I miss that ignorant, handsome face. I park as close to the law building as I can and wait, ignoring the ogling looks I get. I'm only here for one student. I do wink at a few girls passing by, but when I see him, everything else fades.

He has headphones in, his steps measured and hard. There's a whole space around him, everyone avoiding him, and people dive out of his way as he storms across campus.

Fuck, he looks good.

Wearing some loose camel pants and a white sweater, he screams money and elegance. I want to mess him up so badly and see him dirty and bare. His tattoos create a stark difference, a walking cliché, and I love it.

He's so focused, he doesn't see me, so I push away from my car and drop into step next to him. That doesn't even get his attention, so I pluck an earbud from his ear, shoving it into mine. I don't know what I expected, screaming rock music maybe, but my eyebrows rise at the piano piece before it's abruptly ripped from my ear. He stops before me, and I grin, stopping too. Both of us block the path and create a show as people look between us, but I don't care.

All I care about are his dark eyes that slice me to pieces, not finding me good enough. His lip curls in derision. "What? No cuffs today?" he jokes.

"Nah, they are in my car in case you feel like having some fun." I shove my hands into my racing jacket, since I didn't bother changing before I came straight here. Technically, I'm supposed to be resting, but I had to see him. Something about him riles me up but also calms me down at the same time. I don't know what it is or how to explain it.

Bones is not a nice person, but I like that he doesn't hide it. There's a tranquility in his dark eyes I crave.

He doesn't speak again, so I lean in and he leans back, grinding his jaw, but I don't stop until he's almost bent backwards. When he begins to fall to avoid me, I slip my hand over the base of his spine under his raised sweater, feeling the soft, warm skin there. I pull him close until he is pressed against me. "Did you miss me?" I murmur, my eyes dropping to his lips. I wonder what they would taste like.

He wrenches himself from my grip, putting space between us. "Like stepping in dog shit."

"I'll take it."

He snorts and starts to walk away, so I fall into place next to him.

"I think you did, and that's why I came."

He ignores me, so I roll my eyes and move closer so we are practically walking on top of one another.

"Where are you going?" I keep talking, wanting to hear his deep voice.

"Why are you stalking me?" he retorts.

"Haven't I made that obvious, beautiful?" He glares at me, and I smirk at having his eyes back on me. "I missed you, in case you were wondering."

"I wasn't," he snaps. "I'm busy with class. Go away."

"I'll walk you to it. I've always wanted to walk the hottest guy to class and steal a kiss." I grin.

"If you try to kiss me, I will have you flat on your back in a second," he warns.

"Jesus, baby, I didn't know you liked to get that rough. You want me on my back?" I step in front of him, walking backwards so he has to stare at me. "You just have to ask. My car is right over there."

"Skylar, go away."

"Not until you admit you missed me."

"No. Leave."

I stop, blocking his path once more. He tries to move left, and I move with him. He goes right, then I go right. He sighs, pinching his nose before staring at me like he's two seconds away from decking me. Shit, I bet he would look so hot hitting me. I'd even fucking thank him.

"Say it, say you missed me and I'll leave you alone for now, or I can stalk you into class. I bet they won't mind. I'm pretty persuasive. I can flirt with you during your lecture—"

"You wouldn't dare," he hisses.

"Try me," I retort. "You have no idea how far I'll go to get what I want, which is you."

His jaw works, his nostrils flaring as he debates which is the lesser of two evils.

"I have all night, baby," I purr. "Your choice."

"You'll leave?" he asks.

"For today." I grin. "I'm waiting."

"I missed you," he says quietly.

Smirking, I lean in. "I didn't hear that."

"I missed you," he snaps louder.

Cupping my ear, I lean back. "I'm a little deaf from all the engines. What did you say?"

"I missed you!" he yells, and everyone turns to look. His cheeks heat, even as I grin, and he glares and hurries past me. I let him go, knowing when to stop pushing. I just wanted to remind him I was here and I'm not going anywhere. I want him to think about me as much as I think about him. Even if it's in anger, I'll take it.

"Good to know. Want me to wait and take you home later?" I call to his retreating form. He ignores me as I chuckle. "I'll take that as a no." I grin as he walks away, shoving his earbuds back in and flipping me off. "See you later, baby!"

CHAPTER 7
BONES

As if my day wasn't bad enough with five back-to-back lectures, I now have to attend my monthly meal at my father's house. I hate it, and I debate canceling, but I know he will make me pay. Popping some pain relief for the headache I feel brewing, I slide from my car and head up the driveway to the showy mansion.

Townsend is not subtle, not in the least. No, he likes to flaunt his power and wealth and hold it over people, including me. He loves that he has me on a leash like that.

The fucker.

I don't bother knocking. I simply open the front door and storm into his house. I incline my head at the staff, looking for any familiar faces, but as always, they are new—nobody lasts long here. When I was a child, it was to stop me from getting attached after he saw how close I was with the cook. After I left, the turnover rate became higher, since my father is not an easy man to please, so it doesn't surprise me that I don't recognize anyone.

I pass the marble statues and paintings hung proudly in the reception area. This house was always more like a museum—a showcase of his wealth and power. There are pictures with presidents, CEOs, and every powerful man you can think of displayed on these walls, as well as paintings that sell for upwards of millions. It's a collection of wealth without taste.

I hate how cold and empty it feels.

This was never a home, it was simply a house, which makes me even sadder because I realize the one I have now is the same—cold, empty, and a place to rest my head.

Silent Rose became my home, but after everything that happened, even that is changing, and I find myself clinging to the last shred of warmth, needing that support, family, and escape.

I step into the formal dining room, and my shoulders tighten when I realize he is already waiting. He looks impatiently at his watch and then me. He doesn't say it, but it is a silent slap to the face.

I'm late, and he's not happy.

I can practically hear his monologue. *I am a very busy man, son. Do you know how much money I could be making? Instead, I'm here making time for you and you're late.*

Nodding my head in greeting, I slide into the chair at the other end of the long oak dining table. We face each other with at least twelve seats between us on either side. A flower arrangement and candles are perfectly placed in the middle.

The fire roars behind my father, giving him a satanic appearance. The chandelier is turned down low for ambiance, and Mozart, if I'm correct, floats through the room as the curtains flutter in a slight breeze from one of the many windows spanning the right side of the room.

The rug under my feet slides as I tug my chair in, and I take great delight in messing up the perfect room even a little. I sit up tall, stiff, knowing better than to defy him. I used to take great joy in acting out, in snubbing his perfect posture, but it got me nowhere. He would react, but in the end, it didn't change anything, so now I play along for two hours every other week. I am his perfect son so he will leave me alone the rest of the time, and he feels his fatherly obligations are complete.

I do not speak. I know better. One does not speak unless spoken to. You must remain alert, polite, and, better yet, calculating. Every word must be thought through, must have a meaning—an attack and a counterattack.

"How are your grades?" he asks, breaking the standoff.

No hi, how are you, or are you well. He doesn't even ask how I'm feeling after surviving a serial killer.

It shouldn't surprise me, but my shoulders slump slightly. I guess you can take the kid from the house, but you can't take the house from the kid. Somewhere deep down, I still crave my father's love and approval, and I hate that even more. I will never meet his perfect standards because they are impossible, but I still try. He glances at my exposed forearms and the tattoos there, his lips tilting down in disgust, but he has no other outward reaction.

I remember the day I came home with them. He took one look at me and left. He didn't even speak, and we didn't see each other for many months. I thought that would have felt good, but instead it only hurt me knowing he cared so little.

For him, it's all about appearance and structure, and I am a blot on his perfect, impeccable image.

The son he never wanted.

"Good," I say.

"Only good? They should be excellent. Clearly you are not working hard enough. I will contact your professors in regard to extra work you can undertake to improve them."

I know better than to argue, yet I find my mouth opening anyway. "I'm studying more than most, and my grades are the highest in the class—"

"Yet they could be higher. Correct me if I'm wrong." His eyebrow arches, daring me to lie to him. No doubt he has already looked over my last reports and submissions. Hell, he will probably email them back to me with corrections and notes on how to improve.

I never win an argument with him, not once, so why do I keep trying?

"How is work?" I ask instead, offering an olive branch. I don't know why, since there will never be any love between us, but it will hopefully stop him from reprimanding me all night and shift his attention to what he's passionate about.

"Clumsy," he replies as he leans back, no doubt referring to my change of topic, "but effective." There's a gleam of pride in his eyes at that. "We just started working with some big companies. They will be announced soon. I am building this for you—"

I tune out as he rants on about how he's building this empire for me, so we can work side by side, his perfect protégé. He will never give up on it.

I eye the maid nervously waiting for him to finish speaking, and when he does, she scurries forward. "Sir, are you ready for your first course to be served?"

He eyes her distastefully. "Of course, it is already six minutes late."

"You were speaking," I remind him, saving her from his ire. "You taught them it is rude to interrupt, have you not?"

He tilts his head, watching me as he waves his hand, dismissing her. "Your need to save those below you has not been taken away, I see. I thought you would have learned your lesson since your... friends' issues."

"Issues? You mean when we were almost murdered by a serial killer?" I offer coldly.

He curls his lip, hating those crude words. "It is your own fault. You shouldn't have involved yourself with the likes of them."

Oh, of course, because anyone Mr. Declan Townsend has not deemed worthy is not to be trusted nor engaged. He believes friendship and love are weaknesses, and once that rubbed off on me and I believed it too, until that all changed. Now he is gone as well, and I am left alone once more.

"I should have told that to the serial killer," I retort.

"Do not be pedantic, Silas."

"It's Bones," I remind him.

"I named you Silas Townsend. I will not call you some silly nickname," he snaps. "You sound like a thug."

I laugh. "You'd know all about thugs. Aren't you in bed with most of them?"

"That is not funny in the slightest. My company works on many pro bono cases—" I ignore his rant as the maid appears behind him with a plate, hesitating when she realizes he is angry.

"Food is here," I interrupt him, and from the tightening of his lips as he quiets down, I know I will pay for that later.

Another of his rules—you do not interrupt elders.

"Well, serve then," he snaps without looking at her. She hurries forward, terror in her eyes. I don't blame her. My father is a terrifying man. I know the depth of his power and anger, but I don't care anymore. He can't take anything else from me.

I lean forward, my eyes widening in horror as I watch the young maid stumble over the edge of the rug as she tries to balance too many plates, and the one above my father's seat crashes and breaks on the table and floor.

The silence is loud for a moment, nobody daring to speak or move. The young girl looks like she's ready to cry, her eyes wide in horror and fear as my father slides his chair back, looking at the mess in displeasure.

Everybody knows Declan Townsend despises mistakes more than he despises messes. He demands perfection, and as he looks up at her, I see her physically flinch.

"I'm so sorry, sir. I will clean this up right away. I'm so sorry—" She wrings her hands before her in horror, tears leaking from her eyes. All he does is stare, something that has made CEOs weep and flee, so when she starts to tremble, I don't blame her.

Lurching to my feet, I go to intervene when his gaze moves to me. He's about to reprimand me, but his phone rings, breaking the silence. He releases us all from his rage as he picks it up and checks the ID.

As he pushes from the table, he doesn't even spare me a look as he answers the call, talking as he walks away, leaving the mess and me behind, a far too familiar scene. The maid hurries out of the room. Sighing, I throw my napkin down and head to his broken plate. Kneeling, I start to pick up the shards as the maid hurries back, horror in her gaze when she sees me.

"Sir, please allow me!" she begs, dropping to her knees as if she has committed a great crime. She pushes my hands away, her eyes wide and terrified. "Please, if he sees—"

"Let me help," I offer kindly. "I'm sorry for his attitude. You didn't deserve that. It was a mistake."

She ducks her head in shame, her cheeks heating. "I should have been more careful. Please, sir, let me. I will be in more trouble if anyone sees you like this."

Leaning back on my heels, I watch her swiftly clean up the mess, stand, and leave without looking at me again. Fuck this. Where is the humanity? Where is the basic kindness?

I can't even offer a helping hand to the staff. They are so terrified of my father and his precious only son.

I'm left standing in the empty, cold dining room, staring down at the small bleeding cut on my finger from the sharp edge of the plate. It should be bigger, I should be cut to pieces by him, but as usual, those wounds don't show. Instead, I watch the blood roll down my finger and hit his perfect rug before turning away.

He'll be gone all night. Work is more important for him, but at least it frees me.

As I head out the front door, I hear him screaming somewhere deep in the house and shudder, and that is exactly why I will never let another angry male into my life.

My appetite is gone after being around my father, but I know I must eat, so I scarf down some burgers on the way home. Unlocking my front door, I drop my keys into the bowl, not bothering to turn on the lights as I kick off my shoes and pad into the dark, empty apartment. My eyes stick on the photos, the only ones in the entire place, on the side table. There's one of me when I'm younger, without tattoos, and my arms are around the only person in this world I cared about.

I look so young and happy, my smile wide, but as I pick up the frame, I see the light catch on my reflection. Gone is the smile, and now I'm as cold as my father, just like he wanted. Putting it down carefully, I look around my apartment, wondering if this is the life I will always live.

I'm exhausted from being around my father and feeling far too raw. When my phone pings, I rip it from my pocket and frown at the unknown number.

> Unknown: I got your number from Alek. I stole his phone. Hope your class was good.

It pings again.

> Unknown: I'll have a race soon. You should come and watch. I know I'll be much better with you to impress.

> Unknown: You can even take the winner home with you.

> Unknown: That's me, by the way.

> Unknown: It's your Skylar.

I snort, a smile curling my lips even as I shake my head. My shitty night suddenly disappeared. He has this way about him, making me want to laugh even in the shittiest of situations. I mean, he did even that night.

> Bones: I would not, under any circumstances, come and see you race.

He types back quickly, clearly waiting for me to reply.

> Unknown: Name your price. I'll pay it. You want a car? A house? A kiss?

> Bones: How about your silence?

> Unknown: Deal, I'll leave you alone for two days if you come to the race.

> Bones: I was joking, not making a deal.

Unknown: Too late, you should know better as a lawyer. I'll see you there. Alek knows the information. Feel free to wear my name on your shirt. I can always sign it for you later or take it off you. Whichever you want.

Bones: I'm blocking you.

I hesitate when I lock my phone and I don't.
Why? I don't know. Maybe his insanity is rubbing off on me.

CHAPTER 8
SKYLAR

I put my phone away for the trillionth time today, refraining from calling or texting. We made a deal, whether he likes it or not, and I'm beginning to understand Bones enough to know that if he gives his word, then he'll keep it.

I distract myself by practicing. Mackie and I drive all day, working together on tactics and enhancing each other's driving style. Noah is right. We don't have long to prepare for the qualifiers, so we need to be the best we can be.

It's a long day, and I'm exhausted, but after showering and changing into some loose jeans and a tank top, I meet him and the others in the kitchen area. Mackie is sitting alone, pizza and beer spread out before him, and I slump into the chair opposite him.

"For us." He nods at them.

"Thanks." Grabbing a slice, I demolish it in a second and drain my glass before topping it off and grabbing another. The others are on their computers, so we leave them to it as we eat. They are all work and no play, but Alek isn't here, probably at home with his baby. He's religious about getting home before it's late so Evan doesn't have to sleep alone since he has bad dreams. I don't blame him. If I had that to go home to, I would rush home as well.

Biting the pizza, I meet Mackie's eyes as he wipes his mouth. "We should get to know each other better."

"Are you hitting on me?" I tease.

"You wish, pretty boy." He laughs. "You're not my type, trust me." He glances at Noah, and my eyebrows rise. Interesting. I don't call him out though. "I'm just thinking, if we know each other better, it might help us. I really want to win—"

"For you or him?" I ask, glancing at Noah. Mackie's eyes widen in panic, and I laugh. "I don't think anyone else has noticed, don't worry."

He sighs, rubbing his head. "Both. He wants this win so badly, but I also want to win. I'll do whatever it takes, even be friends with your street ass."

I grin and pour him another beer, tapping my glass against his. "To friends then. Ask away."

"Do you have a partner?" he asks, grabbing another slice.

"Not yet." He raises his eyebrows, and I lean in. "I'm wearing this guy down. He doesn't know it yet, but he'll be mine."

"How romantic." He snorts. "Does he even like you?"

"He does. He just doesn't want to admit it." I laugh. "But I don't give up easily. You?"

"No." He glances at Noah again before he takes another drink. "Why do you want to race?"

"I'm good at it," I answer as I sit back. "I used to race to earn money. It was either that or starve." I remember that time in my life before I shake it off with a grin. "I realized I was good at it. I worked hard and became one of the best, and it became my safe place, you know? I was happy there. Untouchable. I felt strong and in control when I never had in any other part of my life. I didn't love it immediately, but now, I couldn't live without it. It's part of who I am. I wake up thinking about when I can race, and I go to sleep thinking about it. It isn't just a hobby or a job for me."

"It's a life. It's passion. It's who you are." Mackie nods. "Me too."

"How did you get into it?" I ask as I grab another slice.

"I watched it all the time growing up, and when I was old enough, I applied here. Noah took me under his wing, seeing something in me. He taught me himself, and now I want to repay him for that." He shrugs.

"Sexually?" I grin.

He spits out the sip he just took, coughing as I laugh. I glance over and notice Noah staring, worry in his gaze as it lingers on Mackie. Interesting.

Patting Mackie's back, I let him cough it out.

"Dude," he grouses when he can breathe.

"Sorry, couldn't resist." I chuckle. "So, do you have any family?"

"Really?" He wipes at his face, still coughing.

"Friends, remember?" I smirk, grabbing another slice and putting it on his plate.

"I have a younger sister. My parents are a couple of hours away, but we're close. You?"

"Not really," I admit, not wanting to go into detail. He must hear something in my voice because he watches me before he nods.

"Favorite drink?" And so it goes. We eat, drink, and talk, and surprisingly we have a lot in common and get along well. I was happy to work with him, since we match on the track, but knowing we can be friends as well leaves me on a high, even as I drive home that night, weary but happy.

Once I'm in bed, my eyes drift to my phone, and I wonder if he misses me. I don't know, but what I told Mackie is true—I won't give up.

Not easily.

I want Bones, and he will be mine. He just doesn't know it yet.

CHAPTER 9
BONES

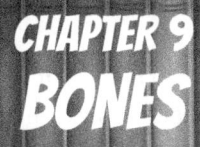

I check my phone once more before slamming it face down on the mat, stretching out my legs. I sip my water as I eye the now empty gym. I just taught two back-to-back classes, and usually I'm exhausted enough to finally sleep without my insomnia getting the better of me, but I haven't been able to for the last two nights.

He hasn't texted me.

He hasn't called.

He hasn't turned up at school.

He hasn't gotten arrested.

Nothing. It's like Skylar simply stopped existing, or worse, gave up on me.

I don't know why it bugs me. I don't even like him. I guess I just got used to his annoying habits—that's all. I changed my life to accommodate him, and it's irritating me. Nothing more. Nothing less.

It also isn't the reason why my hands are bruised from sparring all night or why I went so hard on Alek he walked out, telling me to deal with my shit another way.

Groaning, I roll to my back, my arm over my head.

I don't miss him. I'm just in a bad mood after seeing my father.

"Missing me, beautiful?"

Great, now I'm even imagining his voice—wait.

I drop my arm and sit up, finding a smirking Skylar above me. I didn't even hear him come in, which isn't like me—a testament to how distracted I am.

"What? Quiet for once? That's not like you. Did my stunning appearance render you speechless? I have that effect." He grins, running his eyes over me as I stare in shock. "You look damn good in a gi, baby. I think I might have to take up a new hobby. You can be my teacher. I'll even call you sir."

I stare, and he laughs, his head thrown back. His hair is pushed back from his face and wet, as if he just got out of the shower, and he's wearing nothing but some loose pajama pants and a tight black shirt. He looks fucking good, and I hate it. I hate that I check him out and that I'm curious if he wears this to sleep or not.

Did he come from being with someone?

That only pisses me off further, and I don't know why.

He sticks his hand out, but I smack it away and climb to my feet without his assistance. "Why are you here?" I snap.

"Oh, someone is pissy tonight." He leans in, his eyes sparkling like he knows a secret. "I missed you."

"Sure," I scoff, barging past him and making sure to hit his arm.

I'm surprised when he yanks me back so fast, I don't even have time to react. I hit his solid muscles and freeze as he tightens his arms around me, keeping me pinned against him.

"You know," he murmurs into my ear, "you could just say you missed me." His silky voice wraps around me, hardening my cock as his tongue traces the shell of my ear as I remain silent. "No? Well, I kept away to keep our deal. Two days of silence, but knowing you missed me this much makes me happy. I missed you too, baby."

"I didn't miss you," I snarl, hating the fact that I relax slightly at his confession. I had forgotten about his offhand comment. Clearly, he hadn't. Needing to put space between us, I grab his arm and flip.

He yelps as he flies over me, his back hitting the mat, then he blinks up at me incredulously. "Get out. Go back to whoever or whatever you were doing. I'm busy."

The smirk he aims my way tells me he reads too much into my words, and I turn away, cursing, when his leg hooks around me. I try to recover, but it's too late. I fall back, hitting his body, and he wraps his arms and legs around me from below like a teddy bear. I struggle but it's no use. He's built.

"Let go," I demand, freezing in his arms.

"Not until you admit you missed me," he teases, "and that's why you are in a mood."

"I am not in a mood because I missed you, Skylar," I retort. "I'm in a mood because I am allowed to be. You have no effect on my life at all."

He pulls out his phone and lifts it to show me his screen, where there is a picture of me, my face like thunder as I bark orders. "No? This says differently. Alek texted me, which was a good thing, too, because I was missing your pretty face. I was having to make do with stalking your social media, but it didn't measure up to the real you," he purrs, licking my cheek as I jerk away. "You had two days of peace. Never again, beautiful. It was torture for me."

Freeing myself, I roll us and pin his hands above him, glaring down at him. "My mood has nothing to do with you. I didn't miss you."

"You can pin me like this any time, baby," he flirts, his eyes dropping to my body and the gaping robe, tracing my muscles. I ignore the shiver of heat that shoots through me at his hungry look. "You look good on top of me. You'd look even better riding me."

"Fuck, you're an asshole." I climb off him and step back.

He leans up onto his elbows, looking far too fucking sexy for his own good as he grins at me. "Yes, I am. A deal is a deal though. I stayed away for two days, so you need to come watch me race."

"I never agreed to that." I smirk. "Check your texts. No verbal or written contract was made."

He laughs, his eyes twinkling. "Alright, baby, then let's make a new deal, all verbal and shit so you can't go back on it."

"No." I cross my arms. "Now get out."

"I'm not leaving until we have a deal." He jumps up, and I know he won't. "You're stuck with me, I guess. I'll even follow you home."

Pinching the bridge of my nose, I look at the ceiling for strength when an idea comes to mind. I drop my hand and eye him. "Fine. A deal. First person to pin the other wins. If you win, I'll watch you race. If I win, you'll leave me the hell alone—forever."

"Deal," he responds right away.

I smirk. "Aren't you confident?"

"Baby, I've been dreaming of pinning you down since I met you. I'm not losing." He steps back, tugs his shirt off, and throws it away, distracting me for a moment. "Look all you want. I can wait."

"Let's do this," I snap, stepping onto the mat.

We bow out of respect. When I straighten, I slide my leg back and wait. He seems like the impatient type and too emotional, relying on brute strength, so Skylar will be easy to pin. I have more practice and stamina.

What I didn't take into account was his raw determination.

He feints left and then right, teasing me as he circles me until I grow annoyed and kick my foot out. He skips over it, flipping around me. I manage to right my footing as he kicks my side, and I narrow my gaze.

"I think you missed me a lot, beautiful," he teases as he avoids me, and I step back, calculating my next move. "I think you've thought about me every day, and I bet you even checked your phone a thousand times. Did you dream of me? I bet you did."

My anger takes over and I snap, which I realize is exactly what he wanted. He avoids my clumsy, emotional attack and sweeps out my legs. I land on my back, shocked to my core since no one has ever managed to mat me before, and then he's above me.

He grabs my hands and pins them to the mat above my head, his legs trapping mine. I buck and twist, but he doesn't move. "I win," he murmurs, his gaze dropping to my lips. "Don't feel too bad, baby. There was no way I was going to lose with you on the line. Only an idiot would."

My protests and anger die, my eyes lowering to his lips without meaning to. We are close, and he smells good.

His words trail off as we stare at each other, desire sparking between us, and I lick my lips, drawing his gaze. He groans, following the movement. "Don't tempt me, baby."

"I wasn't," I reply, but my voice is husky and my gaze drops to his plump lips once more, unable to resist.

What would he kiss like?

His head lowers toward me. "Last chance, baby. Move away if you don't want this."

I should push him away, but my eyelids flutter closed and my lips part in anticipation as he lowers his head. I shiver below him and grip his hands, needing to hang on to something.

I wait, anticipation pounding through me along with my heart until he's all I can feel, smell, and taste, but his lips don't touch mine.

I open my eyes in confusion, and he grins like he was waiting for that. "See you at my race, baby," he purrs before kissing my nose and climbing to his feet. He grabs his shirt and disappears as quickly as he came, leaving me flustered and downright pissed.

Fuck!

I cover my face, but my fingers trace over my nose and the warmth from his kiss.

What would it be like to kiss Skylar?

CHAPTER 10
SKYLAR

S lamming my car door shut, I grip the wheel as my chest heaves. The desire I feel is so strong, I'm almost shaking from it.

My hand covers my heart, which is crashing inside my chest, and goose bumps cover my skin, even the slightest brush of air making me shudder. My cock is also hard and uncomfortable in my pants.

I am so turned on, it's not even funny, all from playing with him, wrestling him . . . almost kissing him.

Leaning back with a groan, I wipe my sweaty face with my shirt. My eyes shut as I remember the sight of him below me, the pressure of his hands gripping mine like a lifeline, and the way his lips parted . . .

My fingers drift along my lips, feeling the warmth of his skin. I've kissed a lot of people, but none have affected me like this, and that was only on the nose. What will it be like when I really kiss him?

I think Bones might actually destroy me.

I might act like I'm in control of this game between us, but he has all the power. One word, one look from him and I would be on my knees, begging for more. I can't let him know how easy it would be for him to destroy me.

He drives me fucking crazy.

I stayed away two whole days. It was torture, and now I'm this close to what I want.

I have to stop myself from going back in there, flipping him onto the mat again, and taking what I want. *Patience*, I remind myself. If I rush this, I'll lose him, and I'm playing for keeps, not for a night.

I can't hold back this desire, though, so I shove my pants down, freeing my rock-hard dick.

Gripping my length in my fist, I stroke myself with hard, rough movements, imagining his tattooed knuckles wrapped around me.

Pressing my face into my shirt to muffle my moans, I thrust into my hand, which is practically his since he held it. My eyes are squeezed tightly shut as I remember the hard play of his muscles below me and how the gi parted to tease me with glimpses of toned, tattooed skin.

I bellow into my shirt as hot ropes of cum pour from me, my orgasm ripping through my body. I'm panting and shaking as I slump back into my seat, all my energy depleted.

Despite my release, red-hot desire still rolls through me, hardening me once more. Turning my head, I pick up my phone and open the call list. I could call any of them and fuck them all night to relieve this pressure, but there is just one thing—they aren't Bones.

They won't satisfy me, and it will be like fucking a cheap imitation of him.

Dropping my phone, I look back at the gym for a moment before I fasten my pants and turn on my engine.

No, I'm not fucking around anymore. I'm saving myself for him— the one I really want.

It doesn't take me too long to get home, and I pull my car into the underground parking garage. My bike is next to it, and my second car is on the other side. Alek said both were a waste of money, but he's one to talk because his Skyline is his baby.

That's what we have in common, our love for engines.

Besides, I have the money. I came from nothing, and I know hunger more than I know the feeling of being full, so when I actually started to have money, I treated it like gold and barely spent it, knowing how quickly everything could change. Eventually, that edge of panic lessened, and I started to spend it like it was nothing, high on the feeling of it. Maybe I went overboard, but I can afford it, and I deserve it after everything I've endured to get here.

The beep as my car locks follows me as I stroll through the well-lit garage to the private underground elevator. This one is closest to my spaces and only goes up to my floor. It might seem extreme, but what can I say? I like to play.

I scan my keycard and shoot up so fast, my ears pop. I have to scan my key again, and the doors open right into my apartment. Stepping out onto the wood floor, I drop my shirt near the door before kicking off my shoes and putting them away. I hang my keys up on the board and pass the burning fire. The city is spread out to my left, the floor-to-ceiling two-story windows letting in light. There is a seating area to the left and a dining table to my right, but in the center is my pride and joy.

My original 1956 Aston Martin DBR1 is on a podium. It was a bastard to get up here, but it looks damn good in my living room. Smirking, I imagine all the ways I could bend Bones over it before I have to rearrange my cock and head through the open doorway to the kitchen. I grab a cold water and down it as I move up the wooden, winding staircase to the second story.

There are five bedrooms up here. I turned one into a game room, another into a cinema, and then two spare rooms and my room. I head to the open door at the end, past the en suite with a steam room and sauna, and stand before the city view, sipping my water.

I should shower and head to bed. I need to be up early for work, but I stare outside, wondering where he is.

I know I won't settle down until I know he got home okay, so I give in to my needs and pull out my phone.

> Skylar: You can't get out of our deal now, beautiful.

He doesn't reply, and I glance from my phone to the city before thumbing out another message.

Skylar: Did you get home okay?

He doesn't reply immediately, and I toss my phone to my custom-sized bed before stripping and hitting the button for the shower. I hurry through it, and with my towel wrapped around my waist, I grab my phone again. There are a million other texts, but not from the person I want.

Skylar: I will just keep annoying you until you reply. Did you get home okay?

Skylar: I can do this all night, baby.

Bones: FFS.

Bones: Yes. I'm home. Now leave me alone.

Grinning, I flop back on my bed, holding my phone above my head with a goofy grin.

Skylar: Why would I ever want to do that?

Skylar: Are you in bed? Can I see?

Bones: In your dreams.

Skylar: Oh, it definitely will be. I've been imagining what you wear to bed. I have this weird fascination with it being silk.

Bones: That sounds like your kink. I wear nothing.

He's replying to me! He's actually talking to me.

Bones: Now go to sleep, Skylar. I hear racing starts early.

Turning over, I almost giggle before grabbing my phone again, shocked that he cares that much to find out.

> Skylar: How would you know? Have you been asking Alek about me? If you want to know anything, you ask, baby. I'll tell you anything you want.

> Bones: I don't want to know anything.

I raise my brows, pouting as I go to send a message, when another comes through.

> Bones: Where were you before you saw me tonight? A hot date?

> Bones: Never mind, forget I asked. I don't care.

My heart nearly explodes. Oh, he fucking cares. Is that jealousy? Why does it make me want to throw a fucking party? Bones might act like he hates me, but he cared enough to ask.

> Skylar: Jealous if I was? It could be you if you weren't playing so hard to get.

> Bones: Like I said, I don't care. Forget I asked.

Biting back my grin, I turn over. My towel falls off, and the cold AC blows across my ass as I kick my feet like a schoolgirl and I hurry to text him back.

> Skylar: I wasn't on a date. Haven't been on one since I met you. All I see is you.

I admit it without reservation. I might have unsuccessfully tried to fuck him out of my system when I was drunk, wishing they were all him, but he's all I want, and I realized it very quickly.

> Bones: I don't fucking care. Fuck anyone you want. Oh wait, you already do. You're a man whore.

> Skylar: Keep being mean to me, baby, and I'll fall in love with you.

Bones: Masochist.

> Skylar: You love it, otherwise you wouldn't be replying. You wouldn't be asking. You wouldn't have wanted me to kiss you earlier.

> Skylar: We both know how this will end, beautiful—with you on your back under me. Just accept it.

Bones: Who said I would be the one on my back?

Jesus fucking Christ.

I am so in love with this boy already.

> Skylar: Now how am I supposed to sleep with an image like that in my mind?

Sliding back to my headboard, I lean against it and snap a picture of my legs with the cityscape in the background. I'm careful not to show my cock. If I push him too hard, he'll close up again.

I quickly send it and wait. A minute or so later, my phone vibrates in my hand, his message popping up.

Bones: Why the fuck are you naked?

Bones: Actually, it doesn't even surprise me. I hope your balls shrivel.

I burst into laughter before I hit reply.

> Skylar: My balls are fine, don't worry, beautiful. I can show you if you want.

Bones: Do not fucking dare.

> Skylar: Fine, I'll behave.

> Skylar: Now it's your turn, baby. Give me something or I'll be up all night wondering. You don't want to be the reason I crash tomorrow, do you?

> Bones: You're a fucking asshole.

> Skylar: I'm waiting, beautiful. I can wait all night if I have to.

There are a few minutes of silence, and then my phone vibrates in my hand. I navigate to it, ignoring everything else, and my heart fucking explodes at the picture.

He's flipping me off, the camera pointed at the city through his windows, his legs covered by a black blanket. I stare at the picture longer than I should, since it's just his legs and nothing more, and I try to work out his location using the window.

> Bones: Now fuck off. I'm going to sleep. If you wake me up with another message, I'll never speak to you again.

> Skylar: Mean. Goodnight, beautiful. Dream of me.

I know he's serious, so I put my phone down on the wireless charger, not wanting to ruin this between us. I turn off the notifications on everything like normal before going into my settings and changing it so only his messages and calls will come through—just in case.

CHAPTER 11
BONES

M y phone vibrates again as I'm leaving. Sighing deeply, I pull it out.

> Skylar: Good morning, beautiful. I had great dreams about you.

> Skylar: I love breakfast. What do you eat for it?

There's a picture of him with a smoothie and pancakes, which makes me roll my eyes.

The texts have been coming since this morning, starting at 5 AM.

> Skylar: The sun is just coming up. I'm on my way to the track. I wish you were in my passenger seat. Want me to swing by and get you? What time do your classes start?

> Skylar: I'm at the track, text me when you wake up. Want me to order you some breakfast?

I didn't reply no matter how much I wanted to. It would only encourage this behavior, and if I've learned one thing, it's that if you give Skylar an inch, he'll take a mile.

> Skylar: So mean ignoring me, baby. I miss you already. How's class?

Ignoring his message again, I open the other one that came through not too long ago.

> Anders: Tonight. 7 PM. Sky Bar on Cresset Street. We are having a meal. Be there, no excuses.

> Bones: I'm busy.

I'm not, but it can't be anything good. Alek and I are friends, but not the type to meet up for a meal, so I don't plan on going.

> Anders: Be there or I'll give Skylar your address.

Fuck.

He will, and then I'll never get rid of the clingy race boy. I debate which is the lesser of two evils as I walk without looking.

> Bones: Fine.

I lower my phone and stumble to a stop as a grinning, brightly dressed Lally pops up in front of me. My eyebrow arches as I look for Evan, since they are joined at the hip, but it's just her. My brows draw together as I frown.

"What's wrong?" I ask. Lally is a little like Skylar, always in trouble.

She laughs. "I'm not in trouble, I just came to give you these." She pulls her hands from behind her back and thrusts a huge bouquet of sunflowers at me. I have no choice but to take them, frowning deeper.

"Uh, why are you giving me flowers?" I ask as she starts to walk backwards. I chase her as she laughs.

"I'm not. They are from Sky. He said you wouldn't take them from him. I'm late for class. Bye!" She waves as she runs off, knowing I was going to hand them back.

Sighing, I peer down at the flowers before heading to the closest bin to throw them away, but I hesitate. They are really nice flowers. How did he know they are my favorite?

The flowers didn't do anything wrong . . . .

I put them under my arm instead and stomp to my car to drive home since my classes are done for the day, my bouquet in the passenger seat the entire time.

I tell myself the only reason I'm going is so Skylar doesn't turn up at my house every day. I know the Sky Bar has a dress code, though, so I slip into one of my many designer suits. I leave the shirt off, adding my own twist, and slick my hair back. I have no idea why Anders wants to meet in a place like that. It's not his usual scene, not to mention there's a waitlist.

It bugs me as I grab my wallet and phone and walk through my dark apartment.

My eyes catch on the sunflowers sitting on my dining table, brightening the whole place, as I pass, and I almost smack myself at my own idiocy.

Hurrying out before I decide to ruin their innocence, I grab a taxi since I'll need to drink to get through this meal with Anders.

The Sky Bar isn't far. It's in the heart of downtown Pine Valley on the waterfront, which always has packed bars and restaurants since they are the best. I wander past them, the cool night air wrapping around me. I ignore the looks I get due to my tattoos and intimidating face. Some even move out of my way, but I ignore that as well as I walk through the glass door with a neon sign reading "Sky Bar" above it.

I stride to a bank of elevators and I hit the button. Once I'm inside, I notice there is no button, and we ride it to the very top. The door opens into the reception area, where two men in suits and a woman in a skintight black dress wait behind a wooden podium. There are sofas to the left filled with people waiting, but I move past them.

"I have a reservation. 7 PM, Anders."

"Of course," the brown-haired woman replies. "This way, sir. Your party is already here and expecting you."

I follow her through the double doors, and we are transported into another world. Tables are littered throughout, and we are surrounded by glass, letting us see the night sky. The interior has bright pink and purple flowers spread everywhere, and it's decorated with dramatic displays to take pictures with. There is even a carousel to the left which people pose in front of.

We head past all that and down some steps leading to the outside courtyard. I weave through tables behind her, my eyes catching on the incredible view. The railings are covered in the same flowers, but they don't obstruct the skyline. We finally come to a stop, and I'm so distracted I almost run into her.

"Sir." She nods.

"Thank you." I offer her a polite nod and turn to face Alek. "What is this—" I freeze.

Alek Anders isn't sitting in the leather chair of the intimate, two-person table with candles and flowers.

It's Skylar.

My jaw drops as I gape at him, and his eyes sparkle as he runs his gaze down me. "You look fucking good, beautiful. I like that you dressed up for our date. I did the same. Do you like it?" He stands, opening his arms to show me his outfit.

I thought I couldn't be more shocked, but I am. He's in a full suit, even wearing a waistcoat, in a deep gray silk that makes his dark eyes stand out. His hair is styled in a half bun with strands falling down, and his piercings sparkle in the light.

"I'll take the silence as shock over my sexiness." He grins. "I've heard the food here is good, but we can always go somewhere else."

"Where is Alek?" I ask, even though I know the answer.

"Oops." He winks. "No Alek, just me."

That bastard is dead.

He set me up, and his friend made him.

Turning, I start to stomp away. There's no way I'm staying with Skylar—

"If you leave, Alek will give me your address," he calls. "Your choice."

Grinding my teeth, I hesitate before turning and storming to the table, poking my finger into his chest. "You have one hour. Understood?"

"Understood." He grins. "Sit down, beautiful."

Snarling, I reach for my chair back to sit, wanting to get this over with.

Skylar hurries to my chair and pulls it out for me. I sit and jerk it out of his hands. He doesn't care, grabbing my napkin from the table and unfolding it. He lays it across my lap as his mouth brushes my ear.

"You look good enough to eat." He dances out of the way of my elbow and slides into his own seat, his hand playing with his napkin as he watches me with that annoyingly bright smile.

"How did you bribe him to betray me?" I snap as Skylar leans back, looking far too smug and handsome in his own right.

"I knew something he didn't want Evan to know." I narrow my gaze, and he holds his hands up. "Nothing bad, trust me. It's good, but he wants it to be a surprise. Otherwise, he would never betray you, but when it comes to Evan . . ."

"He would do anything." I sigh, leaning back. "So what do you want?"

"To see you, of course. You didn't reply, so I had to find a way." He smirks. "Did you like the flowers?"

"I put them in the trash," I lie.

"Ouch." He covers his chest like he's wounded, but he's still smiling at me when our waiter appears.

He looks between us. "Are you ready to order?"

"We'll have two of your best steaks, medium for me, rare for my boyfriend. The works on the side. What do you want to drink, baby?" He arches a brow, daring me to argue.

My nostrils flare, annoyance filling me as I glance at the waiter. "Whiskey."

The waiter nods and rushes away, no doubt feeling the tension.

"Don't ever order for me—"

"Do you not like steak?" Skylar asks.

I grind my jaw. "Yes, it's my favorite. How did you know I take it rare?"

He grins at me as he leans closer, like he's sharing a secret. "I've made it my mission to know everything about you, baby. You should know that."

Ignoring his response, I glance at his glass of water. "Aren't you drinking?"

"Not tonight." He leans back, smiling mysteriously. "I don't need it when I'm with you."

Rolling my eyes, I lean back in my chair and check my watch. "You're down to fifty minutes."

"That's long enough." He grins. "You can do a lot in that time."

"Really? I thought you would be a quick draw," I quip, and he laughs, his head thrown back. Despite my annoyance at his blatant manipulation, I find myself staring at him. He really is beautiful, but he knows it, and when he catches me looking, I glance away.

I'll never admit that I like it or that no one, not even my ex, ever ordered for me. They didn't know me well enough, but somehow, this asshole does, and I don't know what to feel about it.

"This has to be the best date I have ever been on." He grins, propping his chin on his hand and watching me.

"It isn't a date," I snap.

He just smiles, and I find myself shuffling under his attention before I realize it and stop my movements. I refuse to show any weakness because Skylar would pounce on it.

"What do you want from me, Skylar?" I ask. "To be friends?"

"Baby, I don't want to be your friend. I want to be your everything. I want to be your lover, your boyfriend, and your forever. I want to be the one you turn to when life is hard and the one you trust with all those secrets. I want the story behind every tattoo covering your delicious body. No, Bones, I don't want to be your friend. I want to be yours."

I search his eyes, vulnerability coursing through me for a moment. "Why?" My voice is soft and tentative. "I'm rude to everyone, I hate everything, and I push everyone away. I—"

"Because you're worth it," he interrupts. "No matter what you think, you're worth the effort, and no matter what front you put on for everyone else, I see you . . . I know you."

"No, you don't—"

"I do," he interrupts again, reaching over and covering my hand. "I saw the real you that night, the man willing to do anything to keep his friends safe—a strong, confident fighter with a fragile side. I see you, Bones, the real you that you try to hide, and I want him. Be mean to me and push me away, but it won't stop me. I'm not giving up." He leans back, taking the warmth of his hand with him, and I tuck my hand under the table, covering it with my other one. Picking up his glass, he takes a sip of his water and swallows. "So how was your day and your classes?"

"You're unbelievable," I say, but it doesn't sound like an insult anymore.

CHAPTER 12
SKYLAR

I'm starting to think nobody has ever taken the time to really know this man if something as small as knowing how he likes his steak shocks him.

What kind of losers has he been dating?

Never mind, I'll make up for them. I'll spoil this boy so thoroughly, he'll never want to leave me. Their loss is my gain.

I am surprised he stayed after he realized it was me. He probably didn't know I was bluffing. Alek would never give me his address, but Bones doesn't know that, and it gets me what I want, which is him sitting opposite me, on a date.

He looks so fucking good, it's distracting. I can't look away, even as I eat my steak. I'm useless with all the knives and forks, but he makes it look like a work of art, reminding me he comes from money. He sits tall and confident, his manners impeccable. He can't hide his smooth rich-boy upbringing even under that tattooed skin.

I love the difference.

"Did you always want to be a lawyer?" I ask.

"No, my father is one. I wanted to be anything but a lawyer growing up, partly to annoy him and partly so I would never be like him," he answers, wiping his mouth with his napkin after he speaks.

"So why are you studying to be a lawyer? Is it because of him?" I ask, my eyes locked on his lips as he takes a sip of his whiskey.

"No, I want to be able to protect those I love, and this is the only way I know how," he replies automatically and then seems to realize it. Clearing his throat awkwardly, he looks away for a moment. "Have you always wanted to be a racer?"

"No," I admit truthfully. I will never lie to him, even if he doesn't like the answers. "I never wanted to be anything growing up. I just wanted to be safe and not hungry. Racing kind of fell into my lap, and it made money, so I got good at it, but I didn't enjoy it at first. Now I do. It's part of me, and I couldn't imagine my life without it. I live, sleep, and breathe racing and cars. When I'm behind the wheel, I feel unstoppable and invincible."

It's a feeling I can't really describe, but I try. I have an inkling he's never felt that free before.

"What made you start liking it?" he asks softly.

"It doesn't matter who you are behind the wheel. It doesn't matter where you come from or the money you have. You leave it all out on that road. Whoever crosses the finish line and wins is a better driver, and I like that. I like that it made us all equals."

He watches me for a moment, his expression seeming to soften. "I didn't expect that from you, but it makes sense. I can't say I understand where you came from, but you seem to be doing well now."

"It was hard for a long time," I tell him as I lean back. I refuse to be ashamed of where I came from, and I have a feeling he won't care. "I quickly realized the only person I could depend on to survive was myself. I either got up and did the work and made it happen or I faded away like everyone else on the streets." I shrug. "It made me who I am today, and I'm not ashamed of that. What about you? What was it like growing up as a Townsend?"

"I'm ashamed of my past," he answers after a pause, "of how I grew up with more money than sense. My father used it like a weapon against everyone, including me. You had to earn privilege in his eyes, earn the right to speak or be heard." He takes a drink, glancing at the city. "Sometimes I wonder what my life would be like if we never had money. Would it be easier? Better? Would he be the father I always wanted?"

I read between the lines, and my heart aches for what he has gone through.

When he glances back at me, he smiles bitterly. "Stupid to complain about that, right?"

"Not at all," I reply. "Money changes people."

"Not you." He tilts his head, watching me. "I've seen the way you interact with people. You don't act like anyone from my world, with money born or earned. You're still kind and down to earth."

"Are you complimenting me, baby?" I tease.

He rolls his eyes, but a small smile graces his lips. I don't like that sad look in his eyes—not one bit. "I mean it. You didn't let it change you."

"I did and I didn't," I admit. "Money comes and goes, but experiences and people don't. That's what I think. Even if you have money, are you really living without passion or happiness? They always say money can't buy happiness, but they are liars. It can, but it can only buy so much. It buys places and people but not their hearts, and it can't buy genuine feelings or interactions."

"Hence bringing me to the most expensive, exclusive restaurant?" he asks, his eyebrow arched.

I grin. "I wanted to show off a little and prove to you I could fit into your world."

"Don't," he interrupts. "Don't fit into my world." I must frown because he bites his lip, playing with his glass. "I like that you aren't a part of it. I like that you're different. I hate my world, so don't try to be a part of it, okay?"

"Okay," I murmur, and he meets my gaze, electricity flowing between us before I grin. "Is that your way of saying you want me around?"

He groans, the moment broken, but I see the smile he tries to hide behind his glass. Two dimples appear in his cheeks, and I swear my soul leaves my body at the sight of them.

"You wish," he responds as our plates are cleared away. I order him another drink. I don't want him drunk, but I want him to enjoy himself.

Does he realize it's been two hours? I don't bring it up, scared he'll leave.

"What do you want for dessert?" I ask.

"What, no ordering for me?" he retorts.

"I can guess, but I'd rather you get what you want so I can remember for next time," I reply.

He rolls his eyes again, sitting back heavily. "There won't be a next time, but I don't really like dessert, only chocolate."

"That's because you're too sweet without it," I joke, making him roll his eyes again. Scanning the menu, I pick an indulgent chocolate cake and order it for him.

When it comes, he frowns and looks at my empty place setting. "You're not having anything?"

"Nope, I just want to watch you." I rest my chin in my hands and do just that.

"Creepy," he snaps, but he picks up his fork and takes a bite. The groan he lets out makes me hard as hell.

"Good?" My voice is choked. He doesn't even notice as he nods and takes another bite.

I brush my thumb over his lip. "You made a mess, beautiful," I murmur, showing him the ganache on my thumb as I lean back and suck it clean, wishing it were his skin instead, but I can be patient.

For now.

I watch as he swallows, eyeing my thumb in my mouth.

"You're right. It's good. Delicious even," I admit with a wicked smile.

He stabs another bite and hesitates before holding the fork out to me. I swear I want to scream in excitement, but I hold it back as I lean in and take the bite, using the excuse to hold his hand on the fork, my thumb stroking it as I reluctantly lean back and chew. He takes another bite, eating from the same fork.

We are basically kissing.

Licking my lips, I watch my boy eat, and when he's done, he sits back, placing his hand on his stomach. "I ate way too much," he complains.

"Need me to rub it for you?" I smirk.

He throws me a glare, but it holds less heat. I wish the night would keep going, but the peace appears to be coming to an end, and he seems to realize it at the same time. "It's time for me to go." He stands suddenly, thrusting his chair back.

My eyes widen as I blink in panic, and he throws me a contemplative look before turning and walking away. I hurry after him, paying as I go. He's already gone, but I take the next elevator and catch him on the street, grabbing his arm and spinning him.

"Wait, how are you getting home?"

"Taxi," he snaps, trying to tug from my grip, so I turn us and press him against the wall of the building. My arm rests against the brick to stop him from escaping. He sighs, eyeing me. We both know he could break from this if he wanted to.

"Let me drive you." I grin as I inhale his addictive scent. This close, my boy is flawless. Does he look this pretty when he wakes up? I can't wait to find out. "I don't know if you've heard, but I'm an excellent driver."

"No, thanks." He ducks under me and hurries away.

Swearing, I grab my keys and rush around the building. Getting into my car, I rev the engine and speed onto the one-way street. His phone is out as he stands at the edge, looking both ways for a taxi. Smirking, I pull in front of him, ignoring the honks as I reach over and push the door open.

"Get in, beautiful," I order.

He leans down, glaring at me. "Skylar," he growls.

"I love the way you say my name. Get in, baby. I'll behave, I promise. I'll take you home and leave. I won't even get out of the car, but I'm not leaving without your hot ass in my passenger seat."

His jaw grinds as he debates his options before putting his phone away and climbing in. Grinning, I reach over and grab his belt. My eyes lock on his, our faces close enough to kiss. His pupils dilate and his lips part, and I debate kissing him, but the click of his belt jolts us back to the present. He turns away.

Grinning, I sit back and pull slowly into traffic.

I will not risk the angel in my passenger seat. I'll drive more carefully than I ever fucking have.

"Which way, babe?" He's quiet, and I lean over, my arm across the back of his seat. "Or I can take you to my house—"

"It's called Hellfire Apartments, Slaughter—"

"I know the place," I admit with a wide grin. I know it very well. In fact, I almost bought an apartment there before mine. His eyes narrow on me, but I don't elaborate.

He sinks deeper into his seat, looking around my car. "Cold, beautiful?" I crank up the heat when I notice his hands tucking under his legs and turn on his seat warmer. I check on him to see him staring at me. "What?"

"You being nice is freaking me out."

"Want me to wax poetically about how many times I've thought about fucking you in that seat?" I reply, and his grin is worthwhile.

"That's more like you," he comments as we zoom through downtown traffic and pull up at the private entry to Hellfire. The guard waves me on when she sees Bones in my passenger seat. I pull up at the reception area, and he goes to get out, but I lean over, covering his hand with mine.

"I had an amazing night. Thank you for coming." I sincerely mean it.

"I had no choice."

"I really enjoyed it," I finish with a grin. "Next time we go on a date, baby, it will be because you want to."

"Doubtful. Goodnight, Skylar." He smirks as he gets out and, without another look, walks inside.

"Goodnight, beautiful," I murmur as I watch him to make sure he gets in okay. When he's out of sight, I grab my phone.

Opening my screen, I pull up my messages to my financial advisor and friend.

> Skylar: If the apartment in Hellfire is still open, rent it for me. I'll be moving in.

I kept my promise and behaved, but that doesn't mean I will forever.

CHAPTER 13
SKYLAR

I t's early, so I didn't expect to see anyone as I crouch and lay flowers in front of Tommy's colorful memorial in the art building. I didn't know him for long, but he was fun and clearly an amazing friend. More than that, he deserves to be honored and remembered, so I come every week and place fresh flowers to thank him for doing what he did. I will always remember him, even if everything else fades. I know Evan visits almost daily, and sometimes I see Lally here, but she's usually crying, and we share a silent understanding not to bring it up.

Alice comes as well, though she doesn't speak.

It's just me today, though, and I straighten some of the images others added of him as I sit back on my haunches. "Hey, buddy, your wall is growing. Soon you'll take over this place." Smiling, I straighten a few more pictures before standing. "I'll be back next week with more. How about roses next, huh?" Shoving my hands in my pocket, I turn to leave, only to find Bones there, staring at me with an unreadable expression.

"You're here early," I comment. The school hasn't even officially opened yet. I know classes don't start for another few hours, although people are in labs and the library.

"I was at the library when I thought I could swing by"—he glances at the wall—"and make sure it was okay."

"What do you mean?"

"The school board was trying to get rid of it, something about it being against the rules. I made sure they wouldn't touch it, but I wanted to make sure they hadn't without me noticing," he replies.

"Bones, you big softie." I smirk. "Do the others know?"

"No. Why would I tell them?" He frowns, not understanding why his friends would be proud and thankful.

Foolish, beautiful man.

"Come on, I'll walk you out." I move to his side, and surprisingly, he falls into step with me as we hit the path and walk under the trees blowing in the breeze.

"You come every week?" he asks, filling the silence.

"I do." I glance at him and smile. "I wasn't as close to him as the others. I only met him a few times through Evan, but he was funny and an amazing soul. My friends loved him very much, and he saved us all that night, so I come to remind him I will never forget what he did. It seems right."

"Who's the softie now?" He bumps my shoulder, and I find myself smiling. "Are you on your way to the track?"

"Yeah, we're practicing pretty much twenty-four seven at the moment. Since I'm a newbie, it's important to find a flow with my partner and the team. I'm a good racer, but it's not enough to win. It's about the team as much as it's about me."

"Profound. I expected you to be all 'it's not the car, but the driver. I'm the best.'" He smirks.

"Nah, I can win, I know that, but I want to win the right way," I reply. "I want them with me. They welcomed me in like family, and we've gotten close really quickly. It doesn't feel right to go rogue, so even though I hate early mornings, I drag my ass there every day and do what I'm told."

"You? Do what you're told? I don't believe it for a second."

I laugh, and we share a grin.

"It doesn't come naturally, I'll admit." I wink as we wander down the path. "Luckily, my partner, Mackie, is really good, and we fit together well."

"You must spend a lot of time with him," he remarks, but there's something in his voice that makes me rerun his words through my head.

Smirking, I turn and walk backwards so I can keep him in view. "He's in love with someone else, and so am I. We are friends, nothing more."

"I didn't ask," he scoffs, but his shoulders loosen, and he grabs me when I stumble over the edge of the path. "Walk normal, idiot."

"So, is this what it feels like to walk with the popular kid? The bad boy of Pine Valley? I am so lucky. Should I swoon?" I joke.

"I wouldn't know. I don't really walk with anyone." I raise my brow, and he sighs. "I have friends, but I prefer being alone. It's just easier." He shrugs. "Besides, most people take one look at me and turn the other way. They call me Bones because they say when I'm through with them, that's all that's left. It stuck, and I kept it to spite them."

I can't believe he's telling me this, so I keep pushing, wanting to know everything about him.

"What's your real name?" It's something I've always been curious about. I could have found out, but for some reason, I want him to tell me himself.

"Ah, now, that would be telling," he teases.

I stop before my car and turn to him. "How about a deal?" I offer.

"You and your deals. I think you do it just because you know us lawyers can't resist a good wager."

"True, that and I'm desperate to hook you somehow." I lean back against my hood as I watch him. "If I win that race you're coming to next week, I get your real name—all of it. What do you think, beautiful?"

"That's all? My name? I expected you to demand more." His meaning is clear, and I wink as I run my eyes down his frame.

"Baby, when you give me your body, it won't be through a deal. It will be because you want me. No, I want your name."

"And if you lose?" he asks, his eyebrow arched.

"I won't." I grin.

"If you do?" he retorts.

"You pick." I push away from my car, and I don't stop until we are almost pressed together. "Tell me what you want, angel."

He glances at my lips, and even though I expect him to tell me to leave him alone, he surprises me when he speaks. "I get to drive your race car if you lose. At least one lap."

"Deal." I lean in and kiss his cheek. "To seal it. See you later, beautiful. Have a good day." I slide into my car and pull out, waving at him before taking off to work.

I'm happier than I've been in a long time.

"Sky, are you coming?" Toni, one of the mechanics, calls, and I lift my head to see them lingering by the door. "We are all going for a drink."

"Nah, you go ahead. I want to practice some more. The race is getting closer." I shrug.

They wave, and I stare after them, wondering when my life changed so much that I would turn down a party and a drink. I'm just now realizing there are more important things. Everyone else is gone, and the garage is dark. Hell, even Alek and Noah left hours ago.

I'm the newbie, however, and although I can race with my eyes closed, I want this to go well. I want to win, not just for me like I thought, but for all of us. Noah works day and night to give us everything we need, and every single mechanic works their ass off to make it happen. Mackie spends day in and day out adapting his racing style so we can work together. It's a team effort, and they are only as strong as their weakest member, so I need to buckle up and keep my head down.

I spent all day on the track, and then I hit the gym. Now the books are spread before me. Some detail the tracks we'll face this championship, while others have other racers' stats and car information. The one I'm reading now and memorizing has the rules.

There are none on the streets, but here, they are long and detailed, and if you break one, you're banned or worse. I won't let that happen.

I might not like to play by rules often, but for this, I will.

Leaning back, I close my eyes and recite the page I just memorized. I run through it until I have it right, and a few hours later, my head is pounding and I physically can't take in any more information. After packing them away, I head to my locker and put them inside before seeing the light on under Noah's door.

Frowning, I knock and swing it open, finding him staring at his computer with just a desk light on. "Hey, I thought everyone left."

"So did I," he murmurs, glancing at me and hitting pause on something on his laptop. "Everything okay?"

"Yeah, I was just running through some prep for the championship," I admit, and the smile he gives me makes me want to shuffle in embarrassment. It's filled with pride, and something about making Noah proud of me heals something broken in my chest.

No one has ever been proud of me, not ever.

Noah is as he beams at me.

Leaning into the doorway, I eye Noah, clearing my throat and changing the subject before I do something stupid like sob. Daddy issues, am I right?

"How come you're still here?"

"I could ask you the same thing," he retorts before leaning back in his chair with a groan and rubbing his face. "I should say something profound like the boss doesn't leave until all his team does, but really, I'm just watching reruns of recent races to try and suss out the opponents' strategies so we can adapt and win."

"Need a hand?" I offer as I push from the door and take the seat next to him.

"You sure?" he murmurs. "It's not exactly fun."

"It's a good idea, and I can get a feel for them. On the streets, the better you know your racer, the better your chances are of winning." I shrug.

"Sometimes I forget you're a street kid." He smirks, rubbing my hair until I lean away with a mock glare. "Alright, but when you get bored, you can leave. Don't feel bad."

"I'm betting you'll fall asleep, old man, before I get bored," I tease.

"Old man? Jesus fucking Christ. Kids these days," he mutters as he hits play.

For the next two hours, we watch race after race, stopping to talk through strategies to counter the ones we are seeing. Some use the same tactic every time while others have a pattern, and some are wild cards, but if we can learn to predict their movements, then we stand a chance.

"Next one?" he murmurs.

"Sure thing." I drop my pen to my notebook and lean closer to the screen as the next race loads up.

Just then, my phone starts to ring, playing *Lover Boy*. There is only one person it rings for. I quickly snatch it up and answer, uncaring about Noah listening at my side.

"Angel, are you okay?" I ask worriedly.

He never calls me, not ever, and panic winds through me. What if something is wrong? What if it's like that night and he's in danger? My heart starts to pound when there's just heavy breathing.

"Bones, talk to me," I plead.

There's a grunt then the sound of music before a door is shut. "Sky, it's Alek," my grumpy best friend says, only making me worry more.

"What the fuck do you have Bones's phone for? Is he okay?" I get to my feet, my eyes wide.

"Shit, calm down, man, sorry. He's okay, just very fucking drunk. Bones, stop—shit, okay, take it." There's fumbling, and then heavy breathing again.

"Skylar," Bones slurs, and my eyebrows rise. All the time I have known Bones, I've barely see him drink, and never anything past one or two. I can hear how drunk he is in his voice, and when he giggles, I swear I fall back into my seat.

What the hell happened to make him get this drunk?

"Yes, angel?" I murmur. "Alek says you're drunk."

"I had a few." He hiccups. "I'm fine."

"Uh-huh, you're always fine. Pass the phone back to Alek, baby," I say softly.

"No, it's my phone, talk to me," he snaps, and my lips twitch at his petulant tone. He's such a fucking brat. "Why aren't you here tonight? Are you on a date?"

"If by date you mean sitting with my boss in his weird smelling office and watching race reruns, then yes," I joke.

"Hey," Noah mutters. "Does it smell weird?"

"You had that weird concoction for dinner. I smell that," I admit before focusing on my phone call as Noah sniffs. "Baby, give the phone back to Alek."

"Why? You don't want to talk to me? Fine." There's a grunt.

"Baby, I want to talk to you all the time, okay? I just need a minute with Alek, so be a good boy and hand him the phone." I talk slowly, trying to placate him.

There's more fumbling and then a deep sigh. "You see what we are dealing with? He's a mess."

"Why did you let him get so fucking drunk?" I snap, completely annoyed.

"Holy shit," Noah mutters, and I throw him a glare. "All that soft, loving voice and now look . . . so mean."

I flip him off and turn away.

"You don't let Bones do anything, you know that. I don't know why he got so drunk," Alek replies.

"Text me the address. I'm on the way. Stay with him and don't let him have another drink," I warn.

"Easier said than done—Bones, don't piss in the pool!" The phone goes dead.

I glance at Noah, and he laughs.

"Go," Noah says with an understanding smile. "If I had someone I cared about enough to take care of, I would."

"Who says you don't?" I counter with an arched brow.

"I don't know what you mean," he mutters, his gaze fixed on the race.

"Uh-huh, maybe I mean the person you keep the fridge stocked with his favorite drinks and snacks for, even though it means you're importing them, or the fact that you watch him on the cameras every morning and night to make sure he gets in okay."

"I look after all my team," Noah mutters, sparing me a look.

"With such a personal touch? I never got any snacks." I wink as I pull my jacket on. "Stop fighting it. Trust me, life is too fucking short to have regrets when the end comes. Live while you can because when it's over, it's just fucking over."

"Don't go getting all sentimental on me, kid," Noah mutters as he watches me pack my bag and grab my keys. "I didn't know you were dating anyone, and I've never heard you use that soft voice before."

"I'm not technically dating him yet. He's mine. He just doesn't know it yet," I admit with a grin, and he laughs.

He snorts. "Lucky him."

"I know, right?" I wink, throwing my bag over my shoulder. "See you tomorrow, old man." I duck out of the door as a book hits it, making me grin wider. I love giving him shit, although I can't help but grin, knowing one day he's going to give into those feelings and chase that little race boy rather than pushing him away.

I'm just getting into my car when my phone dings with a text.

Alek: 451 Slaughterhouse Rd.

Alek: Be quick or I'm dumping his ass in the pool.

My engine roars to life as I hit reply.

Skylar: On my way. If you touch my boy, you're dead, Anders.

CHAPTER 14
SKYLAR

I park my car as close to the front of the party as I can get, ignoring the looks and calls from people gathered there. I take the steps three at a time and push through the front door. I'm taller than most here, so I scan the crowd quickly as I make my way through the frat house. I finally spot Alek's big head in the kitchen and walk his way.

He almost grins when he sees me, which should have been my first warning. He's leaning against the kitchen counter in his leather jacket and jeans with Evan at his side in a sparkly tank top and loose pants, glitter all over his face.

"Oh, thank fuck." Evan sighs, leaning into Alek, who drops an arm around him and kisses his head, a natural move that makes me extremely jealous. "It's your turn for Bones duty. I'm going to dance with my boyfriend. Have fun and good luck." Evan pats my side. "You'll need it."

Turning my eyes from them, I find Bones, and my mouth drops open.

Evan was right. I'll need all the luck I can get to be a saint tonight with my boy.

He has on a white button-down, but it's ripped open, showcasing his stacked chest and tattoos, and black jeans that are glued to his body as he winds his hips and shakes his ass.

Is he twerking?

I swear my brain malfunctions, and I find myself just staring at him until a big guy starts to head his way, and I snap out of it. I narrow my eyes at him in warning, my face cold. It's a familiar look, one I've never used around my friends. It's a look I learned on the streets, and sometimes it was enough to scare them away before they tried anything. It works this time, and the big bastard blanches and scurries away. I reach Bones, my hands falling to his hips to stop his movements as I lean closer for him to hear me over the music.

"Let's go, baby."

His eyes snap open, and he blinks at me. His face is red from the alcohol, and his eyes are blown wide. "Skylar?" he mutters, and even slurred and drunk, hearing him say my name sends a shiver through me.

"Uh-huh." Taking his hand, I pull him from the dancing throng and into the kitchen so he can hear me better. He stumbles, his hand warm in mine, but he doesn't let go, and I want to scream in victory. "It's time to go. Say goodbye."

"No," he snaps as he tugs his hand away. Looking around the kitchen, he plucks a random cup from the side. "I'm staying. I'm drinking and having fun. You can leave."

"Baby, you don't need another drink." After handing it off to the closest person, I cup his face. "Why don't you play with me instead?"

"No." He pouts, pushing me away. "I want to drink. I can do anything I want."

I follow him around the kitchen, plucking more cups out of his hand until he spins and glares at me. His finger pokes into my chest, and I glance down at it then back at him. "You don't get to tell me what to do. You're always getting into trouble. Why can't I?"

Leaning closer, I slide my hand under his shirt and across his warm, tight waist to the base of his back, then I pull him until he falls into me, his lips parted as he stares up at me. "There's only room for one troublemaker in this relationship. Now, you're drunk, and it's time to go. I'm all for you having fun, but when you can barely stand? Yeah, I'm taking you home. So say your goodbyes."

"I'm not yours to order around," he slurs, sassy even now.

I smirk. "That's where you're wrong, baby."

His eyes narrow and he lifts his hand, his fingers clumsily running across my lips. I still, my heart hammering as I stare into his face. He doesn't know what he's doing, but it doesn't stop me from wishing he would keep going. He pulls my lower lip down slightly, rubbing it. "You have a pretty mouth."

"Baby," I murmur, trying to be gentle. "I'm trying my best to behave here."

His eyes rove across my face. "You're very handsome. It's fucking annoying."

Biting back my smile, I tug him into a hug, propping my head on his shoulder so my mouth meets his ear. "I'm very sorry. Now, can I take you home so you can sleep this off? As fucking adorable as you are drunk, I can't wait for you to remember tomorrow and be embarrassed and take it out on me."

"Asshole," he mutters, pushing me away.

"There you are."

He goes to grab a cup again, and I sigh.

"Alright, I tried the nice way. Don't say I didn't." Pulling him closer, I button up his shirt so he doesn't get cold and then bend down, sweeping him up and over my shoulder. He cries out, hitting my ass, and then I turn and walk through the party.

No one stops me. Alek grins and tugs Evan out after me as I stomp toward my car. I can hear them laughing, but I ignore them and Bones as he shouts.

"Skylar, you fucking asshole, put me down! I want to drink. You're not my boss. Put me down right now. I will kill you!" He screams the entire time, and I open my car one-handed and slide him down my body before pushing him into the seat. Leaning over, I buckle him up and kiss his forehead as he rants.

"Hold on, baby." Shutting the door, I roll my eyes when I see Evan with his camera out. "Send me those." I grin as I look at Alek. "Text me his address. I know the apartment building but not the number, unless you want me to take him to my place, and we both know he'll murder you if I do that."

"Tricky bastard. You probably planned all this just to get close to him," Alek mutters, but he pulls out his phone.

"Well, I'd just be taking lessons from you, Anders." I grin. "Like that time you purposely broke Evan's skateboard so you could buy him a new one—"

"Get going!" Alek snaps, covering Evan's ears, who just grins.

"See ya." Waving, I jog around and get in, locking the doors as Bones tries to get out. His hands hit the window, trying to get Alek's and Evan's attention.

"You're all assholes!" he yells at them. "Don't let this psycho kidnap me!"

I pull into traffic, but his hands tug at the door, so I reach over and capture both of them, put them between my thighs, and shut them to trap them. "If you can't behave, I will stop and tie you up, understood?" I warn him seriously. "I will not let you put yourself in danger because you're drunk and annoying. Behave."

"Skylar," he whines.

"I mean it, Bones," I reply as I drive to his apartment.

He slumps back in his seat, and I release his hands.

I crank the AC and spare him a look. "There's water for you in that bag and some crackers. Let me know if you feel sick or anything."

"I never get sick," he snaps.

"It's okay," I murmur as I rub his back. We are on the side of the road over two blocks from his house. He vomited in my footwell since he couldn't hold it. I ignore it as he leans out of the car into the street. Pushing his hair back, I hold the water for him. "Get it all out, baby. It's okay."

He coughs and throws up again. I rub his back before grabbing some tissues, and when he slumps into his seat, I wipe his mouth and face. He doesn't even move.

"Are you okay for me to keep going? We should get you into bed."

"I'm fine," he whines.

"Okay." Bagging the tissue, I pass him the water. "Hold that and sip it," I caution as I lift his legs and put them in the car, careful of the pile of vomit.

After hurrying into the driver's seat, I pull back into traffic, driving as slowly and carefully as I can to calm his stomach. At the next red light, my phone rings, and I hit answer.

"Just wanted to check you got him home okay," Alek says.

"Almost there. We had to stop for him to be sick," I reply. "We didn't make it. Luckily, it was only once in my car. I think he just needs to sleep it off now."

"Shit, he vomited in your car? I spilled water once and you tried to murder me!" Anders barks out a laugh.

"Shut up," I mutter.

"Oh, to be whipped," he jokes. "Alright, have a fun night."

He hangs up, and I sigh and spare Bones a glance to see him looking far too pale again. "Almost there, baby, hang on."

Luckily, we have no more vomit incidents, but I do have to carry him into his apartment. I had to search him for his keys while he tried to beat me, and I struggled to get us both inside. I peer around at the dark, open-plan living and kitchen area before he groans, and I focus back on him.

"Where's your bedroom?" I ask, but he ignores me, curled in my arms. "Never mind, I'll find it."

I head down the hall, eventually finding it, and I lay him on his mattress. He doesn't even react as I pull off his shoes and socks, lining them up at the end of his bed—he strikes me as someone who wouldn't like a mess.

Leaving him for a second, I grab more water, some pain relief I manage to find in a cupboard, and a few wet washcloths. Everything is meticulously organized but cold and empty.

I head back to his side to find him struggling from his shirt. "Hey." I grab him, and his eyes open halfway.

"Hot," he whines.

"Okay, okay, let me help you." I unthread his arms and throw his shirt to the floor to deal with later as he collapses back onto the bed, his chest heaving and flushed from the liquor. I try not to look, I really do, but I stare for a moment before clearing my throat. I put the water and pills next to his bed before grabbing one of the washcloths and sitting at his side. I start to clean his face, since it can't feel nice being all sweaty and gross after being sick.

"Why did you get drunk?" I murmur as I wipe his face with the compress.

His eyes are closed, but he responds, "Girl from my class kept demanding your number and asking if you were single. It was annoying."

Biting back my victorious smile, I continue wiping as his brow furrows. "So you got drunk because you were jealous?"

"No," he snaps. "She can have you," he grumbles and rolls to his side. My eyes widen when his arms wrap around my waist, his head on my thigh. He holds me tightly despite his words.

"So kind of you." I hum as I stroke his hair. "I'll stick to you though."

"You'd like her," he mutters. "She's beautiful."

"Not as beautiful as you," I tell him as I lean down and kiss his forehead. "When will you realize you are the one I want? I'm not going anywhere, angel. I don't want anyone else's number or even their vomit in my car. It's you. It's been you since the first moment I saw you." I know he probably won't remember this tomorrow, but I can't stop myself. "I've never felt like this before. That first moment I met you, I felt like I was hit by lightning. You restarted my heart, and you don't even know it. Don't be jealous, my beautiful boy, because there is no one else in this world I want the way I want you. I'm yours. You never have to doubt that."

"You're just a friend," he mutters. "Friend."

"Angel," I murmur into his skin. "I don't look at my friends the way I look at you."

His eyes open slightly as he presses his face against my thigh and peers up at me. "How do you look at me?"

"Like you are the most precious, beautiful thing in my entire universe," I admit.

He stares up at me for a moment before glancing at my lips. His intention is clear, and it takes a herculean effort to pull back when he tries to kiss me, but I manage it.

"See?" He pouts, rolling away from me and sitting up with his arms crossed like a bratty child. I never knew he had this side, but drunk Bones is so fucking cute and different from his usual grumpiness that I have to hide my smile since he's busy telling me off. "You don't want to kiss me. You don't really want me. I bet you want her!"

I cover his mouth with my fingers and kiss the back of my hand as his eyes widen. When I drop it, I rub his lips.

"I want to kiss you more than I've ever wanted anything, baby, but our first kiss won't be while you're this drunk. You'll remember it and you'll give me consent. Tomorrow, when you're sober, ask me to kiss you and I will without hesitation."

His arms uncross slowly and drop as he stares at me. His pout is so fucking cute, I have to look away.

"Now, you need to sleep." Grabbing his legs, I yank him down until he hits the bed, then I tuck the sheets around him and fluff his pillow. He watches me silently the entire time, looking far too vulnerable and almost scared. Sitting at his side again, I lean down and kiss his forehead, unable to help myself.

"Sleep," I order.

His hand darts out and grabs mine as I go to stand. "Stay?" he whispers softly. "Will you stay with me? I don't want to be alone tonight."

"I'm not going anywhere." Kicking off my shoes, I climb onto his bed and lie next to him, my arms under my head so I don't pull him close. I won't take advantage of him like that, but it doesn't stop him—two seconds later, he rolls and drapes his whole body over me.

"Thank you, Sky," he whispers softly, pressing his face closer.

"Anytime, angel," I whisper as I glance down at him. "Sleep."

One of us should, because I know damn well it isn't going to be me tonight, not with everything I want in my arms. I won't miss a fucking second.

Whatever reason he got drunk, I'm stupidly thankful since it got me this, even if it's all I'll ever have.

It's enough.

CHAPTER 15
BONES

My head fucking hurts, throbbing in time with my heartbeat as I slowly open my eyes, knowing I probably left my blinds open like a moron. When I'm greeted by comforting darkness, I frown and sluggishly sit up.

I'm in bed in my jeans, my shirt and shoes are gone, and the blinds are shut. Huh, I guess I was a good drunk last night. Usually, I'm sloppy, since I take after my father, and it's one of the reasons I never get drunk. I never want to be like him, but I was last night.

I was so fucking stupid, but as all the girls and some of the guys from my class kept going on and on about how amazing and hot Skylar was, well, I lost it. They only saw him for a second when we were on campus, but it was enough. They wouldn't leave me alone about him, so I turned to drinking.

Turning my head, I spy the water and pills on my nightstand, and my frown deepens. There's no way past Bones did that for future Bones. I'm never that thoughtful. Speaking of, how did I get home?

Oh God . . . Skylar.

Oh, fuck.

Everything comes back, and I fall into my bed, covering my face in shame.

I scream wordlessly into my hands. This is why I don't fucking drink. I either get angry or sloppy. At least I didn't hurt anyone or start a fight, but did I really try to kiss Skylar?

No, it has to be the alcohol. It's blurring my memory.

Dropping my hand, I stare up at my ceiling and try to remember him leaving, but it's blank.

There's no way he's still here, right? He probably snuck out in the middle of the night, disgusted by my behavior, and will never speak to me again. My head starts to pound harder, and my stomach takes that moment to growl. Ignoring my self-pity and hatred, I swing my legs out of bed and sit up. After taking the pills and drinking the water, I head to the bathroom, washing my face and peeing. I shuffle down the corridor in search of greasy, unhealthy food to make me feel better.

When I reach my living room, I freeze in shock for the second time this morning.

The blinds are half lowered here, letting in a lot of bright sunlight, which illuminates my spotless apartment. It's never dirty, but I definitely threw some cushions around looking for my watch yesterday and left my clothes on the couch. It's all gone. My cushions are even plumped, and drying before the open windows on hangers are my clothes from yesterday and last night.

Flowers fill vases on my table, but it is the person to my left I stare at. Skylar Warren is shirtless as he sings along quietly to his phone, which is playing music.

His back is to me, his impressive muscles bunching with his movement as he flips pancakes. I realize there's eggs, bacon, breakfast potatoes, and French toast sitting on the counter before my chairs, and my stomach rumbles loudly as I gape.

He's still here.

He cleaned my apartment.

He washed my clothes.

He's making me breakfast.

I'm speechless as he turns to plate the pancakes, and then he stills, a wide, unchecked smile tilting up his lips. "Morning, angel. Did you sleep okay? I didn't wake you, did I?"

"What is all this?" I mutter.

"Breakfast," he answers with an arched brow.

"I mean, this . . ." I wave my hand around.

"Ah, I was up early. I guess I'm getting used to starting work, so I cleaned and helped while I was waiting. I figured you would be hungover and not in the mood to." He shrugs. "Come eat."

"Shouldn't you be at work?" I ask, desperately searching for a way to get him to leave.

"Uh-uh, I was waiting for you to wake up. Don't worry, my boss understood. I'll eat with you and then go." He pushes out a chair as he sits on the other one. "Come eat, I can hear your stomach from here."

Skylar Warren is in my home, invading my space, cooking for me. People don't come here. They don't stay the night, and they never cook me breakfast.

He waits then sighs. "Bones, sit. I'm not going to pounce on you or anything, just eat. Don't make me carry you again."

My cheeks heat, and I glance away in embarrassment. When I still don't move, he starts to stand, so I hurry over and sit. He instantly puts a plate together for me and pours me some water and orange juice. "Drink all of that, your body will need it."

I can't even look at him, but I pick up my fork, intending to play with my food until he leaves, but after one bite, I'm ravenous, destroying it all. When I glance up, he's grinning at me.

"Good?"

I nod, embarrassed even further, and he reaches over, pressing his thumb to the corner of my lip and wiping. I blink as he pulls it back to show the berries from the pancakes, and as I watch, he sucks it clean and then continues eating like nothing happened.

My eyes drop to his lips before I look away. Did I really try to kiss him? What was all that shit he said? Was it just to calm me down or get what he wanted? But he turned me down, so maybe not?

I don't know, but I don't want to either. I dare not ask, it's too much, and I'm still too sensitive from drinking.

"Oh, a few of your bulbs were out as well, so I changed them for you and ordered more because I noticed you were low," he says without looking my way.

I frown. "The maintenance man changes them."

"So? It needed to be done," he replies as he takes a sip of juice and looks at me. "Can't you do it?"

"I can. I just . . . didn't notice," I admit, feeling ashamed.

He grins. "Don't worry about it. I'll come change them anytime. You have a lot of other things to do."

"Why would you change them?" I snap, dropping my fork to my plate.

He looks from it to me. "Because I like taking care of you," he admits without an ounce of shame or embarrassment.

"I don't need you to look after me," I mutter, knowing I'm taking my annoyance out on him. It's not his fault I got drunk and threw myself at him, but he's here, so he gets my wrath.

It's nasty but true.

He doesn't seem to care, however, as he keeps eating, and when he's done, he washes our plates while I just stare at him. He checks his phone and swears, grabbing a folded shirt from the side. He shoves it on and slips on his jacket. "I have to run, baby. My boss is nice, but I have a practice race this afternoon. Make sure to shower and rest, and call me if you need anything." He hurries around, kissing my head before I can react, and then he's gone like a whirlwind, leaving me looking around in silence.

Why doesn't it feel comforting?

I tell myself I'm showering because I need to, not because he told me to. Balling up my jeans and boxers, I head to my hamper in my bathroom, only to stop at the bright blue sticky note pressed to the lid.

Rolling my eyes, I throw my clothes into the hamper and head to my shower, only to find a bright blue note attached to the outside of the glass.

Is he trying to flirt with me through notes? Ignoring it, I shower quickly, scrubbing every inch of me since I feel sweaty and gross. After I get out and wrap a towel around myself, I spot another note on the mirror. I don't know how I missed these earlier, but I blame the hangover.

Ripping them all down, I stomp into my bedroom to see one on my lamp next to my bed.

Snarling, I open my top drawer and shove them all inside, right alongside the card he sent me with the flowers. Slamming it shut, I towel dry and dress in some sweats before collapsing onto my sofa and turning my TV on.

I hate lying around. I'm usually studying, working out, or teaching classes, but I don't feel one hundred percent, nor can I bring myself to see anyone today after the ass I made out of myself last night, so I hide in here, watching Netflix mindlessly.

I try to relax, all while my brain screams at me that I should be working, cleaning, or doing something.

No, it isn't my brain. It's my father's voice.

Lovely.

It makes my headache ten times worse, and the entire time I lie here, it berates me until I'm not really relaxing. I'm just trapped.

When my doorbell rings, my heart starts to pound and I leap to my feet, scanning for any mess or something to grab to make me look busy before I remember I'm in my own apartment and answer to no one. I guess old habits die hard.

Rubbing my head in exhaustion, I walk to the door and check the peephole to make sure it isn't Sky. It's a delivery guy, so I open it and frown when he shoves a brown bag at me. "I didn't order anything."

"Oh, I was told to give you this." A blue note is handed to me, and the guy grins. "Enjoy the food!" I watch him go before shutting the door. Putting the bag on the counter, I peer at the Post-it Note.

> DON'T FORGET TO EAT, HOT STUFF. HOPE YOUR DAY IS AMAZING.
>
> — SKY :)

Sighing, I open the bag and peer inside. There's some soup, a sandwich, fruit, a smoothie, and a cake. Shaking my head, I close the bag, refusing to eat it. I shouldn't give in to him and let him think he can do this or he'll just keep pushing further into my life, demanding more. You give the guy an inch, and he cooks breakfast in your kitchen. What happens if I eat his dinner? I get married?

Not a chance in hell.

My determination lasts all of five minutes. The food smells too good and I'm starving.

After I demolish it, I stare at the note before my phone buzzes. I ignored it all morning after I opened a message from Alek with a video of me being thrown over Skylar's shoulder, my mortification too strong.

> Skylar: Are you having a good day?
>
> Skylar: Have you rested?
>
> Skylar: Are you hungover?
>
> Skylar: I need to work late, but let me know if you're awake later and I'll swing by with some dinner for you.
>
> Skylar: Make sure to sleep and drink plenty.
>
> Skylar: I miss you.
>
> Skylar: You were cute last night btw.
>
> Skylar: Feel free to get drunk anytime.
>
> Skylar: Was the food okay? I ordered from the diner you go to all the time. They mentioned that was your favorite.

Throwing my phone down, I stare at his unanswered messages. Why do I keep getting pulled back in? Last night was terrifying enough, and waking up to him here? No, he's getting too close. I'm letting him get too close. I need to stop this.

Call it panic over what happened and about those confessions I heard that can't be real, but I reach over and block his number. I throw my phone down before I can change my mind.

Dropping my head back, I close my eyes.

There, it's done.
Skylar Warren is out of my life.
He's no longer my concern.
He and his confusing feelings can disappear.
I'm better alone, a prince in his ice castle.

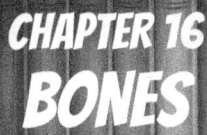

CHAPTER 16
BONES

"**Y**ou are in a suspiciously good mood."

"Huh?" Blinking, I drag my gaze from my phone and the morning text and picture from yesterday to see Alek next to me. He came to drop Evan off, and we happened to run into each other when my phone buzzed. I'll admit I grabbed it fast, my heart racing for some reason I don't quite understand myself.

"You're not glaring," Alek points out as I pocket my phone without responding.

"That means I'm in a good mood?" I arch a brow.

"For you? Yes." His grin is cruel as he nudges me. "Is it a certain racer?"

"Shut the fuck up right now," I snap. "It's just a nice day."

We both turn to look at the dull, cloudy sky and the spitting rain, and Alek eyes me as if to call me a liar. What the fuck is wrong with me?

"Why did you call him anyway?" I mutter.

"I had my own boy to take care of. Besides, you kept telling me to. Don't you remember?" My frown makes him chuckle, and he clears his throat before making his voice higher. "Fine, if I'm so annoying, call Sky. He'll come and play with me. Call him, I dare you."

"I didn't say that." I look away as he nudges me again.

"You're funny when you're drunk, although I don't see you drink that often. Is everything okay?" he asks, concern in his voice.

"Fine, everything is fine," I respond automatically as I push away. "I better get to class."

"I'll see Sky at work. Want me to tell him anything for you? Pass a note? Declare your undying love—" He grunts as I ram my knee into his balls before turning away in a genuinely good mood as he curses.

I head toward the building where my first seminar is, and I'm halfway down the winding path when a man pops up in front of me. My first thought is to swing—mainly because if you invade someone's personal space like that, you deserve to be hit—but I dial it back, knowing my anger management coach would have some interesting things to say about that.

I don't hate everyone per se, just most people, especially those who talk to me or grin at me like a psychopath after jumping out like a clown in a serial killer film.

"What?" I snarl.

"Bones, right?" the guy asks, a cap pulled low to obscure most of his face. He's wearing what looks like a delivery driver's outfit, and he has a helmet clutched in one hand. "You look exactly like he said you would, which makes my life easier. Here." He thrusts a bag at me, and with a salute, he walks away.

What in the ever-loving fuck?

Cautiously opening the bag, I peer inside, only to sigh. There's a lunch box with a sticky note on the top, and I don't even have to guess who it's from.

Shutting the bag, I pull my phone out and type out a message, unblocking him quickly to send it.

> Bones: You know I'm capable of getting my own lunch, right?

> Skylar: But why should you when I can? Have a good day at school, study hard.

> Skylar: I like taking care of you.

I stare at the message, rereading it for what feels like a hundred times before putting my phone away and heading to my seminar, bag in hand.

I do eat the lunch, but only because I end up helping someone go over their notes longer than I expected, and by the time I have a break, I wouldn't have time to leave for food.

It's nice, and I hate that he knows what I like.

Scrunching the bag, I go to throw it away before I hesitate and reach inside, pluck out the note, and then throw the rest away. Shoving the note in my wallet, I head back to class for another busy afternoon.

I don't even realize I'm smiling until someone points it out.

I guess I should be thankful I almost forgot the date. I went all day without remembering. It was only when I got home and was listening to the news that it clicked.

It's the sixteenth.

I knew it was coming, I was dreading it, but I forgot since I was so busy. I guess that's a blessing and a curse, but now as I sit at home, alone in the dark, staring at the calendar, all I can think about is that I wish I hadn't noticed at all.

What is it about grief that does that to a person?

I miss them all the time, but on this date, it's so bad, I feel like I can't breathe, and the memories come flooding back. I can usually shield myself from the pain, but today is the worst day of the year.

The calendar stands beside a glass bottle of expensive whiskey. I know I shouldn't drink it because it won't help. It might numb me and make me forget for a little while, but it will all still be there when I wake up.

Besides, one embarrassing, drunken mess per week is my limit.

I stare at the bottle, wishing it could help take this away.

Turning away from it before I give in, I head to my bookshelf and tug out the small, cheap book of maps from the array of expensive ones surrounding it, then I open the pages, letting them flutter until the picture falls out.

Gripping the cheap photo booth image, I sit heavily on the sofa, my eyes tracing his face like I have done a thousand times in real life and in images. He doesn't change or age, but I do. I no longer look like the bare-skinned, smiling kid in this picture. I'm covered in ink and scars now, and I'm angry and cold.

He would hate who I have become.

My shoulders hunch and my eyes burn with tears I refuse to let fall. I have cried enough to last a lifetime, and I promised myself I never would again, not after that night, but staring at this picture when we were so happy . . .

It fucking destroys me.

Why can't I have that?

What did I do to deserve to lose the one good thing in my life that made me happy? I was sad and lonely before him, and then he came in like a fucking ball of sunshine.

He wasn't perfect. He was stubborn and youthful and stupid sometimes, but he made me smile for the first time ever. He saw all of me and made me laugh. He held me when I admitted how much I hated my life and my father. He loved me when I didn't even love myself.

Why did he do that?

Why did he give me a glimpse of happiness then leave me?

"Why?" I whisper.

It's been three years, so deep down, I know the worst has happened.

He's dead. I can feel it. He never would have left me alone otherwise, not when we had our entire future planned out together.

It's not knowing for certain, though, that's the worst. There's always this lingering doubt, and I check every face. It's like my life is just passing me by and I'm still waiting at that bus stop for him to show up so we could leave together.

But he never showed.

I waited all night, and he never came.

At first I was mad and hurt, but when he didn't answer his phone, I became worried. No matter how angry we were at each other, he always answered. I went to his house, but his stuff was still there, half packed in a bag on his bed, like he was ready to leave with me.

He was planning to. I know it.

The police investigated at my instistance, but it was soon dropped. They just assumed he ran away, but I knew differently. His family life was as bad as mine, and he wanted out just as badly. We had that, and then he was gone. Something happened to him, and I'm starting to think I'll never find out what.

Dropping the photo, I flip through the book, seeing his handwriting alongside mine—notes on countries we wanted to visit, the best time of year, and bus schedules. Every inch was planned out.

I press my head to the cover of the book, and a tear finally falls.

Three years ago today, I stood at a bus stop, ready to run away with the love of my life.

Three years ago today, my heart broke for the final time.

Three years ago today, I lost everything that made me happy.

Three years of living without a heart and the constant what-ifs about what happened.

Standing, I toss the book down and head to the bottle. Fuck it. Tonight is a night for drinking, but as I grab the whiskey, Sky's voice fills my head for some reason.

I like looking after you.

Why am I thinking of him now?

He doesn't even remind me of Aro. They are polar opposites, but here I am, thinking about Sky when I should be thinking of Aro. I can't seem to care, however, as I reach for my phone like I'm reaching for a lifeline.

I need Sky.

I don't want to be alone anymore.

"Baby?" he answers, worry in his voice.

"I need you."

CHAPTER 17
SKYLAR

Climbing from my car, I tug off my helmet and wipe my sweaty face on my arm as I frown at Mackie. "We felt slower that time."

"We have been at it for ten hours," he says with a tired smile. "I know you want us to be the best, but it means balancing practice and rest."

"I know, I know. You sound like Noah. How about one more time?" I plead. I just want to make sure we win—not just for us, but for Bones as well, since he'll be here too.

"Alright, alright, one last time," Mackie warns as he pulls his helmet back on. I'm about to pull mine down when I feel my phone vibrating in my pocket. Grabbing it, I go to silence the call when I realize who it is, and then I swiftly answer.

"Baby, what's wrong?" I ask.

Bones never calls me, not ever, and my heart hammers in fear. What if something happened to him? What if he's hurt?

"I need you." His voice is flat, but I still hear a lot of fucking pain.

I flag Mackie down and shake my head. "One second, baby." Covering the phone, I tell Mackie, "Let's call it a night. I have to go."

"Wait, Sky," he calls as I leave my helmet and rush across the tarmac to the garage. I head to the locker room, holding the phone to my ear as I start to strip from my suit.

"What's wrong?" I ask again. "Are you hurt? Are you safe?"

"I'm fine. I don't know why I called," he admits, his voice so soft and quiet I barely hear him. "Sorry, I shouldn't have. You're busy—"

"Wait, wait, keep talking to me," I implore, kicking off my boots. "I'm glad you called." I sit and quickly undo my suit, putting him on speaker so I can undress and hang it up.

"What's going on?" I ask as I shove my head into my shirt and pull it down before tugging on my jeans. I'm hopping to get them on when there's a knock.

"Sky, Mackie said you're in here. Is everything okay? He said you left pretty suddenly," Noah calls worriedly.

"Shit, you're busy. I'll go." Bones hangs up, and I curse as I shove my boots on and throw my jacket over my shoulders, closing the locker door to see Noah.

"Yeah, sorry, I have to go," I tell him, and he must sense my worry because he nods.

"Need me to drive you anywhere?"

"No, but thanks, boss. I'll see you tomorrow," I call as I hightail it out of there, waving at Alek who watches me with a frown. By the time I'm in my car, I'm redialing Bones, but it goes straight to voicemail.

Fuck.

I speed through downtown as quickly as I can, and once I pull up outside Bones's building, I type in a text.

> Skylar: I'm outside. Either come out and talk to me or I'll come up. Your choice.

I give him five minutes. I even turn on a timer on my phone, watching it count down.

Something is wrong, and he called me, which means he wants to talk. I'll wait all night if I have to. Bones never asks for anything, so if he's reaching out now, it's important, and I want to ensure he's okay.

He sounded tired and sad, something I never thought I would hear from him. He has it together at all times.

The timer is just hitting thirty seconds left when the front door opens and Bones peers out. He sighs deeply when he sees me but heads over, wearing some loose pajama pants and a half open shirt. He isn't dressed for the weather, which worries me more.

Something is definitely wrong.

He opens the passenger door. "I'm sorry. I shouldn't have called you—"

"Either get in or I'm making you," I order, and he startles at my tone but slowly slides into my car before shutting the door. He won't look me in the eyes though. Turning the heat on, I reach over and buckle his belt, meeting his gaze. His eyes widen and drop to my lips for a moment, and I quickly lean back, not wanting to ruin this by taking liberties when all I want to do is kiss that look off his face.

"Wait, where are we going?" he asks when I pull out of the parking area.

"For a drive until you're ready to talk about whatever is bothering you, or if you never are, then at least you won't be alone tonight while something is wrong. Either is fine with me. Driving around always makes me feel . . . freer, so I thought it might do the same for you."

He's quiet for a while, which is fine. I just want him to know I'm here for him. Whatever is happening, he isn't alone.

That's all I want to be for Bones, a shoulder he can lean on.

I drive for a while, and he seems content to work through his thoughts and just be in my presence. Eventually, I park at the overlook above the city and turn off the engine, then I turn to him. "Come on."

He startles at my voice, his eyes sweeping over me. "Huh?" he croaks.

I slide from the car, and a moment later, he follows, hesitating in his open door. Letting him decide, I climb onto the hood and lie back, my arms under my head as I stare up at the sky. It's quiet. There are no sounds of traffic from the city, just us and the insects. A few moments later, I hear his door shut and the crunching of gravel under his feet before he climbs up next to me.

Turning my eyes to him, I find him sitting awkwardly, staring out at the city. I reach up and tug him back. He falls with a gasp, sprawling next to me. "Skylar," he snaps.

"Shut up and relax, angel," I tell him as I turn my gaze back to the sky.

He's quiet again for a minute before I hear his grumbling voice fill the air. "You know people come here to hook up, right?"

"And how would you know that?" I tease, nudging his shoulder without looking.

He sighs deeply but settles back onto the car, our arms inches apart. I let him continue to think because I don't want to be a burden to Bones, but a safe place. If he needs to sit here all night in silence, then we will.

I almost jump out of my skin when he slides closer. I don't move, and I barely breathe. When I glance down, I find his arm between us, so close I could touch him.

I drop one arm from under my head to the hood, placing it close to his, and I can feel the heat from his skin. Ever so slowly, I inch my pinky across the slippery hood until I feel the softness of his, and then I hook mine around his finger. Stiff as a statue, I wait for him to yell at me, hit me, or pull away, but he surprises me when he does none of these things.

He just lets me connect us without a word.

I want to scream in joy, but I also know that means something is probably very wrong.

"If you ever need anyone to talk to, I'm here," I say softly. "I've been told I'm a good listener."

"By whom?" he scoffs, and I feel his eyes on me. I turn my head, finding him turned partially on his side to face me.

"Everyone." I grin, and he arches a brow. "Okay, Evan told me like one time, but the point remains—I'm here for you. I know something's wrong, and sometimes it helps to talk about it. Keeping it bottled up just makes you feel like you're drowning and all alone. Let me be your life raft."

"Cheesy bastard," he mutters, but his lips roll in as his eyes sweep over my face. "I hate today."

"Friday?" I ask, confused.

His smile is small and bitter. "No, today's date."

I wonder if he will tell me if I ask him, but in his bright eyes, I see a drowning man, searching for a helping hand. He's all alone and icing over in that water, and I refuse to let him sink when I'm right here.

"Why?" I ask.

He watches me for a moment, and I don't think he'll answer when his voice finally comes. "It's the day I lost the most important thing in my life."

Frowning, I cover his hand and squeeze as he swallows hard. "Lost?"

He nods, searching my eyes as if looking for strength. "He was just . . . gone. To this day, I don't know what happened to him. Everything was so great. I was happier than I'd ever been, and then it was all gone and I was lost and alone, and I still am. I'm still waiting for him to show, still waiting at that bus stop, my bag in hand. I can't move on because I don't know what happened," he rambles, and I try to make sense of what he's saying. His voice is trembling and so thick at the end, it's hard to understand.

Twining my fingers with his, I kiss the back of his hand as I stare into his eyes. "Have you ever spoken about this to anyone?"

He shakes his head, watching me carefully.

"You loved this person?" I can tell that much—it's in his voice.

He nods this time, and when his mouth parts, it's like the floodgates open.

His eyes turn glassy, and my heart clenches at the agony in his gaze.

How long has he been heartbroken and hurting?

"I loved him, and I lost him, and it really fucking hurts." The tears finally break free and spill down his face. His lower lip trembles, and I can tell he's trying hard to keep it together.

Sitting up, I tug him into my arms. He's stiff for a moment. "I have you. I'm here, just let it out. There's no one else around," I promise softly as I press my mouth to his hair.

His arms wrap around me, and he buries his face against my chest. His back shakes, and he holds me tighter as his soft sobs reach me. Even now, he keeps them in check, but at least he lets them out. I hold him through it, stroking his back.

"Shh, that's it, let it out. I'm right here, you're not alone," I murmur, raining kisses across his hair as he soaks my shirt.

We sit under the moonlight, overlooking the city that has scarred us both. I hold him as he falls apart, and my heart hurts for him. I struggle to breathe through it, and I feel tears fall from my own eyes. I try to hide them as he cries, but he must sense it because he pulls back.

"Why are you crying?" he whispers as he stares at my face.

"For you," I reply. As I stare into this man's eyes, I realize that this might have started as something to pass the time, but this man right here has stolen my heart and soul and become everything for me, so when he cries, it destroys me. I want to find everyone who has hurt him and make them pay, but I know he can fight his own battles, so instead, I offer the only thing I can—my arms.

"I never expected you to be someone who cries," he admits as he wipes his face, embarrassment heating his cheeks.

"It isn't weak to show your emotions to someone, Bones. It's brave and makes you strong and so much more lovable."

"What's the point?" he rasps. "There's nothing left of me to love."

"That's where you're wrong," I whisper as I rub under his puffy eyes. "You don't see yourself as I do, as we all do. There is so much of you to love, Bones, and I will keep showing you every day until you understand."

He watches me for a moment, his eyes red, and he has never looked more beautiful.

"You beautiful, beautiful boy," I whisper, unable to help it.

He finally laughs. "I'm a mess."

"I like you messy," I admit with a grin and wipe away his tears. "I like seeing this side of you that no one else does. When you're cute, jealous, drunk, or sad, it just makes you more real to me and less untouchable."

"Why are you so nice to me? I'm horrible to you," he asks, leaning into my hands, and the fact that he doesn't even seem to realize what he's doing makes my heart race.

"I think you don't know how to be loved and that you're mean because you're scared. Deep down, you want someone to love you. You're just terrified to let them. That's why I'm nice to you, because I see past the snark, past the cruel words, and to the man underneath who teaches self-defense so no one has to feel scared again, the man who stood with his friends in the face of a deranged serial killer, who fought silently to keep the memorial up, never asking for a thank you. You are so deserving of being loved, Bones, my beautiful boy. I know this world has been cruel to you, but I promise I will never be. I will never hurt you, leave, or betray you. I will be right here, like the statue in the wind, unchanging and unmoving. I know you think that I don't take anything in life seriously, but you're wrong. I take you seriously. From the moment I laid eyes on you, you changed me. You made me want more. I can wait for you, I can wait forever if I have to, but don't ever think you can push me away because you can't. I'm not going anywhere."

I can feel his heart pounding as he stares at me. He's looking for a trap in my promise, a trick, his lawyer brain searching for loopholes in my promise, but there aren't any.

My words might never be as eloquent as his, but I meant every single one of them.

I will stay at his side, even when he doesn't want me.

I'm about to drop my hands and lean away to give him space, knowing I'm probably overwhelming him, when he speaks.

"You told me to ask you in the morning."

"Huh?" I ask, completely confused.

He swallows, his tongue darting out to trace his lips, and I follow the movement, my heart starting to pound for a whole other reason.

"If I wanted to kiss you when I was sober, you told me to ask in the morning," he says, his voice confident.

My eyes dart up to his, hope blooming in me, one I dare not feel, but there's a softness in his gaze, a want I can't deny, and neither can he.

"Are you asking, baby?" I question carefully, needing to be sure.

I don't want our first kiss to be because he's sad, lonely, or drunk—not when it will mean everything to me. I want it to be the same for him.

"If I was?" he murmurs, glancing at my lips for a moment as we seem to draw closer together until our breaths mingle, the air becoming tight with tension.

"Then I'd be the happiest man on earth," I admit, "but I want you to be sure. Kiss me, Bones, because you want me. You're giving me hope, know that, so don't ask if you aren't certain."

I don't think I could bear him turning away from me after.

"Skylar, will you kiss me?" he asks breathlessly. When I just stare, he starts to pull away. "I—"

Closing the small distance between us, I press my lips to his before barely pulling back in case he changes his mind. "Anything you want from me, angel, all you have to do is ask. You know that. I will always give you whatever you need or want, even me." Sliding my hand up his cheek and into his hair, I brush my mouth across his.

His lips part, his eyes sliding shut, and I want to scream in victory. Instead, I pull him closer as I deepen the kiss.

I swallow his gasp, sweeping my tongue in to tangle with his. My cock hardens in my pants, but I ignore it, ignore my body and my wants.

This isn't just sex between us.

This is so much more, and my heart knows it as I taste the first kiss of the man I am falling in love with.

The man whose kiss I want to be my last.

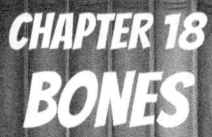

CHAPTER 18
BONES

Maybe this is wrong and I should stop him.

My heart still belongs to another, and I don't have enough of it left to protect and love someone else, but I am so tired of being cold, alone, and in pain, and Skylar is alive.

He is so warm and offering me everything I didn't know I needed.

Maybe it's fucked up for me to claim this from him when he's so serious about me and I'm using him to feel, but I can't seem to care as I kiss him back.

I wish I could say this didn't make me feel anything, and I wish I could say it doesn't compare to my first love, but the truth is, I can't even remember the shape of his lips, the way he tasted, or the way he kissed, but this?

I'll remember this and the way he moans softly, tugging me closer like he can't get enough of me.

"Angel," he whispers into my lips, and I shudder.

Pleasure rolls through me for the first time in years. "Say it again," I beg. There's something about the way he says it, rolling the nickname over his tongue, like it's the only word he will ever need to speak.

"Angel," he whispers again, and I kiss him hard, pushing him back into his car. One of his hands slides down my back and cups my hip to tug me closer, his other stroking through my short hair as his tongue tangles with mine.

We kiss leisurely under the stars. I expected him to push for more, but if anything, he slows me down when I get too eager.

I don't pull away. I let him consume me.

I let him remake me from the inside out.

I let him claim me with a touch and make me feel.

For the first time in years, I feel something other than agony, and Skylar Warren is the reason.

We don't talk on the way home, we don't need to, and I like that he knows when to speak and when to just be. He's usually a big yapper, and I'm just stuck there listening, but as he drives me home in the early morning, I find myself watching him.

There's more to him than I first thought.

Lifting our joined hands, he kisses my knuckles without even looking at me, his lips lingering on them. I look away with a small smile. It's almost over too quickly as we pull up outside my apartment. He releases my hand, and I hesitate, not wanting to go, but he climbs from the car. I watch him with a frown as he heads around the hood and opens my door for me, offering me his hand.

Looking from it to him, I unfasten my belt and lay mine in his. He pulls me from the car, keeping my hand hostage as he shuts the door behind me.

Skylar walks me to the door and turns me to him, his thumb rubbing back and forth across my fingers. "I'll leave you here. I won't ruin this or push you, and we both know if I went up, I would. This isn't what tonight was about, baby." Lifting my hand, he kisses it again, his dark eyes on me. "I'm glad you called me tonight. I'm just on the other end of the phone whenever you need someone to talk to."

"Thank you," I murmur, feeling shy for some reason. "For . . . tonight."

Smiling, he tugs me into his arms and kisses my forehead. "Go get some sleep and remember to eat before school." He slaps my side and steps back, and I watch him for a moment, frozen. "Go on."

Nodding, I turn and head inside, glancing back at the elevator to find him still watching me. I lift my arm and wave. He blows me a kiss back, and I step into the elevator, almost smacking myself.

I fucking waved like a moron.

Shaking my head, I lean back as I rise quickly, and when it opens, I blink and get out, robotically finding my key, unlocking my door, and padding through the dark apartment.

These four walls were once my haven, but now they just feel empty.

Pressing my fingers to my lips, I stare blindly out at the rising sun.

I survived another dreaded sixteenth, but this time, it felt different.

I was finally able to let go a little and start to heal, and it's all because of him.

What is he doing to me?

CHAPTER 19
SKYLAR

T he race is tomorrow, and it's our only chance to qualify. We have to place or we're out of this year's championship running, so the entire team is feeling the pressure. Alek is grumpier than normal, snapping at everyone as he triple-checks everything. Noah is putting out fires everywhere, the mechanics are working overtime, and Mackie and I have been practicing around the clock.

Slumping back into the leather chair before the racing simulator, I stretch out my aching hands. We've done speed training, resistance, and then practice and repeat. I've barely seen Bones these last few days, but this is important, and I hope he understands that too.

I miss him, but I want him to be proud to have me at his side. Besides, I need to win, and I want to claim my winnings from him. Rolling my shoulders as I stand, I lean into Mackie's chair, watching his progress as he maneuvers the wheel, his eyes intent on the two screens in front of him.

Our crews are running their last checks. We'll have team practice once more, and then we'll head home to prepare for tomorrow.

I'm terrified but also excited, more than I have ever been. I am never nervous before races, but this is different, and everything is riding on it. This is my chance to prove myself, my chance at a new life, so everything I want hangs in the balance.

Hours later, we are all exhausted and ready to crash when Noah claps. "That's it. We are calling it a night. All we can do now is rest. We have double and triple-checked everything, and now everyone needs sleep. I don't want any tired eyes tomorrow. No partying or staying up all night. I want everyone to get at least a solid eight hours of rest." He looks around at his team. "This is Starfire's year to claim that championship title for our own, and I know we can do it. We're stronger than we have ever been. Our team is the best, and our racers?" Everyone looks at us. "They are going to bring it home for us, but this is a team effort. Without one, we all fail, so I want to thank all of you for the overtime and effort you have put into this. I know what it takes and how draining it is, but I promise when we hold that trophy, it'll all be worth it." He puts his hand on mine, grinning. "Now indulge an old man."

Everyone adds their hands, and he starts to bounce them as he looks around at us. "Starfire Racing!"

We repeat it despite it being cheesy, and my smile is wide.

Is this what it's like to have a family?

It feels . . . good.

All I need is my boy and the title, and I'll have everything I want.

Today is the day. Despite Noah's warnings, I could barely sleep last night. I grabbed a few hours early in the morning, but I was showered and dressed and out the door before the sun even rose. I'm the first to arrive at the garage, and I sit on the hood of my car, looking out at the track we're racing on today. It's one we've practiced on, so I know the twists and turns. Our team's garage stands to the left, our banner above it.

Red Check Racing's garage is empty next to it, and Blizzard is to the right. There are ten teams competing today. Some of the smaller ones only have one racer, but Blizzard, Red Check, and Starfire are the big three with two. Everyone knows the three of us will be competing for the podium.

I plan to show them how I will snatch that title away.

The rumble of a bike makes my head turn, and Mackie climbs off, stowing his helmet as he heads my way. We bump fists, and he glances at the track. "Are you ready?"

"As I'll ever be," I reply. "You?"

"Ready." He grins. "Let's show those assholes who's going to make them our bitch."

Laughing, I clap his shoulder. "Head in, I'll be there in a minute."

I watch him go as I pull my phone out and glance at my unanswered texts to Bones, which is not unusual, but I find myself hoping for one today. I need his strength and assurance.

> Skylar: You're coming today, right?

Shit, does that sound too needy?

> Skylar: I hope you are. I'll look for you.

Shit, that's even worse.

> Skylar: I'm nervous, but I know looking at your face will make it all disappear. Please come.

I'm making it worse, so I tuck my phone away before I completely embarrass myself. I slide off my hood and head over the gravel lot to our garage, where our cars are sitting. I'm not surprised to see Noah inside, but I head over to the changing room when I notice him and Mackie bent together, whispering and looking far too close.

It's about time that man realized what was right in front of him.

In the locker room, I hang up my jacket and keys and strip, changing into my undersuit as I slam my locker and glance in the mirror. I look just like the boy who climbed into cars in the street, but I feel completely different.

I was a cocky, stubborn asshole the first time I raced. Now, all I feel is excitement and nervousness. I wish I could see Bones for a minute. He would probably call me out on my shit, but it would make me feel better.

Hope fills me as I turn to the door of the locker room as it bangs open, but I slump when I see Alek.

"Well, shit, don't act too happy to see me, asshole," he snaps, but he grins and claps my shoulder. "Don't be nervous, you've got this. I've seen you race a million times."

"It's a little different now," I reply as I play with my gloves.

"Nah, just pretend it's the streets. It's no different, man, just you and the car. Nothing else matters." He squeezes my shoulders. "Take a minute and then come out. Everyone is starting to arrive. Head out there and show the other racers who you are. Just like on the streets, they sense weakness, so don't give them anything."

"Too fucking right." I nod, and he heads out. I look back in the mirror and force a smile. He's right. It's my time to show them all who the new racer is.

My reputation must precede me because I feel the others looking at me. They all know I'm a street racer, and it seems some don't think I belong.

Too fucking bad because I'm not planning on going anywhere.

I make it obvious as I inspect my car and then watch them right back, waving and taunting them. I give them nothing to pounce on as the time passes. The stands fill up, and I can hear the crowd from here. The cameras roll in, and interviewers circle the pits, searching for their new fan favorites. Bloggers and influencers hold their phones up as they walk between teams, and when one homes in on me, I smirk.

Leaning back into my car, I grin at the girl as she points the camera at me and blows me a kiss. She squeals, turning it back around, and suddenly every eye is on me.

I know what I look like, I'm not an idiot, and it seems my appearance has a positive effect here. People crowd our pit, and Noah throws me a thumbs-up. We need fans and supporters, so I play along.

"You're the new Starfire racer, right?" someone asks from the small crowd.

"I am. My name's Skylar Warren." I wink.

"There's a rumor you're an illegal street racer."

"Now, if I was, would I admit that?" I tease as I stretch. I wink at a girl who gasps when my abs flash by mistake.

"You think Starfire stands a chance? They haven't qualified in the last two years. Top teams like Blizzard and Red Check are here, so are you really in the running?" an older man asks, a mic on his jacket.

"I think you shouldn't count us out. They didn't have me the last two years," I joke.

"Arrogant," someone mutters.

"No, it's not arrogance. It's just the truth." I push from the car and straighten, flashing them a beaming smile. "But see for yourself. We plan on taking first and second place today. When we do, talk to me then. Starfire Racing plans on winning it all." Waving at the cameras, I head over to Noah, ignoring them pointing at me.

"Good job," he mutters, draping his arm over my shoulders. "Are you ready?"

I smirk. "Ready to kick some ass."

"Starfire Racing first and second? What a joke." The dark voice makes us both turn, and I raise an eyebrow at the man in a suit standing in our pit, helmet in hand, with "Blizzard" scrawled across it.

"I'm not laughing." I shrug. "Are you laughing, Noah?"

"Not even a little," he replies.

"No, but I will be when I smoke you today," the Blizzard racer sneers, waving at the cameras.

"Sorry, I don't have a clue who you are," I remark.

His mouth drops open as I step closer.

"What I do know is that you seem to be lost, little boy. You better get going. You wouldn't want to sit out on getting your ass kicked, would you?"

"I don't know who the fuck you think you are . . ." He stomps toward me, not stopping until we are squared up. "You're nothing more than trash they dragged off the street. It won't work. I'm taking that championship again, and when I'm done with you, you'll remember my name."

"That's hard when I still don't know it." I grin, not giving into his anger. I won't cause a scene, but I do move closer. "Standing this close to me, I might start to think you want to kiss me. Do you?" I tease, and he stumbles back as I grin. "No? You aren't my type, sorry. Now, if you'll excuse us, our team would like to speak. Feel free to stick around if you really want to. Maybe you'll learn something." I turn my back on him, dismissing him, and Noah chuckles.

"You know who that is, right?"

"Of course I do. I'm not an idiot," I mutter. "Conall is the best. He's won the last three years."

"And has a mean streak, so don't get on his bad side," Noah mumbles.

"He got on mine. That idiot doesn't know who he's messing with. Don't worry, old man." I slap his back and step away. "We'll get you that title."

"Sky?" I look at him. "Look out for Mackie, will you?"

"Don't worry, boss man. I got your boy for you." He curses, and I head to my car as Mackie comes from the changing room. "You ready?"

"As I'll ever be." We crash helmets. After nodding at Noah, we step out of the pit and into the spotlight. It's a small distance to the track where our cars wait, but we don't look at the crowd, ignoring the screams as other racers do the same.

I don't let myself look, not until I'm at my car, then I scan the stands. I find Noah at the side with Alek and Evan, waving a flag, but it's the person beside them that makes my heart pound.

He came.

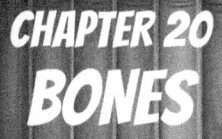

CHAPTER 20
BONES

He stares at me, and I stare right back.

Nerves fill me, but I refuse to let them show. Why am I here? I could blame Alek or Evan, but the truth is, I was planning to come anyway. I even texted Evan to ask what I should wear. He suggested a shirt with Skylar's name. I didn't go that far, but I made an effort and put on a leather jacket. I can tell it wasn't in vain as his eyes run down my body. His friend or co-racer, whatever they are called, tries to tug him along, but he stands still, watching me.

My gaze roams over him, my mouth turning dry. He looks good in the white and orange suit, his helmet held in his hand. I'd been straining to catch a glimpse of him in the pit while Alek and Evan got us set up trackside so we didn't have to sit in the stands, but now, looking at him, I have to admit I want Skylar Warren.

The crowd cheers, and some even scream his name, but he never once looks away from me. He doesn't even seem to blink, but I see relief in his eyes and know I made the right decision to come. When I lift my hand shyly and wave, it seems to break his spell. Ignoring the young guy at his side, he hurries to the barrier separating us from the track.

He doesn't look away as he vaults the first barrier, grabs onto the railing, and hauls himself up, grinning at me. "Hi, beautiful. I'm so glad you came."

"Hi," I say, glancing around in embarrassment when I feel every eye on us. "Skylar, everyone is looking."

"Let them. They can look at you all they want. They just can't touch." He winks.

"I meant at you." I sigh deeply, pinching my nose in annoyance.

"Nah, baby, trust me. They are looking at you, and I don't blame them one bit, but you're looking at me. Like the suit? I could keep it on later—" I smack his chest, and he laughs, kissing my cheek even as I jerk back. "I needed that for luck."

"Go," I order, pointing at the track sternly.

He pouts. "Kiss me properly for luck?" he asks cutely. "I need it. I'm nervous."

"Go," I order once more.

"Baby," he whines. "Wish your boy luck."

I glance at Alek and Evan, who are grinning, and those around us with cameras. Rolling my eyes, I turn back to Skylar, grab the edge of his suit, and pull him in. His eyes widen in shock and desire as I lean close, only to stop. "Go race. I didn't come here to see you lose."

I let go then, and he sighs dramatically. "So demanding. Fine, beautiful, I'll win for you."

"Warren, get your ass on that track!" the man Alek introduced as Noah barks, but he sounds more amused than anything.

"Sure thing, old man, just had to say hi to my boy. Alek, take care of him while I'm racing and make sure no one messes with him." He winks at me and drops back, letting his feet hit the tarmac. With one more grin at me, he turns and prowls onto the track. I watch as the others gathered there watch him with fear, desire, or curiosity.

It's clear Skylar Warren is an enigma to them, and they are all watching him. He's a wild card.

"Is he nervous?" I ask Alek. "He doesn't seem like he is."

"He is. He just covers it well," Alek replies.

"You don't step foot into the wolves' den and not be nervous," Noah remarks, covering his mic. "There is nothing like your first qualifier. I was so terrified, I threw up after, but he's playing it well and not giving them an inch of weakness. It's part of our plan to intimidate them and play up his reputation. Everyone here knows he's a street racer, so he's playing the cocky bad boy to throw them off. It will work." He nods at someone glaring at Sky, who's leaning against a red car. "Even Blizzard is thrown off. They've never seen him race, so they don't know what to expect, and that makes them nervous. There's quite a legend building about Sky, and I bet after today, there will only be more."

"What do you mean?" I murmur, glancing at Noah.

"Skylar Warren is one of the best racers I have ever seen, and with Mackie, he will be unstoppable. If they can rein in their shit, they won't just be champions, but world champions."

I guess I never really gave much thought to the fame Sky will gain from this, but as people scream their names, I start to see how it will be.

Will he leave me behind?

I don't know, but the thought squeezes my heart in something akin to terror. Shaking it off, I focus on him and the track. I tried to research it as much as I could, purely to make sure he doesn't win the bet unfairly of course, but I don't know everything, so I'm glad Alek is at my side.

He and his partner hit their helmets together. "That's Mackie," Alek explains. "Noah's protégé."

I nod, keeping my eyes on Skylar as he puts his helmet on and blows the guy from Blizzard a kiss then climbs in. He's toward the back with Mackie, but he doesn't seem to care as he revs his engine and waits. Everyone else clears the track, and the lights flicker on above them, the four wide bulbs each displaying a racing flag as the commentator's voice fills the stadium, but I can hardly listen until I hear his name.

"We have a new racer today—Skylar Warren for team Starfire. It's his first qualifying match after joining Starfire a month ago. Most aren't putting much stock into the new racer, but we'll see what today holds. Can Starfire place, or will they fizzle out again and be forgotten?"

"Assholes," I mutter as I focus on Skylar.

"Ignore them," Noah says. "Our boys know their job, and they have no problem showing everyone they are wrong." He uncovers his mic. "Mackie, stay on Skylar's ass no matter what. Block those moth-erfuckers and stick to the plan. Skylar, show the fuck off. It's time."

"You got it, boss man." His voice crackles through the mic. "Tell them to hold onto their asses because I'm about to make them my bitch."

Shaking my head, I bite my smile back as a big screen starts to count down. The lights begin to flash red, then orange, and suddenly the flag drops, they flash green, and they are off.

My heart seems to crash in my chest as I keep my eyes on the blue cars. There are two of them, Sky and Mackie, and they keep level as they shoot down the straight, only breaking apart to overtake three cars until they are in the middle of the pack.

"That's it, keep it there. Let them fight it out and then sweep in to take the lead," Noah commands, glancing from the computers to the track.

I watch as they take the first corner, Sky's car drifting around someone before he levels out and shoots off. He and Mackie create a barrier in the middle as the top five cars keep changing positions, seeming to fight it out for the next three corners.

Sky must get bored because on the fourth, he undercuts a car and speeds past to level out with the top four. Two are red cars, and the others are black and orange.

"Skylar, easy," Noah warns.

"Ah, come on, old man, this is too easy. You think I've even put in any effort yet?"

He keeps pace with them around the next corner, and then Noah grins. "Alright, boys, time to show them. Take first and second."

"About fucking time," Skylar retorts.

"Let's do this," Mackie says.

As I watch, Skylar levels out next to the red Blizzard car, and even from here, I can see him waving at him as they pass, and then he slams his hand into the throttle and shoots off, taking the lead.

I can't help it, I cheer with everyone else before coughing when I feel Alek watching me. "I got caught up," I mutter.

"Sure." He smirks.

Looking back at the track, I see Mackie slipping past them, and it's no wonder Noah is so proud of him. He levels out behind Skylar, blocking anyone from getting past and allowing Sky to speed and show off. It's a good plan, and it's clearly working as they take the next lap, the red and orange cars fighting to get past Mackie. The Blizzard car manages to on the third and final lap.

"Shit, sorry, Sky," Mackie snarls. "This fucker won't stop riding me."

"Take care of yourself. I have Conall." I can hear Sky's smirk from here.

"Skylar," Noah cautions.

"Ah, don't worry, just going to show him some street moves."

He seems to slow, and Blizzard pulls up beside him as they take a three S-bend. Skylar's engine revs, and he drifts right next to him, almost touching Blizzard's car. He's clearly showing off, and on the last turn, he slips behind him, letting him think he's won. My eyes widen as Skylar spins in a circle and out on Blizzard's other side then shoots past him.

He takes first once more, leaving the Blizzard racer so focused on Sky that he doesn't even see Mackie hunting him. Mackie swerves left and right before shooting past and down the straight. Skylar slows, leveling out with Mackie.

"Take first place, Sky," Mackie calls. "I'm happy in second. You fucking deserve it."

"Noah?" Sky asks.

"You heard him, take first."

Sky takes off, and Mackie slips in behind him, both crossing the line, and the crowd goes wild.

"And Skylar Warren has done it, taking first place! Starfire claims both top spots in an unprecedented takeover. They dominated the track—"

I'm screaming alongside everyone else, jumping and whooping as Sky and Mackie spin and slide to a stop, other cars following over the line.

"Skylar Warren, the underdog, has done it, beating the undefeated reigning champion from Blizzard—"

"Yes, baby!" I scream, and someone laughs.

When I turn, I gape when I find Alek recording me. He puts his phone away and blinks innocently as my eyes narrow.

When the last car stops, they start to climb out, and my focus is dragged back to Sky. He climbs from his car, and he and Mackie smack each other on the back before Sky picks him up and spins him around, and Noah shakes his head, grinning as he pulls his mic off.

"They fucking did it," he whispers.

Sky drops Mackie, looking at the crowd, and I don't blame him. They are all screaming for him, but his eyes land on me. Uncaring about the other drivers coming over to congratulate him, he hurries my way, leaps over the barrier again, and throws his gloves and helmet down. The crowd screams louder the closer he gets.

Some girls behind me squeal. "Holy shit, he's coming over again! He's so hot."

"Think he'll be at the after-party? We could team him."

"If not, we'll sneak into the locker room again—"

My eyes narrow as I turn to glare at them before a noise makes me turn around to find Skylar hauling himself up the rail again. This time he sits astride it, grinning down at me. Call it excitement or annoyance at those girls, but I fist his suit and drag him closer as his eyes widen, and when my lips meet his ear, I feel him shiver.

"Show off," I murmur, and when I pull back, my lips brush his cheek.

Panting, he stares at me, covering my hand on his suit when I go to release him. "I won. I want my prize, beautiful."

"Sky, get down there for the photo!" Alek barks.

Skylar waits, arching an eyebrow. "They can wait until my boy is ready."

"Skylar," I snap.

He smirks. "I'm waiting."

I hear the crowd chanting his name, every eye on us. Grinding my teeth, I speak quietly between us.

"Silas Townsend," I offer, and his smile is slow and so fucking sexy.

His lips touch my ear, and it's my turn to shiver. "I'll see you at the after-party, Silas. I want this pretty ass at my side all night so I can show you off."

"Warren!" Noah warns.

Skylar laughs as he drops and heads back to the track as Noah curses and points at me. "If you have any control over that idiot, make him behave."

"I don't think anyone can make Skylar behave," I counter.

"Not when it comes to Bones," Alek scoffs.

"Lord help us and whipped racer boys," Noah mutters.

"True." Alek nods. "But then again, you'd know all about that."

It's my turn to gape at Noah, and he quickly looks away.

The crowd screams again, and I look at the track, knowing I'll be at that party just like he said, especially when I hear the girls behind me chattering again.

Skylar Warren might not be mine, but he won't be anyone else's either.

Not while I'm here.

CHAPTER 21
SKYLAR

I take the quickest shower of the century then pull on some jeans and a team shirt, leaving my jacket off. I head back out into our garage, and the celebration is underway. We qualified, and we also took the top two spots. The other teams were furious, and we had two hours of interviews, promotional products, and tours before we could head back here. I should be exhausted, but if anything, I'm even more pumped. My adrenaline is still running high, and as I scan the crowd, I'm only looking for one face—my beautiful boy's.

"Skylar!" Mackie grabs me, passing me a beer. "We did it!" His grin is wide and happy, as it should be. He could have been first today, we both know it, and the fact that he let me win means a lot. I know wherever Mackie goes, I'll go too. We are partners.

"We sure did." Taking a sip, I muss his wet hair as he laughs and pulls away. "Go get your reward from our boss."

He frowns, and I wink, laughing as I walk past and find Bones with Alek and Evan near a car. Someone else steps into my path, though, and I sigh before meeting Noah's gaze.

"I know my face isn't as pretty," he teases, "but I just wanted to say you did good, kid." He claps my shoulder. "We'll go over your performance tomorrow." I groan. "But you did really well, so enjoy it." He

131

glances at Bones. "One of us should." Stepping away, he lets me slip past him, but before I can take three steps, a whole ass circle surrounds me.

Mechanics, team members, and even some pit lizards all vie for my attention. I smile politely and answer their questions, posing for the pictures for content. I hate every hand that touches me, and when one wanders, I gently but firmly pull it from my body, smiling at her to soften the blow.

"Are you going home?" She giggles, leaning into me. "I could go with you."

"No thanks," I reply with a grin. "I already have someone to go home with, and no offense, but you can't beat him. I wouldn't even try if I were you because he can be a real asshole."

She blinks incredulously, staring at me as I wink at the crowd. "If you'll excuse me." Stepping away from them, I look for Bones again. I find Alek and Evan heading my way. Frowning, I glance behind them to see Bones heading out the door.

Shit, is he leaving?

"Sky." I blink, dragging my gaze from Bones to Alek. "Check your phone then get your boy."

Unsure what he's talking about, I pull my phone out and open the file. It's a video, and as I watch, my grin grows.

He's cheering for me, and when I win, he screams and jumps around, showing more emotion than I've ever seen him display before he turns his lethal glare on the camera. I freeze it and screenshot that glare then set it as my background before putting my phone away.

"Thanks, man." Clapping Alek's shoulder, I glance around for Noah.

"I've got you. Have fun," he says.

Leaving him and Alek to fend off the fans, I head after my boy.

I don't need a party of fans, I just need him, and it's about time he realized that.

He doesn't get to leave, not without me.

I catch up to him outside, the gravel crunching under my feet. His back is stiff, the night closing in around him.

"Are you leaving?" I call out, and he stops but doesn't turn. He's in front of the track, not the parking lot, which is something, I guess. I don't stop until I'm at his side. "Without even a goodbye? Cruel, baby."

"It seems like you had enough adoring fans that you didn't need me," he snaps as I turn him around, his eyes spitting fire at me.

His jealousy is a fucking beautiful sight.

"Sounding a little jealous there, angel," I murmur, crowding him. He doesn't step back. Instead, he tilts his chin up slightly, never willing to back down, and fuck if that doesn't make me hard.

"Me? Jealous?" he scoffs as he runs his eyes over me. "Why the hell would I be jealous of something that anyone and everyone has had?"

"Not everyone," I murmur as I step closer, letting my nose touch his. "You haven't tried me yet. Want a test drive?"

His hands press against my chest, trying to push me away, but I don't budge. "You fucking wish."

"Too fucking right," I admit as I rub my nose against his. "There's nobody but you, Bones. When will you realize that? All I saw today was you. It's all I ever see. Even when I crossed that line, you were all I thought about. Your jealousy, while hot as fuck, isn't needed. I'm yours."

He swallows hard, his eyes widening as I rub my nose against his again then pull away.

I grin as I step back, capturing his hand when it comes up to slap me, and I interlace my fingers with his. "What did you think of the race?" I ask.

Sighing, he stops fighting me and looks back at the track. "It was good. You showed off a lot." He glances at me. "I guess you did okay."

Covering my heart, I act wounded. "Only okay? Damn, I guess I'll have to work harder next time to win both the race and your heart."

He snorts, looking at the track, but I see the smile lingering on his lips. He can't hate me, even though he wants to.

"You look a little sad," I comment as his smile drops.

"Eh, I guess I was looking forward to racing your car." He shoots me a look. "Who knew you would win."

"Everyone, baby. I wouldn't lose, not with you on the line." I squeeze his hand. "But that doesn't mean I can't give you what you want." I tug him after me, and I feel him fight my grip.

"Skylar," he hisses. "Where are we going?"

"You'll see," I reply with a flirty grin over my shoulder. He fights me the entire way to the outside pit, where our cars are. Swinging him around, I wrap my arms around him and notch my head on his shoulder as he looks at my car.

"What do you say, baby? Want to give it a try?"

He glances at me, his eyes narrowed. "You mean the car, right?"

"For now. You can try me later." He sighs, and I chuckle as I step back. "Come on, beautiful, no one is around. You can head out to the track."

"Wait, really?" he asks, his eyes widening in excitement.

"Yep, but you have to suit up." I wouldn't make anyone else, but there is no way I'm letting my boy get even a fucking papercut. Capturing his hand, I pull him over to the lockers and grab what he needs before giving it to him. "The changing room is there, be quick." I smack his ass, and he stares at me for a moment before heading in.

I've never been happier to win a bet.

Pulling his helmet down, I push his hair from his eyes and make sure it's secure as he watches me. "Are you sure this is safe? I don't even know how to drive it," he mutters.

"I'll be right there with you. I won't ever let anything happen to you. You trust me, right?" I ask as I secure the helmet and peer into his eyes.

He nods after a moment, and I grin.

"Then let's get you on the track."

I drive the car out, and then we switch. He seems uncomfortable in the seat, so I reach over and cover his hand. "Just stop thinking. For one moment, turn off that big brain and do something crazy without analyzing every angle or possible outcome. Just . . . feel."

His eyes narrow on me. "Some of us don't always give into our impulses, Skylar."

"You should." I shrug. "It's a whole lot of fun." I run my eyes over him, and he slaps my hand away, focusing on the dark track.

"Are you sure this is okay?" he asks again.

"Alright, let's go back. Maybe one of those girls wants to come play with me—" The car shoots off, and I laugh as I'm pressed into my seat. He winces at me at the jerky movement, and I reach over and cover his hand.

"Easy, like a lover. Press it slowly," I instruct, and we level out before the first corner, but we barely edge above fifty.

"Baby, go faster," I tell him. "I know you're a lawyer and shit, but break a few rules every now and again. Go as fast as you want and leave everything else behind. There's only me, you, and this engine."

He glances at me, gripping the wheel hard before bringing his eyes back to the track. "But if I—"

"Silas, let go," I order.

Something about my stern command makes him nod, and I watch the dial move higher and higher. I can practically hear his pounding heart as we take a corner, the tires squealing. He glances at me in worry, and I whoop, holding onto the handle.

"That's it, baby. You've got it!"

He nods and speeds up as we hit the straight, taking it hard. I keep my eye on him just in case, but when we slide around a corner, I can't help but laugh.

His smile slowly grows as we fly around the track, his grip loosening as he relaxes into it until he's laughing with me, speeding around in the dark.

There's only us and the track, and when he glances over at me, his smile is wide and carefree, his eyes shining with excitement and freedom.

I stare into his face, and I know that although I wasn't the one who broke his heart, I will be the one to fix it. I would protect him from anything that tried to dim that smile ever again.

His laughter spills free, and I join in as we skid across the line and slam to a stop. I jerk in my seat, laughing harder. He's panting but smiling as he looks over at me.

He glances at my lips, his tongue darting out to trace his. Grabbing his helmet, I drag him close and kiss him, swallowing his moan. My tongue tangles with his before I pull back, pressing as close as I can. Our breaths mingle between us in the silent cab of my car.

"I get it," he whispers into my mouth. "The thrill, the excitement . . . That feeling? It's addictive."

"Not nearly as addicting as you," I say as I rip the helmet off and toss it to the back, angling his head so I can kiss him deeper.

His hand slides up my arm, across my shoulder, and into my hair, and I grunt into his mouth, sucking on his bottom lip. I taste his sweetness and his whimper as I let it go and tangle my tongue with his as well.

I eat at his mouth, desperate and wild. I want to climb into his skin and feel him. Every drugging kiss has me wanting more, until I vibrate with the need to rip his clothes off and have him, but I pull away, knowing he isn't ready. I can look, though, and I do. I take in what's mine, the beauty of my boy and his swollen lips and glistening eyes.

"You can't look at me like that," he growls before I steal another soft kiss.

"How do I look at you?"

"Obsessive, consuming . . . like there is no other person in the entire world," he admits softly. "You look at me like no one else exists, and it's . . . it's—"

"True," I finish as I take his hand and press it to my chest. "Feel my heart. It only beats like that for you. I've driven cars up to three hundred miles an hour and I've raced for my life, yet it never pounds for anything or anybody else. Only you. Only ever you."

"You are a fool, Skylar Warren," he says, pushing me away and trying to put distance between us—distance I won't allow. I drag him back as his eyes widen, and I slide my lips across his cheek to his ear.

"I am a fool for you." I kiss his cheek. "If you don't get out of this car right now, you'll end up in the back seat, beautiful," I warn before I climb from the car and head around, opening his door. I reach in and undo his belt then offer him my hand.

He lets me pull him out, anticipation in his eyes, but I simply shut the door and hold his hand. "Come on, I'll drive you home."

As I turn away, I swear I see disappointment in his eyes.

CHAPTER 22
BONES

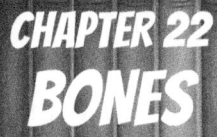

My heart hasn't stopped pounding since I sat in his car on that track. The freedom I felt . . . ? How did he know I needed it?

How does he always know what I need before I do?

How can he read me so easily?

It terrifies me, but I can't stop myself from falling into Skylar Warren's orbit, like he's the sun and I'm the planet. He burns so brightly, it will consume me, I know it, but I can't stop myself. He kisses my hand as we ride the elevator up to my apartment. I'm silent, staring at his profile. He must feel it, but he says nothing, just rubs his thumb across the back of my hand in soft, maddening strokes.

He's beautiful.

No, Skylar Warren is not beautiful—he's magnificent. He's all power and sharp angles, a beauty like I've never seen before. He's all warmth, that lingering smile doing things to me. His muscles pull at his shirt, and even in a T-shirt and jeans, he looks like a fucking model.

He is the most beautiful person I have ever laid eyes on, and I have been lying to myself about not wanting him. I thought if I didn't look hard enough, I could keep denying it, but I can't.

I want him more than I've ever wanted anyone.

This isn't puppy love or lust—this is desire, a flame I can't stop. It melts the ice inside me, terrifying me, but when he glances over at me and flashes straight white teeth in a wicked smile, I don't care.

Let him melt all of my edges.

I'd thank him for it.

His smile drops, his eyes lowering to my lips like he can read my thoughts. His expression turns hungry, and my heart pounds harder as desire rolls through me. I look at his lips, wordlessly begging for him to kiss me, but the ding sounds and we both jump.

Chuckling, he pulls me from the elevator and to his side, walking me down the hall to my door. His hand is still in mine as I stare up at him. I shouldn't say anything, since he's probably tired. He's had a long day and been busy with practice. I shouldn't invite him in.

I shouldn't demand he finish what he started.

"You should head back," I say, but it sounds lame even to my own ears. "You've been busy, and it's late. I bet it's a long drive."

His eyebrow arches, a confused smile playing on his lips. Can he hear the excuse in my words? Can he tell I'm fighting every single instinct not to throw myself at him?

I never bet my body, but it feels like I did.

"What?" I finally ask, annoyance flaring through me. It's my knee-jerk reaction to being vulnerable, but unlike anyone else, he doesn't let it drive him away. He simply grins wider and steps back.

"Not really," he finally says as he pulls out a key, unlocks the door opposite mine, and swings it open to unveil the dark apartment beyond, one that's been empty for a few months since the bar owner who lived there moved out.

He winks slyly at me, putting the key away. "Now I can be as close to you as I want."

I don't even know what to say. He bought the apartment across from mine and moved in without me knowing to be closer to me?

Embarrassment heats my cheeks, and maybe a little . . . satisfaction —not that I'll ever tell him that. It might encourage him, and Skylar is already crazy as it is. He needs no encouragement when it comes to me.

"Fine, night," I call as I shove into my apartment and shut the door, my voice slightly high and tense. Pressing my back to the wood, I hear his laughter and bang my head back, closing my eyes.

I almost threw myself at him. Even now, the wood between us doesn't feel like much of a barrier. He's right there, I know it.

He wants me.

I want him.

I hear his voice, teasing and silken, making me shudder. "I'm just across the hall if you get lonely tonight, beautiful."

I feel him move away, and then his door shuts, and only then do I slump.

Did he realize how close I was to giving in?

Even now, I lift my hand, ghosting my fingers over my lips, which are still sore from his kiss. I can't remember any other before him, not even my first. All I can see and remember is Sky. In a daze, I change into some shorts and fall into bed.

I toss and turn, my cock still hard as desire pounds through me alongside something else.

Want.

I want Skylar Warren, and not just his body and kisses. I want his smile. I want his eyes on me all the time. I want that obsessive edge of his. I want him to do everything for me—stalk me, chase me, never give up. Maybe it's fucked up and probably a huge red flag, but I can't seem to care.

I want to be the center of his entire fucking universe.

I want . . .

I want . . .

Fuck!

I toss and turn, trying to sleep, but it's no use. His voice is in my head, taunting me while he's not even here, until I can't take it anymore.

CHAPTER 23
SKYLAR

The apartment is mostly bare. I haven't had time to move much in yet, but it has the essentials, so there is no way I'm leaving my boy for extra comforts. I roll over in my brand-new sheets, my eyes going to the open blinds and the city beyond.

I won't be able to sleep tonight.

My fingers trace my lips. I wish he had worked up the courage to act on those thoughts I saw in his eyes, but we are going at his pace. I won't push him, but fuck if I don't have blue balls.

I've never been this patient before . . . . I've never cared to be.

I can get ass anywhere, but this is different. I want to earn Bones. I want him to want me. I want him in a way I've never wanted anyone else in my entire life. He drives me crazy and makes me want to do stupid shit just to keep his eyes on me. Bones makes me want to take on the world, just to see him smile.

It has me all fucked up inside, but I don't care.

Rolling to my back, I groan and drape an arm over my eyes, plunging me into darkness, but all that does is make me think of him and wonder if he's asleep yet.

Is he in bed?

Is he thinking about me the way I am about him?

Dropping my arm, I sigh deeply. Even after the greatest win of my career, all I want is him. The high I had after winning was insane, but it was nothing compared to seeing him celebrate with me. For a street kid with no family, I nearly fucking cried when I saw his pride.

My doorbell rings, and I frown, sitting up and swinging my legs out of bed. I walk through the dark apartment to the front door, hope blooming in my chest before I squash it. It isn't him. It's probably security coming to complain about my car again—they have twice already. For the amount I pay to be here, I'd think they would look past it.

It's on the tip of my tongue to tell them that as I rip my door open, only to freeze as I stare into my boy's eyes.

He's wearing nothing but a pair of low-slung shorts. His hands are balled into fists at his sides, and his dark eyes are narrowed on me.

"Beautiful—"

"Don't fucking speak," he snaps, and then he lunges forward, kissing me. I stumble backward from the force, falling into my apartment as he pushes me deeper inside. I'm patient, but I'm not a saint. Groaning, I grip his chin and deepen the kiss as I kick the door shut behind him, backing him up into it. The bang of his head hitting the wood is loud, but we don't break apart. Our tongues tangle in a deep kiss that has me moaning into his lips. He kisses me hard, eating my mouth desperately, gripping my arms like he's scared I'll stop.

Doesn't he know I can't?

He came to me.

He kissed me.

He reached for me.

He's mine, and there is no more escaping me.

Sliding my hands down his sides, I grip his thighs and hoist him up. He gasps into my mouth as I feel his legs lock around my back. Blindly, I walk through the apartment, shoving his shorts up so I can grip his ass.

It's so fucking soft and muscular. I groan into his mouth as we stumble into my bedroom. When my knees hit the bed, I throw us down. We fall into the tangled sheets, our hands all over each other. His legs still grip me like he's afraid I plan to escape, and his kiss turns feral and needy as he scrapes his nails down my back.

Pulling away, I stare down at his beautiful face. His cheeks are pink with desire. I'm not a fool, he came here to be fucked, but I won't let him go after so he needs to be sure. "Are you sure, beautiful?" I ask, my voice rough with desire and obsession. "I need your words. I need to know."

It's important. I need him to know whom he's here with and that this isn't a one-night stand. If he gives himself to me, I'll take all of him forever.

"I've never been more confused," he admits, his Adam's apple bobbing as he swallows hard. "But of this . . . of you . . . I'm sure." His legs tighten around me. "You haunt me," he says. "I see you every-where I go, and every voice I hear is yours. I look for you in crowds. I search for your smile. You are haunting me, Skylar Warren, and I don't care anymore. I'm yours."

Snarling, I slam my lips against his, silencing his whimper. My hands slide down his body, exploring his warm skin. I sit up and gaze down at the perfect being spread below me.

Fuck, I want to take a picture and make it last forever, but I know he'll kill me, so I place a kiss over his pulse and slide down his body. I grip the edges of his shorts and meet his eyes as I start to tug them down.

His cock springs free, and I almost come from the sight. He's long and thick with piercings running down his length. I want to taste him, so I sweep my tongue up his length as his hips rise and roll my tongue over his tip. I suck his precum off, and his flavor explodes in my mouth before I reluctantly pull away and slide his shorts off.

"Jesus fucking Christ, Silas Townsend, look at you," I murmur, running my eyes over every hard, toned inch of him. "You're a goddamn masterpiece. You should be a model, not a lawyer, but then again, I wouldn't want anyone seeing what's mine. Maybe I'll just chain you to my bed so no one can ever look at you again."

"Skylar," he warns, his eyes flashing. I love that sass, and when he reaches for me, I'm gone. "Fuck me or I'll leave."

"So impatient," I murmur, but I know better than to keep pushing him on this.

Gripping his legs, I shove him farther up the bed. His eyes widen from the force and strength, his chest heaving with his heavy breathing.

I trace his tattoos with my tongue as he groans, his head falling back and chest arching up. Smirking, I lick his abs and kiss his pecs before I circle his nipple with my tongue and bite down.

"Sky!" he moans.

"Fuck, do that again. Make that noise, baby. Say my name," I beg, licking the bite mark. Turning my head, I do the same to his other one until he cries my name again. The sound of it fills my apartment, making my dick jerk in my boxers. As I kiss up his chest, I reach down and shove them off, throwing them to the floor with his shorts. I kiss up his neck and across his face to his mouth. Our bodies slide together, and his hard cock presses against mine. The friction of them rubbing together has me grunting into his mouth.

I've wanted this for so long that I can't hold back.

Breaking the kiss, I peer down at him. "I won't go slow or soft, baby. I want you too badly for that. It's going to be fucking hard."

"It better be." He smirks, and I groan as his smirk only grows. "Skylar, I didn't come here for you to make love to me or some shit. Fuck me. Fuck me like you drove on that track today. I want Skylar Warren, not a pretty lie you think I'll like. I want the man everyone fears or wants. I don't want who you think I want you to be." He licks my chin. "Fuck me like you own me."

I slide my hands around his throat, dragging him up so my lips almost press to his. "I do own you. Are you just starting to realize that?" I kiss him again before sliding my mouth down his throat.

"No marks," he snaps as I nip his skin.

Just to piss him off, I dig my teeth in, and he groans, hooking his leg around me and rubbing his body against mine as I mark up his throat.

"Sky." His skin vibrates against my mouth, and I can't hold back.

Next time, I'll take all night, but I need to be inside him, hearing my name on his lips while I claim his spoiled ass.

I reach over to my nightstand and the brand-new box I bought. I open it within Bones's view, so he can see there's no confusion, and then I drop it back inside before I pull out a condom in the packet.

I offer it to him. "Put it on me, angel," I order.

Leaning up, he bites the corner off and spits it away, then he pinches the condom and starts to roll it down my length. The sight of his hands on me has my hips moving, and when it's rolled all the way down, he kisses the tip of my cock.

His tongue darts out, tracing my length as he watches me. I know he's doing it to wind me up, and it's working. I push him down without any gentleness. He bounces on the bed as I grip him. If he wants to play that way, then we will.

Rolling him over, I bite his ass cheek, making him cry out as he fists my bedding. "I want my marks all over you," I growl, my voice thick.

I pull the bottle from my drawer and place it next to us, then I push his legs apart and drag my tongue down his ass and circle his hole. He groans, burying his face in my bed, and grips the sheets as I lick him until he pushes back with a gasp. Smirking, I pull away and open the bottle, squirting it on him as he jerks. I drizzle some across my cock and stroke my length as I slide my other hand down and lift his hips, and then I keep moving so I can grip his cock and pump his length.

"Sky," he pants, pushing back. "Fuck me already."

"So impatient, baby," I tease as I lick his spine. I line my cock up with his ass, letting him feel every hard inch of me that will be buried inside him. "I'm big, but you're going to take all of me, aren't you? Don't tap out now, you're tougher than that. I want this pretty ass wrapped around me all the way to my fucking balls."

"Fuck." He pushes back, giving me an impatient glance over his shoulder. "Then get inside me."

Smirking, I lean back and grip his hips before I start to push into him, feeding him inch after inch of my cock. Some can't handle all of me, but my boy was made for me. He whimpers and pushes back to take more, so I pull out and push back in.

With each thrust, I work deeper until I'm locked in his ass.

I stare down at my beautiful boy as he shudders. He glances over his shoulder once more, his mouth parted and raw. Sliding my hand up his back, I grip his hair and yank his head higher as he cries out, and then I thrust back in.

I speed up, forcing him to take every inch of me until I'm just pounding into him. I can't hold back. He's so fucking tight around me, and seeing him stretched out below me with my name on his lips drives me fucking wild.

"Fuck, fuck, fuck," he chants, trying to escape me, but I haul him back and onto my dick.

"This is your fault for teasing me and winding me up," I snarl. He cries out loud enough for the neighbors to hear.

Fucking bill me for it, but there's no way I'm stopping.

He can scream until the police arrive.

Snarling, I hammer into my boy's pretty ass, circling his cock with my free hand and squeezing until he shouts as I take him. I tilt my hips until I hit that spot that has him writhing and crying out. His fists beat the bed even as he pushes into me.

"Sky," he begs.

"So fucking quiet and stoic in everyday life, but a fucking screamer in bed. Aren't you, baby? I fucking hoped you would be. Let the whole building hear. Let every fucker in Pine Valley hear you beg for my fat cock."

He hisses and glares at me, but his eyes roll back as I slam into him so deeply he whimpers. His dick pulses in my fist, and I know he's close. Sliding my hand down, I cup his balls and squeeze before releasing and pressing his face into the bed, then I pummel into his ass.

I alternate between looking at his spread cheeks and my dick slipping in and out and his arched back and closed eyes.

Fuck.

Nothing can compare to this, not even the feeling of racing. He's ruined me, and he doesn't even fucking know it.

I want to spend the rest of my life inside him, making him scream for me. Fuck racing. Fuck anything outside of this bed.

I'll keep him chained here, spread for me to use.

"Sky." His voice wobbles. "I—oh fuck—"

"I know, baby," I growl with the force of holding back. I don't want to come, not yet. I want this to last forever. His hips push into the bed, and when I lift them higher and slam into him, he screams for me.

The sound echoes around my walls as he comes. I stay buried in his clenching ass, drinking in his reactions—his parted lips, heaving chest, the way his sweat drips down his spine, his closed eyes . . .

I watch his pleasure until he slumps into the bed, his head turned slightly as he pants.

Smirking, I run my eyes down his frame before bending over and blanketing his body with mine.

I drag my tongue up his back, licking away his sweat before I bite his ear, making him whimper. "You look pretty when you come, but I'm not done yet. Open your eyes and watch me as I fuck you. I'm going to make sure you remember this for the rest of your life. I'm going to make you addicted to me like I am to you."

He groans but doesn't open his eyes, so I force him up to his knees, one hand on his throat. I slide my other hand down his chest until I can grip his soft cock and his release. I swipe my fingers in it before bringing them to his parted lips, shoving my fingers inside his mouth.

His eyes fly open, but his mouth closes over my fingers. "Do you taste good, beautiful boy? Taste how well I fucked you and remember what I did to you. You're mine now," I whisper wickedly into his ear as I start to roll my hips again, driving into his ass from behind. His knees spread, taking me deeper as he laps at my fingers before I pull them free.

"You want to know how I taste?" he asks, and his hand moves, doing something before appearing over his shoulder, his fingers glistening with his cum. "Find out."

I suck his fingers into my mouth, wrapping my tongue around them as the flavor of his cum explodes along my tongue, making me groan and bottom out inside him. He gasps, and when he pulls his hand free, I keep one of mine on his neck, the other on his hip.

"Tease," I snap, biting his shoulder in punishment. "You'll regret taunting me."

"Prove it," he dares, bringing his icy eyes over his shoulder to meet mine. "Or are you all talk?"

My eyes narrow in warning as his bruised lips tilt up.

Oh, he wants to play like that? Fine.

Pushing him down, I drive him into the bed with hard thrusts, holding nothing back. I let him feel every inch of me, every drop of my strength and obsession. His constant cries fill the air as he tries to hold on, clinging to my bed for dear life as I ravage his ass.

It's his own fault.

I can't stop, couldn't even if I tried.

"Sky," he begs, his voice choked. All I can do in response is slam into his jiggling ass until it's too much.

Fire crawls along my spine, and my balls draw up. My release rushes toward me until it hits me like a fucking train. I push into him as deep as I can get and empty my cum inside him as my eyes shut in ecstasy.

So much pleasure pours from me, I know I'll never be able to live without him.

His whimpers bring me back, and I blink my eyes open, my heart pounding like a roaring engine. Fighting my own weakness after my release, I run my eyes over my boy.

He's slumped into the bed below me, covered in sweat and my marks, his eyes closed.

I sweep my tongue across his chin and the drool slipping from his mouth. "I'm not done with you yet, beautiful," I warn. "You knocked on my door and came into my apartment. You're mine." Pulling from his ass, I tie off the condom and fling it away before rolling him.

His eyes open, but he seems too tired to fight me as I slide down his heaving chest and lick his dripping cock, tasting his release.

Keeping my eyes on him, I play with his piercings as he starts to harden again. "There you are," I murmur. "This time I want you to ride me. I've imagined you bouncing on my cock since the day we met."

I stroke his cock as he hardens and then slide up his body. I kiss him before sitting back against the pillows, my legs spread.

He turns and looks up at me, glancing at my hardening dick. I crook a finger and wait.

His lips thin, but he climbs to his hands and knees and crawls up the bed, straddling my lap before teasingly pressing his ass against me.

"Is this what you want?" he asks, his voice sharp like a blade. He's annoyed at being ordered around and wants to tell me to fuck off, but he also wants what I ordered. My pretty little brat hates that.

Sweeping my gaze down his muscular body, I nod greedily then reach for his thighs, but he slaps them away and shoves them up over my head, interlacing his fingers with mine and pressing them to the wall above me.

"Keep them here or I'll stop," he orders.

Without retrieving a condom, he rises, trapping my hands with one of his, then he reaches down, pressing the tip of my hard dick to his ass before he sinks down onto my length, taking every inch of me. His eyes stay locked on mine as I bite back a moan, fighting the urge to lift my hips. That tilt of his lips lets me know he's in control here and deadly serious. I grip his fingers harder as he starts to move with slow, rolling thrusts that leave me groaning. I glance at his muscular, perfect body, watching the play of muscles as he rocks on my cock.

"You say I'm yours, but you're mine, Sky," he says, his voice thick and deep.

"Too fucking right I am," I growl, lifting my hips to take him deeper. Smirking, he licks a path down my throat to my chest. His mouth wraps around my nipple and he bites, making me hiss before he licks it better then turns his head and does the same to the other peak before lifting his head.

"You want to mark me? Then I'll mark you." He turns my head and bites my neck, making me cry out and thrust him into the air. Chuckling, he licks the bite and leans back, riding my cock faster.

Freeing my hands from his, I reach out and grip his hips, urging him on as his splayed hands press against the wall for leverage and he fucks me harder.

I'm only made for his pleasure, nothing else—for him to use, break, and ruin.

His eyes are locked on me, hard and hungry, as his hips wind and roll, taking my cock deeper with each bounce. I slide my hands up his back, feeling his muscles bunch as he rides me.

I grip his shoulders and tug him closer, and our lips crash together in a swift, brutal kiss. When he rises and loses his rhythm, I know he's close, but I'm right there with him, and when he bites my lower lip, I'm lost.

"Fill me," he whispers as he soothes the bite. "Let me feel you come. I want to see it this time."

I can't deny him anything. I drag his mouth back to mine and drive up into him, letting go. His cry matches mine as I pump into his ass with my release. I feel his cum cover me as he jerks in my grip. Both of us are caught in waves of pleasure until we break apart, breathing heavily.

A look passes between us.

Both of us know what this means.

There is no going back now.

Wrapping him in my arms, I tug him to my chest where he slumps with a sigh, which shows how tired he is.

I chuckle. "Look at you, like a little, purring kitten, all that brat gone. I fucked it right out of you."

He huffs but doesn't lift his head, and when I stroke his back, he sighs happily again. "If I'm a cat, you're a dog, relentless and dumb."

"You forgot loyal," I tease, kissing his head. "Sleep, you're going to need it."

"No, you're done. I got what I wanted. I'll leave . . . when I can move," he mutters, but he yawns, and I bite back my smile.

"Sure, whatever you say, beautiful," I murmur softly, stroking his back as he snuggles into me despite his words.

He's asleep within seconds. I kiss his hair in satisfaction, unable to look away from Bones in my arms.

My phone buzzes.

I drag it over, keeping my eyes on my boy.

> Alek: Congrats again, brother, on winning the race.

I smirk. I want to tell him that I won much more than that.

I didn't just qualify tonight—I won my boy's trust and heart, and I will never risk it.

I plan to go all the way.

CHAPTER 24
BONES

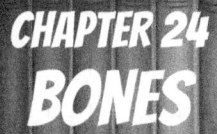

I wake with a gasp. Confusion swirls within me for a moment as I blink, and then I glance up at Skylar as he rises over me in the dark. He holds his dick in his hand as he lifts one of my legs, pressing my foot to his chest, leaving me open and exposed as he lines up with my ass and pushes inside me while I'm still waking up.

I cry out loudly.

My hands scramble across the bed as I fully wake. I don't think I was asleep long, but he doesn't seem to care as he fucks me.

"Please, Sky," I whimper, unable to stop it. I clear my throat, wanting to sound more in charge, but it comes out as a whine. "I'm tired."

"Shh." He covers my mouth as he drives into my ass, the force making me lift up in the bed. Pain and pleasure mingle inside me. He's the biggest I've ever had—not that I'll tell him that—and I knew I would be sore in the best way, but he seems like he's unwilling to leave me alone for even five minutes. His eyes look crazed in the dark as he drives his cock deep inside me. "I can't help it, baby. I need you so badly. Just hang on a little longer. I'm so fucking close."

Whimpering, I bite down on his hand, even as I lift my hips. I complain, but I'm hard and wanting, squeezing around him to the point of pain.

"It hurts," I whine like a brat, but I can't seem to stop. "Please, Sky."

"I know," he growls. "I tried to leave you alone, but you were rubbing on me, driving me crazy, so I can't stop. Take it, baby. I'll lick it better after."

I nod my head, and he grunts. "Good boy. Look at you, all bent up for me." Grabbing my other leg, he pushes it up and to the side. "Wrap your hands around them." I do as I'm told, holding my legs up and apart as he fucks me. Pleasure spirals through me. I feel as if desire is all I know when he touches me. I feel him deep inside me, so deep I know I'll never get him out.

His taste is still on my tongue, and his cum is on my body, yet neither of us care as we come together. I knew it would be like this between us, neither of us able to get enough.

The sight of him above me, his muscles bulging as he drives into me, does something to me, leaving me weak and crying out until I come with a groan, dropping my legs. Snarling, he shoves them up and hammers into me with reckless thrusts before he groans. He buries himself deep inside me, and then he comes, keeping his dick in my ass as he collapses on top of me. His lips seek mine in an open-mouthed kiss as we shake from the aftershocks.

"Good boy," he praises, his voice hoarse, and it shouldn't make me feel good, but it does. He slowly pulls from me, and I cry out at the sharp pain. Leaning down, he kisses my sore ass as he watches me. "You did so well."

"Bastard," I snap.

He smirks. "I know."

Sky wraps his arms around me, dragging me back, and slides his hand up my chest. For some reason, I find myself reaching for it, twining my fingers with his as he presses a kiss to my bare shoulder.

"Sleep, beautiful. I'll let you rest for a while."

"You better," I warn.

He chuckles and kisses my shoulder again before biting down. "It's your fault. You feel too good around me."

"Asshole," I mutter, but I'm smiling as my eyes close again, and here, in his arms, I fall asleep.

Everything has changed, and it makes me scared for daylight.

I shouldn't have been worried. Skylar is the exact same as he always is. Part of me thought he would pull away when he got what he wanted, but I was wrong. The smell of food wakes me, and when I wander into his kitchen, I discover he's cooking for me. It reminds me of that day not too long ago when I got drunk and he took care of me.

"Morning, beautiful," he calls when he sees me lingering in the doorway.

Nodding, I sit at the bar with a wince, and he serves me a plate.

"It isn't much, but please eat. You need the calories after last night."

I shoot him a glare, and he winks as I dig into the food. I'm starving, and when I'm done, he washes up and heads over to his couch as I look around. It's practically empty, even more so than mine. It only has the basic furniture that comes with the place. How long has he had it?

"Bones," he calls, and I spin to see him sitting on the sofa, his legs spread as he watches me.

He crooks his finger and pats his lap. My dirty mind heads straight to last night as I swallow, and my cock hardens. He smirks, no doubt reading my expression. "Don't offer what you can't give, beautiful," he remarks. "Come here."

I head over, confused and hesitant, but when I reach him, he grabs me and throws me down over his lap so I'm spread across it like a naughty kid.

"Skylar," I snap in annoyance and embarrassment, but he smacks my ass, making me gasp.

"Behave or I'll change my mind," he orders, and when he tugs my shorts down, I shudder. He doesn't do what I think, though, as something slightly cold drips along my ass, and his long fingers rub it over every bit of me that's sore, making me relax.

"Good boy," he murmurs, ignoring both our hard cocks as he takes care of me.

When he's done, his lips press against my ass then he tugs my shorts up, and I sit up and slide to the cushion next to him, feeling embarrassed and unsure. He watches me as he leans back.

I hesitate, not knowing what to say or do, and he watches me hungrily. "I should get ready for school," I blurt out and stand, embarrassment heating my cheeks.

I hurry to the door, needing to get away before I climb back into bed with him. He follows me to his door, and just as I'm about to open it, he slams his hand into the wood as his other slides down my half naked body.

He cups my cock through my shorts as I press my forehead to the door. "Need me to take care of this before you go to school, beautiful?"

"Fuck off," I snap, annoyed at myself and my body for wanting him so badly, but when his hand slides into my shorts and grips me, I moan. My head hits the door again as I give in, unable to fight him and this desire he causes in me.

I have never struggled with lust this badly, never wanted to, but it's like he unlocked it, and now I'm desperate all the time.

"Oh fuck . . ."

"I take that as a yes." He chuckles into my ear, rolling his hips into my ass so I can feel his length. "All you ever have to do is ask, beautiful. I'll always take care of you. Whatever you need—money, protection, love, my body . . . I'll give you everything."

Voices outside make my eyes widen, but he doesn't care. He squeezes my cock harder, wringing a moan from me as my legs widen to give him better access despite my better judgment.

I thought I could fuck him out of my head, but I was so wrong. There's no going back.

My eyes close as I try to fight it, but I can't. I thrust into his hand as his other palm glides down to roll and cup my balls as he works me, and within seconds, I spill into his hand with an embarrassing whimper.

I elbow him as soon as I know my legs won't give way, and he laughs as I spin and yank my shorts up.

Stepping back, he licks my release from his fingers as he watches me. There is a knowing look in his eyes that says I'll be back for more, and I hate that he's right. "Have a good day, angel. I know I will."

Ripping his door open before I say something stupid, I rush to my apartment, his laughter chasing me.

CHAPTER 25
SKYLAR

After my boy leaves, I clean up and pour a mug of coffee. Standing at the counter, I stare out at my apartment, knowing I probably look like a lunatic.

He came to me.

He wanted me.

He's mine.

He didn't even fight me on it. He let me have him over and over. It meant something, even to him, and watching him hightail it out of here this morning was just the cherry on top.

I sip my coffee, smiling like a fucking idiot. After I finish my mug, I shower and dress, and then I lean against my door, looking at my phone. Like clockwork, his door opens ten minutes later, and I open mine, grinning at him. "Fancy seeing you here, neighbor."

He sighs, slams his door, and points at me. "Stop it."

"Stop what?" I ask, shoving my hands in my pockets.

"Being adorable and shit," he mutters, and when he realizes what he said, he turns and stomps down the corridor. I hurry after him, slinging my arm over his shoulders. He shrugs it off, but I wrap it around his waist instead, and he fights me as we walk to the elevator.

"You think I'm adorable?" I murmur into his ear.

His elbow hits my side, and I double over, breathing heavily as he steps into the elevator with a wicked grin on his lips.

I step in after him and don't stop until I'm behind him, my hands on his hips. "I think you're adorable, blushing for me and acting all shy when you were screaming and clawing my back a few hours ago."

He shudders as he spins, poking my chest until I hit the wall, but I can't make my smile drop. I love this side of him just as much as I love every other facet.

"Skylar Warren, stop it," he warns. "Just because I had sex with you doesn't mean I'm yours."

"Ah, baby, that's where you're wrong," I murmur. "I told you what would happen if you climbed into my bed." Leaning forward, I watch his nostrils flare in anger as I grin. "I told you it means you're mine."

The elevator dings, opening on another floor, and he turns, ignoring me as someone else steps on. The guy looks between us, arching his eyebrow before hitting a button.

Smirking, I move over to Bones once more so I stand at his side, my hand sweeping across his hips to his ass. He slaps me, but I keep a grip even as he grunts and fights me. The guy turns to look at us. I wear an innocent smile, and he looks between us again before shaking his head and facing the front.

I stick my hand in his pocket and rest my head on his shoulder. He studiously ignores me, but I see his lips twitching, and I know I'm getting to him.

He's probably overthinking, which is his strong suit, so I'll be an idiot if it makes him calm down and just be here with me, not lost in his thoughts.

The door opens, and the man steps off. Bones goes to rush after him, but I hook my arm around him and drag him into my arms, my lips brushing his ear. "You can run all you want, angel, but I'll chase you. Be a good boy at school today. I'll see you tonight." I kiss his cheek then leave him there. I whistle as I walk to my car.

"Fuck you, Skylar Warren!" he yells.

I wave as I smile. "You already did! Love you too, beautiful."

Despite qualifying yesterday, I'm at the garage bright and early. Most of the team is already here, with Mackie nursing a coffee and looking far too hungover. Ruffling his hair, I sit and steal a pastry from the middle of the table, eating it whole.

"Good night?" I ask around a mouthful of food.

He gags and turns away. "God, stay away."

Laughing, I wipe my chin and lean in. "You look wrecked. Did you get drunk?"

"Maybe," he admits, staring at his coffee before looking around to ensure we are alone. "I made a move on Noah. It backfired, so I got fucked up."

"Shit, what happened then?" I ask.

"He found me in the garage with a groupie." Mackie blinks. "She was checking out the car, and I was drunk. He ordered her to go home then dragged my ass out of there. It was so embarrassing. I don't remember much after, but I woke up at his place and left before he could scold me."

"You're a bad drunk." I chuckle. "What did he say about you making a move?"

"He said I was drunk and didn't know what I was saying," he mutters as he lifts his head. "I had one drink, one fucking drink, and he acts like I don't know my own mind . . . like I'm still a kid."

"So show him you're not." I shrug. "You like Noah, right?"

He nods.

"Then prove it to him. Don't let him lock you out. He likes to keep everyone safe. I also think he doesn't believe he deserves to be loved. He will be hard to crack, so you'll need to be persistent." I smack his shoulder. "But you can do it. Don't back down or let him talk you out of it. If you want him, fight for him."

Nodding, he stares at his coffee again. "You're right. I'm tired of trying to do everything right to get his attention and still not being enough. It's time I showed him what I want."

"That's my boy." I clap his shoulder. "But maybe shower first." I scrunch up my nose. "You stink."

"Gee, thanks." He hits me. "You had a good night?"

I smile secretively as Alek drops into a chair opposite us, and before we know it, the whole team is here. Noah stands in front of us, clapping to get our attention. His eyes purposely avoid Mackie, but the fact that he has to fight not to stare makes me smirk. He eventually gives in, checking him over to make sure he's okay, even if he doesn't want to.

Noah might not want to admit it, but he has feelings for Mackie.

I wonder when he'll give in.

"Alright, I'm glad we all had a good night." There are some chuckles. "But the time for celebration is over. We qualified, but that just means we need to work harder." Everyone groans, and Noah smirks, the masochist. "Our next race is in two weeks—"

Alek slides his chair over so he can whisper in my ear, distracting me. "You're smiling like a crazy person. Did you have a good night?"

"Maybe," I reply.

"Sky, tell me you didn't corrupt Bones," he grumbles.

"Maybe he corrupted me," I mutter, and he slaps me so I slap him back, and before I know it, we are both slapping the shit out of each other until someone clears their throat. We break apart, turning to Noah.

"Interrupting something, are we?" he says sternly.

I lean back with a smile. "Noah, you look a little tired this morning. Did you have a long night?"

His eyes dart to Mackie and back to me, and I grin sweetly. "Moving on . . ." He turns away, and I wink at Alek, who rolls his eyes.

"Asshole," he mutters.

"How's my Evvie? Maybe I should stop by—"

He covers my mouth, his eyes narrowed. "If you go near him with your whore penis, I will chop it off," he warns.

Covering my cock, I groan. "My boy wouldn't like that. He likes what it does to him too much. Besides, I'm only a whore for him now, no one else."

"How fucking romantic," he deadpans. "Now, can we stop talking about your dick?"

"You brought it up. Would you prefer we talk about yours?"

He watches me for a moment. "Why are we friends?" he asks.

"Because you're a grumpy bastard that no one else will put up with?" I retort sweetly.

"Ass," he mutters, but he shoots me a grin just as a mechanic skids into our impromptu meeting, stopping Noah mid-sentence.

"Boss, come quickly!" he yells. "It's Manny—oh God, please come!"

Alek and I share a look, and then we are on our feet, running.

CHAPTER 26
BONES

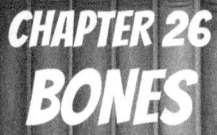

I chew my nails. It's a bad habit, one I thought I'd broken, but apparently not.

I slept with Skylar more than once.

I knew what it meant when I knocked on his door, but I was so tired of fighting everything in my life—to be strong, to be the perfect son and the perfect student—I just wanted something that was my own.

Something just for me.

Maybe I should regret it, but this is different than a one-night stand. I don't regret it. Not one bit . . . .

I want to do it again.

I rub my face, ignoring the tense looks thrown my way. I can't concentrate on this lecture. It's important, but my mind just keeps spinning around and around. Last night was about more than just sex, which was phenomenal, but the way he looked after me and gave me what I wanted, even though I hadn't won.

Day after day, Skylar Warren fixes me. Every sweet text and reminder to eat. What he doesn't know is that every time he does something like that, he heals a pain inside me he didn't cause.

This world has been cruel to me. I was raised amongst lions and forced to find my teeth, but Skylar shows me it's okay not to bite everyone.

He shows me what life could be if I were happy, if my dad didn't hate me and my first love didn't break my heart and disappear.

For the first time since I was young, I feel like someone finally sees my wounds and wants to heal them.

Groaning, I drop my head back.

I'm so fucked.

Today was a total bust. I didn't even take one note. I was lost in my own thoughts the entire time I was in class. I want to go home and fall into bed and try to fix this mess inside me, but I can't. I have responsibilities.

Silent Rose started as a place for rich kids to become more powerful, but over this last year, it's truly started to mean something. When everything with Evan went down, we became a real family, protecting one another, and it's only grown since then. It's become an integral part of all our lives.

"Hey, Alice." I nod as she sits at Evan's side, chatting. She was inducted after Evan and I put her forward. She's smart, capable, and exactly what we need. She might not have a family name behind her, but she has us.

I know Alek wasn't too happy about it, but I promised to keep my eye on her, even though he's supposed to be keeping his distance and letting her make her own mistakes now. She's definitely changed. She's bolder and more confident, but tonight, there's a shadow in her eyes.

"You okay?" I ask as I sit on her other side. Evan shoots me a searching look, but I focus on her. "You know we're here if you need anything."

"Everything is fine. It's fine." She shakes her head, forcing a smile. "Just . . . It's something I can deal with. Don't worry, it's nothing bad."

"What about you?" Evan asks as he looks at me again. "I saw a certain racer boy stealing you away last night."

"Shut up," I mutter. Glancing away, I run my gaze over the others gathered here.

"Skylar?" Alice screams, and every eye swings to us. She covers her mouth with a muttered, "Oops," and when they look away, she smacks me. "I knew it. Tell me everything."

"No." I frown at her, but like Evan, she doesn't seem to be scared of me anymore.

Seriously, why isn't anyone scared of me any longer? I blame Skylar. He started it.

"He's so cute and totally obsessed with you. Loads of students saw him race. He's all everyone's talking about."

My frown only grows, and Evan laughs. "I know that look—that's the look of a jealous lover."

"Not a chance," I snap, but my teeth grind together, and I glance at Alice. "Everyone?"

"Everyone." She nods. "He's a total hottie, Bones." She nudges me. "But it's obvious he's obsessed with you, even . . . even *that* night." Her smile fades, and her expression turns haunted.

It's a look we all have—us survivors.

I sling an arm around her shoulders as Evan hugs her other side. "Want me to call Lally to take you home after the meeting?"

Evan mimes cutting across his throat, and I frown.

"No, it's okay," she replies.

I ignore Evan and continue. "Let me, she can walk you—"

"She won't come," Alice snaps, her eyes on her shoes. "She's avoiding me. She pulled away after that night, but now it's all fucked. I don't know. It's fine. I don't need her. I don't need anyone. I'm fine. I'm totally fine."

How often did I tell myself that?

How often did I look in the mirror and lie?

Evan and I share a look, but we let it go. We know if we push this, it might push her away. We have to wait until Alice is ready to talk about it, but Lally . . . What's wrong with her?

Is it Tommy or something else?

It's still on my mind after the meeting as I see everyone off. Shoving my hands into my pockets, I walk the path from the art building, ignoring everyone and everything.

"Hey, beautiful." The familiar voice snaps me from my thoughts and my head jerks up. Skylar pushes from his car and heads my way, grinning widely.

"What are you doing here?" I ask, knowing I sound unfriendly right now, but my mind is a mess, and seeing him doesn't help.

He makes everything clouded.

"Taking you home." He leans in and kisses my cheek when he reaches me, his smile wide.

"No thanks, I want to walk." I step past him, but I really should have known better. In the next breath, I'm hanging over his shoulder.

"Alright then, if this is the way you want to do it, beautiful." He smacks my ass and throws me into his passenger seat before he reaches over and fastens my belt. He ruffles my hair as I stare at him incredulously. "Good boy." The door shuts, and he runs around the front, getting in and pulling away while I just gawk at him.

"You— That— It's kidnapping!" I yell.

"It isn't kidnapping if you want it," he replies as he rests his hand on my thigh and squeezes. "How was school?"

I blink at him as he waits for me to answer. "Fine," I say.

"Good. I had an amazing lunch today. I should take you there—" He carries on talking while I just stare at his profile.

Why does he keep fighting for me?

Why doesn't he give up?

Why does that make my heart pound?

God, I'm so messed up, but he doesn't seem to care, and honestly, I'm starting not to as well.

CHAPTER 27
SKYLAR

Glancing over at my boy, I see him staring at me, and I can't help but grin. "Keep looking at me like that and we won't make it back to your apartment, beautiful."

"I'm not sleeping with you, Skylar," he warns, his arms crossed as he purposely stares out the window.

"Who said anything about sleeping?"

Grinning, I focus on the traffic, and once we are back at the apartment building, I take his hand and lead him into the elevator. He sighs but doesn't fight me, and when the door shuts, I glance at him, my eyebrow raised. He stares back, and I back him into the wall as we quickly ascend. My arm presses against the wall above his head as I lean in, and his eyes start to close.

"You aren't sleeping with me? But you want to, don't you? Look at you, all ready for me to kiss you," I tease.

His eyes open, and he pushes my chest. Laughing, I lean back but capture his hands, kissing the backs of them. When the door opens, neither of us move for a moment. I keep hold of one hand and tug him from the elevator and down the corridor. He's quiet, and when we reach my door, I glance at him, my eyebrow arched in question.

I'll let him go home if he wants to.

"Fuck it," he mutters, and suddenly, he's on me, slamming me back into my door as he kisses me.

I fumble with the lock behind me, but the sound turns into a groan as he nips my lower lip. I manage to get the door open without looking, and we tumble inside, both of us hitting the floor. He kicks the door shut, but that's about as far as we make it.

He tears at my shirt before moving down and unbuckling my jeans. Groaning, I capture his wandering hands and spin us, pinning him to the floor. "Slow down, beautiful."

"I need you," he says, his eyes hungry as he arches up to kiss me, biting my chin. "Don't make me wait."

"Never," I promise as I release his hands and sit up, straddling him. I reach over my shoulders and tug my shirt off, throwing it away before I finish unzipping my jeans. I lean down and push his shirt up, then I kiss along his quivering abs as he gasps. He reaches for me, tugging at my hair to get me moving, but I take my time. Pushing his shirt up, I drag my lips up every inch of his chest before he sits upright, and I help him take it off and toss it aside with mine.

His hands slide up my back, his nails digging in as I gasp, and his perfect lips run across my throat before he bites down on my Adam's apple. Gripping his hair, I yank his head back and stare into his bright eyes. "Behave."

"No." He pouts. "I won't unless you make me."

"Does anyone else know you're such a fucking brat?" I mutter, and my eyes narrow. "They better not."

His smirk is mean. He licks my neck, causing me to groan. "Why don't you find out?"

Cursing, I push him down and roll him. He gasps as I yank his ass up and push his jeans down. I bite next to my mark from last night—a warning. Reaching into my pocket, I pull out my wallet and extract the condom I put in there this morning just in case my boy felt needy. I open it one-handed then roll it onto my length. Sitting back on my heels, I yank him up so his back is pressed to my front as he trembles on his knees.

I grip his cock, pumping him as he groans and leans back into me, rubbing his pretty ass against me.

My boy has gotten brave, and I fucking love it.

"Are you going to behave?" I murmur into his ear. "You only get my cock when you do. Otherwise I'll leave you like this, and I'll wind you up all night."

"You wouldn't dare," he mutters, even as he cants his hips, thrusting deeper into my fist.

"Try me," I growl, then I slide my hand up and grip his throat, squeezing gently. "I might be willing to follow you around like a little puppy, baby, but in here, in the bedroom, you're mine, and you'll only get my cock if you're good. Now, are you?"

I feel his jaw grind as I grin against his neck. "Yes," he snaps.

"Yes, what?" I prompt.

"Yes, I'm a good boy," he growls.

Fuck, my cock jerks at his words.

I nip his ear then suck it better as I lift him and place him on my cock, letting him feel my hardness. He shivers against me, reaching up and gripping my arm. "Stop making me wait. I did what you asked."

"Very true. You were such a good boy, and good boys get rewards." Forcing his thighs wider, I rub my dick along his ass until he rotates his hips, seeking me without words. Knowing I'm pushing him and not wanting to make him angry, I settle him on my tip and slowly push inside of him. He whimpers loudly, and I bite his ear.

"Shh, beautiful, it's going to feel so good. Remember how good I felt last night when I was buried in this tight ass?"

He nods, and I release his throat, circling his cock and squeezing. His ass clenches around me, and he relaxes enough to let me slide deeper.

"Good boy." I suck his neck as I press forward until I'm all the way inside him. I still then, letting him catch his breath, stroking his length until he starts to move.

"Skylar," he says, pushing down on me. Guiding him with my other hand, I rock into his ass, fucking my boy.

I release his cock and slide my hand up, stroking his incredible chest as he cries out and takes me even deeper.

I can't hold back. I can't be gentle.

He's just too fucking pretty impaled on me.

I wrap my arm around his chest and grip his other shoulder, forcing myself deeper.

I hold him like that as I fuck him, speeding up until he's whimpering for me. Sliding my hand down, I grip his cock and pump it in time with my thrusts. "I love the noises you make. You're so controlled, but when I'm inside you, you can't stop it. Yeah, that's it, baby, cry for me. Let me hear everything you keep trapped inside."

He thrusts into my hand wildly, his cock jerking in my grip, and I know he's close. Closing my fist over his tip, I squeeze hard.

His cry fills the air as he spills over my fingers. "Good boy," I praise, kissing his neck as he slumps against me. "We aren't done yet though, not until I fill this pretty ass with my cum."

Releasing his length, I watch him slump forward to the floor. I pull from him and roll him over, and when his half-lidded eyes lock on me, I lick his cum from my hand before grabbing his thighs and pulling him to me, impaling his ass on my cock.

"Skylar!" he yells, his ass gripping me tightly.

"That's it, baby, scream my name. You're mine, aren't you, beautiful?" When he doesn't answer, I roll my hips, and he groans. "Say it."

"No," he counters, opening his eyes and meeting mine.

"There he is." I groan as I speed up, unable to resist. He's a fucking sight spread below me, his cock hardening for me as I claim him.

I need more. I need him closer. I want his mouth on mine and his hands on me. Gripping him tightly, I stand.

His legs wrap around me, and I carry him over to the counter and drop him on the edge, laying him back. I pull him farther onto my length as I lick his exquisite chest. "You taste like mine," I murmur as I lick his skin, powering into his ass as he moans. "You feel like mine." I run my eyes over him. "You certainly look like mine wrapped around my cock, spread out on my counter like a fucking feast."

He glares and sits up, the new angle making us both pant as his lips press to mine in a hard kiss. "Skylar, you idiot, I'm not yours, but you're mine, aren't you? One look and you come running like a dog in heat." Meeting my thrusts, he takes me deeper until my fists hit the counter as I try to control myself. "Look at you. Tell me, race boy, who really belongs to whom?"

I try to kiss him, but he turns his head with a smirk. "I've always been yours. One fucking look was all it took," I admit without a hint of shame. "You never have to doubt that. I don't need to look to see my obsession, beautiful." I slam into him, and he groans. He turns his head, and my eyes drop to his lips. "Now kiss me. I've been thinking about your mouth all day."

"Then say it," he retorts, turning my words on me. "Say you belong to me, Skylar Warren."

"Possessive little thing," I mutter as I try to kiss him, but he covers his lips. Stilling, I stare into his eyes. "I, Skylar Warren, belong to you from now until forever. Now kiss me."

His smile is slow, but he drops his hand and kisses me, and that fire roars back, my hips moving in fast, brutal thrusts before we break apart before I trail my lips down his neck.

He groans loudly, and I feel it vibrate in his throat as his nails slice at my back, ripping into me as I power into him. "More," he demands. "Fuck me harder, Sky."

I'll never deny my boy anything, so I pummel into his sweet little ass. Tilting his hips, I make sure to hit that spot that makes his eyes cross and roll back, his hard cock leaking between us.

"Oh fuck, fuck, fuck." His words slur as he rips up my back, lifting his hips desperately, and I know he's close again. My balls draw up, my own pleasure demanding to be felt, and I only hold it back with gritted teeth. I must look insane above him, my jaw clenched as I slam into him over and over, until his cries echo around my kitchen. His ass grips my cock as he explodes all over us, and I can't hold back anymore.

I bury myself as deep as I can into him, and with my own bellow, I come so hard I see stars. My legs shake, and I fight to stay on my feet. Pleasure flows through me like lava as I pant. When it finally subsides,

I force my eyes open to see him below me, a small smile curling his lips.

I memorize the pure, unguarded happiness in his eyes.

Breathing heavily, I rest my chin on his chest as his hands stroke my shoulders and back. "Now that's a welcome home."

My eyes are on the ceiling, my hand strokes his back, and our legs are entwined. One of his thighs is over my hips, and his arm is draped over my chest where his head is. I never expected him to be a cuddler, but I fucking love that he is. I want him closer.

I always want him in my arms like this.

"You're quiet," he murmurs, and I feel him looking at me, so I drop my eyes. My hand slides up to stroke his hair. "What's wrong?"

"Just thinking about something that happened at the garage," I admit.

He props his chin on my chest, peering up at me. "What happened?"

"A freak accident. A jack dropped onto a tech's hand when he was checking one of our cars. He had to be rushed to the hospital. He might never be able to use his hand again." I can still hear his screams, still feel his blood as we pulled him from the car.

"Jesus, that's horrible, Sky," he murmurs. "You didn't get hurt?"

Shaking my head, I lean down and kiss his forehead, watching his eyes close for a moment. "No, but I'm going to visit him tomorrow. Noah is going to cover his expenses, and he'll always have a job and a place with us, but mentally, that must be hard."

"Such a softie," he teases, kissing my chest.

"Don't tell anyone." I grin. "I have a reputation, you know."

"Oh, I know, big bad Skylar Warren. Racer, street boy, sex god." He smirks as his teeth dig into my chest, and I hiss. He kisses it better then grins at me. "Your secret is safe with me."

He rests his head on my chest, and my eyes return to the ceiling. "How was school?"

"Fine," he replies, and I expect him to shut down, but he starts to trace patterns on my chest. "I saw Alice. I think she and Lally are fighting. Alek told me to keep an eye on it."

"I'm sure they'll be okay. Lally lost someone close to her, and that doesn't easily disappear. It fucks you up," I murmur.

His gaze lifts, and I know he hears the truth in my voice, the one I hide under laughter and teasing. "You lost someone?"

I smile, but it's bitter. "I was a street kid, baby. What do you think? A lot of people around me died, and some were friends. That's why I did everything I could to get out."

He's quiet for a moment. "I'm glad you are out of it. You're doing amazing, Skylar. Everyone is so proud of you. I'm proud of you . . ."

Why the fuck does that make me want to cry?

I do what I always do instead, and I cover it. I roll us and pin him as he smiles at me. "Yeah? Want to show me how much?" I flirt.

He smiles and kisses me. "I mean it, Skylar. You can hide or change the subject, but I'm proud of you. I can't imagine what it took to survive what you have and get out, but you're doing incredibly well. Look how far you've come. I'm proud of you. You're a good person, Skylar Warren, and when you forget it, I'll remind you."

"Yeah?" I croak.

"Yes," he murmurs as he cups my cheeks. "We can remind each other—the rich boy nobody ever wanted and the street kid racing as fast as he can. We'll be each other's safe zones. How about that?"

"I thought you'd run again," I admit weakly.

"I'm done running," he whispers, staring up at me. "Besides, you would only catch me." That makes me grin, and his smile fades after a minute. "I'm scared. I won't lie, you terrify me, but I'm done fighting against what I want, and what I want is you. So, I'm here with you. Let's see where it goes."

Staring into his bright eyes, I can barely believe what I'm hearing. "Say that again."

"Don't push it." He smacks my chest and pulls me down so he can lie against me again. "I'll deny it if you keep asking, but I'm here. That's enough for now, right?"

"More than enough," I agree, kissing his head. "For what it's worth, you terrify me too. I've never worked so hard for anything in my entire life . . . . I never wanted to."

He chuckles, kissing my chest again. "Well, don't stop now. I like it."

"You've got it." I wrap my arms around him as he yawns, and within minutes, his breathing evens out and he snores softly. I hold him tightly, a bright smile I can't contain on my face.

What I told him is true: my past is pretty fucked up. I've seen some things I can never forget, but the more I keep moving, the more I'm reminded it's behind me. I have a bright future ahead of me. I can leave the past out on the track and now with him—my safe place.

My phone buzzes again. It has been going off all evening, but I've been ignoring it for my boy, not wanting him to think I'm not here when I'm with him. He deserves all of my attention.

Kissing his head, I reach over to check my notifcations.

> Noah: He's out of surgery. He's going to be okay. He didn't lose his hand, but it's messed up. Get some sleep.
>
> Alek: Thought you should know that it's your boy's birthday in two days.

I sit up, gaping at my phone.

"Skylar?" Bones murmurs sleepily, peering up at me.

"Go back to sleep, baby," I whisper, closing my phone and kissing him. "I'm not going anywhere."

Two days. I have two days to make my boy's birthday amazing and prove I'll work hard forever for him.

I can do it.

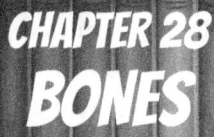

CHAPTER 28
BONES

Skylar Warren is like the Energizer Bunny. He's up every morning before me, and my breakfast is made as well as my lunch. He drives me to school and drops me off, then he goes to work and picks me up after, all while texting me incessantly.

I said I would give this a go, and I meant it. I can't deny there is something between us, and being with him makes me happy. We have no labels, but I'm not keeping it a secret.

At night, he fucks my brains out, scrambling them so much I end up crashing in his arms rather than heading back to my place. I think it's his plan, to be honest.

Evan heads toward me, grinning widely. It's a short day at college today, and I'm not surprised he found me. He makes a habit out of seeking me out. I think he misses Tommy, not that he will ever admit it.

"Happy birthday, you magnificent asshole!" he shouts when he gets near enough. My eyebrows rise as I stare at him. The bundle of sunshine stops before me, his bright eyes sparkling and his icy hair catching the sun.

I'm the total opposite. If he's the sun, then I'm the darkness, but he doesn't seem to care as he starts to sing loudly and off-key for me. I glance around with a wince. I would never stop him, though, because he looks too fucking happy doing it, and when he finishes and grins at me again, I mutter, "Thanks, forgot it was today."

I pretend I forgot it was my birthday, like I don't care. I didn't, though I wish I could. I had the insane urge to tell Skylar this morning, but I couldn't bring myself to do it.

"What? How?" He punches my side, and I stumble back a step. Evan might be a ray of sunshine, but he has the ability to beat the shit out of most guys. I have a theory that if he really wanted to, he could even beat me. He just hides his anger better.

Shrugging, I focus on my phone, which I had been looking at before his sudden appearance. "Bones, seriously, it's your birthday. Don't you want to do anything?"

"I hate my birthday," I admit, and it's true. It's just another reminder that I'm another year older and I spent another year without people I lost. First, my mother, and then my love. I might have friends and Skylar this year, but that doesn't mean I'll celebrate. "I always spend it alone. My father used to insist on spending it together, for his image, I guess, but he never turned up, so I stopped going. It's just another day."

"Shit, that's fucked up," Evan says, "but it isn't another day. It's *your* day, your birthday—"

"What's so great about that?" I retort with an arched brow.

His mouth drops open before he shakes his head. "There is so much wrong with everything you just said, I don't even know where to start. And I thought I had parental issues." Slinging his arm around me, he sighs. "At least let me buy you dinner."

"Oh, um, I'll probably be . . . ," I trail off, unsure what to say. My eyes scan the lot for the familiar car that is never late picking me up.

"With Skylar? He texted me. He's going to be late today. Work ran over. Alek will drop you off at your place after," he says happily.

Nodding, I let him lead me away, even as my shoulders slump. I guess I was excited to see him. I may not want to celebrate my birthday, but it might have been fun to spend it with him, even if he didn't know.

Bones: Hope everything is okay at work.

He doesn't reply.

(image)

"I am so full, princess, rub my belly," Evan whines from the front of Alek's car.

Grinning, Alek reaches over and slides his hand across Evan's flat abs, making him groan. "That better, pretty boy?"

"I don't know. You could rub something else—"

I cough loudly. "Did you forget I'm here?" I snap from the back seat.

"Oops." Evan grins as he glances at me. "Kinda, sorry."

"At least someone should get some on my birthday," I mutter as I flop back, my arms crossed. I'm not pouting.

I'm sulking.

Skylar didn't text me back. He never fails to respond, usually seconds after. It makes me worry, but when I see his car in our apartment parking garage, I feel annoyed. So he's just ignoring me? After I said I would give this a try, he got so comfortable he decided to stop putting in the effort?

What an ass.

I'm definitely not sulking, not at all, just pissed.

"Here." Evan hands over a gift bag. "From Alek and me. Happy birthday."

I blink down at the bag then look up at Evan as he grins at me mischievously. "Go on, head inside."

I eye him and Alek, who seem far too excited. They've been like this the entire meal. Maybe they just really want to get home to fuck. It wouldn't surprise me, since they are like rabbits. "Thank you. You didn't have to."

"We're friends." Evan sighs. "I wanted to get you something."

Alek smirks. "I had no choice. He made me."

Grinning, I slap his shoulder. "Thank you, I mean it, and for the meal."

"You're welcome. Now fuck off, I want to take my boy home," Alek says.

"Asshole," I mutter as I slide from the car and wave at them.

I will not go to his apartment tonight. Fuck him. He thinks he can ignore me?

Fine, I'll ignore him right back.

I don't need anyone. I never did. I'm fine on my own. I can spend my birthday alone. I always have. This won't be any different.

"Well, goddamn, beautiful, it took you long enough." My head snaps up as Skylar pushes from the wall next to his apartment door. "Alek texted that you left the restaurant thirty minutes ago." He grins at me, almost bouncing on his toes. "Come on, hurry up."

"For what?" I mutter. "I'm going to bed in my apartment. I'm tired."

"Uh-uh, no, you're not." He reaches for me, but I duck under him and head to my door.

"Yes, I am," I snap. "Goodnight, Skylar."

"Baby," he whines, sounding adorable.

I ignore him as I fumble to find my key, and he sighs.

"Bones, look at me."

No. I don't say it out loud, but I refuse.

Suddenly, I'm spun around and tossed into the wall next to his door.

His arms wrap around me, pressing me against the wall as his forehead rests on mine. "Are you sulking, my little brat? Is it because I didn't reply to your text?"

"No," I snap, pushing at his chest, but he simply grins, and I slump into the wall, glaring at him. "Well, why didn't you?"

Fuck, why did I say that? He'll get the wrong idea for sure, and from the happy glint in his eyes, I know I'm right. He kisses the tip of my nose.

"Adorable, you are fucking adorable. Why don't you come and

see?" Pushing from me, he captures my hand and interlaces our fingers, refusing to let go as he opens his door.

I try to resist, but he just yanks me inside, kicking the door shut behind me and releasing my hand as I stare at the boxes covering nearly every surface of the living room. All of them are wrapped in black and gold with my name scrawled across them.

"What is this?" I whisper in shock.

"Surprise!" he yells. "Sorry I didn't reply. I was finishing setting this up, so I asked Alek and Evan to distract you."

I gape at the number of birthday presents spread around his apartment. "What the fuck, Skylar?"

"One for every year I missed," he says as he turns to me, grabs a big bow, and puts it on as I arch my eyebrow. "And this year's present . . ."

Biting back a smile, I shake my head and look around again. "How did you even . . . Alek."

"Alek." He grins as he wraps his arms around me. "You like it?"

"I—" I stare past him again in shock.

He got me a present for each year he missed. He remembered my birthday.

I'll never admit it, but deep down, I'm happy.

As a kid, I always wanted someone to make a big deal out of my birthday. As I got older, I pretended I didn't care, but seeing the effort other people's parents, friends, or partners would put in . . . Yeah, I was jealous and always trying to convince myself I wasn't, but staring at Skylar Warren and the apartment overflowing with presents and love, I have the overwhelming urge to cry.

He gave me this without prompting or being told. He didn't care about my protests or the act I put on. This isn't for his reputation or the cameras. It's because he wants to see me happy.

"Sky," I whisper.

"Happy birthday, baby." He kisses me softly. "I'm so glad I get to celebrate with you this year and the rest to come. I promise to make each birthday better than the last."

I stare into his dark eyes, lost for words. "I hate my birthday," I admit.

"Evan told me what you said, but listen to me." His hands cup my face so I'm really listening to him. "Your birth should be celebrated because you're a fucking miracle, and you are the best part about my life. Do you hear me?"

Nodding, I glance back again, and he grins. "Come on, let's open your presents."

He leads me over to the couch and pushes me down, shoving a little box on my lap. I glance from it to him, and he waits excitedly, so I carefully pull the paper open and fold it next to me.

"Rip it, baby!" he encourages.

"But it's too nice," I admit. "I think we should save it."

He grabs the paper and carefully folds it for me, and I smile as I open the box to find a key ring inside. It has his car's number on top of a race flag, and I grin. "I'm already sensing a theme."

Grinning, he grabs another box, and I open this one just as carefully. It's a framed photo of us, and I stare at it, confused. "Skylar Warren, was this the night we almost died?"

"You were super cute when you were angry," he says as I gape at the picture. It's in the back of the car, with me on his lap, glaring past him as he grins behind me.

"Jesus," I mutter, but the picture is whisked away and another box quickly replaces it, bigger this time.

This one holds a jacket. I unfold it to see the patchwork designs on the leather. It has Starfire Racing, his name and number, and some flags and flames on the back. It's cool as hell.

"For you to wear when you see your man race," he says eagerly.

Nodding, I lay it down, eyeing the presents worriedly. There are so many of them, I don't know what to say. I feel awkward. I've never really received a gift before, never mind so many.

I think he can sense I'm overwhelmed because he suggests, "Why don't we save the rest for later?"

Nodding, I play with the edges of the jacket draped over my lap. "I'll be back, just going to the bathroom." I watch him go before stroking the embroidery. It's my colors, my style, and I want to wear it.

I want everyone to see his name on my back when I'm at the races, so they won't get any ideas.

Maybe I am a possessive bastard like he said.

Suddenly, the lights go out, and I jump to my feet, flashbacks from that night filling my head. Skylar, wearing a corny birthday hat, comes around the corner from his bedroom. "Happy birthday to you, happy birthday to you, happy birthday, my boy, happy birthday to you." He stops when he's before me, holding a huge, round chocolate cake with my name on the top and hearts all around it.

Candles burn brightly on the surface as I stare at it.

"Happy birthday, beautiful. Come on, blow them out and make a wish," he whispers softly.

Closing my eyes, I lean in and send up a wish before blowing out the candles. My eyes open as he cheers and turns to the counter.

"Tell me what you wished for!" he says as he puts the cake on the counter and grabs two plates.

"I can't tell you," I say, feeling embarrassed. "It won't come true."

That, and I don't think I could survive him knowing.

He pouts, but he lets it go. "You want to cut it, beautiful?" I just stare at the cake, tracing the letters across the top. "Bones?"

"I've never had one before," I tell him, peering at the smoking candles and the incredible frosting below.

"What? A chocolate cake? I wasn't sure—"

"No, a cake."

"To yourself?" he asks with a frown.

"At all," I admit, meeting his eyes.

The heartbreak in his gaze as he stares at me makes me shift uncomfortably and look away.

I hesitate as I stare at the cake. It's so beautiful, I don't want to cut into it. "Baby." His voice is soft, but I can't bring myself to look at him, shame heating my cheeks. His hand gently cups my chin and turns me, his eyes tracing over my face. "I promise you will never spend another birthday alone, and every single year, you will have a cake. I will never, I mean never, let you miss out on anything else. Do you understand?"

I peer up into his eyes and nod, believing him.

Every day, Skylar Warren fixes something within me, something others broke.

Grinning, he slides his fingers into icing, breaking the perfection for me, and bops my nose with a wide grin. "Asshole," I mutter, then my voice turns soft as I stare into his eyes. "Why are you so patient and kind to me when I'm nothing but cruel?"

He searches my eyes for a moment, a small, understanding smile flitting across his lips. "Because, baby, I think you act like that because you've never been shown kindness or how to accept love, and I'm willing to teach you." His grin only grows. "Besides, I never liked sweet things," he murmurs as he licks the frosting from my nose. I inhale deeply as he leans back. "I much prefer sour."

I glance away, but I know I'm smiling as I turn to the cake and start to cut it. His arms wrap around me, and his chin rests on my shoulder from behind. Once it's cut, I stare at the decadent chocolate, thinking through his words.

"But you grew up in a worse situation than I did and you turned out well," I mutter in annoyance.

"Baby, it doesn't matter how much money you had or didn't have —a house without love or safety is just as bad as the streets I grew up on. Besides, I didn't turn out well. I have my own issues, ones I wish you didn't know about. I hate the idea of you thinking less of me. Before I had you, I was drinking every day. I told everyone I was fine, just having fun, but the truth is, it was the only time I felt anything . . . . It was the only time I was truly happy, not just forcing an act for everyone around me. I was tired and lost and bored, and you came along. You're my vice now. Maybe that's unhealthy, but I don't care. You make me happy, and taking care of you, protecting you, and cherishing you make me the happiest. Fuck our upbringing, and fuck our pasts. Let's focus on the present and being together, okay? We can learn how to love together."

Closing my eyes, I lean back into his arms, letting him comfort me.

He's right. We should look to our future, not what happened before. I'm happy with Skylar. He makes me laugh and enjoy things again, and he's added some feeling into my numb world.

I don't know where this will go, but for the first time in a long time, I'm excited.

My skin is still scarred from the touch of another, and my heart is still broken from that love, but being surrounded by his warmth is bringing me back to life. It's healing those wounds and giving me another chance at love, but along with that comes fear.

This could be taken away again, and I could lose this before it truly begins.

Every good thing in my life is taken or ruined. I don't want that to happen with this . . . with us.

Feeling that desperation, I turn and kiss him. It's fast and hard, but his hands cup my cheeks and he slows it down until we are both panting.

"Thank you for caring, and thank you for remembering my birthday when my own father doesn't. Thank you for always making the effort, even when I don't make it easy. I might not be able to say it a lot, but I didn't like my life before you, Skylar Warren. You brought joy into it, and I'm . . . happy when I'm with you. Really happy."

It cost a lot to admit that, and I see that knowledge in his eyes as he kisses me softly, treasuring my words. "You make me happy too," he whispers against my lips. "I've never been this happy. You make me believe in a future, and you make me want to be a better person to deserve you. I won't ever give up on you. Give me your worst, I'm not going anywhere."

My words will never be able to encapsulate everything I want to say, so instead, I show him with my body.

I kiss him hard, and desire roars through me as he grips my thighs and lifts me onto the counter, chasing my lips. My head falls back as his lips glide down my throat and back up. My gaze lands on the cake. Using two fingers like he did, I cup some of the frosting and press it to his lips as he leans away.

Gripping my hand, he sucks my fingers clean of the frosting. My cock jerks at the sight and I pant, licking my lips.

It's always like this between us, the desire so strong I can't even breathe.

I've never wanted someone the way I want Skylar Warren.

Kissing the tips of my fingers, he drops my hand as we crash together again, our mouths meeting in a brutal kiss until I push him away, breathing heavily as I tug at his shirt, tearing it down the middle and exposing his perfect chest.

He grabs a handful of the cake and holds it to my mouth. I take a bite as I watch him. "Good boy," he purrs before lifting his hand to his mouth and smearing the frosting there.

Gripping his cheeks, I trace my tongue across his lips and chin, licking it up. Our lips meet in a messy kiss as we gasp, tugging each other closer. His hand moves past me again, and I wait, anticipation running through me at the hunger I see in his gaze. His hand returns covered in chocolate frosting, and a devilish smile curls his lips. Dragging it down his chest, he eyes me and arches one eyebrow, taunting me.

Driven by desperation and desire, I drop to my knees before him and trace my tongue across his muscles. The taste of him mixes with the chocolate, creating my new favorite flavor. Sliding farther up, I circle his nipple with my tongue before biting down. He hisses and reaches down, yanking me to my feet, and his lips meet mine again in a hungry kiss. When he pulls away, he kneels and tugs my pants down, freeing my hard dick. His tongue darts out and licks his lips as he stares at me.

When his eyes meet mine, I grip the counter so I don't fall. Seeing the big, powerful Skylar Warren on his knees for me has me feeling like a god.

"Cover your hand in frosting, baby," he orders, his breath wafting over my cock as he speaks. I reach back blindly, smashing my hand into the cake before I offer it to him. "Stroke yourself."

Eyes on him, I wrap my hand around my cock and stroke my hard length. I groan as I tighten my fist.

"Enough," he demands, and I stop instantly, dropping my hand.

Keeping me trapped in his feral gaze, he leans in and licks a long line down my dick, tasting the frosting before he sits back with a hum. "Delicious, angel," he praises as he grips my cock at the base, holding it still for his tongue, and then he proceeds to torture me by licking every drop of frosting from my cock. His tongue traces over me until I mutter obscenities, my hips rolling as I try to suppress my desire.

"Skylar," I beg, and it's like he was waiting for it. His lips wrap around my tip and he sucks hard, making me arch away from the counter as my eyes slide shut in ecstasy.

Chuckling, he opens his mouth wide and takes me all the way into his throat. His wet, hot mouth seals around me as he sucks hard before pulling back. His head bobs as he takes me deeper each time. I force my eyes open and onto him, not wanting to miss a moment. He ignores his own desire completely as he sucks me, playing with my cock and piercings until I thrust into his mouth.

His other hand grips my thigh, and he tugs my legs open wider before his fingers trail up the inside of my thigh and to my ass. I shiver in want, and pleasure spirals through me as I look down and anchor my hand in his hair. It falls around his face, giving him a roguish appearance, and my dick jerks at the sight. His mouth pops from my cock as he smirks.

"I knew you liked my long hair. You like to pull it, don't you?" he teases.

"Shut up," I say. "Fuck, please, for once, just use that mouth for something other than talking."

Laughing, he sucks me into his mouth, and my head falls back with a groan.

He grips my ass, his fingers sliding up my crack and parting me as he circles my hole in time with him pulling from my dick and swallowing me again. I push into him, begging wordlessly, until I can't take any more. I'm about to yell at him when he presses inside me.

His fingers push into my ass, making me cry out as they bury deep, twisting to rub the spot that has me jerking and forcing my cock farther into his mouth.

"Sky!" I cry out as he takes me all the way down his throat, his fingers digging into that spot until red-hot pleasure explodes through my body, like a lightning bolt hitting me. I bellow, my cock pulsing in his mouth as I fill his throat with my cum. It seems to go on forever, trapping me in an endless orgasm until I struggle to breathe. The pleasure is intense, and when it finally subsides, I slump back, barely able to stand. His fingers slide from my ass as he pulls his mouth from my cock and places a gentle kiss on my tip before rising to his feet like an avenging angel.

"Happy birthday, beautiful," he whispers, his lips swollen as he grins. His eyes are filled with nothing but happiness and love as I tremble in aftershocks against him, knowing I'll never be able to eat birthday cake without getting hard.

I start to fall, and he sweeps me into his arms, carrying me to the sofa as he keeps his possessive gaze on me. I suddenly understand how Evan feels when Alek looks at him.

Sky stares at me like I'm his everything, like nothing else exists in the world other than me. It's addictive but also powerful—a feeling I never want to let go of.

CHAPTER 29
SKYLAR

I t's been another hard day at work. I haven't told Bones yet because I don't want him to worry, but accidents keep happening —far too many to be coincidences.

They have to be purposeful.

First, it was the tech and his hand. Next, one of the engines crapped out after it had just been checked, and then our track was flooded. Today I went in to find my tires all fucked. Noah has this look in his eye, like he knows something but he won't speak to me about it, and it makes me feel annoyed and worried.

Who is fucking with us?

Who is willing to damage our property and hurt people?

Why?

Is it because we qualified? It has to be. That's the only thing that's changed. It puts me in a shitty mood, though, and there's only one thing that can cheer me up—my boy. I head over to the gym he's giving a lesson at tonight, knowing I shouldn't, but I need to see him.

I need to be around him, even in a room full of others.

I need him to make it all better and remind me that there is still good in this world.

I leave my jacket and everything in the car, and at the class doorway, I kick off my shoes so I'm in my tank and jeans. I lean into the wall and just watch my boy. He's standing before the class in some shorts and a vest, with rows of women of all ages before him, listening intently.

I don't blame them. If he were my teacher, I would have paid attention in class too.

"Does anyone have any questions?" he asks kindly, his voice softer than I've ever heard it.

I lift my hand, grinning as all eyes turn to me. "Yes, I have one. I'd like to take this class," I say.

Bones's eyes narrow in annoyance, and he crosses his arms. "This is a women's self-defense class."

"Feels a little sexist," I retort. "You don't mind, do you, ladies?"

"Not one damn bit," someone says.

"If you take your shirt off, I'm good with it," another comments. She's easily old enough to be my mom. I like her style, but my boy is possessive and jealous, even if he won't admit it, so the shirt stays on.

Winking, I wag my finger at her as Bones sighs. "You want to be a part of this class?"

I grin. "Absolutely."

"Fine," he grumbles, an evil grin curving his lips, and I shudder as a bad feeling builds in my bones.

My boy is cruel and vicious, and I love it.

I stand before the class at his side. "Everybody, say hello to Skylar. He will be our volunteer today as I show you some new moves. Say hello, Skylar."

"Hi, ladies," I say with a grin despite the fact that I know I'm about to spend the next hour getting my ass handed to me by my boy. At least he'll have his hands on me. "Go soft on me, baby. I won't be able to play with you later if you don't."

Bones's angry eyes cut to me, and I just grin as giggles sound out in the class.

An old lady, easily seventy, lifts her hand. "Bones, is this your boyfriend?"

"No."

"Yes."

We answer at the same time, and I grin as he glares at me. "How about I show you how to silence an attacker?"

"Oh, I know this one. The throat?" a young girl asks.

"Very good. Let me demonstrate." My eyes widen as Bones grins evilly at me, but I don't move away as he brings his hand toward my throat. I gulp, but he stops when he's just barely touching me. "One smooth hit will disable them. Alternatively, you could use your elbow." He steps back. "Now, last week we were practicing throws. I want to show you another one." He looks at me. "Attack me from behind."

"I do that every night," I tease, and his glare makes me chuckle as I head over, grabbing him.

He reaches up, holds me tightly, then flips me. I hit the mat hard, the wind knocked from my chest. I just lie here, struggling to breathe, as he explains it to them again.

Fuck, my boy is strong.

Why is that so sexy?

"Just like that. Now let me demonstrate again slowly." And so it goes. I am up and flipped over and over until he has them practice, and then he moves through them, correcting their hands and postures. I see their confidence grow and their excitement when they manage it.

My eyes track my boy. I'm so fucking proud of him, I don't care about my aching muscles. He's giving them their power back and giving them confidence. Does he even notice the devotion in their eyes as they watch him or the relaxed, happy atmosphere he creates?

He says he's cruel and cold, but as I watch him, I know everyone else, including him, is wrong.

An hour later, I'm lying on the mat, panting and sweating. He beat my ass for an entire hour. I have no doubt he used more force than necessary, but every time he smiled in victory, I let him do it.

"Here." I open my eyes to see him thrusting a water bottle toward me. I lift my arm to take it but groan and let it flop back to the mat.

Rolling his eyes, he lowers to his ass as his class talks and packs up. His arm slides around me and lifts me into a sitting position as he opens it and hands it over.

I take a drink and groan. He reaches out, brushing away drops of water from my chin and lips. "You sore? I might have gone too hard on you," he admits, worry in his gaze. He's concerned he will drive me away and that, once more, he will be too much.

"Don't worry, beautiful. You can beat me up anytime and kiss it better later." The class giggles, some hooting and shouting.

"Anyone who shouts will run ten laps," Bones snaps.

"I'll run them for you, shout away!" I yell from the mat as I grin at him and wipe his sweat away. "You did good today, baby. I'm proud of you. You've created an amazing thing here."

He shrugs and looks away, embarrassed under praise, so I turn his face back to me.

"I mean it. You're giving them the skills necessary to protect themselves. That's amazing, Bones. I'm so very proud of you."

"Thank you," he mutters.

"You guys are so cute," someone calls, and I grin as I glance over at the class.

"What do you think?" I ask, slinging my arm over him and pressing my cheek to his. "Do we look good together?"

"Yes!" they yell.

"See? They think so too," I flirt. He shoves me away, but he's grinning. He tosses the water at me and goes to see them out. He walks some to their cars before coming back.

He locks up, turns the lights off, and offers me his hand. "Come on, let's go home."

He called it home.

With me.

CHAPTER 30
BONES

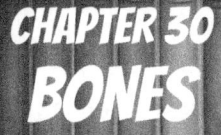

We fall into a routine, something I'm not used to. I'm not accustomed to someone waiting on me, eating every meal with me, or going to sleep with me, but I like it. I can't seem to pull back and draw boundaries.

I spend every night in his arms and bed, and I let him take me to and from college, parties, and Silent Rose. I let him do everything he wants because seeing him happy does something to me. I did that. I made someone that happy by just being with them, and it warms my heart.

Others have started to notice. Someone in my class even told me today that I'm smiling more. I didn't realize I was, but I guess it's true. I think about him and smile like a crazy person.

I told him he didn't need to pick me up today, since I had to stay late and study, but as soon as I'm home and changed, I head over to his apartment, opening his door with the spare key he gave me. Some of my presents remain unopened on his table. I've been opening one a day, but he doesn't seem bothered. He drinks down my every reaction, and when I came out this morning wearing the shirt he bought me, I swear he screamed.

"Skylar?" I call when he doesn't rush to greet me. I don't hear him, and it's quiet. Maybe he isn't back yet.

I see his keys in the bowl, though, and panic fills me. It's too quiet. Where is he?

My heart races as age-old terror lifts its head, the past and present colliding as I hurry through his apartment, calling his name.

I hurry through his bedroom, and a noise makes me rush to the closed bathroom door. Yanking it open, I freeze, my heart slamming as terror turns to annoyance.

He's in the shower with his head tipped back, the water running over his incredible muscles. He hasn't heard me yet, so I just stare and drink him in. I have the insane urge to join him. I shouldn't, but . . .

Yanking my shirt over my head, I kick my jeans off and head his way, opening the door and stepping in behind him. His head turns, and he opens his eyes.

"Hey, baby," he says so softly I shiver and press against his back as he kisses me.

"Hey, yourself," I murmur, sliding my hands around him to link them together when I feel something on his side. Frowning, I turn him to see a bandage on his hip. "What happened?" I ask.

"Ah, nothing." He cups my cheek and kisses me again. "I missed you."

"It's been like six hours."

He grins. "I still missed you."

"I missed you too," I admit reluctantly. "Now what happened? This isn't nothing."

He tries to kiss me to distract me, so I lean back, making my glare brutal. "Skylar Warren, if you ever want me anywhere near your penis again, you will tell me."

"Baby," he whines then sighs. "There was an accident at work. That's all."

I know he's holding something back, but at least he told me. Running my eyes over him, I frown. "You're okay?"

"Fine, just a scratch. This is just to be safe. You could always kiss it better though," he teases.

I drop to my knees, seeing his eyes widen as I turn my head and press a kiss over the bandage. I feel his cock hardening, but I ignore it for a moment as I press another kiss to his wound and peer up at him as I caress his hip with my fingers and circle his dick.

His breath comes out in a whoosh as he stares down at me, hunger in his gaze.

"Tell me what happened," I murmur.

"Accident," he blurts out.

I blow on the tip of his cock until he shudders and reaches for me, but I sit back.

"What happened?"

"Shit. They teach you this at law school?" he rasps, his head falling back. "Don't be mean."

"I've only just started." I smirk as I dart my tongue out to taste the desire on his tip. "Tell me what happened and I'll suck your cock."

"Mean."

He doesn't tell me. Instead, he watches me torture him, lapping at him with my tongue. My hand softly circles his shaft, and his hips roll forward, but I don't give him enough to get off, and he eventually grows annoyed. Reaching down, he yanks me to my feet as my eyes widen.

He shoves me into the wall and falls to his knees, then wraps his lips around my cock. I know he's trying to distract me, and it works. For a time, I let him because Jesus Christ, his mouth . . .

I lose myself in it as he turns the tables on me, and within minutes, I'm screaming his name and coming down his throat. When he stands, he looks at me victoriously before he casually washes my body and wraps me in his towels like I'm a baby.

I fucking love it.

Lying in his bed sometime later with my head on his chest, I run my hands around the wound. "You really won't tell me?" I ask sadly. Does he not trust me? I must say it out loud because he sighs and pulls me up so we lie face-to-face on our sides, holding my hand.

"I didn't tell you because I didn't want you to worry," he replies. "Not because I don't trust you, okay?"

"But you worry about me. I want to worry about you, okay? Please tell me. I hate secrets and not knowing." I know he understands it comes from my past being filled with uncertainties and not knowing what happened.

Kissing my hand, he leans against his pillows, his hair sticking up all over. "There have been some accidents at the garage. We thought they were coincidences at first, but I think someone is targeting us. This happened because I saw a hoist give way, and I yanked a tech out before it could crush him. I got a little hurt from it."

"Skylar, you could have died!" I sit up, but he pulls me back down.

"But I didn't. I'm okay," he promises. "Just let me hold you. It's been a hard few days."

"You should have told me," I snap in annoyance. "Do you know who it is? Who's doing it?"

"No, but we'll find out. There aren't many people it can be. Noah will handle it. I know that. I'm just . . ."

"What?" I demand.

"I'm worried. At this rate, someone will be dead before the next race."

My heart stops, but he kisses me.

"It won't be me, so don't look so worried. I'll be extra careful, okay? I'm going to speak to Noah about it in the morning. We'll figure out who it is and stop them. They want to scare us, and they want us to pull out of the championship, but it won't work. They won't scare us off that easily."

He might not be scared, but I am.

What if something happens to him?

What if it ruins his dreams and career or worse?

What happens if it gets him killed?

I stare into his eyes as he wraps himself around me, and I know I can't live without Skylar Warren. He's become important to me in such a short period of time that the idea of anything happening to him terrifies me.

CHAPTER 31

SKYLAR

"Get dressed," I order Bones, who lounges naked on my bed like an oversized cat—hell, he pretty much is. He likes to be pet when he demands it, and he likes sleep and food and can hiss when he wants. "As much as I love the view, beautiful, we are going out." I slap his ass as I pass him.

"Going out where?" he asks as he rolls over to keep me in sight. His eyes darken when he notices I'm wearing nothing but a towel.

"Behave," I warn as I lean over him and nip his tempting lips. "We are going on a date. I realized last night I haven't taken you on an official date as a couple, so get dressed." I head to my closet, but I feel him hesitate, and I look back. "You don't want to go on a date with me?"

"I do," he admits as he leans up. "But people will see us. I know you're open about your sexuality, but will it be good for your image—"

"Silas Townsend," I growl as I stalk his way and lean over him until he has no choice but to focus on my words. "I don't give a fuck about my image. All I give a fuck about is what's in my arms right now —you. Get your beautiful ass dressed so we can go on our official first date."

He smiles as he leans up and kisses me. "Fine, but it better be good. I have high standards."

"Go," I order, smacking his hip as I grin and head to get ready.

Excitement courses through my veins as well as nervousness. I've never been on a real date, since he admitted the one we went on before didn't count. I want to impress him.

He was born rich, and I want to prove I can take care of him and give him the same life he is used to. I want my boy to have everything in this world, and tonight, I'll show him that.

Bones looks good enough to eat. His dark red shirt is open, exposing his tattoos and stunning chest, paired with dark slacks and shined shoes. It's hard to keep my hands off him, but I try. His eyes, however, are filled with hunger as well, and not for the fancy five courses we are working our way through, but for me.

I lean back, letting him look.

I'm his, after all, and this is all for him.

My fancy, new black button-down is open all the way down. I have my boots on, but my hair is slicked back, half up and down, and I know I clean up well. If the way he has been looking at me since I knocked on his door is anything to go by, he likes it a lot.

"You like the restaurant?" I ask hopefully. It's supposed to be the hottest new spot in Pine Valley, recently opened with a waitlist for months. It took me days to pull strings to get a reservation out here on the roof terrace. The vibe is intimate and screams money with low lamps and heaters, private tables separated by flowers and artful bushes, and an incredible view of the city. Everybody here is suited and dripping in diamonds. He fits right in. My boy is so fucking beautiful, I debate bending him over the table and eating my dessert right now.

"I've been wanting to come here," he says as he looks around. We've had our first course, some tinier than life salad, but watching him nearly come over the taste of it was worth it. I'd eat tiny rich meals for the rest of my life if he made that face again.

Wrapping my feet around his under the table, I nurse my mocktail.

I won't drink with my boy here, but he's nursing a red wine and seems super relaxed and happy, which makes me think I'm doing something right.

"So how am I doing so far? Impressing you on our first official date?" I ask with a grin.

"You're doing okay," he replies coolly, and I grin wider, knowing he likes it. I'm learning to read every nuance of Bones, and when he looks away like that, it means he's lying. He shakes his head, but he smiles as he looks out at one of the best views of the city. I just stare at him because he's better than any view. I could watch him for the rest of my life. "It's beautiful."

"You can say that again," I murmur, and he glances over to see me watching him.

"You corny ass. I was talking about the view."

I smirk. "So was I."

He gives me an exasperated side-eye, but I lean back as the next dish is served. I wait for the server to leave before spooning up some of the foam and fish.

Cupping my hand under the spoon, I feed him the second course, wiping his mouth as he chews. "Good?"

"Really good," he admits after moaning.

"You make that moan when I'm deep inside you," I comment casually.

He smacks me, looking around in shock as I laugh. Hooking my foot around his chair, I drag it closer to the table so I can run my leg up his.

"Skylar," he warns, but he's smiling, and I can't help but smile back.

I've never been this happy. I want to spend the rest of my life doing this—racing all day and coming home to him, sharing our lives.

"Silas?" a barked voice calls. We both whip around, and my smile drops as I eye the man. Bones chokes, however, and when I glance over, he's sitting upright, his face cold and closed down, but I see fear in his eyes. I run my gaze over the man again, already hating him. The older man spares me a look, and the way he dismisses me by averting his gaze lets me know he doesn't approve.

That's fine. I don't either, whoever he is.

"Father," Bones responds curtly. All traces of happiness are gone.

Ah, so this is the devil who raised him. I hate him instantly and debate making Bones an orphan.

What little I know of Bones's childhood is cold and unpleasant. His father, a dick-torian, was cold toward his son. No wonder Bones almost appears sad to see him here, tonight of all nights.

"What are you doing here?" Bones asks. His father arches a brow, and Bones swallows. "I meant to ask if you are here for business or pleasure."

"Then say it as you mean it. You know better," his father warns, his words cutting and sharp, and I watch them sink into my boy like a weapon. "Words hold meaning. They should be chosen carefully. I thought I would have taught you that by now." He looks at me again, his nostrils flaring. "I had a business meeting with a potential client. Why are you here? Shouldn't you be studying, not . . . playing around?"

"Yes, Father," Bones mutters, but he seems shaken and withdrawn. I hate it. I hate how quickly this man ruined my boy's happiness.

"We aren't playing around. We're eating. Food is important, no?" I ask his father.

"I wasn't speaking to you," he snaps angrily. It's clear he's a man used to getting his own way and inspiring fear in others.

"Father," Bones cautions.

"Well, that's too bad because I was talking to you," I drawl with an arched brow. "You can glare at me all you want. It doesn't intimidate or scare me. I grew up surrounded by stronger men willing to do anything to get what they want. Since you didn't introduce yourself, I won't either, but Bones and I are busy, so I suggest you go back to your business meeting."

His eyes narrow, and he leans into me, trying to physically intimidate me. No doubt it has worked on everyone in the past. He carries power and money like a weapon, but what I said is true. I grew up on the streets, surrounded by drug dealers, gang bangers, and murderers, so not much scares me anymore, not even the devil dressed in Versace. "Now you listen here, little boy. If I were speaking to you, you would know it. I was speaking to my son—"

"More like ordering him around." I lean close to his face, and when he flinches back a bit, I smile in victory. "Did you even wish your son a happy birthday?"

"Sky, it's okay." Bones's voice shakes, and I want to throttle this man. Can't he see how scared his son is? What kind of father wants that?

"No, it isn't. You are his father. Did you even call him? Text him? Send him a card?" I arch a brow. "No, so clearly you know nothing about your son's life. You shouldn't be making adjustments to it, now should you?"

He leans back, eyeing me. "Birthdays are trivial events. I have important work. My son understands that." He turns to Bones. "You should keep your . . . friend on a leash."

"Woof," I bark, and he shoots me a glare as I smile. "You can go now. I'm sure you have *important work* that's much more pressing than talking to us. Besides, I didn't invite you to stay, and you are annoying me and spoiling my view."

He splutters, and the reaction only makes me smile and lean back. His face turns red in annoyance, and with one last glare at me, he gives Bones a pointed look and marches inside.

Smirking, I look back at Bones to see he's pale. "Skylar, I'm sorry—"

"Don't you ever apologize for your father." I cover his hand with mine and lift it, kissing his knuckles. "How about we get out of here?" I ask. He looks upset and uncomfortable. "Let's go somewhere he can't follow us."

Nodding, he stands. I keep his hand in mine as I pay the bill and head out with him at my side, quiet and withdrawn.

"Were you really not scared of my father?" he asks sometime later as I'm driving, his head turned as he watches me.

"Not even a little. Trust me, he's nothing compared to the gangsters I used to eat dinner with when I was a kid." I wink. "But forget about him. Don't let him ruin our night. You are allowed to enjoy life, beautiful, and go out and have fun. It isn't all about work and school."

He swallows but nods, and I drive us deeper into the city, away from the glitz and glamor, from the rich and the famous and the fancy places he's used to. "Where are we going?" he questions after a while.

"Somewhere different. You grew up in places like that, but I grew up in places like this. I'm not saying either are bad, but tonight, I think you could use some home cooking and community," I tell him.

He doesn't fight me on it, and I want to see him smile again, so I take him to the one place that always made me happy. We pull off the side streets in the area I grew up in and to the restaurant at the bottom. It's more of an old building with half the front missing, but nobody steals from Mama's. She fed us all, after all. It's her motto, feeding starving street kids or businessmen alike.

The front has a metal gazebo the community built after a bad storm, and tables are spread under it, picnic style. There are black chalkboard menus, and even at this time, it's busy. A live band plays in the back as home-cooked food is served. Climbing from my car, I take Bones's hand as he gets out.

"What is this place?" he asks, his eyes wide.

"Mama's," I answer as I pull him after me. "When I couldn't afford food, she would feed me, never complaining or asking for anything in return. When I grew up and started making money, I gave it back here. It's always been a good place for me. It reminds me of how a home should feel—safe, happy, and with love in every meal. I think you could use that tonight," I say as I head inside, ducking under the opening and heading toward a free table in the back.

"Sky!" I smile and wave at those I know, clapping shoulders as I sit and pull Bones down opposite me on the small picnic table. His eyes are wide as he looks around.

"What do you want to eat?" He didn't get to finish his fancy meal. Besides, even if we did, we would still be hungry.

"Um . . ." He glances at the menus with a wary expression, and I grin.

"Want me to order?"

He nods, and I grab the pad from the table, scribbling down our order before heading toward the counter.

"Skylar!" Mama calls as she pushes the server aside and kisses both of my cheeks before checking me over. "You lost weight. You haven't been eating properly," she admonishes in the way only a mother can.

She will always be a mother, even without her son.

"Been missing your meals," I admit as I hand over the sheet. "Make this with extra love. I brought someone special."

"Special?" She leans around, and I point out Bones. She grins at me, slapping my side. "He's handsome."

"He is." I grin and hand over a wad, but she waves me off like normal. She could earn a fortune, but she doesn't care about money. She just wants to feed our community and save as many as she can through her home-cooked food and care.

I'd be dead if it wasn't for this woman who saw a scrawny, angry kid and kept bringing me food, even though I wouldn't speak.

Rolling my eyes, I shove the cash into the tip jar, and she sighs as I hustle to my table to avoid her scolding. Not five minutes later, our food comes out, the trays heaping with more than I ordered. Mama leans into my shoulder as it's served.

"You're Skylar's boy?" she asks kindly, analyzing him in a way only she can. Within two minutes, she knows everything about him and what he needs. It's her gift.

"Yes, ma'am. I'm Bones. It's nice to meet you. The food looks incredible, so everything he said must be true," Bones says with a soft grin.

Mama swoons, hitting my side. "Call me Mama, everyone does. My boy, you picked good. Don't be an ass to this one. Keep him."

"I plan to." I smirk as she kisses my head, sending warmth through me. The familiar gesture brings both happiness and sadness, as I have forgotten how my other mother did that.

"Eat up. We've missed you, although we've been watching your races. I knew you could do it. We are all so proud. Look." She points to the back wall, and I grin when I see the flag with my number on it. "Enough, eat." She walks off, but I hear my name, and I wave as the people she's talking to whoop and call out.

"I feel like I'm with a celebrity." Bones grins, but he seems more relaxed, and when he takes a bite, his eyes widen. "What is this?"

"That is Mama's love." I laugh. "Best food in the city."

Blinking, he shovels the food into his mouth, and I watch proudly while eating my own. When he's done, he leans back. "I am so full," he remarks.

Just then, Mama returns. "You haven't eaten a lot. Let me get you some more—"

I catch her arm and kiss her hand. "We're full, Mama. It was incredible, as always."

She frowns, looking at our plates. "I'll pack some to take home. Can't have my boys going hungry," she mutters and hurries away.

"Looks like she's adopted you too," I say. "She's like that. You'll be hers now, no escape. She's a mother to everyone here."

He smiles and continues to do so all night as I talk to the usuals and people I know. He watches me in a way that makes me want to kiss the shit out of him, and when I come back from the restroom, he's talking to Mama. She's fixing his hair and smiling brightly, clearly loving him as I head back over.

"He's so smart," she whispers to me. "Marry him before he realizes you're an idiot."

"Mama." I sigh. "Where's the love?"

"Uh-uh, it's a good thing you're pretty. Bones, you remember what I said, okay? And come back any time. I'll keep a plate for you."

"Thank you, Mama," he says, smiling widely.

Shaking my head, I grab his cup and head over to top it off. As I'm there, she leans into me. "I love him. He's perfect for you. He has fire and sass . . . . I think he's hurting though. I think deep inside, he has the same pain you have. Be kind to him."

"I will," I murmur as I hold the drinks. "I'll make sure no one hurts him again."

"That's my boy." She grins. "I approve. Now enjoy your night. Go."

Shaking my head, I head back to him and hand him his drink just as the music starts up again.

"She's lovely," he says, indicating Mama. "She really takes care of everyone here?"

"She grew up here, raised her kid here—her son was shot when he was a teenager—and she opened this place for him, since that's what he always called her, so all of us street kids could have a safe place like he needed. That's why we all call her Mama. She was a mother without a son, so we gave her hundreds so she'll never feel alone again," I explain.

"I didn't know," he whispers, eyeing her sadly.

"She doesn't talk about it a lot. He was a good kid who fell in with the wrong crowd. We all make sure to take care of her and this place. Don't worry, she isn't alone."

He nods, but he's watching her sadly, so I take his hand and kiss the back of it. "Feeling better?"

His smile is slow but there. "Much. Thank you for bringing me here. I like learning more about your past and life. Everyone here loves you. It's strange. I've passed my neighbors for years but don't even know their names, yet here, you all know everything about everyone."

"Community." I shrug. "It's important. Without it and the love we all share, what's the point?"

"I guess I wouldn't know," he says as I rub the back of his hand. He watches me as we lapse into silence. The band kicks into another song, this one fast, and whoops fill the air.

Bones and I smile as everyone gets up and dances, laughter filling the air as they move through the tables under the sky.

Holding out my hand, I get to my feet. "Dance with me, beautiful."

He rolls his eyes, but he lets me pull him up, and in the middle of the street, I wind him in circles, twisting and dipping him. His laughter rings out with everyone else's as we move to music, everything else forgotten.

He just lets go, trusting me as we dance together, his cheeks red with happiness. I want to take a picture and never forget it. His hand holds mine as I lift it and turn him again. He laughs and then does the same for me. I spin under his arm, grinning as the music fades and we pant, sharing secretive smiles.

I tug him deeper into my arms as the music slows to something soft and loving, then I slide my hand from his and drape both arms around his waist. His own slide around my neck, and he rests his cheek on my chest, our bodies pressed together.

Rocking under the moonlight, I hold him closer and move us to the soft music. No one cares here. Tonight, we can be anyone.

"I don't want to ever let you go," he whispers as he lifts his head. I massage the back of his neck as we sway.

"Me either," I admit.

We stare into each other's eyes before he leans in and kisses me. It's the first time he's kissed me in public. It's soft and chaste, but it's there, and when he leans back, I can't help but grin.

"Thank you, Skylar, for showing me what life can be if I let it. Thank you for loving me when no one else does."

"Always," I vow as he leans into me again.

We sway like that for hours, neither of us wanting the night to end.

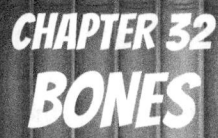

CHAPTER 32
BONES

The place empties as the night goes on, but we make no move to leave. "I came here a lot as a kid," he tells me as we take a break from dancing, "when I was too weak to fight back and needed safety or food. I know a lot about fear, baby, and what I saw in your eyes with your father was fear."

I swallow as I stare at him, and he smiles, kissing my hand. He's always touching and comforting me, like he can't resist, and every time he does, my heart skips a beat.

"You might not want to admit it, but we are partners, so lean on me and let me be there for you. When the world hurts you, I'll heal you and pick up the pieces. I'll make you laugh, even when you want to cry. I'll do anything, and I'll always be right here," he promises, and I see the truth in his eyes.

He means it.

When everyone else left, he stayed.

When everyone else would have given up, he fought harder.

I kiss the back of his hand, like he does with me, and the spark in his eyes tells me I need to do it more often, like when I kissed him earlier. It's happiness mixed with surprise, and I crave that look. "Let's go home." That's all I can say, but I plan to spend all night showing him just what his words mean to me, just what *he* means to me.

We wave goodbye to Mama and head down the side street where Skylar parked, holding hands, when someone steps out before us. His expression is grim and angry, there's a spider tattoo across his left cheek, and he's in loose pants and a leather jacket. Another man steps out at his side, and when I glance back, my smile drops when I find three more burly, angry guys surrounding us.

"Skylar," I whisper.

"I know," he murmurs calmly and squeezes my hand.

"Skylar Warren," the man with the tat says. "Never thought I'd see you again."

"The feeling is mutual, trust me. Nobody wants to look at that ugly face."

One of his men chuckles at Sky's words, but his eyes narrow.

"Still a smart-ass, I see." He lifts a pipe and points it at Sky. "We have a debt to settle. You wrecked my car."

"Nah, you wrecked it by trying to outdrive me." Skylar rolls his eyes. "You should have known better, accepted that you lost, and moved on."

"No, I'll get my winnings one way or another," he warns, and then he dives at Skylar. Sky pushes me out of the way and ducks under the swing. My back hits the wall as I turn in horror and watch them circle him.

"Really? You want to do this tonight? Come on, I'm out with my boy. How about a rain check?" Sky jokes.

"You're dead, and then your boy will be too."

Sky loses his smile at that, but when he glances at me, he winks. "Stay there, baby. I'll be right back," he says, even going so far as to blow me a kiss, but he ducks under the pipe again.

He bends and weaves, moving backwards to avoid them, but he doesn't fight back. I know Skylar can fight, I've seen it, so why isn't he?

"Fight back!" I yell.

He grunts as a pipe hits his side. He winces but smiles at me. "No can do, beautiful. I can't get into trouble. I promised you and Noah."

My jaw drops as another pipe hits his side. "Fuck that, fight back! Kick their asses!" I shout.

"Stay there, baby," he warns me as he ducks under a pipe, grabs it, and tosses it away. It clatters against the wall near me, but that only pisses them off more, and their attack grows brutal.

There is only so much he can do, though, to avoid all five of them and their weapons. He grunts as they rain blows on his back until he's forced to his knees. His head is bleeding, his back is no doubt fucked, and his arms can't take much more.

Ignoring his orders and whatever this means for my career or future, I grab the pipe he tossed. "Fuck this!" I mutter. "Hey, fuck heads," I call as I head toward them.

They ignore me, however, pounding on Skylar, so I slam the pipe down on one's back, making sure to only use some of my strength. I don't want to kill them, unless they hurt him worse.

He stumbles back, and I hit his arm. He cries out, clutching it, and they turn their attention to me and away from Skylar, who's shielding his head on the ground, refusing to break his promise to Noah and me.

One of them leaps at me, so I hit him with the pipe until he stumbles back. "Get him!" the leader yells, and he lunges for me.

Swinging again, I slam into his chin, and he flies backwards as I bring it down again. "Do not fucking touch him, do you hear me? He's mine!"

"What are you going to do, rich boy?" one of the thugs asks as he stares at me, holding his busted arm.

"That's right, I'm a rich boy, and I'm a fucking lawyer. That means I can put your ass in jail and make it stay. I have enough money to destroy you. Remember that next time you come after him," I growl, holding the pipe as Skylar groans and stumbles to his feet, trying to pull me behind him, but I push him behind me and hold the pipe out.

He might not be able to fight, but I can.

"Fuck this." The leader heads toward me, raising the pipe, but I'm half turned, pushing his friend away who's coming at us too. "You'll die with him." I turn in time to see the pipe heading for my face.

Skylar's hand slams out, his reflexes faster than I have ever seen, and he catches the pipe midair and kicks him back. "Never touch my boy," he warns, and then, despite his promise, he grips the man's hand and snaps it, breaking his wrist.

"Hey, assholes!" A whistle cuts through the air, and we turn to see Mama with a kitchen knife and two cooks at her side. "You leave my boys alone, you hear? If I see you again, there will be trouble."

They look from her to us, and one of the guys grabs the one with the tattoo. "It isn't worth it. Let's go."

I watch them leave, and only then do I drop the pipe. Skylar groans but leans down and uses his shirt to clean the pipes before he tosses them into the nearest grate as Mama and her boys look at us. "We'll make sure they don't come back. Head home, boys."

When she's gone, I rush to Skylar, looking him over. Blood trickles down his forehead, and he's holding one of his arms, but he seems okay, especially if the goo-goo eyes and crazed, lopsided smile are anything to go by.

"You're hurt. Stop looking at me like that," I tell him.

"I'm yours, huh?" His grin widens.

"Unbelievable. They must have hit your dumb head. Come on, Romeo." I wrap my arm around him and lead him to his car. I settle him in the passenger seat and get in the driver's seat. "We need to get you checked over at the hospital—"

"No, no hospital. They will ask questions. I won't get you in trouble," he replies, shuffling in his seat, and I frown.

"Sky, you could be hurt. You need to see someone," I beg.

"Fine, I know someone." He leans forward and plugs in the address. "Drive my car carefully, baby."

Rolling my eyes, I put on my belt and reverse carefully, then I follow the directions to the address. He doesn't complain, but every bump makes him wince, and I'm really worried something is broken.

Can he still drive if it is?

Will he lose his chance?

Terror fills me. He's worked so hard for his dream. He can't lose out on it now.

He just can't.

I should have killed those pricks.

"Ouch, damn, old man," Skylar whines, jerking back. "Give me some warning."

Noah huffs, tossing the cotton ball aside. "I told you not to fight!" he snaps.

Skylar pouts. His shirt is off, and he's sitting backwards on a chair, his arms and back exposed, showing the worst wounds. Noah looked worried and then pissed when we pulled up, but he let us in and grabbed a first-aid kit without a word, barking orders.

"I didn't, old man, promise." Sky offers him his pinkie.

Noah glares, and I clear my throat. "He didn't. He was jumped. I was there, but he refused to fight back."

"Don't you defend him!" he warns as he stands. "Nothing is broken. You'll be bruised and sore, but you got lucky. Here, you deal with him. He's pissing me off."

"Nope, he's yours." I grin, but then it fades. "I'm worried about his injuries since he refused to go to the hospital."

Noah looks from me to him. "You really didn't fight?"

"Promise, old man," Sky states seriously. "I wouldn't risk our chance like that."

Noah sighs and picks up another cotton ball and gets back to work on his wounds, cleaning them. They look shallow, but they must hurt like fuck. He got lucky—I know that. If they had the chance, they probably would have killed him.

Skylar whines again.

"Shut up. Don't be a wimp," Noah grouses.

Wandering around his living room, I nearly whistle. This is a nice fucking place. I guess being a race car driver pays off. It's large and on the good side of town, and the amount of cars outside is impressive.

The pictures on the mantel are more remarkable than everything else though. It's not money; it's achievements. There are photos of him with trophies and medals.

No wonder Skylar looks up to him and came here—he trusts him.

When he's done, Noah sits back. "You can put your shirt on."

"Why? Feeling inadequate?" Skylar teases.

"I see the beating didn't affect your ego." He sighs. "Shame. Why did you get jumped?"

"Eh, just some old issues." Sky frowns. "I'm sorry, boss man. I can't change my past."

"I know. I knew it when I took you, but I'm proud of you for keeping your word. You did good, kid."

Skylar perks up at that, and I hide my grin at how much he looks to Noah for guidance. He probably doesn't even realize it.

Skylar Warren hasn't had a clear father figure and it shows. It appears Noah has taken that or the big brother role for him.

Putting his shirt back on, he winks at me as Noah hands over some pills. "Take these with water and rest."

"You got it." He pockets them as he glances around. "Nice place, old man."

Noah just rolls his eyes as we head to the door.

"Wait, wait . . . Whose shorts are those?" Skylar grins widely as he nods at the striped pair of shorts lying on the floor, which are too small to be Noah's.

"That's it, get out." He pushes Sky out of the front door and blocks it as he tries to lean around him.

"Interrupting, am I? Is it Mackie?" He wiggles his brows.

"Yes, it's Mackie. He got drunk, so I had to pick him up," he answers with a deep sigh. "He stripped, and I had to chase him and put him to bed. It seems I'm doomed to babysit idiots tonight."

"Uh-uh, I don't remember you looking after any of us this closely. Why did you go get him when he was drunk?" Sky challenges.

"Don't push it, Warren. Go home and rest. I'll see you in the morning."

Skylar is on his front with his arms stretched out and his back on display. There are a myriad of bruises and cuts, but it could have been a lot worse, and as the morning light trickles across him, I can't help but lean into his warmth.

I was so scared last night. I could have lost him. They were determined to kill him, and he refused to fight back, the brave fucking idiot. I've never been scared like that before. I'm worried about what he has been through before if that was normal for him.

How did Skylar Warren survive the streets?

More importantly, how did he turn into such an amazing man?

I brush my lips down his back, careful of the bruises there, and listen to him sigh as he snuggles deeper into his bed. His voice comes, sleepy and deep and so sexy. "Morning, baby."

"Morning," I whisper against his skin. "How do you feel?"

He turns over with a groan, opening one eye and pulling me into his arms. "Better now," he says.

Rolling my eyes, I cuddle against him, and he sighs happily. "I was scared," I admit. "Next time something like that happens, promise me you'll fight back, Skylar."

"You and my future are more important," he murmurs. "I won't ruin what I have. I can handle a beating or two, don't worry."

"How many enemies did you make on the streets?" I ask.

He's quiet, and I groan. He laughs, holding me tighter. "It's nice you're worried about me."

"Don't change the subject," I snap as I prop my head on his chest and look at him. "I can't lose you, okay?"

"You won't," he murmurs softly, cupping my cheek, and I lean into his touch. "I'm not going anywhere. Now, about breakfast . . ." His smile is wicked and slow. "Can I eat you?"

My sigh fills the air, followed by his laughter.

CHAPTER 33
SKYLAR

"Jesus, Skylar, put on a shirt. The marks on your back look like you were attacked by a cat," Alek scoffs behind me.

I wipe my hands as I turn away from the engine and lean against my car. "Not a cat, but a brat. I wear them proudly."

"Christ," Noah mutters as he walks over, crossing his arms. "I'd be more worried about his face. You finished getting beat up now?"

"I followed the rules," I mutter, but my smile can't be dimmed, especially as I remember the way my boy kissed every single wound this morning.

He rolls his eyes, and we all turn as Mackie shuffles past. Sunglasses cover his pale face, and his shirt is on backwards. He waves at us absentmindedly and slumps into the kitchen table.

"Speaking of, did you have a good night, old man?" I tease.

Noah ignores me for a minute, frowning at Mackie, so I nudge him, and he turns his glare on me. "I was taking care of a member of our team."

"Oh, I bet you took care of him. He can't really walk today—"

"I will add another black eye to your bruises," Noah warns, pointing to my face. "Don't say this to Mackie."

He's deadly serious.

"Why? Worried it will hurt him?" I retort, not backing down. This man needs to recognize his feelings before it's too late. He has to stop pushing Mackie away and pretending he's nothing more than his boss or Mackie will give up, and Noah will lose his shot at happiness. Noah is so sure about putting everyone else first and protecting this garage, he doesn't even consider his own feelings. Usually, I wouldn't care, but I like Noah a lot, I respect him, and Mackie is my friend. I want them to be happy.

"Skylar, I'm warning you." His voice drops an octave, and his face closes down.

I simply smile. "So you *can* get angry when it comes to your boy." Clapping his shoulder, I chuckle. "Just making sure."

Noah sighs and looks to Alek for help, but he just shrugs. "I have been trying to shut him up since I met him. Nothing has worked, so don't look at me."

"My boy can. He does this thing with his—" I wince when Noah slaps the back of my head.

"Focus on your work," he mutters as he and Alek walks off, grumbling about me being annoying.

Grinning, I turn back to my engine, grabbing my rag before my smile fades as I look at my arms.

As I eye the bruises, I recall what happened last night and pick up my phone, heading outside. I promised Bones and Noah I wouldn't fight, but that doesn't mean I'll let them get away with this.

Not to mention, they tried to hurt my boy.

No, I might not have as much power as some people around me, but I think they forgot who I am.

I'm Skylar fucking Warren, and these streets and that boy are mine.

I wait for him to answer, but I don't let him speak.

"It was a stupid fucking move you made last night."

"Who is this?" he asks, the sound of springs moving in the background indicating he's still in bed.

"Who the fuck do you think? You tried to take something away from me last night, and you tried to hurt me."

"Skylar?" he mutters.

"The one and fucking only." I know my voice is dark and danger-ous. It's a place I never wanted to go to again, the person I had to become to survive, but if it keeps my boy safe, I will do anything.

"Look, man, fair is fair—"

I cut him off. I don't want his bullshit. He made a stupid move, and he should know the price.

"If you ever so much as come near me or him again, I will destroy you. Is that understood? We both know I can. Forget the races or payback, I will make your life a living hell. Did you get my note this morning?"

"How the hell do you know where I live, man?" he snarls.

"That's not all I know. I know your mother's address. I know your girlfriend's address. I know where you hide your illegal shit. One move from you and I will send it all to the police and get you locked up for life. I know enough about you to make it happen," I warn.

"You turning rat now, Skylar?" he hisses.

"I'll be whatever I have to be to keep my boy safe. Remember that. Don't think I've gone soft just because I straightened out. I have more money and connections now than I ever did, and I will use every single one to burn your world to the ground. This started on the streets, but it will end in a body bag. Understood?"

"Fuck, fine, understood. I'll let it go. I don't care that much. You aren't even running the street anymore, so I can earn my title back."

"Good boy," I praise. "You do that, and we won't have any issues, but if you don't . . . well, I'll be seeing you soon." I hang up and take a deep breath, then I let the anger go. When I turn back and head into the garage, I'm smiling Skylar again.

"Why are you both in my office? What sin did I commit in a previous life?" Noah mutters as he eyes Alek and me.

"We are here for a sacrifice—"

"An intervention," Alek supplies helpfully.

"Right, an intervention. It isn't about Mackie, don't worry. I scheduled that one for next week. No, this one is serious." My smile drops. "These accidents are getting worse. You can't look me in the eye and tell me we're not being sabotaged. Someone is targeting us."

"I know." He sighs, and I blink. "They are trying to make us pull from the championship, which is why I haven't said anything. I don't want their scare tactics to work."

"People are getting hurt," Alek mutters. "I know we've spoken about this, but we have to do something."

"You don't think I am?" Noah retorts. "You think I've just been sitting back, watching my people get hurt, and doing nothing?" We both share a look, and Noah curses. "I've been working in the background. I won't let them get away with this. I'll stop them before anything else happens, but I need you to focus on your jobs and keeping the team excited and happy. I can't do that and this. I need you to support me. The best way to end this is to show them we aren't scared and to win that title."

"Noah, this is serious—"

"I know." He cuts Alek off, rubbing his face, and it's only then I realize how exhausted he looks. "I've spoken to the police and installed new cameras, alarms, and safety features. I'm trying the best I can, but I promise I won't let whoever this is get away with it."

"We all know who it is," Alek mutters. "One of those other top three fuckers are scared after the qualifiers and don't want to lose. Let us help you, Noah."

"You will, just give me a little bit of time, okay? I have something I'm working on in the background, just . . . trust me, alright?"

Alek and I share a look, but we nod and stand. "Okay then. Enough seriousness, it's cramping my style. It's time for coffee." I wave goodbye and head out, joining Mackie, who is nursing a mug of coffee. I pour one, leaning back as I eye him.

"Had a good night, did you?"

"I drank way too much. It was dumb," he admits, his eyes still shielded by his sunglasses. "I ended up at Noah's," he says quietly so no one else hears. "He tucked me in like I was a kid."

"Maybe he's into that. Maybe it's his kink," I comment, and

Mackie flips me off as I laugh. "You're getting to him, just keep trying."

"Maybe I should give up. It obviously isn't happening," he says, staring down at his coffee.

"Do you want to? If you do, I don't think you're the man Noah or I think you are. Mackie, you don't back down from anything, so why start now?"

"Great pep talk. Maybe we can have this again later when the room stops spinning," he grumbles, making me laugh.

I chuckle. "Okay, okay, later. You need to fix your hair though. You look like a fucking tumbleweed."

"My hair? Look at yours. It's in a man bun," Mackie mutters. "You need a haircut."

"Nah, I'm growing it for my boy. He likes to pull it." I duck under the spray of coffee Mackie spits out and grin as I sit back and sip mine.

"I'm too hungover for this," he says.

"Funny, that's what he sounded like when—"

I hit the floor as my chair is kicked from under me by a passing Alek, but I can't stop laughing.

"You're such a loser when you're in love," he mutters as he watches me.

"Absolutely." I grin up at him from the floor. "I'm his loser."

The garage fills with groans that only make me laugh harder.

CHAPTER 34
BONES

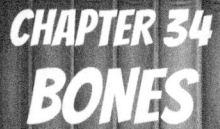

I have been dreading this night since I saw my father when I was on a date with Skylar. I know he'll have something to say, some sly remark or comment. I've never hidden my sexuality from him. In fact, I shoved it in his face like a dare. He never liked my ex, though he only met him once or twice before . . . well, before, but it's clear he didn't like Skylar.

He doesn't like anyone who stands up to him.

I hesitate like a scared little boy, standing before my father's house, knowing the devil is waiting inside to spring a trap and make me miserable. I still came, though, because I have a promise to keep.

Taking a deep breath, I pull out my phone and reread Skylar's text. He might not have known I'd need it, but I do, and I use it to strengthen me.

> Skylar: I have to work late, beautiful, but I can't wait to come home to you. Just sleep over at my place, and when I get in, I'll get to hold you and make this day so worth it.

Biting back my smile, I pocket my phone. I can do this. I can handle anything he throws at me. Let him toss his words like weapons, but he won't crack the shield I've built. I'm really happy, something that is still scary to me, but I am, and I won't let him ruin it just because it's not what he wants for me. He doesn't control my life.

I repeat it as I head inside.

I can feel the tension in the air, even as I enter the dining room. I nod my head at the staff, sit in my chair at the other end of the table, and wait since he is looking at his iPad.

When twenty minutes pass and he says nothing, I grow irritated and bored. "How is work?"

His eyes finally lift to me, and he arches a brow in question. I swallow down anything else I would say as his eyes drop to his iPad again. Ten minutes later, he sits back, running his gaze over me in a way that makes me nervous. My father likes to tear me apart, I'm used to it, but something in his expression seems different.

"Sir, are you ready for your first—"

"No, we will wait," he interrupts without sparing the maid a look. It's a different girl tonight, and I hope the one from before is okay, though she is probably better off not working here.

His words, however, are my first clue that something is wrong. Declan Townsend is never late for anything, nor does he push anything back. His schedule is strict and set in stone.

"Are we waiting for someone?" I ask.

Without a word, he stands and buttons his suit as he wanders toward me, his eyes hard and determined. He's approaching me like he's in the courtroom, and that's my second clue something is happening.

Laying his iPad before me, he watches me impatiently. My gaze lowers to the screen and widens in horror and shock. There's a picture of Skylar on it, heading into work at Starfire. He reaches down and slides it over to another picture of him getting out of his car in their parking lot, then him at my school, and another of him and me walking. He flips through so many pictures, I start to feel sick.

When and how did he get these?

"Are you stalking me now? Paying someone to take creepy pictures of me?" I snap, pushing the iPad away. "That's low, even for you."

Sitting on the edge of the table, he eyes me. "Knowledge is power. Without knowledge, we have a losing hand, and I never lose, so let me tell you what I know. Skylar Warren is currently driving for Starfire Racing, and before that, he competed in illegal street races. It seems he was quite good as well and made a lot of money—money he now spends on you." He opens up pictures and news articles. "There are some mysterious assaults, deaths, and drug arrests that could never be tied to anyone, but I can tie them to him."

I shake my head. I know about Skylar's past and what he did to survive on those streets. He didn't tell me all of it, but it was enough for me to understand. My father doesn't care though. He lists every single thing about Skylar in black and white, making him seem like a criminal.

"Why are you doing this?" I ask, interrupting him.

"To show you how easily I could destroy Skylar Warren's life. This iPad has every dirty little secret, past sin, and crime—everything the world would clamor to know. His career he so painstakingly built would be ruined . . . all because of you."

"Why would you want to destroy him?" I whisper, already knowing why.

"Because he is in my way and in your life, and I do not like it."

"Why? Do you really hate me being happy?" I gesture at his iPad. "You want me to be miserable and alone like you?" I thrust to my feet, glaring at him. He doesn't react to my anger, doesn't rise to meet my outburst. He simply smiles.

"Yes, if that is what it takes. You have a bright future ahead of you. I will not let you ruin it over someone like this," he sneers as he looks at a picture of Skylar again.

I can't help but laugh bitterly. "Did you ever think he's worth ruining it over?" I retort, I know I'm getting worked up, but I'm pissed, and fuck his calm, rational arguments. I don't care about his game. I'm sick of trying to please him. He doesn't get to fuck up my life and take away the one thing that makes me happy. "My bright future isn't what *I* want, but what you want."

He stands, his movements slow and measured, his face cold—it's the expression he wears when he knows he's already won. "You listen to me, boy. I've done too much to make you into this for you to destroy it now. This is your first and only warning. Stay away from Skylar Warren. It won't be you I'll ruin, but him."

He turns, picking up his iPad and heading back to his seat as I stare at him in horror and panic. "We will take our first course now," he calls, seemingly happy as he sits.

"I'll never be enough, will I? I guess I always knew it, but listening to you now, I'm sure. Nothing I ever do will be enough," I croak, years of repressed self-flagellation and hate pouring from me. I did every-thing I could to make him proud, to make him love me, but he never will. I'm not his son or even a person to him. I'm just another thing to control and move across the board.

He places his iPad down and leans his chair back. "Enough with this tantrum—"

"It is not a tantrum!" I sweep my hand across the table, the crash of the glass loud, but he doesn't react.

"No? It sure looks like one. You can cover your body in tattoos and act all tough, but under it all, you're a scared little boy who still needs his daddy's approval, who still needs me—"

"That's where you're wrong. I never needed you. I *wanted* my dad to be proud. I *wanted* my dad to love me, but I've realized I don't need you to. I'm surrounded by enough family and love for two lifetimes with or without you, and that's kind of fucking freeing," I snarl.

"It doesn't matter though, does it?" he replies calmly. "You can't escape me, and if you try, I will destroy this boy you care so deeply for. It is your choice."

He'll destroy Skylar to get what he wants, and I would be the reason why. I would be the reason Sky lost everything he's worked hard for. He would lose it all because of me.

I'm not worth that. Nobody is.

Worst of all, he would hate me, and I don't think I could bear that.

I just stare at my father, and he offers me a cruel, mocking smile.

"I will excuse you tonight. I am not in the mood for your attitude.

You may leave and think about what we discussed." I glare at him, feeling like I might cry or throw up or both. "You can go."

Without a word, I tear out of there, knowing there is no arguing with him. This is his law. Either I play along or Skylar loses everything.

Sky . . . Oh fuck, Sky.

Hurrying through the front door, I stop at my car, my heart shattering in my chest. I feel sick and cold.

I was so fucking happy, so fucking filled with life when I came here, and now it's all gone.

"Fuck!" Slamming my hand into my car, I feel my skin split and my bones ache, but the pain drowns out the agony in my heart and head, so I do it again and again.

I slide down and sit with my back to the car as I stare up at the lights of his mansion.

He'll do it, I know he will, and Skylar will lose everything.

I can't let that happen.

I care about him too much to let that happen, which means I'll have to break Skylar Warren's heart—the one he gave me without strings or expectations. I never thought it would hurt this badly, but tears flow from my eyes unchecked as I struggle to breathe.

It's then I realize the true depths of my feelings for him and just how much I've come to care, and now it will all be gone.

I'll be completely and utterly alone and broken again.

Eventually, I picked myself up and drove home. I didn't go to Skylar's, and I ignored his knock later that night, as well as his texts and calls. Eventually he gave up, assuming I was asleep.

I don't sleep, how can I? My bed is cold and empty, and without his arms around me, I don't feel safe. Before the sun even rises, I leave my apartment, avoiding him. It's a dick move, but I can't face him. He'll know, and then he'll try to make it better. He'll try to protect me. It's who he is.

I won't let him.

No, this is for the best. It's better if it ends now.

As the day passes, I'm like a zombie. My phone is switched off since he's blowing it up. I barely eat or take in what is said in my classes. I'm just drifting.

I wonder if fighting to survive, each and every day, and putting on the façade while striving for tomorrow is even worth it. It's expected, it's what's done, you can't just give up, but what if it isn't worth it? What if ten years from now, I look back and realize none of it was worth it? I feel like I'm just the side character in everyone else's story, waiting to add to their life. Isn't that sad? It keeps me up at night, wondering why I keep going . . .

For a while, I did it because of him. I kept going for him, but now he's gone again, and I'm dragged back under the waves that seek to drown me.

I wander across campus, lost and without purpose, tired and so fed up it must gather around me like a cloud because everyone gives me a wide berth.

"Bones!" The familiar voice makes me whirl around, my whole body coming to life as he jogs toward me, looking worried, all before I realize what this means.

I should have known he wouldn't let me go this easily, and it only makes it harder. Can I really look into his eyes and break his heart?

Turning away, I speed up to escape him, knowing I don't have the strength to look him in the face and hurt him like everyone else.

"Bones!" He yanks me around, looking confused and sad. "Talk to me, baby. What the fuck is going on? Did I do something?" He presses closer despite my struggles, and for a moment, I relax into his warmth, soaking it in. I won't ever be warm again after this. "Talk to me, beautiful. Tell me what I did so I can fix it, okay?"

Staring into his eyes, I almost cave and tell him everything. It's on my tongue, but as I look into his handsome face, I know I can't do this. I can't drag him into my fucked-up world. I can't let him ruin everything he's worked for—not for me and not because of my father. He deserves better.

"Nothing's wrong," I admit.

"Yes, it is. I know you. What's going on?" He shakes me slightly. "Baby, talk to me. I'm too attached to you for you to act like this."

I remind myself this is for him and his future. It's what has to be done. I can't ruin his life, even if it means he'll hate me forever. I'll keep him safe.

"I never told you to get attached to me, okay? I don't care for you like that. What we had was fun, and the sex was good, but that's all it was." It's like stepping on sunshine. I see pain flash in his eyes.

"You're lying," he snaps.

"Am I?" I harden my features, realizing I must look like my father right now. The mask threatens to break when he cups my cheeks, but I force it to stay in place.

"Talk to me," he begs.

"I am. It isn't my fault you won't listen." Gripping his hands, I pull them from my face and let them drop, the warmth from his touch marking me forever. I know I'll feel it until the day I die. "Sky, you're fun. That's all. Did you really think you could ever be anything more? I got what I wanted and now I'm bored. Take a hint."

He flinches, another barb hitting him. I know exactly where to dig.

I've never hated myself as much as I do in this moment as I watch his face crumple, yet he still doesn't let go. "I don't know what's going on, but I must have done something. If you tell me, I can fix it. I promise."

"You aren't listening." I laugh bitterly. "What's it going to take for you to listen? You've had so many one-night stands and flings, Skylar. Don't you see that's what this is for me? You of all people should know what it's like to use another for their body."

I expect him to get angry, but he just stares at me.

"What?" I demand.

"You're mean, Bones, but you're never cruel, not like this. Baby, talk to me. I can see you locking yourself away."

"That's where you're wrong. I am cruel." I try to step from his arms again, but they tighten.

"Let me go, Skylar," I demand, my voice cold, and his eyes tighten in pain as he searches my gaze. Yesterday morning was paradise. We kissed leisurely, had breakfast together, and took our time exploring each other. I admitted to wanting more, to needing him. I let him in, and now I'm pushing him away. I know he's confused. I would be too. He's also hurt, but he's still more worried for me, thinking it's his fault, and that hurts even more.

He's blaming himself.

I need to make him hate me, but I don't know if I'm capable of it. I would never want to see his eyes fill with disgust and hatred like everyone else's when he has only ever looked at me with love and kindness.

"You are so dumb, Warren. Look at you. You are pathetic."

Stepping back, he drops my hand, severing the connection between our bodies. I suddenly feel so cold, so alone, that I want to drag him back, but I don't. I step away, watching as tears glisten in his eyes as he stares at me. He's broken and confused, but he refuses to give up, even as I hurt him. "Bones, please, talk to me."

"Get it through your head. This is—was nothing, and it's over. Go back to racing, and I'll go back to my books."

"No," he snaps, reaching for me, but I step away again.

"Stay away from me. Don't become like Mr. Rose, obsessed with something that never existed. I was and never will be yours. I don't even want to be. I just wanted to have fun. Let it go," I snap and turn, forcing myself to take slow, measured steps away when I want to run.

Each time my foot hits the ground, taking me away from him, another piece of my heart crashes inside my chest, shattering and breaking.

I didn't just break his heart. I broke my own as well.

At the end of the path, I can't take it anymore. I turn, expecting him to be behind me or standing where I left him, but he's walking away, and my hand flies to my aching chest as I struggle to breathe.

It's strange seeing him walk away from me. I've never seen him from behind because he was always walking toward me.

CHAPTER 35
BONES

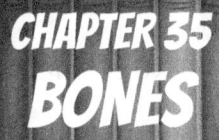

I did it. I broke Skylar Warren's heart. I finally made him give up on me.

I tell myself it's for the best as the whiskey glass tumbles to the counter from my numb fingers as I sit in darkness. Is he across the hall now, thinking of me? Or has he already moved on, forgetting me inside another?

The thought sends agony splintering through me, and I grab the bottle, downing it before letting it hit the counter.

I'm alone once more, but that's fine. That's how it should be. Everyone I love is better off without me. They leave for a reason. I am unlovable. No, it's better this way. It's how I've always been.

Alone.

I choose to be . . .

The truth is, I embraced the depression and loneliness because it was easier to wallow in that pit. It was easier to hurt than to move on. There was even a type of beauty to the loneliness and agony I surrounded myself with. Such strong emotions keep me tethered to the bottom, because it's easier to be on the ground than to risk falling again.

But I did. I fell, and now he's gone.

They say suffering makes you stronger, better, but sometimes it just fucking hurts. Sometimes the pain doesn't teach you a lesson, it just destroys you, and in those flames, I wasn't remade. I was left.

I'm beginning to realize love can either be a scar or a temple, not both.

Deep down, I crave love and intimacy, but I'm terrified because it means I'm vulnerable, so I pretended I didn't want it and filled my life with everything else to drown out that voice. I pretended so hard, I started to believe it—until him.

The truth is, I'm scared to show anyone the real me, because what if my deepest fear is true and I'm unlovable?

Clearly, I am.

Alone not lonely. Alone not lonely.

I repeat it as I stare into the darkness, hoping if I say it enough, I'll believe it.

Alone not lonely.

Alone not lonely.

Alone . . . *I'm lonely.*

I'm fine.

I'm always fine.

I survived before Skylar Warren, and I can survive after him.

I'm fine. I'm totally fine.

I say it to everyone who asks, even though I see the disbelief in their eyes. I say it so much, it becomes stuck on repeat.

I am fine.

I'm always fine.

As I stare out at the city two days later, I break down.

I'm not fucking fine.

I'm not fucking okay.

He's all I want. He's all I need.

I want him here with me.
I ruined it.
I'm not fine.

CHAPTER 36
SKYLAR

I wish I could say I didn't have time to think about Bones with everything going on, but that would be a lie. He's all I think about. I haven't been able to eat or sleep properly. Is he eating and sleeping enough? Is he lonely or pushing people away again? Has he leaned on his friends?

"Warren, head in the game," Mackie barks, and I blink, bringing him back into view.

"Yeah, I'm with you," I mutter, and he frowns. Our cars wait for us to test some new tweaks before next week's race.

"Skylar, you look like shit. Have you been sleeping, brother?" he asks as he steps closer. "Is everything okay? You know I'm your friend. You can talk to me."

"Everything is fine." I force a smile, not wanting anyone to worry. I don't want to share what happened because it might make it real. Besides, I'm not planning on letting Bones go.

I know Alek has been worried, especially since I keep asking about Bones. He knows something is wrong and will probably corner me, so I stay out of his way.

Mackie eyes me. "Liar," he says, "but if you don't want to talk, then let's race instead. Leave it all on the track."

"On the track." I nod as I bump my helmet against his.

We walk to our cars and slide inside, and I wave at Mackie as I climb in. We aren't pushing it today, just a friendly race to test the limits of the cars, which is good since I haven't slept. My reactions will be slower, but hopefully I'm still well enough to get through today without anyone pulling me aside to call me on my shit.

We pull up to the line as the lights flash red, amber, then green. I'm off just a second after Mackie. Shaking my head, I try to pull it together. I focus on the track, not letting any other thoughts invade. I can't. It's dangerous. They will still be here when I'm done.

Normally, the speed and adrenaline push everything else away, but not this time.

He's all I can think about, even as I accelerate too fast around a corner and almost spin out. I manage to regain control, but Mackie is far ahead because of it. Swearing, I slam my hand into my helmet.

"Focus, Skylar," I bark.

I try to catch up, but he has a good lead. He's driving well, and he's speeding back down the straightaway when smoke suddenly billows from his hood. The car jerks and then spins. Horror fills me as I watch him, knowing he's fighting to stop from flipping.

He whips back and forth before hitting the barrier and stopping. I can hear shouts from the team. I know they are racing over, but I'm closer. I slam on my brakes, fishtailing, and I'm out before my car is fully stopped. Ripping off my helmet, I toss it to the track and sprint to Mackie's car.

I eye the smoke as I lean in, panic pounding through my heart, and then I see him move.

"Brother, you okay?" I shout. "Mackie!"

"I'm okay. I'm okay." He coughs, his eyes wide as he blinks and turns to me with shock on his face. Ripping his door open, I unfasten his harness and help him out, guiding him away from the car and leaning him against mine as I check him over. There's a trickle of blood on his forehead, but otherwise, he seems okay.

He got damn fucking lucky.

"Damn, brother, it's a good thing you're a good driver. That could have been bad."

"I don't know what happened. It's like something blew in the car and all my control went." He leans over, dragging in deep breaths.

His name is screamed over and over, and Noah shoves me aside. I hit the ground hard from the force as he grips Mackie's head.

"Kid, you okay? Talk to me." The panic in Noah's voice makes my eyebrows rise as I climb to my feet.

"I'm fine, I'm fine," Mackie promises, covering Noah's hands on his helmet. "Just a bumped head."

"Jesus, kid, I had a fucking heart attack." He pulls him into a hug, and I turn away as they embrace, giving them the privacy they need. When I look back, Noah is leaning away, frowning. "What happened?"

"I didn't do it—"

"Kid, I know you didn't. You're the best fucking driver out here. I'm asking you what happened, not accusing you," Noah says, his voice soft.

"I don't know. It's like something in the car went crazy, no controls. I was lucky I didn't flip."

"Not luck, skill," I interrupt. "I saw smoke before it happened. Something is wrong with the car." I meet Noah's eyes.

Both of us are wondering the same thing.

Did someone sabotage Mackie's car?

If so, they could have killed him.

This just became a lot more serious.

Mackie went to the hospital to be sure. Noah demanded it and went with him. He's barely left Mackie's side, and I know whoever did this is going to wish they killed Noah, not hurt Mackie. When Noah is done with them, there will be nothing left.

The rest of us are quiet and worried, the garage silent for once.

"I heard there was an accident." Alek rushes in with Evan at his side. Alek took today off for a date. "Skylar, are you hurt?" He inspects me with his eyes as Evan touches my shoulder worriedly.

"I'm okay," I promise. "It was Mackie. There was something wrong with his car." I eye Alek meaningfully, and his lips tighten. "He hurt his head. He's at the hospital now, getting checked over. He's fucking lucky he's alive."

"Jesus." Alek sinks into the chair next to me, and Evan sits on his lap with his arm over his shoulder, both facing me. "This is getting ridiculous."

"Tell me about it. I think Noah might actually kill someone. I feel bad for the doctors. He was barking orders here before he dragged Mackie out." We both grin, and Alek wraps his arm around Evan's waist, tugging him closer. For a moment, envy fills me with how easy it is for them. I know it wasn't always like that, I saw my friend fight to get to this place and I'm happy for them, but right now, watching them hurts.

I wish my boy were here, but he isn't. Alek is eyeing me again, so I force a smile and perk up, not wanting the questions. "How was your date? Sick of him yet?" I ask Evan.

"Not yet." He grins, but he eyes me too. "You okay?"

"I'm fine," I answer.

"Pretty boy, could you get us some drinks?" Alek asks, and something passes between them before Evan kisses Alek and hops up.

"Of course."

We both watch him walk away, and Alek sighs.

"God, he is so hot," Alek mutters.

"No need to be jealous, you're hot too." I smirk.

Alek eyes me, his expression dead. "I'm not being jealous, Skylar. I'm being gay."

He says it so straight-faced, I can't help but burst into laughter. "I needed that," I admit.

"I know. Tell me what the fuck is going on with you and Bones. He was stalking around campus, looking like he was ready to murder someone."

"Is he okay?" I sit up, my eyes wide. "Did you talk to him?"

"Jesus, Skylar, what happened?" Alek snaps.

Slumping, I look at the table. "I don't know," I mutter. "I knew winning him over would be hard, but I was determined. He's worth it. He keeps pushing me away, though, and I know something is wrong . . . . I just don't know what." I shrug, not wanting to explain it all. I don't want his relationship with Bones to change. They both need friends and get along well.

Alek sighs. "I hate seeing you like this."

"Like what?" I mutter, wiping at my burning eyes.

"In person," he deadpans, and I choke on a laugh.

He grins but leans in, laying his hand on my arm. "You were always there for me with Evan and to give me a kick in the ass when I needed one. Let me return the favor. If Bones is worth it, then fight for him no matter what. You don't back down, which is an oddly annoying endearing quality to have. Whatever is happening, talk and figure it out together. I've learned that talking can solve most things. It's miscommunication and lack of understanding that causes issues."

"Jesus, I think that's the most I've ever heard you speak," I joke, but I smile softly. "I know. You're right. Anyway, less about my love life and more about yours. How are you and Evan?"

"We're really good." He grins widely, and so much happiness radiates from him, he glows with it.

"Good, how's Alice?" I ask, changing the subject. I need to deal with this alone, and I love Alek like a brother, but right now, he can't help. It's clear Bones wants space, so I will give it to him.

"Eh, I feel like she's finally going through her rebellious teenage years," he grumbles. "Evan tells me I worry too much."

"You do." I smack his arm. "Enjoy your boy and just be happy, okay? You deserve it, Alek."

"That's the nicest thing you have ever said to me."

"Don't expect it again." We share a smile as Evan sets three mugs down and sinks onto Alek's lap.

"All man talked out?" he scoffs. "Can I pretend I didn't know?"

"Shut it, pretty boy," Alek warns, smacking his hip.

"Or what?" Evan teases.

"Or I'll punish you—"

They share a look, seeming to forget I'm here. Propping my hand on my chin, I lean closer, watching with a grin, and they suddenly turn and see me.

"Jesus, Sky!" Alek barks.

"Don't let me stop you. Punish? How do you do it? Whips? Chains?" I dart up and run as Alek chases me. Evan watches us, shaking his head and sipping his coffee. Laughter fills the garage, and the tension eases a little, but like my heart, it will take time to be normal again.

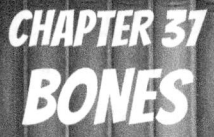

CHAPTER 37
BONES

"I 'm not in the mood, Alek," I snap when I see him lingering at the gym door. It's late, but I couldn't sleep. I thought if I worked out until I dropped, I might be able to.

At least, that's the lie I'm telling myself.

The truth is, I miss him, and I think I fucked up.

I panicked and pushed him away to protect him, but I should have spoken to him and found another way because my life without Skylar sucks.

I've never felt proud or excited to finish anything, just relieved it's over. There was no joy, highs, or lows before Skylar Warren. There was just existence. He taught me what it meant to truly live, and I taught him what it meant to hurt. I got his happiness, and he got my darkness. It wasn't a fair trade, but he didn't seem to care.

He wanted me, scars and all, and I ruined that out of fear. I took a hammer to our carefully growing glass house, walked over the shards, and left him there in the midst of the destruction. I hurt him, and I hate that.

He's the last person in this world I want to hurt.

Alek heads over and stops before me, eyeing me then nodding at what he finds.

"Did you know there was an accident at the racetrack today?" Alek says conversationally, putting his hands in his pockets.

"What? Is he okay?" I leap up, my heart slamming to a stop as I grab Alek and haul him close. "Alek, is he okay?"

"He's fine. It was his partner who got hurt." I blink in confusion. "I was just checking if you cared or not."

Releasing him, I swallow and lean back. "Of course I fucking care."

"Then act like it," he snaps.

I stare at him. "Did he tell you?"

"No, he's protecting you. He wouldn't tell me anything," he replies. "But it's easy to see my friend is hurting, and I don't like it. You're both hurting. Is it worth it? Whatever this bullshit reason you're giving for hurting him, is it worth it?"

I could make an excuse, but it would be lame. He's right. I hurt his friend. I hurt someone I care for.

"I thought so. Wouldn't you do anything to keep Evan safe?"

"Not if it meant losing him. I'd stand with him and we'd tackle it together. There is one thing I've learned through all the shit we went through—anything is possible if you do it together. Things are never better apart, no matter how hard it is or how impossible it seems. I lost Evan once by being stupid, and I will never do that again. Don't make the mistake I did."

"You don't understand," I mutter. How could he? Alek and Evan were meant to be together. They didn't have my father standing between them, threatening to destroy the one I love.

"No, I don't. I really fucking don't. You're miserable and suffering, and he's pissed."

"He's angry?" I whisper. I don't know why that hurts more than him being upset.

"What do you think?" Alek retorts. "There are only so many times you can push someone away, Bones, before they stop coming back."

Panic like I have never felt winds through me. Has he given up on me? Has he walked away for good? Has he realized I'm not worth it? That's what I wanted, right? I can't breathe, and I realize the idea of losing him forever scares me much more than him growing to hate me because of my father.

Alek is right. I'm a fool.

I'm a fucking idiot.

I should have stood at his side. I should have fought. I should have told him.

Suddenly, nothing else matters but getting to him. I'll work to fix this.

I'm not letting Skylar Warren go.

"Where is he? Alek, where is he?" I demand as I shove my shoes on, indifferent to the fact that I'm just in shorts and a tank.

"Well, it's about fucking time," Alek mutters as he pulls out his keys and throws them at me. "I know you walked here, so take my car. He's at the track. I don't do this for anyone. Take care of my fucking car . . . and my best friend. Don't hurt him again." He steps back, smiling. "Go get him."

Clutching the keys, I run out of the gym, hitting the fob before I slide into his car, start the engine, and speed toward the garage and the track.

I get there as quickly as possible, leaving Alek's car at an angle—he can fucking bill me. I rush past the garage. There are no lights on inside, but I can see his car making its way around the track, the headlights splashing across the tarmac.

"Skylar!" I yell, but obviously, he can't hear me. I tried to call him on the way, and he didn't answer. Something strange guides me as I climb over the railing and stand just before the finish line as he skids around the final corner and down the straightaway.

His car barrels toward me, but I don't move.

I tilt my chin up, my stance wide as I stare and wait with nothing but love.

I hear the moment he slams on his brakes, and he skids to a stop right before me, his front bumper almost touching me. He rips the door open, tosses his helmet away, then storms over to me.

"Are you okay? Bones, are you okay?" he demands, checking me over, and when he realizes I'm not hurt, he shakes me, his hands high on my upper arms. "What the fuck were you thinking? I could have killed you!" He doesn't let me get a word out. "Fuck, angel, I could have hit you!"

"I needed to see you. I trust you," I whisper, my voice choked. Everything I want to say fades away as I stare into his eyes.

"Are you fucking crazy?" he snaps and drops his hands, so I grab them and press them to my cheeks. He freezes, his eyes narrowing in confusion as he searches my face.

His headlights shine on us, letting him see everything I try to hide.

"I knew you wouldn't hit me. I knew you would rather die than hurt me, but I couldn't go another second without being in front of you and telling you . . . without fixing this. I'm sorry, Skylar. I fucked up and panicked and pushed you away. I love you, Skylar Warren, and if you'll let me, I'll tell you everything. I'll fix everything. Just tell me I'm not too late. Tell me you still want me. Tell me you still love me." I search his wide eyes. "I didn't mean anything I said. I was just trying to protect you, but I realized I can't live without you. No matter what happens, I can't live without you. I love you."

I trail off, waiting.

Please, tell me I'm not too late.

Tell me he hasn't given up.

Tell me he still wants me the way I want him.

"Say it again," he whispers, and when I stare, he tightens his grip. "Say you love me again."

My lips tilt in a smile. We are going to be okay. I know it.

"I love you," I say, and then I cup my hands around my mouth and scream, "I love you!"

"It's about fucking time," he snarls and yanks my head to him, his lips crashing onto mine.

Groaning, I lean onto my toes as he drags me closer so there isn't an inch of space between us. He kisses me like he's never saying goodbye again, like he knows I'm the love of his life and has been waiting for me to realize it.

He kisses me like I'm his and he's mine.

Moaning, I slide my hands into his hair, pulling on it until he hisses. He breaks the kiss. "Keep saying it. Keep saying it while I fuck you and prove to you that you're never getting away from me." Before I can speak, his lips are on mine again.

It's a hard, dominant kiss that has me softening into him and sliding my hands down his suit to tug him closer.

He kisses life back into me.

I have been cold, dead, and lost for days, but now I'm alive.

I push him back, and he stumbles as I pull the zipper on his suit down to his crotch. I slide my hands inside and press my lips against his, needing more.

I need Skylar Warren to breathe me back to life.

I need him to prove that he still loves me . . . that I'm loveable.

My hands slip deeper into his suit, stripping it from his shoulders as he backs me to his car and bends me over it, never breaking our kiss.

His hand slides under my tank, gliding across my abs and up to my pecs. He squeezes them hard as he breaks our kiss and drags his lips down my neck, biting the top of my shirt. He drags it up, and I help him take it off. He shoves his hand into my shorts, gripping my hard cock as I gasp. My back arches, and my eyes shut.

"Eyes on me, angel," he orders. "You're going to look at me while I fuck you. You're going to remember this moment forever. The next time you doubt us, you'll think about it."

My eyes snap open, colliding with his as he squeezes my dick to the point of pain.

"Sky, please," I beg. "I only feel alive in your hands. Please, please, I need you."

"You've got me," he growls as he bites my chest before kissing the sting away.

Shoving my shorts down, he leans back far enough to peel off his suit and remove his shirt. He doesn't bother stripping anything else off, just yanks his pants down and presses his hard cock against my ass as he kisses my chest.

"Fuck, baby, it was torture being away from you these few days. I kept my distance, giving you the space you wanted. I knew if I pushed, you would run, so I waited. I fucking waited, and now I want my prize for being so patient, so be a good boy and take all of me."

"Sky!" I scream as he slams inside me, forcing himself deep. The edge of pain and pleasure is familiar and so good, tears squeeze from my eyes. He wastes no time and starts to move, setting a hard, quick pace. His lips drag along every inch of exposed skin, biting and licking.

My hands grip his shoulders and his hair, stroking him as I arch up over his car as he powers into my ass. My cock leaks against my abs, jerking with the need to come. His lips press against mine as he claims me.

"Mine," he growls into my mouth as he pulls away. "You're mine, angel. Try to leave me again, I dare you."

"Never," I vow, sounding breathless as I push to meet his thrusts. "Please, Sky."

"Come for me," he demands, biting my jaw. "Let me feel it while I fill you with my cum so every step you take tonight is a reminder that you're mine. I want to see my cum dripping from you."

I whimper as he twists his hips, hitting that spot inside me that has my eyes crossing. My balls draw up as my release slams through me so hard and fast, I choke as I come all over myself.

His groan matches mine as he pounds into me as hard as he can and empties his balls inside me, my name on his lips as he holds me against him.

Our foreheads knock together, both of us locked in pleasure, and his lips find mine for a moment.

"I love you, Silas Townsend. You need to know that. Nothing could ever change it. I'll always be right here, at your side," he promises under the stars.

I know we have a lot to talk about, but we are going to be okay. It's in the way he helps me dress and kisses me softly before taking my hand. He never lets it go as he puts his car away and locks up.

Hand in hand, we walk into the lot, and he whistles. "Shit, Alek loaned you his car?"

I nod.

"I tried to drive it once, and he slapped me so hard I hit the ground. Why did he give it to you?"

"So I could find you," I reply. "Don't tell him, but I have a feeling Alek has a soft spot for you."

"Well, well, isn't that sweet? How about we explore the back of his car?" He chases me to it as I laugh and push him away at the door, but he kisses me. "Alright, fine, drive safe. I'll be right behind you. See you at home."

"At home," I murmur before kissing him again. "I won't run again."

"Good." He grins as he steps back. "You could try, but I'd catch you every time."

CHAPTER 38
SKYLAR

We barely made it through the door before we were on each other again. In fact, we barely made it to the elevator, but afterwards, we lie in his bed, tangled in his sheets.

It was torture letting him push me away, but I knew if I didn't give him the space he needed, then I was no better than anyone else trying to control him. I don't want to clip Bones's wings. I want him feral.

That doesn't mean I was ever letting him go, just giving him time to figure out what he really wanted.

Luckily, it's the same thing I want, which is us. Otherwise, I would have had to kidnap him and tie him to our bed. I don't tell him that bit though. We are in a happy place, and as much as I love arguing with him and the fucking that comes after, I like this quiet happiness between us more.

Everything has been stripped away, and the world can't touch us here. It's just us and our love.

"I need to tell you why I pushed you away," he murmurs.

Lifting my head, I peer down at him, but he isn't looking at me. "You don't have to if you—"

"I do. I owe you that," he snaps before kissing my chest. "My dad came to me. He had a folder on you, Skylar." He looks up at me, and my heart slams in fear.

What did he see? I've never hidden my past from him, but hearing it and seeing it are two different things. Did he not want me because of where I came from? Before my anxiety can completely take over, he kisses my chest again.

"He was going to use it to ruin your life, taking your job and your shot at the championship if I didn't leave you. I told him to go to hell, but I knew he would and could do it. I couldn't let that happen. I couldn't let you lose everything for me. I'm not worth it, so I pushed you away, even if it was the hardest thing I have ever done in my life. It destroyed me, making you think I didn't want you, but I love you, Skylar, and I didn't want to be the reason you didn't succeed."

For a moment, I just stare at him, and he swallows, searching my gaze.

"Say something," he snaps, smacking my chest.

I drag him up and kiss him soundly, swallowing his gasp of surprise. "You brilliant, beautiful fool. How could anyone so smart be so stupid, angel?"

"Fuck you." He pushes me away, but I can see the worry in his eyes. "I wanted to protect you."

"And I love you for that," I tell him. No one has ever tried to protect me, not once in my life, but this man did. He tried to shield my future and my reputation like I give a fuck about any of it without him.

If I wasn't already madly in love with Silas Townsend, I would be now.

Cupping his cheeks to make sure he really listens, I meet his bright eyes and wonder how anyone could ever think this boy is cold. His heart is so fucking pure and big. He just protects it better because he was tired of being hurt, but when Bones loves, he loves so deeply, it's almost a miracle.

"It is my choice, not yours, angel," I murmur, and he frowns. "My choice is to keep you in my life. It isn't yours. Let him destroy my future, let him out my past, I don't care. I don't care about any of it. It means nothing without you. Don't you see that? I love that you wanted to protect me, but if it was at the expense of losing you, then fuck that. He can take everything, but he can't take you from me. Let him try because I have something to fight for, and there's one thing about me he doesn't seem to realize—I never lose."

He searches my eyes. "You aren't mad or worried?"

"I'm worried about you," I answer truthfully. Let his father come for me. He doesn't scare me. I've dealt with gang bangers, drug dealers, and men who would make Declan Townsend weep in fear. He might think he's a big, hard, powerful man, but I can cut him down to size and show him what he truly is—a weak, scared little boy.

"Worried that you let this get to you, that you're still thinking I'm better without you. Let me make this very clear, Silas Townsend. You are mine, and I am yours, and nothing else matters."

"Of course it does. The championship—"

"There will be others, but there will never be another you," I state, and he quiets. "I am in love with you. I want to spend the rest of my life with you. I don't care what your father says. I don't care what he does. I have you, and I have Alek and Evan, and I have Starfire at my back. I know you will all support me." It's something that's taken awhile to sink in, but I have a family now—one that would go to war for me. Noah would never let me go no matter what, Mackie would stand before anyone who tried to question me, Alek would simply kill them, and Evan would make them wish for death. Bones . . . he would be the devil they pray doesn't come for them. "We both have a family that loves us. I am not going anywhere, and neither are you. This—" I gesture between us. "He can't taint it, break it, or ruin it. It isn't his, and you aren't his. You're mine. If you try to leave me again, we both know you won't get far."

He smiles, but it fades, and his eyes fill with something infinitely worse—fear.

"He scares me," he whispers, finally admitting the truth. "I'm terrified of my father, of what he will do to mold my life. I'm scared, Sky."

Anger flows through me, but I keep it in check, biting it back as I lean in and kiss his forehead. "You don't have to be scared anymore, beautiful. I'm right here, and I will never let anyone hurt you. Do you understand me?"

His lips tremble, and his eyes fill with tears, each one that falls a blow to my heart. I kiss them away and hold him, my lips in his hair as he shakes in my arms. "I will never let him hurt you. I would kill him before I ever let him lay a hand on you, emotionally or physically. Your life is yours to control. If you want to say fuck it all and run away, I'll do that. If you want to become a singer, a dancer, whatever you want to do, I'll make sure you can. Your father doesn't have a say in your future. Do you hear me, angel? I will give you everything you want and whatever you need so you will never be afraid again."

"I don't want him to hurt you," he rasps, his voice thick.

"Don't worry about me. I can take care of myself." I grin as I wipe his tears away. "I grew up on the streets, angel. A lawyer doesn't scare me. Now, this lawyer, he does things to me, but none of it involves fear."

He grins, wiping at his face. "Idiot," he mutters, but it seems more loving than anything.

"You're an idiot." I roll him, and he grins up at me. Raining kisses all over his face, I drink down his laughter as he tries to smack me away. I never want to see fear in my boy's eyes again, and I'll do anything to ensure it never happens.

He's panting when I finish, but he's smiling. I kiss him until he can't think about anything other than us. "You should get some sleep. You look exhausted," I murmur.

"It seems I've grown so used to being mauled to death by a clingy koala during sleep that I can't sleep without it," he admits, and I grin wider.

"Then it's a good thing I'm here." Wrapping him tightly in my arms, I kiss every part of him I can reach. "I love you, Silas Townsend, and I will be right here when you wake up."

"Promise?" he murmurs, covering my hand on his chest and interlacing our fingers.

"I promise."

I wait until Bones is asleep, and then I slip from his arms. He reaches for me, so I press a pillow into his hands, and when he sighs and cuddles it, I grin. I take a picture on my phone and set it as my screen-saver, then I grab his phone and head out.

Typing in his passcode, I sit heavily on the sofa in the dark living room. I don't want to wake him up, but this is important. I know the longer you leave your enemies alone, the stronger they think they are. I need him to realize he's nothing and that he has nothing—no power or control.

Pulling up Bones's contacts, I chuckle at the name he saved his father under and I hit call. It rings four times before a deep, snapping voice answers.

"What is it, Silas? It's the middle of the night—"

"Your first reaction is anger when your son calls you in the middle of the night? Not worry? I guess that shouldn't surprise me," I reply.

He's quiet for a moment, and then I hear rustling. "Who is this?"

I chuckle as I glance at the window. "Now, let's not play coy. You know exactly who this is, and from what I've been hearing, you know everything about me."

"Skylar Warren."

"The very one." I smirk as I lean back, crossing my legs as I drape my arm across the back of the sofa.

"Why are you calling me at this hour and using my son's phone?" he snaps.

"Well, we have something very important to talk about. Your son is sleeping, and I won't wake him for your bullshit. You are going to leave us alone. You're never going to interrupt his life again. You will back off, is that clear?"

He laughs. "And why would I do that?"

"Because if you don't, I won't stop coming after you until you have no choice," I reply casually, eyeing my nails. They need a trim. My boy doesn't like it when they cut his back when he rides me.

"Like you said, I know everything about you—"

"Not everything. You don't know what I'm willing to do to protect Bones. You don't know what I would be willing to do or willing to lose to keep him happy. Declan, what would you be willing to lose to keep your son? I'd lose it all. Would you? Because that is what it will come down to. You think you are the only one with power and connections, but you're not. I could pull every dirty skeleton and secret from your closet within a day."

He's quiet for a moment, and I laugh.

"Exactly what I thought, so this is how it's going to go. You will never threaten your son again, and if you ever lay a hand on him or hurt him again, I will do exactly what I just promised and I will laugh as your life burns. You will cease contact with your son and stop forcing him to meet you or do what you want. If he wants to be in your life, that's his choice, and you will honor that."

"And if I don't?" he retorts.

"Then let's see how far you are willing to go. You know everything, and you know what I'm capable of. I'm not afraid to get my hands dirty. Are you?"

"You are a foolish—"

"Maybe," I interrupt, and his sharp inhale tells me he doesn't like it, but I don't care. "You aren't the first person to try to destroy me, and you won't be the last, but I'm never letting your son go. I love him, something you should understand but don't seem to. That's okay. I'll love him enough so he never has to worry about that. I'll give him the life he deserves and the life he wants, with or without you. If you ever threaten him, though, or scare him again, I will ruin you, Declan Townsend. Let me make that very clear because I do not lose." I hang up, refusing to let him get another word in.

It's all about power with a man like him, and I just took his away.

Dropping Bones's phone, I lean back, only to look up at a noise. Bones is hesitating in the hallway, watching me.

"Baby, what are you doing awake?" I murmur as I meet his sleepy eyes.

"You said you would be there when I woke up," he mumbles, sounding adorable as he shuffles over, rubbing his eyes as he yawns.

Damn, I love this man.

I open my arms, and he collapses into them, his head on my chest where it belongs. "Was that my father?"

"You heard?" I ask. I'm not worried. I will always do what it takes to protect him.

"Most of it," he admits. He stares at me for a moment. "What did he say?"

"What could he say? I told you to trust me, didn't I?"

Sitting up, he swings his leg over my lap and presses his hands to my shoulders as he looks at me with love and hope in his eyes. "We are free to be together?"

"Even if he doesn't listen, we are," I reply as I turn my head and kiss his wrist, feeling his pounding pulse. "He won't be a problem, angel. I'll take care of it."

"Thank you," he whispers.

"Why don't you show me how thankful you are and how incredible your boyfriend is?" I grip his wrist and run my tongue over his pulse. His eyes dilate as he peers at me. I place a kiss on the inside of his elbow before kissing down his arm, and then I slide his thumb into my mouth, sucking on it as he watches me.

Popping it free, I lay a kiss on the tip of it, and he swallows hard. He looks so beautiful in the moonlight, the type of man they would write sonnets about.

"There is an old story that says souls were split in two, and we spend our lives searching for our other halves to feel whole again," I murmur as I lean forward, grabbing his hips and tugging him so there isn't an inch of room between us. "You're my other half, angel, the missing part of my soul, and I have been waiting for you for so long."

"Skylar—"

I cover his lips, hushing him, and meet his gaze. "I have never claimed to know much about love. The closest I have ever seen was my parents before their deaths, but I am willing to die for you, beautiful. I'm willing to suffer for you . . . live for you. I'm willing to be whatever you want to be. You are all I think about every waking moment. When the sun shines, I want to be under it with you. When it rains, I want to be your umbrella. When it's dark and scary, I want to be your light. I don't know much about love, Silas Townsend, but I know this"—I smack my chest—"is yours, and I will spend my life searching for answers so I can be the best other half to you I can be."

He watches me with glassy eyes, and I kiss my fingers on his mouth, lingering for a moment. "No matter what happens, no matter if the world tries to tear us apart, remember where you go, I go. You will always find me at your side."

He pulls my hand away, smiling softly. "You know, I tried so hard not to let you in because deep down, I knew you would have the power to destroy me. Ruin me, Skylar Warren, if that's what you want. I don't care anymore. Just don't ever leave me. If I could go back to the night we met, I wouldn't change anything. I don't want to live a life where I don't know the warmth of your arms or the softness of your kiss. I don't want to live without you. You aren't my first kiss, my first time, or my first love, but you are the first person to make me feel whole, and you'll be my last kiss, my last time, and my last love."

He kisses me, sliding his hands up into my hair where they belong. Mine sweep up his back until there is no room between us.

What I said was true. I only feel whole when I have him in my arms.

Silas Townsend is my other half—the better half.

For the first time in my life, I'm generally afraid of losing something. Oh, I survived because I had to, but I never really had a reason to fear it. Now I do. I'm terrified all the time because I never want to break his heart. I never want to leave him alone again, so I'll spend the rest of my life making sure he feels safe and secure. I'll be scared enough for both of us.

When we pull back, I can't help but smile as I reach up and brush away his tears. "No more crying, beautiful. I only ever want to see you smile now."

His smile grows and he laughs.

"I told you that you have the best boyfriend, didn't I?"

He rolls his eyes, but his smile remains. Smacking his ass, I draw his gaze back to me, and indignation flares in his eyes even though he loves it. My cock has been hard since he sat down on my lap, but it throbs in reminder of what I want—him.

I drag my lips up his neck, and his moan fills the air as he turns to give me better access. I bite his earlobe then kiss it better.

"Say thank you, Skylar," I murmur. "Thank you for being mine."

"Fuck you," he mutters, but he grips my shoulders and tugs me closer.

"I plan to fuck you, angel, but first, you are going to thank me." I smirk into his skin, and then I lean back, sliding my hand down his chest. I grip his dick through his shorts, and he moans, jerking into my touch. "Or show me. Your choice."

He watches me for a moment, his lips tilting in a cocky smile before his hands drop from my shoulders.

He slides from my lap, standing before me, and I narrow my eyes as I go to stand, but his hand hits my chest, stopping me. "Sit," he orders.

You damn well bet I fucking sit.

He smirks as he watches me, knowing I might act like I'm in control, but he's the one who is. I would do anything he asked. I would follow his every order and whim, no matter how unreasonable and crazy.

"You want me to show you?" He kneels before me, grabbing my boxers and pulling them down. His bright eyes pin me in place as his mouth presses to the tip of my aching, leaking cock. "Then let me show you."

My head drops back to the couch as he slides his mouth down my length and back up, dragging his tongue along the veins under my dick. I jerk in his hold, forcing myself deeper. I tangle my fingers in his hair as I watch him.

"Angel," I murmur.

He licks the tip of my cock, tasting me, as his other hand slides down and cups my balls. "You wanted me to show you." He kisses the tip of my dick. "Do you see now? Do you understand?" He slides me all the way into his mouth and down his throat.

"Fuck, angel." I drive into his mouth, forcing him to take me. "You were made to be fucked by me. You were made for this. Look at you. So goddamn beautiful. Look what you do to me."

His eyes heat at my words and he sucks harder, squeezing my balls until I'm swearing.

Fuck, I'm so close. His mouth feels too fucking good, but I want to be inside my boy. I want to be buried so deep, no one can ever separate us again.

I yank him up and off me, his eyes widening in confusion and desire. "That pretty mouth is incredible, angel, but when I come, I want to be inside you. I want to be buried in your perfect ass so you know exactly whom you belong to."

Throwing him down onto the couch, I roll so I'm on top of him and rip his shorts off, tossing them away as I kiss his incredible chest. My lips wrap around his nipple, and I suck as he rubs against me, his hands clawing at my sides as his legs fall open, demanding I take him.

I do just that. Lifting his pretty, tattooed hips, I place a kiss on his leaking dick before I line up with his ass and slowly push inside him, his hot hole gripping me as I slide deeper before pulling out and pushing back in. I stretch him as his mouth drops open on a moan, his eyes sliding shut as he tosses his head.

"Skylar, fuck, please, I want you so deep I'll feel you everywhere," he begs. "I need it, please."

I need it too. I need it more than my next breath.

I need to be like this forever, trapped in his body with my name on his lips.

I was made to love Bones, and that's exactly what I do. My hips speed up until I'm pounding into his ass, watching him bounce with the force of my movements.

"Please!" he screams.

Rolling, I pin him against the sofa, trapping him on his side between me and the cushions. I thrust my hips and force myself deeper as he groans. Lifting his leg, I toss it over mine so I can change the angle, letting him feel every hard inch of what he does to me.

"That's it, angel, look how well you're doing. You're being such a good boy, taking me like this. How crazy do you have to be to think I'd ever let you go? I only find this heaven inside you. I'll destroy every single person who ever tries to get in the way of me having what's mine." I suck on his ear, feeling him clench around me.

"Sky, please, babe, please," he begs, pushing back as his head falls against my shoulder.

"I love the way you beg me. You're so fucking stern outside of our apartments, but in here, you're just my baby, aren't you? My needy fucking angel desperate for me to fuck him into oblivion." I bite his neck as he cries out. "I always knew you would be a screamer."

"Fuck you," he growls as I drive into him, forcing more of those addictive sounds from his lips. The neighbors pound on the walls, but it only spurs me on, and I slam into him harder so he makes more noise.

He digs his teeth into the cushion as I fuck him, trying to muffle the sounds until I pull him away. I want to hear them. I want his beautiful voice to haunt me.

"Sky," he begs, reaching up and gripping the back of my head. I bite his neck as I fuck him, and his ass spasms around my cock as he cries out.

Sliding my hand down his chest, I grip his dick, tightening my fist until he bellows his release. I feel the warmth of his cum spill over my hand, and it drives me over the edge. Grunting into his neck, I pump my cum deep inside him. Pleasure races through us. The only time I feel my heart speed up is with him, and it pounds now.

We both slump into the cushions, sweaty and satisfied. I kiss his neck, soothing the wounds there.

He turns in my arms and smiles up at me so brightly, I can't help but kiss him.

"I love you, angel."

"I love you too," he whispers.

We are in this together.

There is no breaking us apart.

Where one goes, the other follows.

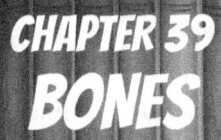

CHAPTER 39
BONES

The only real date I have ever been on was with Skylar. He seems to like that, and he also seems to enjoy spoiling me, so when he surprises me on Saturday with a day off from practice, I can't help but grin. Mackie is resting after his recent scare, so Noah let them have time off. His big race is coming up, but he doesn't seem nervous.

I have no idea where we are going, but I don't really care because we're together. We drive out of the city and to the next one over, where there's a beach and an amusement park. He parks, and I groan, letting him take my hand as I stare at it.

"An amusement park?" I scoff.

"I'm assuming you've never been or enjoyed one, right?" He backs me into his car, wiggling his eyebrows. "I'm giving you all the firsts you haven't had."

I laugh, and he kisses me. I lose myself in it until someone clears their throat. I try to pull away, but Sky lingers, kissing me before moving back slightly to let me see Alek and Evan.

"Are we interrupting?" Alek asks.

"Yes." Sky grins. "But I'm glad you made it."

He winks at me. "I thought we could do a double date. You need some time with friends who care about you."

I melt, and he interlaces our fingers together. I lean in and kiss him. Evan squeals while Alek claps. Rolling my eyes, I flip them off.

"Fuck off. You're just jealous."

"Do I need to make a big sign online to let them know the infamous Skylar Warren is taken?" Alek jokes.

"Good idea." Sky pulls his phone out, snaps a picture of our joined hands, and before I can react, he posts something.

"What did you do?" I hiss, yanking my phone out of my pocket. I see the notification and I click it.

The picture loads on his Instagram, and I'm tagged in the caption.

Official announcement: Skylar Warren is now an honest and taken man by an incredible angel who is @BonesBoii.

"Skylar!" I slap his chest, but I bite back my smile, and he kisses my cheek and steps back.

"Now, let's ride some rides, eat too much food, and have a good day!" he declares, and Alek and Evan head toward the park. I let Sky pull me after them, but nerves fill my stomach.

"Sky." I tug him back to a stop. "My father—"

"No, not today. Today is about us and fun. That's all. Nothing more. Today we are just Sky and Bones, no one else."

"Okay," I agree, knowing he's right. I can't live my life in fear of my father. Sky smiles approvingly, takes my hand, and tugs me after Alek and Evan, who are waiting impatiently.

Skylar pays for me and Alek pays for Evan, even though we both fight them. He's right. I've never been to an amusement park before. My father didn't allow it. Screams fill the air, and the noise of games and rides is overwhelming in a good way. My nose twitches with the scents of fried food and sweets, and I can't deny I'm excited.

Evan bounces on his toes, pointing at the closest ride. "Let's go."

"Baby." Alek sighs, but he lets Evan pout and pull him all the way there.

Once in line, Skylar stands behind me, wrapping his arms around me while resting his head on my shoulder as we shuffle forward. I chat with Evan and Alek, and I know Sky was right. I needed this. I feel the weight lifting off me until I'm just happy.

We hit as many rides as we can. Sky, Evan, and I scream and laugh, loving the adrenaline. Alek looks sick every time, but he goes without protest, happy to see Evan enjoying it.

"No more," Alek begs, looking nauseous after a particularly intense ride.

"But . . ." Evan pouts, and I see Alek's resolve cracking. Chuckling, I grab Evan's arm before Alek has a heart attack.

"I'll go. You both stay here and compare engines or something." I wave at them and let Evan tug me over to the ride.

Evan and I eventually take Alek and Skylar on the teacups after Alek admits he can't handle any more. Evan takes more pictures than I can count, his camera always on his neck. Alek complains each time, but he always lets him while Sky poses.

We find ourselves at the stalls with the games next. Sky picks a shooting game, while Alek and Evan wander off to hook a duck. Sky hands over some bills and checks his gun.

He aims, fires, and knocks all the moving targets down except one. "Damn," he mutters, but he points at an angry-looking bear. When the guy hands it over, he grins and passes it to me. "It looks like you, angel."

"Asshole." I pass over another wad of bills and grab the gun. "Let me show you how it's done."

I fire quickly, knocking down every target, and with a wink at Skylar, I point out my prize and wait.

"I'm so turned on right now," Sky says.

Snorting, I take the teddy the bored attendant hands over and shove it at Sky. "Here, now we match. This one looks like you." His is a goofy teddy, but as he looks at it, his eyes sparkle and he seems so happy, I have to turn away.

He takes my hand, and we wander around before I stop him and grab my phone. I press my lips to his cheek, our plushies held up, and snap a picture, then I run off before he can say anything.

"Not fair. Get back here. Let me kiss you!" he yells after me, and I can't help but laugh.

He chases me down, and I laugh as he catches me, flings me over his shoulder, and heads back to Evan and Alek.

"You good?" Alek asks.

"I'm fine."

"I mean Sky," Alek scoffs. "Is he being a brat?"

"Always, but I love it." He carries me away, and we head to a carousel. Sky puts me on my feet and helps me onto a white horse, while he climbs onto a black one next to me. I shake my head as he grabs my hand as we slowly circle. I can't help but laugh loudly as he sings off-key with the music.

I don't think I have ever been so happy.

We wander the rest of the morning until Evan hands me his camera before the edge of the water at the pier. "Just press this, okay?" he instructs before hurrying over to Alek. They grin widely at each other, and I snap. When they glance back, I snap another, and when they kiss, I snap even more.

I can't help but smile at the happiness pouring from them, and when he returns, looking them over, I can't resist asking, "Can you take one of Sky and me?"

Evan gives me the widest grin, and before I know it, I'm being posed as a million pictures are taken. Lesson learned—never ask a photographer for a picture. Over an hour later, my eyes are blurry and he's grinning, leaning over his camera with Sky.

"Damn, look at this one. Bones looks like a model. Oh, this is the cutest picture I've ever taken."

"Look, angel." Sky shows me one, and my jaw drops at the image.

I look happy.

Our arms are wrapped around one another, and we are grinning at each other. I remember he just said something funny, but the way my eyes sparkle captures my attention before I see him.

God, his eyes.

"Is this how everyone else sees you looking at me?" I murmur.

"Like you are his air?" Evan jokes. "Absolutely. Honestly, the way you two eye each other makes me feel like we should leave you in private. I've never seen someone look at another the way he looks at you."

"Yes you have, baby," Alek corrects. "I look at you the same way."

"We should take one together," I whisper, but my eyes are still on the one of Sky and me.

Do I really mean that much to him? As I raise my eyes, I know the answer.

Yes, I do.

My phone is blowing up, and the comments on Sky's post are insane. He tagged me, so my follower count had skyrocketed. It seems nearly the entirety of Pine Valley's population is now shipping us.

Shaking my head, I put it away and walk next to Skylar, with Evan and Alek behind us, splitting cotton candy. I'm tired but happy. Today has been amazing.

"I'm glad you two are finally together," Evan comments around a mouthful. "I knew you'd give in, though I'll admit I didn't expect Skylar to officially date anyone."

"I don't date men," he replies seriously, and I arch a brow at him. He grins at me. "I marry them."

"Oh God." I try to leave, but he laughs and pulls me back just as an older woman stops before us, glaring.

"Can I help you?" I ask as she eyes us distastefully. My hackles rise, and anger courses through me at the sneer on her lips as she looks us over.

"You shouldn't be doing this in public," she chides, gesturing at us.

"Doing what? Walking? Would you prefer I run?" I smirk.

"No! Flaunting this . . . this sin. The devil will come for you, you know?" She looks so righteous, so sure of herself. Evan appears annoyed, and Alek is furious—I feel the same way. I expect Sky's anger, but he leans into me and smiles at the lady.

"Do you have his number? I heard he's . . . *hot,*" Sky teases. "I bet we'd get along, two bad bitches and all."

"The devil is in you," she hisses.

Sky gasps and places his hand on his heart dramatically. "Really? I didn't notice." He glances at me. "Did you?"

"I don't know about the devil, but I had you in me," I say, and she looks horrified.

"You are disgusting, you vagrant—"

"Enough," Alek snaps. "You can take your outdated opinions else-where. We aren't hurting anyone. You're the one causing the scene."

"But you—you—" She glances between us.

"Is there a problem here?" A security guy approaches us, a big, burly, older man with a handlebar mustache.

"Yes!" she cries, putting on the tears, and we all sigh. "These kids are rude and disgusting."

"That wasn't what I heard. I heard you being cruel to them." He glances at us. "Are you okay?"

"We're fine," I murmur in shock as I glance at her. "Just to let you know, I'm a lawyer. I could press charges, but I won't."

"You . . . You . . ." She looks between us and the security officer.

"Let's go." He nods.

"Yes, take them away. Get them out of here. It's disgusting. There are children here!" she yells, still not understanding.

"I mean you." He frowns at her. "We don't tolerate abuse here. Everyone is free to be who they want. Love is love, ma'am. Maybe you need to realize that because you could clearly use some love your-self. It might change your mood." He steers her away and nods at us. "I apologize. Please ignore her. I will escort her out. Enjoy your day."

We watch her go, and Alek whistles. "Well, damn, maybe the whole world isn't fucked."

"Not the world, but I certainly was last night—" I elbow Skylar, cutting off his words, and he chuckles even as he wheezes.

I walk away, but my smile is wide, and when he catches up, so do Evan and Alek.

"What now?" Evan asks.

"Let's have fun." I shrug. "Let's just go with it. Today is about us, no one else."

"Sounds like a plan to me." Alek nods. "The awesome foursome— wait, that sounded wrong."

We all groan, but it's laced with amusement before Sky and Alek dive into name ideas.

As I watch them bicker, I can't help but be grateful they came into my life and fought to be a part of it, because I couldn't imagine my world without them.

I was so alone before, but now, I'll never be alone again.

CHAPTER 40
SKYLAR

Yesterday was like a dream. I'd never been so happy, and my boy smiled widely the entire day. He forgot about everything else, and I'm glad I could give him that. Our perfect day and night, however, was interrupted by my phone ringing ridiculously early this morning, and if it had been anyone else but Noah, I would have bitch-slapped them.

Work is important, though, so I left Bones sleeping, made my ass presentable, and hightailed it down to the hotel he sent me the information for.

The room is already set up when I arrive, and I throw myself down in one of the chairs behind the tables. Our logo is on screens behind us, and our names are situated before us with little mics. Mackie is already at my side, and he looks a lot better. There's some bruising on his face, but I'm sure Nurse Noah has been taking good care of him.

"You okay?" I ask.

He nods and forces a smile as he faces the people who keep trickling in, the crowd made up of journalists, bloggers, influencers, and fans. News of Mackie's accident spread quickly, and Noah wants to get ahead of it before speculation runs amok, saying that we are pulling out or being shut down for having unsafe practices. Our mics are off for a moment, but I make sure to keep my voice low, not wanting to spoil whatever Noah has planned.

"You know what he's going to do?" I question.

"Not a clue." He nods at Noah, who is talking animatedly to Alek at the side. "But he's been on a warpath for days, terrifying everyone. Whatever it is, I'd say buckle up for the crazy."

"You know it's because of you, right?" I ask as I glance at him. "He was mad before, but the moment they made you a target, he lost every shred of control he had."

"No, it isn't," Mackie mutters. "If it had been you, he would have been the same way. He's just mad someone thinks they can get away with this."

"You are both idiots." I sigh as I slap his shoulder. "When you get married, I'm going to share all the times you morons tried to deny this."

Mackie sputters, making me grin, and when Noah appears behind him and calls our names, he whirls around, his face turning red. Poor boy.

"What?" Noah asks, looking between us before he presses the back of his hand to Mackie's head. "Are you feeling sick? You're hot."

"You think so?" I prop my chin on his shoulder and grin at Noah. "How hot do you think he is on a scale of one to ten?"

Noah frowns, not understanding. "Like a six? Not a normal temperature for sure."

Mackie pushes us both away and glares at me before he focuses on Noah. "What's going on? You didn't tell me anything when you hustled me from your house."

"Staying over, are we? Nice little slumber parties. Noah, do you wear silk or nothing?" I retort.

Noah ignores me and glances at the room, which is almost full now. "It's time to tell everyone what's been happening and start a manhunt. The police have scaled up their investigations, but I don't want anyone else getting hurt." He looks at us. "Go along with what I say and show we are a united front, okay? This won't take long," he tells us. "Then it's back to practice. The room will be left set up for the boxing announcement coming next, so don't break anything."

"Why does he assume we will break anything?" I mutter to Mackie.

"Hmm, I don't know, maybe because you have broken eight—"

"Nine," I correct, knowing where this is going.

"Coffee mugs, two chairs, a shower, and a locker. How did you even break the locker?" he asks, his eyes narrowed.

"Ah, well, see, my boy called me, and he wanted to see what I was wearing—"

"Microphone," Noah hisses, and I jerk up to see some members of the crowd giggling.

"Oops. If you're watching, baby, sorry!" I call, and some of the journalists shake their heads. Mackie's face is beet red, but I just lean back and grin.

"Sorry for that. As you can tell, Skylar has no qualms about over-sharing," Noah offers, and the room breaks out into chuckles. "I won't keep you long. First of all, thank you for coming today. We really appreciate it. For those who don't know, I'm Noah, manager of Starfire Racing, and to my right are Mackie and Skylar, our two racers this year. We wanted to address some rumors and stories that have been circulating about an accident Mackie recently had."

Everyone leans forward, eagerly waiting. They know that whatever's next will be good. After all, you don't call a press conference for no reason, and coupled with the pissed expression Noah is unable to control, they know there is gossip.

"I can confirm that Mackie was in an accident this week during training. The car lost control and spun from the track. We are very lucky it wasn't much worse. However, it was not the driver's fault or even a simple accident. This was an attack. Mackie's car was sabo-taged, causing him to lose control. If he hadn't been such a good driver, he could have died." Noah lets that sink in, and I see horror and confusion on the faces of those gathered.

Reaching under the table, I squeeze Mackie's hand, and he grips mine for comfort.

"We are working alongside local police to investigate this matter thoroughly. There have been a recent string of injuries and attacks at Starfire Racing, resulting in some of our team members being hurt, but this was something we kept quiet at the police's request. However, I refuse to sit back and remain silent while my business, my team, and my family remain under threat. Nobody should ever feel unsafe doing their job, and that is exactly what's happening."

"Why?" someone calls.

"Starfire has qualified at the top and are expected to place with the other elite teams, something we have not done in many years. Skylar and Mackie are at the top of their game, and that threatens this year's championship. If we lose, not only are sponsorships, money, and titles lost, but respect, and in some drivers' cases, their contracts with clubs. I believe that one of the teams below us feels threatened, knowing we will win, and they have decided to scare us away from competing." Noah once more lets that sink in. There are questions, but he ignores them for a moment until he raises his hands. When they quiet down and sit back, he carries on.

"We will find who did this, and we will not let them succeed. Nobody comes into my house and threatens my family. I will make sure they never step foot in this industry again and will face the full wrath of the police for their crimes. Make no mistake, this is a crime. People have been hurt. My family has been hurt. These are weak, scared individuals who think they have power. I will show them what true power feels like."

I turn to Noah in shock. They don't know it, but he just declared war.

It seems going after his boy was a bad idea.

"Skylar, Skylar, what do you think about all this?" someone calls.

"I think Noah is right. They are scared. They know we are going to win and are trying every underhanded tactic to scare us from the races, and we won't let that happen. Fear never wins. They came after my partner, my team, my family. We won't let it stand. Let them do their worst. They don't scare me. My ass will still be in that car on race day, and when Mackie and I take home first and second place, they'll finally realize there is no stopping us."

I glance at Mackie. "What happened was a disgusting show of fear and resentment, but they won't win. We are a family, and we protect each other."

"Mackie, Mackie!" they shout. "Aren't you scared to get back in the car?"

Mackie swallows and glances at Noah, but then he sits taller. "Not in the slightest. I was born to be a racer, and nobody will take that away from me. I feel the strongest and happiest behind the wheel. One accident won't change that. I will bring the title home for Skylar and Starfire. Their scare tactics have only made us more determined, and I know Noah and the police will do everything to keep us safe while we compete."

"Absolutely." Noah nods. "Which brings me to my final topic. We are offering a reward for any information on these attacks. Fifty thousand dollars will be given to anyone who provides us with information that leads to the successful arrest of the culprits. This is being funded by Starfire Racing. We do not care how you know or who you are. We simply want the information."

"Noah!" someone yells. "You must have an idea of who is behind this."

"The way I see it, there are only two teams that would benefit from us pulling out of the championship," Noah replies without an ounce of fear.

My eyebrows rise. That's a shit ton of money, which I'm guessing is Noah's.

Like I said, you don't fuck with his boy.

Noah stands. "We won't keep you any longer. We thank you for coming, and we hope to see you at our next race."

Mackie and I stand, and as one, we follow Noah from the room. Questions are shouted at us and cameras chase us, but we stand tall through it all.

We just declared war, and now we need to prepare.

I'm eating dinner at a local restaurant when he appears. I don't know how he tracked me, but it shouldn't surprise me that he did. He's never been one to let someone else have the last word.

He sits down opposite me, reclining back. Despite him being Bones's father, he looks nothing like my boy. This man is cold through and through, while my boy is simply pretending to be.

"Please, sit." I wipe my mouth.

"I'm not here to play nice—"

"Silly me, I thought we were going to bond for a moment." I wait, my eyebrow arched. "Well, come on then, I'm waiting for the next threat."

"No threat, not this time." He pulls out a black book—a check-book, I realize—and I watch incredulously as he scribbles something, rips one out, and slides it over to me. "This is if you leave my son alone. Break his heart and walk away."

Picking up the check, I look at the numbers. It's a lot of money.

"One hundred grand is that what your son is worth to you?" I ask. He looks smug, like he's won, the dumbass. I take great delight in ripping it up and letting the pieces flutter to the table. "You'll need a whole lot more money than that. I thought you were rich." I pull out my own and grab his pen, filling in the check before I slide it across. "There, triple what you offered me for you to stay away from your son." Standing, I smirk as he gapes at me, open-mouthed. "I have more money than you, I have more power than you, and I have no plans to ever let your son go. Have a good meal. Feel free to put it on my tab."

I leave him staring after me, smiling the whole time.

CHAPTER 41
BONES

"Come on, just one picture," Evan pleads behind me. He's been trying to get me to model for him for weeks now. I keep saying no, but he's getting desperate, and it's fun watching him chase me around. I'll give in because I don't want to hurt my friend and his passion is photography. Even if I hate it, I'll pose for him to make him happy, but I want him to suffer a little first.

I never said I was nice, just a friend.

Shaking my head, I turn to walk toward my car when I freeze.

My ears ring, my heart stops, and I can't blink.

A ghost stands before me, lingering near my car with his hands shoved in his pockets as he waits. He lifts his head and meets my gaze.

His lips tilt up in a soft smile, one I traced more times than my own. His eyes, however, look worried. They aren't filled with joy like the last time I saw them. His hair is different too, shorter and another color. He seems . . . bigger, older.

"Hi, Si." His voice is the same, soft and sweet, and that's when it hits me.

He isn't a ghost, and I'm not back to missing him so much I see things.

It's really him.

He's standing before me like I didn't spend the last five years of my life searching for him, thinking he was dead or worse.

"Bones?" Evan asks, worry in his voice. "Everything okay?"

I stare at him, at a boy—no, this isn't a boy. This is a man. He isn't the boy I loved. He isn't the boy I planned to run away with. This isn't the boy I shared my fears and dreams with in silent, stolen whispers. This is a man.

"Si?" He steps closer, gnawing on his bottom lip, a habit when he's nervous. I know it better than my own.

I continue to stare.

"I'm back," he says lamely, and that's what snaps me out of it.

I suck in a wobbly breath, my chest aching as if I'm splintering apart. My world tips on its axis. All these years, the sleepless nights, the nightmares, the grief, and the searching close in, suffocating me until I feel like I'm wading through that simply to open my mouth.

"Bones, who is this?" Evan asks, stopping at my side. I can't look away. I can't do anything.

"You aren't dead."

He flinches and stops walking toward me. A few steps remain between us now, and I look at the man I loved more than even myself. He's different, but it's him.

All our good times rush back to me, twisting the pain deeper until I feel my eyes burn. My legs begin to shake, and I fear I might collapse.

"No, not dead," he admits. "I had to go for a little while—"

"Why are you back?" I force the words out, barely keeping myself together. I don't want to hear whatever he was going to say.

He isn't dead.

He isn't hurt.

That means he chose to leave me, which has been my biggest fear since I waited at that bus stop.

He wasn't taken or killed. He simply walked away from me, not even bothering to say goodbye.

It's something I've never admitted, even to Skylar, or ever wanted to acknowledge to myself, but this crossed my mind nearly every day since the night he disappeared.

"I wanted to see you," he says. "I missed you."

My chuckle is bitter and filled with pain. "You missed me? You missed me?" I know my voice is rising now, sounding manic. "You left. I thought you were dead or kidnapped or worse. You just fucking disappeared, and now you're back because you missed me?"

His eyes drop to the ground in shame, and I step closer, shoving him back. "Say something!" I shout.

His face lifts, and I see tears swimming in his eyes. "I'm sorry, Si. I really am."

It's all he can say—no excuses or reasons because the reason is right here.

He left me. He broke my heart into pieces and never even gave me the chance to get over him.

I want him to hold me and tell me he's sorry, but then I realize I don't because he's the reason I was broken and in agony in the first place. It fucking hurts.

I shove him again, watching him stumble back as I crack. Years of pain, heartache, and grief consume me.

They say the truth sets you free, but as I stare into this man's eyes, I realize it can also ruin you.

"I think you should go," Evan snaps as he steps in front of me, but I can't speak or look away.

Aro nods, glancing at me then at Evan and back. "I'm staying at Downtown Winter when you want to talk." He bites his lip again. "I'm sorry, Si. I really am."

He leaves just like before, only this time, I see him walk away.

I hit the pavement, feeling a sharp pain in my knees before it blends into the rest of the anguish flowing through me. The hurt in my heart is worse than any my body could ever suffer.

You don't hear a heart break. It happens silently, as if it isn't occurring at all. While your world crumbles, devastation fills you and agony overwhelms you, as if death would be easier, but the world carries on.

My heart shatters, imploding in my chest brighter than any supernova. There is no way to contain this kind of pain. It rises up my gullet and overflows into a cry.

"Bones, what is it? What can I do?" Evan pleads as he drops to his knees before me, his hands on my shoulders.

I should care that we are in public.

I should care, but I don't.

"Home, I want to go home," I whisper, my eyes filled with tears.

I don't remember Alek helping me into the car or the car ride. All I remember is the shame and truth in his eyes as he faced me. I spent months staring into those brown orbs, falling in love.

He left me. I wasn't good enough. He didn't love me enough.

He left.

I'm swept under the wave of agony again, until I don't even feel like I'm being dragged away by the water.

How can so much pain be contained in one body?

It can't. I feel like I'm exploding from it.

"Bones, we're here, okay? Let me park and help you," Evan offers softly from my side where he's sitting in the back, holding my hand. Neither of them know what happened, but they don't care. They are trying to help.

It shouldn't make me feel better, but they aren't what I need.

Turning, I thrust the door open.

I'm out of Alek's car before it even fully stops, hopping the barrier onto the track and rushing toward Sky, who turns to me.

I run into his arms.

I'm home.

CHAPTER 42
SKYLAR

I stare down at Bones, terrified and confused, as he presses his face to my chest, holding me so tightly it hurts. Glancing up, I meet Alek's and Evan's worried gazes. Evan shrugs, and I nod as they walk back to their car, leaving me to deal with it. I'll have to thank them for bringing him to me. I don't know what happened, but he's safe, and that's all that matters.

"Hey," I coo softly as I pry his face from my chest. Tears glisten in his eyes. "Talk to me, angel. What's wrong?"

His pain morphs into fury as he stares at me. "How could he do it? Why? How?" As he speaks, his voice gets angrier, and his hands slap my chest. I stagger back under the force of his blows before rooting myself in place. My brows draw together as I search for answers I don't have.

I look into his eyes, and I see so much rage, but where there is fury, there is always pain, so I let him lash me with his words and his fists until he slows. The anger ebbs into exhausted agony, and when he crumples, I catch him. His tear-stained face turns to me, pale and ruined. "Why aren't I enough?" he whispers.

"Shh, you are enough," I murmur as I kiss his head. "Tell me who hurt you, angel, and I'll make them pay. Tell me what happened so I can make it right."

"Aro," he croaks. "The boy I loved . . . he's back. He isn't dead. He just left me all those years ago. No goodbye, no excuse. He just left." He looks at me. "I loved him, Sky. I loved him so much, and I thought the worst happened all these years, but he just—" He hiccups. "Left like I didn't matter at all. He left me."

"Oh, angel." I tug him into my arms and hold him tighter.

Nothing I say will make this right. I know how much he struggled with never knowing, with the grief and loss of his first love. He pushed everyone away because of it, scared to care again. He shaped his life around the hole Aro left, but for his ex, Bones was simply someone to toss away.

How anyone could ever hurt my boy or leave him is beyond me, but I hold him as he grieves for the answers he always wanted but probably resents now.

In some ways, it might be easier if he were dead.

We stand there, locked together as he breaks. I don't care about anything else. I just hold my boy as he tries to put his heart back together.

He's quiet in my arms until he suddenly steps back, wiping at his face, and eyes me. "Let's break up."

Those three words crush my heart, but I refuse to give them roots and let them grow. He's hurting and lashing out. He's closing down to protect himself. It's Bones's defense mechanism—hurt them before they hurt you.

Well, it won't work on me.

For the first time in my life, I'm genuinely afraid of losing something. Oh, I survived because I had to, because giving up and dying was too easy, but I never really had a reason to fear death. Now I do. I'm terrified all the time because I never want to break his heart. I never want to leave him alone again, so I'll spend the rest of my life making sure he feels safe and secure. I'll be scared enough for both of us

"No," I state softly as I step closer. He retreats a step, so I stop moving. "Never. Hit me, kick me, bite me, scream, cry, do whatever you need to, but I'm not letting you go."

"Skylar," he whispers. His expression is cold, but his eyes scream at me not to let him go, to love him and never leave him. "I didn't realize it until now, but honestly, the only reason I'm still alive is spite —spite for the boy who left, and spite for my father who hates me. I want to hurt him and make him pay every day I'm alive. I want to be a reminder of the thing he lost and can never control. Don't you see, Skylar? I can't love you. There's no room for that."

I see him building his defenses, trying to reason out why I shouldn't be with him, but it doesn't matter to me.

"That's fine. It doesn't mean I can't love you though." I take his hands as he stares at me. My poor, lost boy is searching desperately for land to hold on to. He thinks pushing me away is the answer, but he's an idiot if he thinks I will ever let him go.

"And you're happy with that? With loving someone who will never love you back the way you love him? Being his second or third or even fourth priority? Nobody would be. Don't fool yourself, Skylar. You might love me now, but it will soon turn to hate, just like the love did in me. I'm rotten to the core. I'm not worth it."

"I say you are. I say you're worth every bruise, hurt feeling, and sleepless night. You're worth it all. Look into my eyes and tell me I'm wrong. Look into my eyes and see yourself the way I see you, my beautifully flawed man. I don't love your perfection. I love the man before me. I love the man who loves so deeply, he's willing to spend his entire life getting revenge. I love you, and I'm not letting you go. I will never leave you, not like him. I will never use or hurt you like your father. I love you with everything in me, and I will spend the rest of our lives proving it," I promise.

His eyes are wide as he watches me. "What if I'm not worth it?"

"You don't get to decide that. It's my life and my heart, so I get to choose whom I hand it to, and I choose you every single time." I press my forehead against his. "He hurt you and destroyed your life once. Don't let him again. I'm sorry he left you, baby. I'm sorry you had to find out this way. I wish I could take the pain for you, but I can't. I will, however, piece you back together. It's me and you, don't you see that?"

"I loved him," he whispers.

"I know," I murmur, and I ignore the pain it causes me. I know he loved him, and I hate my own insecurities at the moment, but this isn't about me—it's about him. "I'm sorry. I'm so sorry."

He nods, tears sliding down his cheeks, and I kiss them away. He closes his eyes for a moment, and when they reopen, they are a little brighter, and I know he's going to be okay. "Take me home?"

"Of course," I murmur.

Bones is finally asleep. He cried for hours and refused to eat. I managed to get some water in him, clean his face, and change his clothes. He hugged me tightly as he fell asleep, as if he were afraid I would disappear. I know it will take time to prove that I won't, but I'm willing to put in the work.

My phone rings, and I know who it is without looking. Sliding from the bed, I grab it and head to the other room, not wanting to give Bones another reason to be worried or, worse, use it as another excuse to push me away.

"Noah," I greet.

"Warren, you better have a good fucking excuse for skipping that race." He's furious. I don't blame him. I missed a practice race—yes, practice, but it took a long time to set up and was part of the plan to prove to everyone we aren't afraid. I don't care though. Bones always comes first.

"My boy needed me," I tell him, refusing to lie.

"Goddammit." The phone is pulled away, and I hear him swear before he comes back, panting and angrier than I've ever heard him. "This was important, Skylar. You promised me when you joined to put this first."

"He will always come first," I reply without hesitation. "Always, but I'm sorry I let you down."

"Fuck, Warren!" Noah snaps. "You'd give up your entire future for him?"

"No, don't you see? He is my future." I glance back at the bedroom. "As long as we are together, that's all that matters. He is all that matters. I love racing, I love my job and you're my family, but he's my everything. The one thing I can't do is live without him."

He's quiet for a moment, and then he groans. "It's like you lost your sanity when you met your boy."

I can't help but grin, and I know Noah will forgive me. He understands where we stand now. If he asked me to choose, I would always choose Bones.

"It's bold of you to assume I had any sanity to begin with."

He scoffs, and I know he's calming down. "Fine, fucking fine. Look after your boy, but you will be back here in the morning, and you'll pay for missing the race, you hear me? You miss another one and you're gone." He pauses. "I hope he's okay."

He hangs up before I can say anything, but I smile, knowing he'll get over it.

A noise in the hall makes me frown, and I stride over to the door and peer out, seeing someone's back as he raises his hand and knocks on Bones's door again. I open mine, and he turns to glance back at me.

His hair is light blond and pushed back, and he has deep brown eyes, a tan complexion, and a muscular body, even if he's slightly skinny. He's good-looking.

"Why the fuck are you knocking on my boyfriend's door in the middle of the night?" I snap, crossing my arms.

"Boyfriend?" His eyes widen as he looks me over. "This is Silas Townsend's place, right?"

My eyes narrow as I run my eyes over him, and then it clicks. He's older, but it's the guy from the Polaroid Bones keeps—the one he tore up earlier and I secretly, meticulously put back together. I might hate this man, but I know he's important to Bones's past, and I didn't want him to regret choices he made in anger. This is the bastard who hurt my boy, though, and I can't let that pass.

Stepping out, I pull the door almost fully shut so it doesn't wake Bones. He steps back, looking fearful as he watches me.

"It's you, isn't it? The asshole who left him." His eyes widen. "You're the one who hurt my boy."

"Your boy?" He eyes me worriedly. "I didn't know he was dating anyone."

"That doesn't matter, does it?" I block his path to my apartment.

This man might have had him before, but he let him go. He's an idiot.

"I just wanted to see him," he admits sheepishly. "He looked upset earlier. I wanted to make sure he's okay."

"You think he will be okay when his first love randomly appears back in his life after disappearing without a trace, making him believe he was killed or worse?" I laugh, and he flinches. "You're a fucking dumbass, something I already knew since you left him, but still."

"I made a mistake. I want to make it right," he murmurs, his cheeks heating.

"Then why now? Why did you come back now? You didn't care about leaving him five years ago, so why do you suddenly?" I stare into his shifty eyes and it clicks. "His father called you, didn't he?" I scoff bitterly. "What, did he think you showing up would make Bones leave me?"

Maybe that's my own fear talking.

"Tell me." I step closer. "How much money did his dad give you to leave him alone?"

He swallows, turning pale. "I don't know what you're talking about."

"Yes, you do. You knew exactly where he would be and where to wait. You haven't been in his life for years, so how did you know? You know his apartment, and you conveniently arrived after I turned his father down. How much did Declan Townsend give you to break his son's heart?"

He glances over my shoulder, his eyes widening, and I turn to see Bones standing in the doorway, looking between us in horror.

"Angel," I begin, but he steps out and stares down at Aro.

"What?" Bones snaps. "Tell me he's wrong. Tell me my father didn't pay you to leave then or to come back now."

He remains silent, his eyes imploring Bones to give him a chance and not ask that.

"I'm not, am I?" I look at Aro when he refuses to answer. Maybe I shouldn't get involved, but damn this asshole for breaking Bones's heart and then trying to rub it in once more. "I know because his father offered money to me too. He wanted me to leave Bones and never come back. How much money did he give you? How much did you sell your love and Bones's trust for? Was it worth it?"

I feel Bones staring at me, and I'll tell him the details later, but right now he deserves the truth. "Tell him," I demand.

"Yes, okay? He paid me!" He stares at Bones, words tumbling from his mouth. "I was a kid, and I made a mistake. I was scared and didn't see a way out—"

"We had a way out!" Bones shouts. "But you left me. You broke my heart and left me wondering for years, unable to move on or even grieve. You were a kid, but you weren't stupid. You knew what you were doing." He pauses, his chest heaving, and I hate the pain in his gaze. "How much was my love worth?" Bones asks. "I hope you got a lot, since he's loaded . . . . Might as well make it worth your while."

"Si—"

"Do not fucking call me that!" he roars. "My name is Bones. Bones. Not Si, not Silas. Bones. You also don't get to call me any of that. How much did he give you?"

They stare each other down, and I slide my hand down Bones's back, offering him my strength since I know he's hurting right now. He doesn't push me away, which I'm grateful for, but I see his ex eye that touch, and something flashes in his gaze.

Jealousy? Envy?

It doesn't matter.

"Two million," he admits.

Bones laughs, the sound bitter. "Two million to break my heart? I don't know if I should be flattered or annoyed."

"You should have asked for more." I smirk. "He's worth it, and we both know it." Bones elbows me, but I just grin.

"You're a weak man," Bones tells him. "I can't believe I ever loved you." I watch the man flinch, and I feel a little bad for him before I remember what he did to the person I love. "You aren't even worth this."

"For what it's worth, I really did love you, Si." He reaches for Bones, but I hold out my arm, blocking him from touching him.

"It's worth nothing. You sold yourself and ruined everything we had. I hope it was worth it." He storms back inside, and I watch him go before turning my eyes to Aro.

"If you ever come back here, I'll kill you," I warn him, meaning it. "I don't care what he tells you or pays you—do not come near my boy again."

"He won't let you win, you know?" Aro murmurs. "It's what I realized that night. I didn't stand a chance. He was going to get his way no matter what, make him hate me, so I took the money and left."

"That's where you're wrong. It's Declan Townsend who doesn't stand a chance against me. I'm not weak, not like you. He won't break us or turn us."

"You'll see. He always gets his way."

"I should thank you. If you didn't leave, I never would have met him, never would have fallen in love with him. Your mistake is my everything, so no, he won't get his way. Not this time. Go back to wherever you ran to." I wait for him to leave, and then I head inside after my boy, ready to piece his heart back together again.

I'll spend my life doing it.

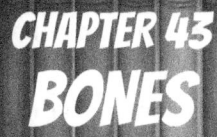

CHAPTER 43
BONES

I crawl into Skylar's bed and bow my head in shame and resentment. Seeing Aro again only rubbed salt into the wound that never healed. It just scabbed over, but he ripped it open and exposed it again, and now I'm an open, bleeding wound once more. This time, I don't know how I'll ever heal from it.

I sink into that darkness that has plagued me since the night he left me.

The truth is, I embraced the depression and loneliness because it was easier to wallow in that pit. It was easier to hurt than to move on. There was even a certain beauty to the loneliness and agony I surrounded myself with, and it was easier to be broken than to risk falling again.

Deep down, I crave relationships, love, and intimacy, but it terrifies me because it means someone has the ability to hurt me again. After Aro, I pretended I didn't want it, that it wasn't important, and I filled my life with everything else to drown out that voice. I pretended so hard, I started to believe it until I met Skylar.

I'm scared to show anyone the real me, good and bad, because what if my deepest fear is true and I'm unlovable? I must be, since he left, and so easily . . . .

"I'm here." Skylar's arms wrap around me, and he holds me in the dark, anchoring me to this world, even as I grieve for another.

"Why did he leave if he loved me?"

I don't even realize I said it out loud until Sky sighs. "I can't answer for him, but for me? I could never leave you. It would destroy me. You aren't easy to leave, Bones. You're easy to love. Fuck him and fuck your dad. They hurt you, but don't let them win, baby. Don't give them what they want. You're stronger than that."

He's wrong. I'm not.

I thought I knew everything, and now everything is a mess.

The boy I loved left me.

The man I hate made him.

My father tried to make Skylar . . .

"How much did he offer you?" I croak.

"Not ever enough," he murmurs.

"Why not? Get some money and be free of me. Seems like a win-win," I reply.

"I don't need money. All I need is you." He turns me and presses his forehead to mine in the dark. "I can't change what's been done, and truthfully, I wouldn't." I flinch, but he holds me tighter. "Because it brought us together. It brought you to me, and you are the best part of my life, angel. Maybe that makes me a jerk, but you have to know I'm not like him. I'm not going anywhere. I love you so much. I would give anything to stop this pain, but I'm right here with you, and it's where I'll stay forever."

I stare into his eyes and question everything I know.

Aro looked me in the eyes, lied, said he loved me, and then left, so why can't Skylar do the same thing?

What if I'm just an idiot? What if I gave my heart to another, just for him to break it?

What if Skylar Warren will grow tired of me one day and leave, just like everyone else?

"I see you spiraling and trying to find an excuse to push me away, but it won't work, angel." He grips my chin. "Try it, I dare you. You're hurting, but closing yourself off won't make it better. You just have to feel it, baby. You can't run or hide from it this time. Just feel it, feel it all. I'm right here."

I try to pull away, but he doesn't let me. He forces me to meet it head-on, and the avalanche of pain flows through me once more.

I have been running from it for so long.

I broke and changed my body and hardened my life, but it was always just there, waiting for me to notice it.

A sob rips from my chest and I throw myself at him. He holds me, rubbing my back as I cry and let out years of heartache.

I really let myself feel for the first time in years.

I am so tired of crying and letting my past haunt me.

I'm so tired of being strong.

I let it all go in Sky's arms, knowing he will be there to catch me.

It isn't fair of me to ask him to help me through my heartbreak over someone else, but he doesn't seem to care, and I can't let him go.

"That's it, angel, let go. I'm right here. I'm right here with you. It's okay. Let it all out," he murmurs as his grip tightens.

He holds me as I grieve like I should have done back then.

He's right. I closed down and tried to not feel, but it all comes back, and he holds me through it.

I'm not easy to love, and I'm not worth all this pain, but Skylar Warren doesn't care, and I can't bring myself to prove him wrong because the truth is . . .

I don't want to live without him.

When I was hurting, he was the first person I thought of.

My safe harbor, my home, and his arms were all I wanted.

Even now, he's the only one I want here.

I don't know how long we lie like this, but my tears dry and my heart settles into a dull ache, yet I still cling to him.

Licking my lips, I force my swollen eyes open and meet his. I must look like shit, but he smiles, and his eyes sweep over my face like I'm the most perfect thing in the world.

"I love you," I whisper. "I don't want to break up. I don't want to lose you. I was just scared."

"I know, angel. I know." He smiles as he kisses the tip of my nose and then both of my eyes, but I want more. I want to feel his lips on mine.

I roll us and kiss him. My lips are salty because of my tears, but he doesn't seem to mind.

Leaning back, I tug my shirt up as he watches me. "Angel—"

"Stop, I need this. I need you. I need you to make me feel alive. I need you to replace today. I need you to remind me you love me. Please, Sky, make me forget." I'll beg him if I need to.

I should have known he would never deny me. Sitting, he slides his hands up my back and tugs me closer. "Anything you want, angel. I'm yours. Let me show you."

His lips meet mine in a soft kiss before he tugs my shirt up. His lips brush across my cheeks and up, then he kisses each of my eyes closed as he lays me back and pulls my pants off. When I open my eyes again, he's above me, stripping off his clothes. Sky arches over me, kissing down my neck as I moan. I focus on the way his hands hold me obses- sively, the slide of his skin against mine, and his tongue darting out to lick my nipple before sliding down my abs.

All of the sensations drive me out of my mind, and I can't think about anything else but him. His hands glide up my thighs, and he throws them over his shoulders as I open my eyes. My lips part to speak, but I groan as his tongue dips inside my ass and circles it. He eats me with long, sure strokes that have me fisting the bedding and arching up. My cock leaks and jerks, begging for attention, and my whole body quivers with pleasure.

"Sky," I beg.

He kisses my ass once more before sitting up. My thighs drop to his waist, and I wrap them around him as he smiles at me. "I've got you, baby," he says as I feel his hard cock press against my ass. He slowly pushes inside me with a soft stroke, stretching my ass before pulling out. Reaching up, I grip his shoulders, digging my nails in as I arch, pulling him deeper inside me. His lips slide down my neck before he sucks my skin, pleasure zipping through me until I push down, taking all of him.

When he starts to move, my cries fill the air. His confident, hard strokes push me up the bed as he fucks me. The pleasure rolls through me like fog, obscuring anything but him and his touch as I reach up and turn his head, kissing him.

Maybe it's not the healthiest outlet, but I don't care.

I find heaven in his arms. I find sanctuary in his kiss. I find healing within his touch.

I want his hands to replace all the others that have been on my body.

I want his kiss to be the only one I ever taste.

I might have given my heart to another before, but not in the way I gave it to Skylar. I loved Aro as a child, but I love Skylar as a man.

"I love you," I rasp into his skin as he bites my neck and fucks me. Our skin slides together and sweat drips down me as my cock jerks between us.

"I love you too, angel," he murmurs. "Use me as much as you need to. I'll be right here every time to wipe your tears and turn your sobs into screams."

I start to smile, but it morphs into a cry as he tilts my hips up and hits that spot that drives me crazy. My beautiful boy watches as I come apart, shattering in his arms with a scream just like he promised.

His thrusts speed up as I ride my orgasm, and then he stills with a groan, pumping me full of his hot release. Collapsing on top of me, he rains kisses across my skin as I wrap myself around him, panting but happy. The pain seems far away, like nothing can touch me while I'm in his arms.

I know Sky is right. I needed to break in order to heal so I can move on.

Aro is my past, but Skylar is my future, and I am not wasting one more second of it.

CHAPTER 44
SKYLAR

I expected Bones to hurt the next day, but if anything, he's determined. He seems okay, but I know that's a lie—he's still hurting, but he's trying.

He comes with me to the garage, and after one look into my and Bones's puppy eyes, Noah lets us off. I do have to clean the bathrooms as punishment, though, but there are worse things. I practice with Mackie until night falls, and then I take Bones's hand and drive through the city, pulling up outside a huge house.

"Are you sure?" I ask him in the quiet car.

It was his idea, but I don't want my boy hurting any more than he needs to. As he looks at me, though, I know he needs this.

He lifts our joined hands and kisses the back of mine. "Yes. Thank you for coming with me."

"Always, angel," I murmur as I lean over and kiss him. "He's still your father. If you want him in your life, it's your choice. I will support you no matter what."

He smiles, but it drops when he turns back to the house. "I hated this place. I was always haunted when I was here. I've grown, but I still have the same feelings when I come back here, and he knows it. He uses it against me."

"I'll be right there with you. He only has as much power as you give him, angel," I remind him.

He nods and blows out a breath before climbing from the car. I follow him, and he takes my hand as we ascend the steps. It's an impressive house, if slightly over the top. He opens the door without knocking and strides down a corridor to a sitting room where we find his father.

A scotch sits before him, and he's still in a suit with his laptop on the table and papers spread across his knee. He looks up, glaring when he notices us lingering in the doorway.

"It's very rude to turn up without an appointment," his father snaps, "and he is not welcome."

"This is important. I'm your son. I shouldn't have to make an appointment," Bones snaps back. "Besides, where I go, he goes."

His father sits back, eyeing us. "What do you want?"

Bones heads over and sits, so I do the same, sitting at his side and holding his hand. He holds mine tightly, and his father notices, but I don't care.

"I know you paid Aro to leave me years ago."

His father doesn't even blink. "And?" he asks when Bones doesn't continue. "Don't tell me this show is all for that? If you know that, then why are you here, looking for answers?"

"Why? I want to know why," Bones replies. "Why, Father?"

"He was holding you back. I knew about your plans to leave with him. You would have ruined your life. It was foolish. I took care of it like I always do." He reaches out and takes a drink before leaning back.

Bones bristles at my side.

"Do you feel better? It was the right decision. Look how far you've come. Now you just need to get rid of . . . him." He looks at me in disgust.

"Skylar is my boyfriend," Bones snaps.

His dad curls his lip in a sneer. "No one in our field will ever accept that. You will be humiliated. Everything I do is to help your career. I can find you a nice gir—"

"All of this because I fell in love with a man," Bones whispers, realizing it at the same time I do.

This isn't about controlling Bones—okay, it is—but it's also about who he chose over his father.

"You will find a nice woman and settle down, and she will help you continue to grow. This is just a phase," his father remarks. "In time, you'll understand and thank me."

My stomach rolls at his implication. He's telling Bones about his own sexuality and trying to dismiss it, as if he can choose whom he loves.

My poor boy. No wonder he got as far away from here as he could. If this is the way he grew up . . . Fuck, I'll make sure he never wants for love and acceptance ever again.

"No, I won't," Bones whispers as he stares at his dad. "I'm gay, Father. I always have been. I can't help the way I was born. I like men—"

"Enough," his father interrupts, and Bones startles at the sharp edge of anger in his tone, but then I see his own ire rise to meet his father's.

"No, it isn't enough. Why is my love less deserving? Why is my love less because it's for a boy rather than a girl? What makes yours so much fucking better than mine? Does it make it less? Make it not real? I love him with everything in me, and if you can't understand that, then I feel bad for you because you've clearly never felt that deep kind of love and never will." Bones gets to his feet, staring down at his father.

His father's eyes narrow on him as he carefully sets his drink down and stands, buttoning his jacket, but his jerky movements betray his anger. "You feel sorry for me? Look around at my life, boy."

"Yes, and you know why? This house, this money, and this stuff is all you will ever have, and it's empty and hollow just like you. So yes, I feel sorry for you, sitting in your big house all alone. I'll be living my life, and fuck anyone who can't accept who I am!" He grasps my hand. "Come on, Skylar. We're leaving and never coming back."

"You will not leave this house!" his father bellows as we head to the door.

Bones turns, his eyes flashing in anger. "I am more than a name! I am a person. I am not an extension of you, and I never will be."

His father's eyes narrow as he steps toward us. "The world will never accept you."

"Then fuck the world," Bones spits, lifting our hands. "I have everything I need right here." I smile at my boy, my heart so full it hurts. He's choosing me over everything. I wish it didn't have to go like this, but some things can't be fixed.

Some people will never change, and although I know it hurts Bones, it also heals him to let go of everything regarding his father and say everything he's always wanted.

Declan Townsend will always be his blood, but we will be his family.

"You know what I realized tonight, Father?" He kisses my hand before he looks back at his dad. "I'll never be enough for you. I guess I always knew it, but listening to you now, I'm sure. Nothing I ever do will be enough. I have tried so hard to be someone you would be proud of, but I can't change who I am, not even for you, nor would I want to. I'm not ashamed of who I am. This is who I am. I love a man, and if that's the worst thing you can find out about me, then I'm glad. Let them come for me. I don't care."

His father stares at him like he's a stranger. "You need me—"

Bones almost looks sad as he interrupts his father. "That's where you're wrong. I never needed you. I wanted you. I wanted my dad to be proud. I wanted my dad to love me, but I've realized I don't need you to. I'm surrounded by family and enough love for two lifetimes with or without you, and that's kind of fucking freeing. I'm sorry that you can't see past your own hatred, bias, and issues to the son who was waiting for you to love and accept him. I'm sorry that you will never understand the pure love we have or how happy we are. I'm sorry for you, Father, because you will always be alone, even when you're surrounded by people. I'm sorry that I will never call you Father again, because you don't deserve the title. You may have created me, but this is my life now, and you don't belong in it. Goodbye, Mr. Townsend."

Bones looks at me. "Let's go home, baby. We won't be coming

here again." I glance at his father to see his shocked expression. He genuinely never thought Bones would fight back. He assumed he would cave and give into him.

He should have known better. He brought one hell of a man into the world.

I am so fucking proud of Bones.

Clutching his hand, I let him lead me outside, and when we reach the car, I spin us.

"Are you okay, angel?" I ask him as I cup his face.

He smiles, but it's a sad one. "I really am. I guess I always knew he didn't love me, but seeing it . . . I'm free, Sky. I'm finally free of him. No more trying to get his attention and doing everything to make him proud. This is my life, and I choose you. I choose me. Fuck him. Let him rot alone in his mansion surrounded by money. You're my family, and you're all I need."

"And Evan, Alek, Noah, Mackie, Lally, and Alice. You are so loved, baby. You do not need him. You have us, and we will make sure no one hurts you. When you're sad, we will cheer you up, and when you get a win, we'll celebrate. We will always be with you."

"I just want to be yours," he says. "That's all for now. Let him live in his glass house. In the end, he will only poison himself." He kisses me right in front of the house that scarred him. "Now take me home and show me just how much I am yours."

"Gladly." I grin as I open the door and help him in, my hand skating down to his ass. "And the day after that, and the day after that . . ." I fasten his belt and steal a kiss. "I'll remind you for the rest of our lives, beautiful."

As I get in the car and drive away, I see my boy look back, but he doesn't seem upset.

He seems almost . . . *glad.*

CHAPTER 45
BONES

Skylar is busy practicing for the upcoming race. It's in a few days, and they are determined to win and prove to whoever is trying to sabotage them that they can't stop them. I'm scared for him, but I have to trust that he knows what he's doing. He won't back down from this, and I love that about him. It's his passion, and I know he's going to win that title.

There will be other titles and wins, but this one is more important than ever now.

> Bones: Don't forget to eat. I ordered delivery for all of you.

> Stalker: God, I love you. I'm going to show you how much with my mouth tonight.

Biting back my grin, I shake my head.

> Bones: Eat, drink, and practice. Don't make me watch you lose. My boy doesn't lose.

> Stalker: Not a fucking chance, angel. I'll win and then spend all night letting you fuck this champion.

"Earth to Bones," Lally calls.

I jerk my head up and drop my phone. "Sorry," I mutter. I don't see Lally much. I don't think Evan even does, to be honest. It's like she's pulled away, which is exactly why I'm here. I know everyone is concerned. "So how are you?"

"Really?" she scoffs. "You aren't the type for small talk. What's up, hot stuff? We're friends and all, you know, bonded over serial killers, but we aren't close enough to be getting all emotional over tea."

She nods at the table on the quad we occupy.

"We are worried, that's all," I admit.

"What, did you stage an intervention?" She laughs. "I'm fine. No one's worried. Don't be so dramatic."

"Of course we are." I frown, but she forces a smile.

"I hear you and race boy are together. Tell me, is he good in bed?" I arch a brow at her obvious tactic, but she looks desperate to escape our talk, so I sigh and allow her to change the subject. Hopefully, Evan will have more luck with her, but as long as she knows she has us, that's all that matters.

"I love him," I tell her.

"Damn, never thought I'd see the day. I guess that means I'm the only single one." She smirks, but it seems wrong.

"Lally, we've been through hell. Serial killer survivors, remember? I'm here if you need to talk or just be with someone. I can never replace Tommy—"

She swallows, and I wince.

"But we're your friends."

"Got it." She smiles, but again, it doesn't reach her eyes. I know what it's like to hide, run, and deflect all too well.

"Bones! Lally!" Alice calls, and I wave as she heads our way with a huge smile.

"Well, I better go." Lally leaps up, grabs her bag, toasts me with her herbal tea, then hurries away, leaving me stunned as Alice reaches our table.

"Lally!" Alice calls to her retreating back, and she seems to slump as she watches her leave.

"She's avoiding you too, huh?" I ask carefully, seeing her pain.

"Something like that," she mutters as she sits, looking dejected. Alice has grown up a lot since everything happened, but sometimes she is still so innocent that she makes me want to protect her.

Reaching over, I pat her hand. "She'll come around, just keep trying."

"Thanks." She perks up. "Look at you, trying to comfort me. Skylar has really done a number on you." She wiggles her eyebrows, and I groan. "It's cute! How are you guys?"

"We were talking about you," I point out.

"And I don't want to, so come on, one of us should be happy," she pleads. "Are you happy?"

"I am," I admit. "More than I've ever been."

"At least that night was good for something. It brought you two together, even if it drove Lally and me apart," she mutters before perking up. "Anyway, what did you want to talk to me about? Is it what we were talking about in the meeting?"

I know pushing will only make it worse. Whatever is going on between them is their business. Sometimes, you just have to let two people figure it out, like Skylar and me. "Yes, I was hoping you would help me."

"You got it. Count me in."

Sky and I managed to sneak some time together early in the morning or late at night. Between my lectures, Silent Rose, putting my life back together, and Skylar practicing, we have been super busy, but it's the night before his big race, and we are finally alone with nothing to do.

My legs are draped over his as we sit on our balcony, his hand rubbing my thigh as he sips his wine and looks out at the city, but I only look at him.

He's the best fucking view.

It's quiet and warm, and I'm in my happy place. There are no outside pressures or prying eyes, just him and me and the love between us.

We didn't start in the best way, but I am so glad he never gave up on me because I can't imagine my life without him. His gaze swings to me, and when he catches me staring, his smile only grows. "See something you like, beautiful?"

"Absolutely," I murmur as I kiss his cheek. "But you look worried."

"Just nervous about tomorrow. It's been too quiet since Mackie's accident and the press conference," he admits.

I frown. "You think they will try something on race day?"

"I don't know. I'd like to think they are afraid, but it doesn't seem like them. I'm worried they will do something. What if Mackie gets hurt?"

"Hey." I turn his face until he meets my gaze. "Noah will have a million precautions in place. It's all going to be fine. You are going to win, and those idiots will get caught. That's all there is to it."

"I hope so," he whispers. "I hate waiting. I wish they would just do something, you know? I keep replaying everything in my head."

Lifting onto my knees, I swing my leg over his lap, silencing him. "Then let me take your mind off it."

I take his wine glass as he peers up at me and sip the liquid before I put it down. Tilting his head back, I press my open mouth to his and force him to drink it from me. When I pull back, his eyes burn with hunger. "You'll be fine, but let me show you a preview of what will be waiting for you at home when you win."

His eyes narrow in desire as he leans back. "Show me then, angel. Show me why I should win."

I smirk down at my boy as I reach behind me and slowly tug my shirt up. I hear his groan as I throw it to the side, wearing nothing but boxers. I shimmy them down next as I stand, and then I kneel before him, sliding my hands up his jean-clad legs. His chest rises rapidly now as he reaches out and gulps his wine. He tosses his glass aside as I reach the buckle of his jeans and unzip them. I tug his jeans down, and he lifts his hips so I can ease them off. Running my tongue up each thigh then back down, I tease him before kissing up his legs, ignoring his hard cock as I slide up and straddle him. My hands fist his shirt before I rip it open to expose his chest. I run my tongue teasingly around his nipple, then he grabs my chin and jerks me up. He kisses me, but I pull away, wagging my finger.

"Uh-uh, I wasn't done," I tease.

His eyes are harsh now, but he leans back, his face flushed from wine and desire as I slide my body across his, rolling my hips and rubbing myself against him as I sweep my hands down his chest. "I love your chest. It's one of my favorite parts of you. So thick, so perfect . . ."

"What's the other part?" he asks, his voice tight.

"Your thighs." I press against his cock. "So big and easy for me to balance on."

"What else?" he growls, watching me with fire in his eyes.

I smirk as I rub against him, winding my hips. "Hmm, I like your arms, the way they bulge as you hold me, and the veins on your forearms."

"What else?" he prompts.

"Your face is nice too," I tease.

He grips my hips, and my eyes widen a fraction before I'm tossed to the side. He flips me and pushes me onto all fours, pressing his dick against my ass as he grabs my hair and yanks my head up until his mouth brushes my ear. "And this? Do you like my cock, angel? Isn't it your favorite part of me?" He pushes the tip inside me, and I bite back my groan, even as I widen my stance on the cushions. His tongue darts out to lick my lobe before he bites down. "Well?"

"I can't remember. I guess you'll have to remind me," I taunt.

"Remember what you said," he warns, and his other hand anchors on my thigh as he pulls away. I frown, about to protest, before he slams into me, forcing his length all the way inside me.

My cry fills the air, but neither of us cares.

He pulls out and slams back in, making me fall forward, but he drags me back up, working himself into me. Pleasure and pain courses through me as his hand slides from my hip and circles my length, playing with my piercings. "Do you remember now?"

"Your hands . . . I like your hands."

"Bratty boy," he mutters as he bites my neck. "Fine, have it your way."

He keeps me pinned under him, not moving, and I frown as I hear rustling.

Sky wraps my discarded shirt around my eyes, blindfolding me. "Focus on me," he snarls as he fights my body, pushing deeper as I arch back and take more. "That way you'll never forget your favorite part of me again."

I can't see, and it seems to heighten every sensation—the soft give of the cushion below me, his skin sliding down my back as he kneels behind me, our scents, and the red wine in the air. It all becomes too much, and when he pulls out and pushes into me, I scream.

"That's it, angel. Scream for me. Let everyone hear. Scream until the cops come," he snarls as he tugs me back onto his length, fucking me hard and fast. The furniture rocks on the balcony with how fast he claims me. My breath comes in gasps, my cries coming out loudly. Without the sight of the skyline, it's easy to forget where we are, but a soft breeze rolls over me and heightens my pleasure.

His hands dent my inked skin as he drives into me from behind.

"Sky," I beg.

"That's it, beautiful. Say my name . . . Scream it," he orders, his voice tight as he powers into me, still gripping my cock. I roll my hips into his hand before pushing back to take more.

I can't handle it anymore. My balls draw up, and red-hot pleasure arcs through me, spilling over as I bellow. I lock up below him as my ass tightens around him, and he groans against my neck, burying himself deep inside me as I feel his cum fill me.

I can't hear much over my pounding heart and heavy breathing, my eyes straining in the darkness as I slump.

His hand slides up my back, and he kisses the nape of my neck before tugging the blindfold down. Sky turns my head and kisses me softly. "I bet you remember now, but I'll remind you every day if I have to," he teases into my kiss.

"You better." I grin as he wraps me in his arms and tugs me down. I cuddle against him, happy and sated, his smile reflecting mine.

CHAPTER 46

SKYLAR

I know my boy is safe with Alek, Noah, and Evan, but I still look for him after my interviews. As expected, many people are curious about the attacks, but I skip over those questions like Noah advised and focus on our race.

We'll be starting soon, so everyone is at the track. I'm alone, and I drink water in the silence for a moment since I know when I step out there, everything will change. One way or another, I will make history today. I have to win this for Mackie, Noah, Bones . . . and me.

"Well, well, well," Conall says, and I turn to see him holding his helmet, heading my way from his pit. "Is the great Skylar Warren nervous?"

"Not even a little." I smirk. "You?"

He grins, running his eyes over me. "Not for a second. I'll win today, while you'll be the last to cross that line—if you make it at all." Whistling, he saunters out, and I watch him go.

A bad feeling builds in my stomach, but I can't let them down. He's just trying to freak me out. It's a last-ditch effort to stop me from competing so they can retain their titles.

Blowing out a calming breath, I close my eyes and remember my boy's words this morning as he helped me dress.

Focus on the finish line, nothing and nobody else. I'll be waiting for you, so come and get me.

He knows how to motivate me, that's for sure. Opening my eyes once more, I tilt my chin up, smile, and step out. The crowd screams and music plays, but the din turns deafening when I step out onto the track. I search the stands until I find him.

He's shouting with the others, wearing my name on his jacket as he jumps between Evan and Alek. I blow him a kiss and head over to Mackie. We bump fists and offer each other confident nods.

"This is what it's all been for, brother," I tell him.

"Time to bring it home," he says. "Lead the way, and I'll protect your ass. Show them what we are made of."

Nodding, I head to my car and shove on my gloves as I take one last look at my boy. He's grinning and clapping with everyone. He's right. I can do this. I've raced a thousand times before.

It's just like any other race, only this time, I won't just be bringing home money. I'll also be a champion.

I know what to do, as does my body.

Shoving my helmet on, I climb into my car and turn on the headset.

"All good?" Noah asks.

"All good here, old man," I tease.

"All good," Mackie replies.

"Remember our plan. Stick to it and you'll cross that line," Noah says. "I don't like their attitudes today. Stay safe, okay? We've taken every precaution, but I want this to go smoothly."

He feels the anticipation in the air as well. It's been too quiet.

Something like this only revs up, it doesn't slow down or stop, but I have to trust that I can deal with whatever will happen.

We get into line, and the lights flash red repeatedly. Noah can't hit me because he's too far, so it's now or never. "Noah, if your boy wins, are you going to reward him?"

"What are you talking about?" Noah snaps. "Focus."

"I'm talking about Mackie. Are you going to give him a kiss as a reward?"

"Skylar!" they both bark, and I chuckle.

"You know everyone can hear this," Noah hisses.

"Good, they'll help me hold you to it. Besides, I plan on dramatically kissing my boy, so no one will be looking at you. You're welcome, Macks."

"I hate you," he mutters as the lights flash orange.

"If you win, I'll reward you both—not sexually. Skylar, get your mind out of the gutter."

"Was going to say you're not my type, old man. I prefer them young, pretty, and a beast in bed." I chuckle as I rev and prepare. We go quiet, my heart slows, and adrenaline pumps through me. My body knows this feeling better than its own heartbeat.

Orange.

Orange.

Green.

I'm off before it fully flashes, Mackie right at my side. We shoot out in front since that's where we're starting, with the others hunting us. I don't particularly like it, but it's something we have worked on and planned for.

Mackie and I form a block that lasts the first lap. Blizzard and Red Check try to pass us, but we manage to stop them from slipping by. On the second lap, they have figured it out, and they trick Mackie into moving and soar past.

Patience, I remind myself. I make it look like I mess up and slow to keep pace with him, and four cars shoot past—two Blizzard and two Red Check. Smirking, I speed after them.

The hunter is back.

"You take those two. I'll take Conall and his wingman," I tell Mackie.

"Got it, brother. Let's clear the way."

I let him get in front so we form a line. He rides their ass the next two corners before slipping past, and I follow in his wake until we are behind Henry from Blizzard and Wills from Red Check. As we shoot onto the next straightaway, Mackie jerks to the left and I swing out, using the momentum to drive behind them.

"Yes, brother!" Mackie calls, and I don't bother looking back because I know he'll block them.

I accelerate, as do they, until we pull away from the pack, Mackie keeping them back. This is between us.

My aim is the Blizzard car, Conall's, and he's my entire focus as we head into the final lap.

It all comes down to this. Pushing my engine as fast as it can go, I let the rest of the world fall away. My gloved hands clench on the wheel as I shift the gear and fly around the next corner. They are just a little ways in front now, but I'm catching up while letting them think they are safe.

That bad feeling from earlier has disappeared. I thought they might have fucked with my car, but as I push it to its limits, I know Noah's precautions paid off.

Toma from Red Check, who's hot on Conall's ass, suddenly swerves and falls back. I keep going, speeding toward him. It could be a trick to make me slow down.

"You see this, Noah?" I ask.

"Keep going," he advises.

"Got it." I shift into the highest gear, the speedometer maxing out, but suddenly, his car swerves and starts to spin. Smoke fills the air as he fishtails across the track in front of me.

Toma is totally out of control, and realization hits me.

It isn't my car they fucked with, or even Mackie's.

It's the other team, and as he slows to a stop in the track, I have a choice—hit him and kill us both or try to avoid it and crash. I'll get hurt, but there is only one option, right? Blizzard did this. I know it. They fucked up Red Check's car, expecting this to happen.

"Skylar!" Noah roars.

My hard-won instincts from the streets are the only thing that give me the ability to avoid killing us both, but as I fishtail to avoid him. I have a white-knuckle grip on the wheel to hold it, but the car hits the edge of the track and throws us.

I'm going too fast, which is what he was betting on.

For a moment, I'm weightless, then I crash back down.

I hear the crunch as my body is thrown. I can barely see, barely know which way is up as I roll before I come to a stop against the outer barrier.

Everything is fuzzy, and my head is still spinning.

There's pain in my shoulder and leg.

I still feel like I'm tumbling, even though I know I'm not, but my body doesn't seem to care. I feel hot and cold at the same time, adrenaline forcing me to shake.

Blinking, I realize I'm sideways in the car. The hood is smashed up into the glass and smoke billows from it. As I slowly turn my head, my vision spins as I see the other side of the car is completely wrecked.

The sound of sizzling reaches me, and I know I need to move.

I can't seem to though. My body won't respond, and my brain is slow to process as well.

"Get out of there, Skylar!" Noah roars.

"Sky, I'm coming. Hang on, I'm coming!" Mackie pleads as I hear engines roaring my way.

I lift my head groggily, scanning the crowd numbly as something drips into my eyes. The audience is on their feet in horror, and there's my boy, hopping the fence and rushing past Noah, his eyes wide and terrified.

I try to smile, but I'm on the verge of blacking out.

Something is very wrong.

I realize I'm not getting out in time as the dripping increases, and oil spills into the car.

My heart crashes just like I did as the truth hits me, causing more pain than this crash did.

I'm going to break his heart, just like everyone else did.

"Sorry, angel," I whisper, knowing it will be my last words.

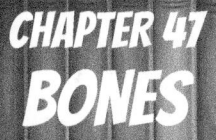

CHAPTER 47
BONES

I see it happening, but there is nothing I can do.

People scream around me as Skylar's car flips over and over. I'm moving before I know it, jumping over the barrier. Arms catch me as I yell his name and watch his car jerk to a stop.

"Skylar!" I bellow. The crowd is crying and screaming. Everyone is waiting. The drivers left on the track are forgotten. Winners and losers no longer matter.

All anybody wants now is not to lose someone.

"Bones," Alek whispers, holding me. Noah is at our side with his headphones off, tears in his eyes as we stare at the wreck.

"No, no, no! He's alive!" I elbow Alex and slip from his arms, scrambling across the track. I don't care about the other cars driving around. He's all I care about. I catch sight of him as I hit the grass on the edge of the track, drawing close, when flames burst from the engine, throwing me backward. I hit the grass and cover my eyes before I scramble to my knees to see bright red flames engulfing the front of the car.

Arms grab me again. I feel tears flowing down my cheeks as the heat of the flames wafts over me, but nothing else matters.

I need to get to him.

"Skylar!" I shout, fighting those trying to block me. His car is right there, and he's in the driver's seat. His helmet turns, and he sees me coming. His eyes widen as flames consume the car, and I see resignation in his gaze. "No!"

Despite my own fear, I break out of the hold on me and run toward the love of my life.

I grip the door, hissing as my palms burn, and when I peel them from the metal, my skin is left behind. I ignore it as I yank it open and find Skylar. Blood drips down his face as he blinks. He's too pale. I take his harness off with fumbling fingers. "Get out!" I roar at him.

"Angel," he rasps, blood steadily dripping into his unfocused eyes.

"No!" I scream as I'm torn away. "Skylar!" I beg as I'm dragged to the grassy ground. "Skylar, get out!"

The flames are spreading across the car, turning into a fireball, and I know it will only be seconds until it explodes. "Skylar," I beg through my sobs.

Please, God.

I pray Skylar isn't taken from me, not when I just found him.

We have both suffered so much. This can't be how it ends.

He was supposed to win. We were supposed to celebrate.

"Skylar!" I shout, and I throw my weight forward, crawling as someone tries to hold me back.

His head turns farther, and he sees me heading his way. His eyes widen and horror enters his gaze, causing the haze to dissipate.

The door budges an inch, and then he's climbing from the window. He collapses against the car before stumbling away, dragging one leg behind.

Hope and horror mix within me as he fights the heat and his injuries to reach me.

In that moment, I know love is not a weakness. It makes gods out of us all because my man walks from the flames when he sees me putting myself in danger.

I break free again and rush over, catching him as he collapses. I spin us, throwing my body across his just as the car explodes behind us. Heat slices through the skin on my back. I feel it but I don't care. I stare down into his eyes as I try to pull off his helmet. My hands aren't working properly, but others appear and pull it off so I can finally see his beautiful, bloody face.

"Baby, look at me. You're going to be fine," I promise, tears clogging my voice.

"Angel," he croaks. "Sorry . . . I didn't . . . win."

Sobbing, I lift him into my lap as I hear sirens and people rushing over. "It's okay. You did so well, baby. We're going to go home now, okay? Just stay with me. We'll go home."

"Okay." His voice is soft, and when I glance down, his eyes are fluttering shut.

"No, don't you fucking dare!" I scold. "Skylar Warren, I order you to open your fucking eyes. You promised you would never leave me, so open your fucking eyes. You fucking stay with me. We are going home. We'll have breakfast, and you can hold me, and we'll watch those shitty shows you like. Please, Sky, please don't leave me like everyone else. I don't want to be alone."

His eyes close, blocking my view of my everything.

"Sky, just hold on." The sirens draw closer as I press a kiss to his head. "They are coming, baby. Listen to them, they are coming. You'll be fine. You'll be fine."

His hand drops from my side, and something inside me drops with it.

Flames continue to run out of control, but I can't look away from his pale, bloodstained face.

This man has become my everything.

He isn't afraid of death, speed, or heights, but he is afraid of losing me.

It's in this moment that I know true fear.

I don't remember much of the ride to the hospital, but once he's rushed inside, I'm left in the waiting room.

People try to talk to me, but I just stare at the doors he disappeared through.

Someone touches my side, and I whirl around to see Evan. His face is streaked with tears, and Noah and Alek are talking to some police officers and nurses.

"Bones, let's get you a seat." He touches my hand and jerks back. "Oh fuck. Your hands!"

I glance down as Evan gasps, and it's only when I look at my palms that the pain registers. They are a blistered, bloody mess. "Oh my God, Bones! You need to be seen."

"Sky—"

"Is being taken care of. He would want us to look after you," Evan orders, completely in control while I just stand here like a fool. "Excuse me!"

A nurse rushes past, and Evan's eyes narrow. "I said excuse me! Someone better take a look at my friend's hands before I find the closest fucking doctor and drag him here!" he roars, and the whole room falls silent before he forces a smile. "Please."

Alek and Noah head my way as the door opens. I see Mackie and the others rush in, but I focus on the doors.

"Are you okay?" Alek asks.

I can't answer him.

How can I be okay? Skylar isn't here, and I don't even know if he's alive.

"Bones, let this nice doctor look at your hands," Evan demands. He tugs me away, but I refuse to go into a side room. Instead, they inspect my hands in the waiting room. They are bad, but I won't lose them. I don't know what they do, but they are wrapped up like a mummy when the medical staff walks away.

"It's been too long. Where is he?" I beg Evan. Jumping to my feet, I head to the door, and a nurse steps out. "How is Skylar Warren?"

"He's getting the best care. Please, take a seat, sir."

"I'm going in to see him." I try to move past her, but she blocks me.

"It's family only," the nurse says.

"I am his family! We are his family!" I tell her. "Please, please."

"No. Take a seat. We will update you when we can," she says firmly.

Arms drag me back and push me into a chair.

"It's going to be okay," Evan promises. "Just let them work, okay?"

It's been hours. We have heard nothing, and my numbness has worn off, morphing into anger and fear.

"Fuck this." I climb to my feet, and everyone surges forward, blocking the doors. It's the fifth time in the last hour they have done this. I think they are worried about what I will do if I get through.

"No, Bones," Alek snaps, tired of telling me.

"Fucking move," I snarl.

"Bones—"

"Don't fuck with me right now, Alek. That is my man in there. That is the fucking love of my life, so get the fuck out of my way."

"Or what?" he asks. "What are you going to do? You're a lawyer, Bones, not a thug—"

"That just means I know how to kill someone and get away with it. If you don't move right this fucking second, I'm going to make Evan a fucking widow."

"Hey," Evan mutters.

"Move," I demand, squaring up to him. We stare each other down, but the door suddenly opens and a doctor peeks out.

"Uh, I think you should come through. The patient woke when he heard you, and he needs to rest."

"He's awake?" I whisper, forgetting everything else. "Skylar is awake? He's okay?"

The doctor offers me a sad, understanding smile. "He's injured, but he will be okay. He's very lucky. Honestly, it's a miracle he wasn't injured worse."

Not a miracle, just Skylar Warren.

He's a survivor.

"Thank you." I rush past the doctor, ignoring everyone else as a helpful nurse points out a room. She was from the ER, so she is probably just sick of dealing with me and knows not to get between us now.

Heading to the private room, I slide to a stop when Noah steps in before me, blocking the door. He meets my eyes, and I glare at him.

"Maybe we should let him rest," Noah begins.

"Noah, Skylar likes and respects you, which is the only reason I haven't punched you, but if you try to stop me, I'm going to cut off your balls and make them into dice to hang from my mirror. Understood?"

Noah's eyes widen. "Jesus." He covers his balls but still hesitates.

There's a hacking chuckle from the room, but it ends in a groan. "You better let him in, old man. My boy isn't playing with you."

Noah moves aside with a sigh, and I burst into the room. Tears fill my eyes when I see him in the bed, all my strength fleeing at the sight of him. He looks so pale. His arm is wrapped, his leg is elevated, and machines are stationed all over. Seeing him like this, I realize how truly close I came to losing him.

He smiles when he sees me. "Hi, angel."

Choking on a sob, I run over and fling myself into his arms. He grunts but holds me, kissing my head. "Shh, I'm okay. I'm sorry if I scared you."

I pull back and smack his chest. "Scared me? Skylar, you terrified me. I was so fucking worried. You were hurt so—"

"Shh, it's okay. I'm here. Breathe with me."

Taking a deep breath, I nod and calm down.

His smile only grows. "I heard you claim me." He wiggles his eyebrows. "All it took was almost dying again. Not a bad trade."

"Don't even joke," I snap.

"Sorry, angel." He looks down as he tries to twine our fingers together. "What happened? Are you hurt?"

"Oh, just some burns from when I tried to get you out of the car," I admit.

"Burns? Angel, God." He sits up with a frown. I'm unsure what he's doing when he swings his legs over the side of the bed.

He struggles to get up, all the while yelling, "Doctor! Doctor!"

"Skylar," I hiss, pushing him back. "I'm fine!"

"Doctor!"

The door opens and Noah bursts in, followed by Mackie, Alek, Evan, and the others. "What's wrong?" Alek asks. "Are you in pain—"

"Bones, his hands . . ." Skylar's eyes are wild as he holds my wrists delicately. "He needs a doctor."

I sigh. "Skylar, I've been seen."

"No, you need to be checked again. Alek, get a doctor," he snaps.

"Skylar," Alek begins, but Skylar glares, and he holds up his arms and disappears. A moment later, two doctors are dragged back into the room and pushed toward me.

"Don't ask me. I'd do the same if it were my boy," Evan mutters at his side as the doctors look at us.

"His hands—his beautiful, perfect hands." Skylar points. "Check them over."

"Sir, I'm a neurosurgeon—"

"Then that means you're qualified," Skylar barks. "I will donate enough money to fund this entire hospital, but I want my boyfriend checked."

"Sky," I hiss, but he ignores me as the doctors share a look before gesturing to the chair next to the bed. I sit, because what else am I supposed to do, and they carefully start to unwrap my hands.

I blush under the scrutiny and all the soft chuckles of those around us as two doctors recheck my hands, even though Skylar is the injured one.

"Oh, angel, look at your beautiful hands," Sky whispers. "Why would you do that?"

I meet his gaze, my brows drawing together. "You were in danger. How could I not?"

"Fuck, that's so romantic," I hear, and when we look over, Alek is wiping at his eyes while Evan grins next to him.

I roll my eyes. When the doctors are done, Skylar finally relaxes enough for me to help him back into bed.

"How are you feeling?" I ask.

"Not as bad as I expected. These are some good drugs." He nods at Mackie. "You okay, brother?"

"Me? You're the one who wrecked," he scoffs.

"And the other driver?" Skylar asks.

"He's fine. Engine malfunction," Noah answers, but there is something in his eyes.

"I see." Skylar nods and spares me a smile. "At least I didn't hurt my pretty face, huh, angel? You know you like to look at it when—"

"Okay, enough." I cover his mouth. "I think the drugs are too strong."

I lean back, keeping my hand over his, then I let him speak to Noah, Alek, Mackie, then Evan. Everyone has something to say, and he's a good sport about it, but as everyone gets settled, I see something pass over him—understanding.

So many of us surround Skylar, and his eyes widen as he looks around at the room filled with love. I know he still struggles to accept it, since he came from a broken home where he had no one, but now he has an entire family around him.

He glances at me, confusion and happiness in his eyes. Brushing his hair back, I place a gentle kiss on his lips. "They are all here for you, babe. You are so very fucking loved. Never doubt that." I kiss him again. "And if you ever try to leave me again, I'll kill you myself, understood?"

"I wasn't trying to leave, angel," he defends. "My car was on fire."

"Not good enough. You don't get to leave me. Death can't have you. You said you were mine," I warn. I'm being unreasonable, but he simply smiles.

"Yes, angel," he promises.

"Good boy." I kiss him and sit down when there's a loud clap at the door.

"Alright, boys, time to go. He needs to rest. You can all come back tomorrow." It's a nurse, and she gives us a nononsense look.

"I'll be in the waiting room just in case," Noah says, but he rounds up the others.

"You too, pretty boy," the nurse calls as she shuts the curtains and walks around the room.

"No." I look back at Skylar. "I'm not leaving him."

"It's family only—"

"He is family," Skylar says with a soft smile. "He's my soon-to-be husband. He can stay, can't he?" He aims a sweet smile at her, and I see her softening when she wouldn't before. That's just Skylar Warren's charm. "I don't want to be alone right now."

"Fine, fine, but no funny business. I mean it." She shows him the buzzer then leaves. I see Noah lingering outside the door and turn back to Sky. His eyes close as the drugs kick in.

"Get some sleep, babe," I murmur.

"You'll stay?" he slurs.

"I'm not going anywhere," I promise as I hold his hand as best as I can.

He's asleep within minutes, and I carefully slide my hand back and cover him with the blanket.

"I'll be right back," I murmur, even though he's sleeping. "You've spent so long protecting me. Now it's my turn to keep you safe."

When I'm sure he isn't going to wake up and find me gone, I slip from the room and find Noah in the waiting room. I nod my head, and he follows me down a side hallway. I turn to face him, knowing my expression is like thunder.

"I want to know everything you know," I demand, crossing my arms before dropping them due to my hands.

"Bones," he begins, no doubt about to give me some bullshit excuse.

"Don't fight me on this. Give me every detail. We're going to catch this bastard, and I'm going to string him up by his balls."

"Why do you always go for the balls?" Noah mutters, but he nods and sits in the chair. I sit in the one next to him.

"I know where to strike to make it hurt, remember that. Tell me."

For the next hour, he runs through everything he knows, and I assemble the facts in my head, working through all the pieces. "So you think it is the one who won the race, Conall from Blizzard?"

"It has to be. If he loses his title, he stands to lose his sponsors. People do stupid things for money. I never thought he would go this far, and I can't prove it." Noah scrubs at his face. "It's my job to keep him safe, and I failed."

I place my hand on his back. "Skylar knows you did everything you could. He looks up to you so much. He doesn't blame you for this. He and I know better than anyone just how wicked people can be. You can't control others' actions, but you did everything you could to protect him."

He nods, but the guilt is still eating him up inside. "I'm going to speak to the police again. They know and are investigating, but I worry he will get away with it without proof."

"We won't let him." I stand. "I better get back before Sky wakes. Don't worry, Noah, it will all work out in the end. Trust me."

"Bones?" I turn as he calls my name. "You're kind of terrifying. I'm glad he has you. Sky might seem strong, but everyone has their breaking point. Everyone needs somebody."

"No, I'm lucky to have him. Go get some rest, Noah. We have work to do."

"We?" he calls.

"We," I confirm. "They came after my family. I won't let that go."

Before he can question what I plan to do, I head back to Sky's room, shut the door, and walk over to his bed.

Climbing in alongside Skylar, I lay my head on his chest as he sleeps. He sighs and drapes an arm around me, pulling me closer. My eyes stay on his face the entire night.

I almost lost him today, and whoever tried to take him from me is going to regret it.

Skylar might be from the streets, but I grew up learning how to cover up crimes. It's time to put that to use.

"I love you," I whisper, "and I'll make them pay for hurting you. I promise, Sky. I'll make them all pay."

CHAPTER 48
SKYLAR

I'm discharged the very next day, which I think the hospital is grateful for since my boy is a drill sergeant when it comes to my care. Camera crews are set up at all times outside, so Noah causes a distraction, and Alek and Evan pick us up out back.

My leg has a slight fracture, and my shoulder was dislocated, but it was put back into place. My head injury was the worst, and I need to keep an eye on it for a concussion, but all in all, I was very fucking lucky. Most would have broken bones, lost limbs, or worse.

Bones's hands were rebandaged today. The doctor assured me they would work fine. I hate that he will have permanent scars because of me, but he doesn't seem bothered by it. I know I should go after Conall, who did this, but I'm tired, and I just want my boy. Besides, the police are involved now. We spoke to them this morning, and they assured us they will catch who is behind it.

I have no doubt he's going to pay for what he did. Fucking with us in secret is one thing, but causing an accident on the track is another. Many others could have died. That is a problem for tomorrow, though, because today, I just want my bed and my boy.

"Have you been online?" Evan asks as he turns in the passenger seat to see us. "You guys are famous right now."

"What do you mean?"

"Well, someone took videos of the accident and caught Bones trying to save you and you collapsing in his arms. It's trending everywhere. You're about to be more famous than ever, Sky."

Bones groans. "More assholes to fight off."

"Don't worry, I'll cheer you on," I joke, and he grins as he rolls his eyes.

"So, what happens now with the next races?" Bones asks, glancing between us. He knows how badly I wanted to win.

"There will be another," Alek replies. "That was only the semifinal anyway. If they allow it, Sky will come back, but he will start last."

"Give them all a miniscule chance." I wink. "Don't worry, your boy will still be a winner."

Bones nods, but I can tell he's worried, so I lean into his shoulder.

"Will you wear a nurse's outfit today?"

"Not a fucking chance," he mutters.

I pout. "But I'm sick."

"You're lucky I'm looking after you at all," he scoffs, but he kisses my head. "We'll be home soon, then you can sleep."

"I'm not tired," I say, but a yawn ruins my denial, and they all laugh.

When we pull up outside our apartment building, Bones gets out and grabs my stuff as I slide to the edge of the open door.

"Sky?" I glance back to Evan and Alek, Bones waiting just outside the car.

"He was really worried. I've never seen him like that. He was going to fight the entire hospital to get to you. Go easy on him," Evan warns.

"Get some rest, brother," Alek calls.

"Thank you for looking after him," I tell them as I let Bones help me out and guide me toward our apartments. I need to connect them or buy another one for us.

We practically live together now, so we might as well have one place we can call home. Maybe I should ask him? Nah, I'll just do it or move everything into mine.

By the time we make it inside, my body is twinging in pain. Bruises cover nearly every inch of me, and whatever drugs they gave me are still in my system. Bones helps me into bed and then snuggles into my side, and before I know it, we are both asleep.

I wake up sometime later to the room being dark and Bones snoring at my side. Slipping from the bed, I open my drawer, pull out the ring sizer, and hurry around to the other side of the bed. Careful of his bandage palms, I slip it onto his finger like they showed me then hide it when he turns over. I make a mental note of the size before I shut the drawer and grab my phone as I head to the kitchen to grab a drink. I'm sipping a glass of water and scrolling through ring pages when he shuffles out.

"Sky?" The panic in his voice is adorable.

"Here, baby." I lock my phone and drop it. "I just wanted a drink."

"You should have woken me. I'd have gotten it for you," he mutters. "You should be resting."

"I'm injured, not dead." I grin. "Besides, you need your sleep. You look exhausted."

"Thanks," he mutters as he heads over and pours a glass of water before hopping up on the counter next to me. I slip between his open legs and press my head against his chest, holding him. His arms and legs wrap around me, and we sit like this in the dark, reminding one another we are here and we are okay.

"Were you scared?" he whispers as I pull away to look at him. "When you had the accident?"

I'd be a liar if I said I wasn't and I tell him as much. "Not for me, for you."

He frowns. "Me?"

"Yeah. I knew if something happened to me, you would blame yourself and lock yourself down. You'd never let anyone close again so they couldn't hurt you. You feel everything so deeply, angel, which is why it always hurts you so much, hence you shutting down.

You have the biggest heart of anyone I've ever met, so yes, I was scared."

Cupping my face, he searches my eyes. "Skylar Warren, you are an idiot, but I love you."

"Good." I grin. "Because I'm aching, Nurse Bones. How about you kiss it all better?"

"We aren't sleeping together, Skylar," he states so firmly, I almost grin, but the desire in his eyes screams something else.

"Who said anything about sleeping?" I tease as I lick his lips. He tries to resist. "I need you, angel. All I keep seeing is you fighting flames to get to me. I need to remember we're alive."

"Your injuries—"

"Aren't important. They'll heal." I kiss him softly, and he whimpers. "You claimed me for everyone to see, so it's time I staked mine, don't you think?"

He huffs as he leans back with a grin. "Like you haven't since the first moment we met?"

"Glad you caught on." I pull him to the edge of the counter and lift him with my good arm.

"Sky," he murmurs. "Your arm."

"I only need one to fuck you, angel. Don't worry." I wink as I carry him back to bed. When I lay him down, however, he pulls me after him and carefully arranges me against the headboard.

"Let me do all the work," he murmurs as he straddles my lap. "Just lie back and let me take care of you."

My hands meet his hips as he strips us so we are both naked. Reaching over to the bedside table, he uncaps the bottle of lube and covers my cock, sliding his hand up and down until my head falls back. The pain in my body is forgotten under his expert touch.

"Angel," I murmur. "Fuck, you're driving me crazy. Please."

I rarely beg, and his eyes flare as he releases my dick and slides forward. His hands hit the headboard so as not to injure my shoulder as he lifts. With my one good hand, I help guide him down. He works himself onto my length, his hot, tight ass wrapping around my cock before he lifts and lowers, taking me deeper each time until I'm buried, and we both pant.

Leaning down, he kisses me as he starts to move. He sets a slow pace as he fucks me, bouncing on my cock while I suck his tongue. He pulls away, his head falling back, and my gaze sweeps down his incredible body. Watching his inked skin roll above me while his hot ass grips me makes my balls ache. I fight off my pending release, letting him ride me.

His gaze clashes with mine as he slides one hand down his chest and circles his dick, stroking himself as he fucks me.

"Angel," I groan. "You look so fucking good above me."

"I know." He smirks. "You love watching me, don't you?"

I nod, unable to speak as I stave off my pleasure, wanting this to last forever, but then he reaches down and rolls my balls. I groan his name as I pull him down, burying deep inside him, and he leans down and kisses me as I fill him with my cum. When his hand jerks between us, he whimpers into my mouth and spills over my stomach.

Our kiss turns sloppy, then he falls forward and lies on my chest. I wrap my good arm around him, kissing his head, our bodies still connected.

"You're a good nurse," I tease.

He chuckles as he lifts his head. "Don't ever try to leave me again, Sky. I mean it."

"Never," I promise as I kiss his forehead. "I'll always be right here."

I've been forced to rest for three fucking days.

I'm going crazy. My only saving grace is having my boy at my side. I think that's why he forced Alek and Evan to come over for a movie day—okay, apparently they volunteered, but still.

I'm sitting on the sofa next to them as Bones heads my way and hands me a drink before he goes to sit. I slap his ass out of habit, and he spins around, glaring as he rubs it while I blink innocently.

"Sky, that hurt," he snaps.

"I didn't hear you complaining last night when you begged for more until it hurt." I smirk. His face turns bright red, and Alek groans while Evan laughs. Evan reaches over, and we high-five as Bones stomps into the kitchen to hide.

Winking at Evan, I get up and slip my arms around Bones, my lips brushing his ear. "How about I kiss it better tonight, angel?" He tries to elbow me, but I turn him and back him into the fridge. "I'll make it better. I'll eat your pretty ass as long as you forgive me and it doesn't hurt anymore."

"I can still hear, just so you know," Alek calls as he turns the TV up. "Get a room!"

"This is our room!" I retort as I wiggle my eyebrows at Bones, who's smiling now.

"We have an exclusive report that lead race car driver, Conall Frost from Blizzard, has been arrested in connection with the accident of fellow driver, Skylar Warren—"

We turn and hurry back to the couch, our eyes on the news. *"It's said Conall threatened Warren, saying he would not finish the race, and when the other car malfunctioned, it caused Skylar Warren to make the heroic choice between hitting a fellow driver or avoiding the other car and injuring himself."*

"I'm a hero." I nudge Bones, who smacks me away.

"Police have not officially confirmed the charges, but it seems likely that Conall was behind the sabotage. Noah of Starfire Racing recently announced their garage was under attack by someone wanting to force them from the championship. We will keep you updated as we find out more, but it doesn't look good for Team Blizzard and Conall."

"Shit," I mutter. "How the hell did they manage that? Surely there's no proof."

"I don't know," Alek mutters. "Last I heard, Noah was searching high and low for evidence, as was Red Check."

"They can't arrest him without something concrete, right?" Evan mutters, no doubt speaking from experience.

Bones is suspiciously quiet, and when I turn to him, he's smirking proudly. "Angel . . . what did you do?"

"Me?" He glances at us. "I just called in some favors. It won't stick forever, but it will provide enough time to find the evidence we need. I also might have asked some people inside to work him over a little."

My eyes widen as I stare at Bones, who simply sips his coffee like a devilish villain.

"Jesus, I always knew he was crazy," Alek mutters.

"Yeah, remind me not to piss him off," Evan responds.

"Marry me," I blurt.

Bones winks and takes another sip. "Now we just need to find evidence." When I just stare, he sighs. "Nobody fucks with what's mine, okay? Drink your tea, it's good for your health."

As he wanders back to the kitchen, I glance at Evan and Alek to see they are both just as confused.

"I'm afraid and turned on," I admit.

"I'm just afraid," Evan comments.

"Team foursome for the win," Alek mutters, making us all laugh.

CHAPTER 49
BONES

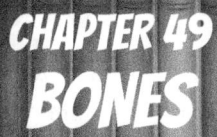

Skylar has finally been cleared to go back to work, and although I want to beg him not to get back into the car, I won't. Racing is his life, so it's a part of mine now, but I'll admit I'm relieved when he comes home that night. I forget all about the case study I'm reading and drag him onto the couch.

We both came so close to losing each other that I know I'll never take another moment with him for granted. I now understand why Alek and Evan never leave each other alone. They nearly lost what they had, and it only made them appreciate it more.

People who are in love used to make me sick, but I guess I'm one of them now.

His head rests on my lap as I stroke his hair. "How was today?"

"Hectic. Everyone wants to see me and check in. Noah and I spoke to the race officials, and as long as I'm medically cleared, I can race, but right now, everything is on hold for the investigation, so I don't even know when the next race will be."

"That's good though, right? It gives you time to heal and focus on racing, not almost being murdered." It's a joke, but it comes out pained.

Sitting up, he pulls me onto his lap, and I curl up against him as he strokes my back. "True, and I get more time with you. I guess I was just ready to win the title, but there's time. Anyway, how was your day, angel?"

"Fine," I grumble, and he raises a brow. "Everyone wanted pictures or to talk to me. It seems Evan was right. I'm somewhat of a celebrity. I don't know why it isn't due to my sparkling personality," I deadpan, and we both grin. "It was fine. I was given some extensions since I will struggle to write for a while. I've been toying with some dictation software in the meantime. I know my dad started me on this path, but I really do want to be a lawyer—not because of him, but because I want to be able to protect those I love. Plus, I'm good at it."

"Yeah, you are, my brutal boy." He smirks, tugging me closer as he kisses my forehead. "You can be whatever you want. It's your choice."

Playing with his shirt, I can't bring myself to meet his eyes. "My father called today."

"Oh?" He doesn't seem mad, just curious. "What did he want?"

"I didn't answer," I admit, and I meet his frown as he watches me.

"Bones, he's your father, you're allowed to want him in your life, but if you don't, that's fine as well. This is your decision. Don't make it for me. I just want you to be happy and loved, and if having him in your life is what you want, then I'll bite my tongue and fight him until we're cordial. I'm not saying I won't slap him around a little first . . ."

I smile and cuddle against him. "I don't know if I do want him in my life," I murmur. "Not after everything, you know? He's had twenty years to form a connection with me, and he hurt me every time he had an opportunity, but he's still my father. Maybe that's stupid, but I don't have to decide right now, do I?"

"Not at all. Take all the time you want. It's your life, your choices."

"I choose you," I say without hesitation. "Every time."

His smirk grows as he watches me. "Who knew such a soft man was inside that cold, closed-off boy?"

I narrow my eyes in warning, and he laughs.

"I love it when you're happy, angel, but damn, there's something about seeing you pissed at me." His tongue sweeps along my lips before he bites down. "It makes me want to fuck it out of you."

"You wish, pretty boy," I scoff.

"So you think I'm pretty? Good to know, but I do prefer sex icon, god—"

"Full of yourself?" I interrupt. "Like I haven't seen any other men as attractive as you?"

"What other men? Give me their names right now," he retorts, his eyes flashing with envy.

"You are the most jealous man I have ever met, Skylar Warren," I mutter.

"You know other men?" he exclaims, and I can't help but laugh as he throws me down on the sofa, pinning me against the cushions. My laughter trails off, but my smile remains in place as I drape my arms around his neck. "I love you too, angel, and I will always choose you. You know that."

"Good." I arch up and kiss him softly. "Now, about your promise to fuck it out of me."

"Well, I can't leave my boy waiting." Gently grabbing my hands, he kisses the bandages then places them above my head. "Keep them there, angel. I know you like to cut up my back and mark me, but we can't have you hurting yourself."

He grins as he slides down, stopping to kiss my skin revealed by my partially unbuttoned shirt. I groan his name just as a phone rings, startling us apart. Sky groans, glancing at my phone then back to me. "Ignore it." He slides his tongue farther down my chest, and I want to, but it starts ringing again.

I grab it and sit up. "What?" I snap.

There's just a heavy sigh, and then an unsure voice says, "Si? It's me."

"How did you get this number?" I ask as Sky shuffles closer.

He presses his ear to the phone, so I hit speaker so he can listen too.

"From your dad—wait, wait, before you hang up, just give me a moment, okay? I've been a horrible person, I know. I just . . . I want to say goodbye. I don't want to leave while everything is like this between us. No matter what you think or what happened, you are one of the most important people in my life, and for a long time, you were the only person. I know I have no right to ask, but I was hoping we could meet up and clear the air. We can say goodbye for real this time, you know?"

I hesitate, looking at Skylar.

"It's up to you, angel," he whispers.

"Si, please? I don't want to walk away like this. I fucked up, and I don't deserve a moment of your time, but I'm asking for it. You were right. You deserve to move on. I want you to be happy."

Biting my lip, I debate his words. "When?"

"Now? I have a plane to catch in the morning," he replies softly.

I scoff. At least he didn't just disappear this time. "Fine, text me the location." I hang up and look at Sky. "You know this means nothing, right? I don't love him, not anymore, and never the way I love you."

"I know." He kisses my cheek. "I trust you, angel. You don't have to explain anything to me. I think it's important you go. He's right. You never got closure. Maybe if you do, it will help you move on."

I sigh. "What did I do to deserve you, Skylar?"

"I don't know, but you can spend all night making it up to me." He wiggles his eyebrows as I laugh and stand, grabbing my coat and keys, and my phone vibrates with a text.

"Need me to come with you?" he asks.

"No, I've got this. I need to do this alone." I kiss him gently. "I won't be long, and then we can start where we left off."

"We better. Love you, angel," he yells as I reach the door.

Shaking my head, I flip him off and head out, knowing he's right. I never moved on, and part of me still feels trapped at that bus stop. It's time to say goodbye once and for all.

I took a taxi since my hands are still wrapped, but when it drops me at the address, I almost can't believe it. The arched stop looks the exact same as it did back then. It's set back from two major roads, so the noise of traffic doesn't reach here, and the suburban houses are dark at this time. He's already here, sitting in the exact spot I did five years ago, but this time, he's waiting for me.

Taking a deep breath, I head over to him.

"Thanks for coming," he says, smiling.

It was once a smile that disarmed me and made me happy, but all it does now is remind me of memories we shared. It doesn't make me happy nor sad—it just is. That's when I realize I've already moved on.

Skylar healed what this man broke, but I owe it to that lovestruck boy who waited all night. I owe it to the kid who didn't know why everyone thought it was wrong to hold his best friend's hand or want to kiss him.

I owe it to myself to close that door once and for all.

Aro is my past, but Sky is my future.

I promised to hear him out, though, so I stop before him.

"Why here?" I ask as I stare at the scratched paint of the seat I spent hours waiting on all those years ago.

"Did you wait for me that night?" he asks, staring at the ground.

"Yes," I answer without shame as I sit hesitantly as far from him as I can.

He's quiet, and I can feel him watching me, so I glance over. "Well?" I prompt. "I'm here. You wanted to talk, so talk."

"Your dad was right. You're sharper now."

I stand to leave, and he catches my wrist to stop me. I glance down at where he touches me.

"I'm sorry, please stay."

I shake off his grasp, feeling like it burnt me and not in a good way, then I sit and wait.

"I wanted to say sorry, Si, for not telling you and leaving like that. It was a shitty thing to do. I had my reasons, but that's not an excuse. I hurt you, and I'm sorry," he says, and I arch a brow.

"Is that all? After all this time, that's it? You didn't just break up with me or something. Aro, you disappeared. I thought you were dead or hurt. I spent years searching for you, blaming myself. I became a

shadow of who I was, so excuse me if a simple apology doesn't cut it.
"

"Will anything I say make it better?" he asks after a pause.

"Probably not," I reply, "but you can start with the truth."

"Your dad paid me, and I took the money. I panicked, Si. I was a kid, and he had all this power and influence and he was terrifying, so I ran."

"Where to?" I ask.

"Does it matter?"

"I suppose not," I say, and it doesn't. Whether it was ten miles or a hundred, he was still gone, and I was left picking up the pieces.

"I did love you, Si. I need you to know that. I was just scared," he whispers.

"So was I. Didn't you ever think of that? I was terrified, leaving my life behind and knowing some people wouldn't like us together. I was so scared, but I knew as long as I had you, it would be worth it," I retort. "Then you were gone, and I was alone again and so fucking confused why I wasn't good enough for anyone."

His eyes search my face, and I wonder what he sees. "I'm sorry," he says, and that's what it boils down to, doesn't it? He's sorry, and I'm done.

There is nothing else to be said. Maybe he sees that, but he suddenly scoots closer.

"I mean it, Si. I'm so sorry. I never wanted to hurt you. I love you." His words are laced with desperation.

He leans in, and my eyes widen as his close, his lips moving toward mine. I shove my hand between us and push him back.

"What are you doing?" I hiss.

"You said you spent years searching for me, so I thought maybe you still cared about me the way I care about you," he says. "I still love you, Si. You're all I thought about every day while I was gone, wondering how you were doing, if you were okay—"

"Stop," I bark as I move farther away. That's the difference between Aro and Sky—not that I'm comparing them because I'm not.

Sky would never spend one single day away from me. He wouldn't miss me because he wouldn't give up.

"You were my first love, Aro, and I should thank you for that. No matter what happened after, you helped me put a name to those feelings. We were kids, and for a while, we found sanctuary with each other, but people change and life moves on, and I have. Yes, I'm thankful we had each other when we did, and I don't know if I would have survived my childhood without you, but I have Skylar now, and I love him more than anything in this world. We are building a future together, and I'm so excited for it. I know he'll never leave or hurt me." I smile at him. "You were my first everything, Aro, but he will be my last. Do you understand?"

"You always said you'd love me forever," he says with a hurt smile.

"I think part of me always will, but not in the same way. I love that you taught me how to smile, how to say I love you, and how to trust someone, but I don't love you—not anymore. I'm just thankful for you. I am not the same person I was then. My favorite color isn't pink anymore, and I don't watch reruns of old action films. I grew up and my heart changed, and now it's his. I don't know if we would have lasted, maybe we would have, but what I do know is that it doesn't matter anymore. We will never know, and I'm okay with that."

"You say you changed, but you are still unapologetically you," he remarks. "I like this newfound confidence. I think I'd like to get to know this new version of you."

There is something so bitterly beautiful about your first love. It teaches you lessons, and I think you always carry them with you no matter what.

Some say your first love is always your greatest, but I think they are wrong.

It's the love that comes after, the one that heals your heartbreak and puts you back together, that teaches you it's okay to fall again.

"I don't want to look back at us and feel pain anymore," I tell him. "I want to be able to smile about it. You brought me a whirlwind type of madness, but he brings me peace. I won't hurt that. I don't want you to be a part of my life."

"Give me a chance to make you happy again," he pleads, covering my hand, but I jerk mine away from his. I tried being nice, but it isn't working. I can't even believe the direction this is going. How does he think we could ever go back to the way we were, even without Skylar in the picture?

"You aren't listening to me. You left me, and I still had all these feelings, all this love to give, and I had to choose to drown in it or share it with someone else. Skylar and I aren't meant to be friends, family, or partners. We are meant to share this life. I couldn't have stopped myself from falling in love with him any more than you could have stopped yourself from leaving. Loving him is effortless and natural. I kept telling him I needed to forget you to move on, but the truth is, he's already healed the hole you left, and there is no more room for you anymore." I pause and make sure he's truly listening.

"I won't apologize for being happy. That isn't my issue anymore. You should figure out your own feelings and a way to take care of them. This is making me uncomfortable and unhappy. I wanted closure, not more pain," I finish.

"I'm sorry. I just love you. I missed you, and you don't even seem to care," he mutters.

"I'm telling you that you are making me uncomfortable and unhappy, and your response is to turn that around and try to make me look after your feelings?" Shaking my head, I look away. "This was a waste of time. There's nothing to gain from this."

A car rolls up and the window slides down, revealing an older lady. "I'm so sorry. I think I'm lost. Can you help?"

I head over to her and crouch down into her window. She points out where she needs to be and I help her, grateful for the interruption. When she pulls away, I turn to look at Aro.

"You dropped this. It fell out of your pocket." He hands me my phone as he watches me. "I really do love you, Si, but you don't love me anymore. I guess I was stupid for trying, but I had to. I don't want to hurt you. Can we just sit for five minutes? I won't be rude or try anything, I promise. I just want . . . I guess I need to say goodbye to this, for old times' sake."

I hesitate before sitting down again. Hopefully after this, he will leave Sky and me alone because I know I will be the one walking away this time, and I'm happy about that.

The boy who was left at this bus stop all those years ago will be smiling, knowing I'm heading to a better place with someone who loves me.

CHAPTER 50
SKYLAR

I hope Bones is okay, but I have to trust him to handle this. That boy broke his heart, and he never had the chance to confront him about it. I hope he's doing the right thing, but even if he isn't and comes home hurt, I will be here to cheer him up.

"Thank you." I hand over the cash and wait as the florist prepares the sunflowers. I thought they might make him happy, and every time I give him flowers, the gleam in his eye reminds me that his man has never had anyone think of buying him something as simple as flowers just to see him smile.

My phone vibrates and I pull it out, scanning the text from him. A smile curves my lips just from seeing his name.

> Angel: I'm done. I don't want to go home yet. Let's meet here instead and just enjoy the water.

I put my phone away when the florist reappears and take the bouquet. "Thank you."

"No problem. I hope they like them."

I wave as I head back to my car. After putting the flowers in my passenger seat, I put in the location and drive over.

It's near a bridge not too far from here. Kids go there during the day to skate and hang out, but it's quiet at night, peaceful. Maybe he needed that. Parking a little ways down, since it's mostly a pedestrian area, I walk along the riverside, searching for him, holding the flowers in my hand.

"Angel?" I call, pulling my phone out. I dial, but it doesn't connect. Frowning, I glance down. Did he forget to charge it again? I scan the area and walk farther down.

He said he would be here, so he will. Maybe he's late?

Pursing my lips, I wander as I wait, the bridge blocking the wind. The water is peaceful tonight with the moon reflecting on it, and I eye the graffiti and tags with a smile, remembering when I used to do the same.

A crunch of gravel under what sounds like a foot makes me frown and step back. I strain my eyes as I search the darkness beyond. The hair on the back of my neck stands on end, and old instincts come roaring back.

"Who's there?" I demand, dropping the flowers to my side as I debate if I should go or not, but if Bones comes and doesn't see me, he might get worried.

Conall steps out from the darkness, a shadow emerging from the rigid structure. "Hello, Skylar." He lifts his arm, and I freeze when I see the gun flash in the moonlight. "Let's talk."

"What do you want?" I snap, refusing to be intimidated, but I keep my gaze on the gun.

"You know what I want. Let's not fuck around." He gestures for me to walk deeper into the shadows. I take two steps and stop as he wags his finger. "Close enough."

"I thought you were in jail," I scoff.

"I got out early. You aren't the only one with a good lawyer." His eyes are wild, and he has the look of a man who's been pushed too far. I've seen it before on the streets. He has nothing left to lose, and it makes him more dangerous than anybody else.

"If you fire that gun, your career is over—"

"It's already over." He laughs. "They'll find the evidence soon enough. That stupid fuck wasn't sly enough—"

"Who?" I ask. If he wasn't acting alone, I need to know who else was involved.

"Some blond-haired freak. He approached me. I think his name was Aro. We made a deal. It seems he wants your boy, and I wanted you gone. Two birds, one car, you see? We fucked with their car so you'd crash and die. He'd get your boy, and I'd get the title."

"All this for a championship?" I shake my head, stepping forward with my hands held out. "Was it worth it?"

"I'm the champion!" he shouts, his chest heaving. "I'm nothing without it. If you win, I'll lose it all. Why couldn't you stop? I just wanted to scare you, but now . . . now I'm going to kill you." His hand shakes.

Despite the anger flowing through him, he's never killed before, never pulled a trigger, and he's hesitating. I use it to my advantage, stepping forward again.

"Stop fucking moving!"

I can smell the alcohol on him from here.

"Your boy is safe. I don't have any issues with him. He's with his ex right now. I just needed to lure you here."

"So you're really going to kill me?" I refuse to cower, and my voice comes out strong. It's not the first time I've faced a gun. "Then what? It isn't too late to change your mind. You'll get some time for what you've done, but there's a difference between trying to fix a race and murder. You aren't a killer, Conall." I step forward again and see his arm wavering.

"Racing is all I have. It's all I am," he whispers. "It's the only thing I have!" he yells. "I can't let you take that away. Not some street thug."

"Conall," I say slowly as I step forward again, glancing from his face to the gun. If I can get it away from him, it's over. "Drop the gun and let's talk about this. We can figure this out. There's a place for both of us. My success does not negate yours—" I lunge for the gun, and he reacts.

I dodge left and then right before sprinting toward him. His eyes widen, and his finger flexes on the trigger. I hear it before I feel it.

I jerk from the force of the bullet. It spins me around, and I hit the ground. The flowers fall from my useless arm as it goes numb, and Conall steps toward me, aiming the gun at my head. "For what it's worth, I'm sorry, Skylar."

I lift my head, staring at his face, and I know this is the end. I'm going to die here on the streets where I always belonged, so close to ultimate happiness I can taste it. I don't close my eyes. If he's going to shoot me, he'll look me in the eye as he does it. I accept it, sending my love to my boy, hoping he knows he was the greatest thing I ever won. No race or championship could compare to his heart, and no matter how short our time was together, I was happy being his.

A roar fills the air and a blur flies past me, tackling Conall to the ground. The gun skids away as they tumble before getting to their feet, and I realize who it is.

"Bones!" I yell, but he doesn't spare me a look. He grabs Conall's hand and snaps it before throwing him over his shoulder. Conall hits the ground hard, and Bones rushes over to me. His eyes are filled with tears as his hands flutter over me, unsure how to stop the bleeding, before he helps me into a sitting position. I lean into him as he staunches the blood.

"I came as soon as I realized what he did. Babe, your shoulder—"

"It's fine. It's a through and through," I rasp. "Just a flesh wound. Angel, go get the gun."

He glances over, searching for it, but it's hidden in the darkness. Conall is groaning on the ground, holding his broken hand to his chest with a whine.

I scan the area before my gaze lands on a flash of brightness in the shadows. For some reason, I focus on the half-crushed sunflowers, my blood now covering the petals as Bones worries next to me.

There's a scrambling noise, and I look back to see Conall reaching for the gun, which was hidden under some trash. He lifts it and swings it our way with his other hand, aiming at Bones, whose eyes widen.

Leaping to my feet, I run right at Conall. His eyes widen as I tackle him back to the ground. The gun goes flying again as it shoots, but I don't feel it hit me anywhere as I slam my fists into his face. Blood sprays me as he screams, trying to block the blows, but all I feel is rage.

He aimed the gun at my boy.

"Nobody touches him!" I yell as I slam my hands into his face over and over. Bones break, and he stops fighting, but I keep hitting him until hands touch me.

"Sky, please, your shoulder."

Panting, I spit on Conall's face and stumble to my feet, letting Bones catch me and start to lead me away as I lean on him.

Conall sputters, choking on his own blood, so I let my boy pull me away, knowing he's done.

The sounds of engines reach us, more than I've ever heard before, and Bones and I turn. Lights shine over us as people climb from cars with their cameras out, Sanjay at the front.

"Sanjay?" I ask.

"Saw this shitbag buying a piece off the street and thought I'd follow him. I had a feeling he was the one fucking with you." I frown, and he grins. "You might have left the streets, Sky, but we never left you. You're family."

I smile in gratitude and let Bones help me to my feet. "It's over," I tell Conall, who pushes to his knees, his face covered in blood.

"No, I have nothing else to lose, but you do. You took what I love most. I'll do the same to you!" He grabs the gun before I can. I don't have enough time to react, but I push Bones to the side as he aims. Suddenly, Conall is hit from the side.

He smacks against the ground hard, and the gun is snatched from him and pointed at his head.

My eyes widen as Alek glances at me and nods. "Bones texted us. Figured you would need some backup. Sorry we're late."

"Police are on their way," Evan calls as he jogs over, looking us over. "Are you okay?"

"Peachy," I joke as Bones slaps my side.

Sirens fill the air just then, and I groan as I look at Bones. "Do you think we'll ever have a moment of peace?"

"Probably not." He smiles as he kisses me. "Come on, babe, let's get you looked over . . . again. Maybe after this we could go a week without injuries?"

"No promises." I grin as I scoop up his flowers. "These were for you. Sorry they are bloody."

"They are perfect," he replies.

We sit in the back of the ambulance, where Bones wraps his blanket around me. I'll be going to the hospital for the gunshot, but I was right. It went through and should heal pretty fast. I was lucky.

We watch as Conall is led away and put in a police car. They'll have questions, and I have no doubt camera crews will be here before long, so I nod at Sanjay who recorded the entire thing. "Better bounce. It wouldn't be good for you to end up on the news."

"You got it, my man. See you soon. Win us that title, yeah? We're all rooting for you." He slaps my good arm, nods at Bones, and rolls out. They came because they thought I was in trouble. It isn't something I ever thought I would see or that the police would just let them go, but I guess they have bigger fish to fry right now.

"Sir, I need to confirm some things," an officer says to Bones, who nods and looks at me.

"I'll be right back, okay?" I nod and watch Bones join the police officer, while Alek sits at my side. He nudges my uninjured shoulder, and I smile.

"Thanks for coming, brother," I murmur.

"Eh, I figured my life would be boring without you. Plus, training a new racer? No thanks." He winks.

I smile, but it fades as I stare into his face. Alek and I were always friends, bonded by trauma and engines, but over the last year, we have become extremely close.

"I mean it. Thank you, brother. We might not be brothers by blood, but by actions. You're always in my corner, ready to help or lend a hand. If I could choose anyone in this world to be my family, to be my brother, it would be you. You might not show it, but I know you feel the same way. You have Evan, and I have Bones, but we'll always have each other too."

He smiles softly and rubs my head. "You've always been my brother, Sky, and nobody messes with our family—not a serial killer or a fucked-up racer with a god complex."

"I'd really like some downtime without being stabbed or shot though," I admit.

"I mean, who lets themselves get shot?" Evan jokes as he heads over, Bones at his side.

"You guys almost have matching wounds now." Bones grins. "But don't go getting shot all the time, you hear me?" He points at me, his smile gone.

"Yes, angel, sorry." I wince.

He grumbles but relaxes as he looks around. "So, it's really over? He was behind it all?"

"Not all," I admit, and he looks at me with a frown. I wish I could spare him this too, but it seems all truths are coming out in Pine Valley tonight.

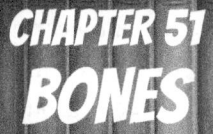

CHAPTER 51
BONES

"Skylar, don't let me see you here again, okay?" The officer nods, and Sky laughs as we head out of the precinct.

We spent hours at the hospital before he was cleared, and then we came to do our interviews, knowing the process too well. "I guess this is the first time you haven't had to bail me out." He grins as he hooks my arm with his good one. "This is where our love started." He wiggles his eyebrows, making me laugh.

He's going to be okay.

When I saw that gun aimed at him, I felt fear unlike anything I had ever experienced before. I didn't even realize my phone was off until I left Aro and the bus stop behind. When I turned it on and saw the text, I called a taxi and headed right there. I had a horrible feeling, and I'm so glad I got there in time. It could have been a lot worse.

I didn't even know Conall was free, but he went straight after Skylar. The police said he knew he was going to end up inside and had nothing else left to lose. When you make something your entire life, losing it could send you off the deep end, and I think that's what happened to Conall.

He isn't the only one who needs to be dealt with though.

"Are you sure about this?" Sky asks as we walk toward his car.

"I'm sure. Let's end all this so we can start the rest of our lives—no more crashes, threats, or guns, just happiness."

"Sounds good to me, baby. After all this, we need a vacation. Let's go somewhere warm where you can wear nothing," he teases as I open his door and help him. He doesn't need me to, but I like taking care of him, and after everything he's been through recently, Sky deserves to be pampered and taken care of for once.

I put his seat belt on for him. The doctor wants him to rest his arm, so it's going to be touch and go until he's fully healed. I know he's worried about what that means for racing, but right now all I care about is that he's alive and with me.

I kiss his forehead before I lean back and smile. "Yes, we'll go on vacation, but only if you wear a speedo."

"Baby, this doesn't fit in a Speedo," he jokes, making me roll my eyes as I shut his door.

When I'm behind the wheel, I glance over to see him watching me with a dopey smile. "You look good in my car. You also look good in my clothes and my bed, but even more so in my arms."

"Drugs make you loopy," I tease, but I lean over and kiss him, unable to resist. "But don't worry because I'm not going anywhere." Turning the engine on, I pull out.

I blow on the spoon and then hold it out, keeping my hand cupped under it so it doesn't spill as he wraps his lips around the utensil and takes a bite of soup. I spoon another and blow on it before offering it to him again. His eyes are locked on me, and the rest of the restaurant is forgotten. This table on the rooftop above the city has become our place, and after the shitty few days I've had, we wanted someplace good. Besides, he won't expect it here.

"Uh, Si?" comes his hesitant voice. I heard him approach, but I don't spare him a glance as I lift Sky's glass and help him take a sip of water. It's important he eats and drinks with his meds.

He holds my hand as he leans back, offering Aro a smug look. Sky doesn't need to be jealous because all I feel for Aro now is resentment and anger.

I almost lost Skylar because of him.

"You texted Skylar from my phone." I hold up my hand as he tries to speak. "You almost got us both killed." His eyes widen. "Yes, I suspected you didn't know about the gun, but we both could have ended up dead. Skylar very nearly did. I don't know what you were thinking, but it stops now. I've made my stance clear, but let me make something else very fucking clear—you will leave Skylar alone or I will make your life a living hell."

"I'm sorry, Si," he says. "I just wanted a chance. I knew with him here, I wouldn't get that. I saw the way you looked at him."

"If you're sorry, then you'll do the right thing," I snap.

"You aren't going to tell?" he asks me, his eyes wide.

"Not me, but they will." I jerk my head at the police nearby, and then I turn away. "Do yourself a favor and tell them everything. Now leave, I'm spending time with my boyfriend." I feel him hesitate, so I glare at him.

"I knew I didn't stand a chance the first time I saw you together, but I had to try." He looks at Sky. "He never looked at me the way he looks at you. You would have run away with me, Bones, but you never would have stayed with me here, facing your dad. You did for him." He nods. "I hope you both stay happy and healthy." He turns and does the only good thing he has ever done for me.

He hands himself over to the police to help their investigation and pay for what he did.

"Hey, angel." I turn back to Sky, who smiles. "You did so well."

I nod, glancing at the food. "I'm sorry my past got you into trouble."

"Nah, both of our lives are messy. It makes living fun. Besides, I understand killing for you. If I were him, I would be the same way. Now, how about you go back to feeding me so I can feed you something else later?" He wiggles his eyebrows as I laugh.

He's the only person who has ever made me laugh when I feel like crying.

Aro was right though. I would never run away with Skylar.

This is our life, our home, and I'll stand at his side through it all.

I'll face down the entire world if I have to.

Love makes people brave and a little bit crazy, but I realize I don't mind as I stare into his eyes.

CHAPTER 52
SKYLAR

My boy is so embarrassed, it's hilarious.

I whistle and cheer with everyone else, clapping and loudly shouting his name. Rows upon rows of chairs are placed on the lawn of Pine Valley College as they prepare to honor my boy.

It seems they wanted to make something good out of a bad situation, and Bones was given an outstanding person award for all his work in the college and local area—teaching self-defense, tutoring, helping catch a serial killer, and then saving his boyfriend. It's a PR excuse for the college, but I can't help but grin as he stands on stage, his face red and eyes wide as he listens to the dean praise him and list all the good he has done.

His father isn't here, but I make sure Bones never feels his absence. Alek and Evan sit at my side, with Lally and Alice. Countless others are here as well, and there are camera crews everywhere, since Bones is practically a celebrity now.

"Silas Townsend, also known around campus as Bones, has become a figure many look up to. He has dedicated his spare time to teaching self-defense classes both off and on campus, fought for cleaner campus initiatives, and is also a champion of the free tutor program. We are honored to have Silas as a student. Recently, I'm sure you have seen his heroics on the local racetrack while saving his partner. This isn't the only time Silas has stepped in during a difficult situation. This campus is still plagued with grief over the loss of one of our own, and Silas is one of the survivors of that terrible night. Everyone, including the police officers, praised his poise, strength, and love for his friends. That is why we are here today, to honor this excellent young man who is a wonderful addition to our college." He steps up to Bones, shaking his hand and posing for pictures, but Bones isn't smiling, and I know he'll regret it.

"Yes, angel! Work that camera!" I yell, and laughter breaks out. I see his lips twitch as he fights to focus on the camera. "That's it! Think *Vogue!*"

He finally breaks into a wide smile, and I can't help but cheer louder. His eyes find me in the crowd, and his lips purse in a happy smile as he winks at me. I wink right back and clap. I finally sit as he heads back to his chair for the dean to continue speaking about pride and inclusiveness on campus

"Did you hear?" Alek murmurs, applauding as he leans in.

"Hear what?" I ask, clapping my hands. My left arm still aches slightly, but it's healing every day. Bones and I have been in a bubble, our very own little world, until now.

"The championship is back on, and the investigation is closed. The final race will be in two weeks . . . . So, Skylar Warren, are you ready to be a champion and get everything you ever wanted?"

I grin at him before glancing back at my boy. "I already have it all right here, but champion has a nice ring to it."

I roll my shoulder back, testing its strength. I'm as close to fully healed as I'm going to get in this short time. I'm worried it will affect my driving today, but it's now or never. They pushed the race back as much as they could—I think they felt bad about what happened—but

they have to hold it before the world championship starts, so today is the day.

Blizzard entered another racer, and he seems like a good guy. I don't blame the entire team for what happened, even though some do. Red Check's driver is back as well, and I'm glad we are all here. I don't want the win to be handed to me—I want to do it the right way.

"Are you ready for this?" Mackie asks as we stand in the pit, holding our helmets in one hand as we stare out at the track.

"Yeah. It has to go better than last time, right?" I joke.

"Let's bring it home." He grins. "Sky . . . there is no one else I would want to race with. I'm glad we are partners."

"Me too," I admit. "I never knew I needed one, but I'm glad I have you. It wouldn't feel right winning without you."

"Then let's get you that title and prove everyone wrong." He bumps my good shoulder and steps out as the crowd goes wild. I let him have his moment as I wait.

"Excuse me, have you seen my boyfriend?" I turn, and Bones mock gasps. "Don't tell him, but you look so hot in your suit. Can I get your number?"

Smirking, I head over and tug him in for a kiss. "I'll let you have anything you want, angel."

"Promises, promises," he teases as he leans into me. "Are you nervous?"

"Nah, I belong out there." I wink, but he arches a brow, and I sigh. "Okay, a little. I don't want to let anyone down."

"Skylar Warren, you are incapable of letting anybody down," he states. "It isn't who you are, so go out there and show them that. Make them remember your name, and then come back here and let me scream it so they know whom you belong to."

"Dirty angel." I press my forehead to his. "Thank you for seeing me."

"I'll be right here," he vows before he kisses me. "See you at that finish line. Don't crash this time."

"Not a chance." I grin, thankful he came. I know it's hard for him to watch me head out there and race again after what happened last time, but my boy is strong, and he's here to support me. I walk backward, and our fingers touch until the last second before I turn and head onto the track, knowing he'll be cheering for me in the stands. It's how it works between us—we support and celebrate the other's achievements. He's my support system, and I know I wouldn't be on this track without him.

I wave and smile for the cameras, and I wink as I pass Noah and Mackie as I walk to my car. I'm just putting my helmet on when the driver from Red Check heads my way.

"I just wanted to say thank you. I have a wife and kid at home who are your biggest fans now. I'd be dead if you didn't make that sacrifice. You're an amazing man, Warren, and I'm honored to compete with you."

I knock his arm. "I just did the right thing. Let's show them what you're capable of, yeah? No ruined cars this time."

"My wife will appreciate that," he jokes as he backs up and heads to his car.

I nod at both Blizzard drivers before putting my helmet on and sliding into the driver's seat. I'm starting at the back, but that's fine.

I'm a hunter, after all, and I'm hunting that title.

It will be mine.

I rev my engine and glance at Mackie. He gives me the okay, and then Noah's voice comes. "Alright, boys, I'm getting déjà vu, but no accidents today, okay? I want both of your asses to cross that finish line, even if it isn't in first place. I have a very nervous Bones and team here, so play it safe."

"When have I ever done that?" I joke.

"Nah, we're getting that podium," Mackie adds.

I hear Noah curse, but he comes back. "Fine, then let's do this. One last time, boys. Show them what Starfire is made of."

Smirking, I stare forward as the lights flash red and then amber.

Anticipation floods me, as does a slice of fear, but I don't let it take root.

Green.

I'm off, chasing them down. I manage to climb a few places on the straightaway, but we get jammed at the first corner. I slip past a few more, gaining on the top five cars as we speed, wanting that title.

My heart starts to race as I come upon the accident site. The track is clear, and there aren't even any marks to indicate it happened, but I remember. My hands curl tighter on the wheel, recalling the weightless feeling and the burn from the flames.

As I hit the corner where it happened, I slow slightly and they pounce, using my weakness. Snarling, I speed after them, managing to catch them on the second lap, and this time, I don't slow at the turn. The past is the past, and it can stay there.

As I cross the line and head into the third and final lap, Mackie levels out with me. There are two cars in front of us—one Blizzard and one Red Check—just like last time. I respect them, but that title is ours. I nod at Mackie, and he slips past me. It's a move we haven't used yet, which is why we saved it. I back him up, like I'm pushing him for their title, and they focus on blocking him on the first two turns. While they are focused on him, I take a turn fast and speed past them, and then I drive off. I can practically hear them cursing as they give pursuit, and Noah screams in my ear.

Mackie manages to slip past Blizzard, and then it's between us three.

"You've got this, Mackie." I believe in him. He's one of the best racers I've ever met, and I have no doubt he will overtake me one day. He just has this edge to him.

"Go, go, go!" Noah cheers as we hit the final stretch. I'm ahead, and I glance back, seeing Mackie level with Toma.

Come on, come on.

I chant it as they start to catch up, their bumpers to mine. Red Check tries to move to my left and I block him, and then Mackie slips up on my right. We hit the gas and speed forward. I cross the line just seconds before him, Mackie right on my tail, then Red Check and Blizzard.

We slow our cars and stop on the next lap with everyone else.

The crowd is screaming, and the screens are already playing our finish as I climb from the car.

Ripping my helmet off, I hit Mackie's arms and swing him around, ignoring the twinge, before we pull away. I thank the other racers as they head over, and then I run to the barrier where my boy waits.

He's smiling, holding his arms open, and I swing him over the barrier and kiss him in front of everyone. "You did it," he whispers.

"Did you doubt me?" I grin just as Alek, Evan, and Noah reach us. Mackie joins our group, and soon, we are all celebrating.

Noah holds up a Champagne bottle, pops it open, and covers us as we laugh, and it's the happiest I've ever been.

I'm a champion, but as I look at Bones, I know with or without that title, I'd still have him, and that's all I need.

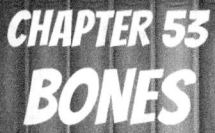

CHAPTER 53
BONES

Today has been a whirlwind, and I watch as Skylar takes the title he deserves more than anyone. He completes interview after interview and takes pictures on the track before he's finally released, and it's time to celebrate.

There's already a crowd in the Starfire garage when we arrive, and Noah goes to entertain with Mackie, Alek, Evan, Alice, and Lally while Sky leads us to the locker room.

"I need to shower. You can help me." He grins.

I roll my eyes, but as soon as that door is open, I'm on him, sliding my hand down into his pants. "I promised my champion a reward, didn't I?"

"That you did." He backs me up into a stall and reaches in, turning the shower on before he pulls my hands up and presses them above me, careful of his shoulder. His mouth crashes onto mine, and I kiss him back, tasting all that is Skylar. My hands curl into his as he kisses down my cheek to my neck. My cock jerks in my pants, demanding his attention.

The party is in full swing, but neither of us care as I tug my hands from his grip. We remove each other's clothes and stumble into the shower, pulling the curtain shut as his back hits the wall. Water sprays across us as we kiss. I feel his scars, new and old, and he kisses my hands as he turns us and holds them above me again.

"You're all I thought about behind that wheel," he growls against my neck as I lift my leg and wrap it around his hip, giving him better access. "Getting across that line and getting to you, being home inside you where I belong." His tongue traces the water along my collarbone before he lifts his dark gaze to me. "Winning means nothing without you, angel. Everything I am and own are yours. You just have to ask."

"All I want is you inside me right now. Show me how fast a champion can be," I challenge him.

His eyes narrow, and he presses me against the cold wall. He's so fucking beautiful, I roll against him, needing him inside me more than I need my next breath.

"Well?" I prompt when he just stares. "They are all waiting, and so am I."

He kisses me again, interlacing his hands with mine above our heads as he pushes into me with one smooth, hard thrust. I'm needy, but he's big, and it hurts in the best way. I whimper into his mouth as he pulls out and slams back into me.

Our kiss turns frantic as we come together, setting a hard rhythm. The sound of our skin slapping is loud as he breaks the kiss to breathe, his dick hitting that spot inside me that has me crying his name and arching up off the wall.

Groaning, he pulls from my body and turns me, then he powers back into me from behind. His mouth slides down my throat, biting and sucking as pleasure courses through me. My balls tighten to the point of pain and my cock throbs.

"Sky, my Sky." I push back, so close I can taste it.

"Come for me, angel. Come for your champion," he demands as he bites my neck, and that sharp stab of pain sends me over the edge. I scream his name as I come on myself and the wall. He groans into my ear as he hammers into me, keeping me upright as he ruins me.

"Fuck, I love you, angel. Love the way you scream for me, love the way you come for me, love the way your body was made for me. I love you so fucking much, and we will be right here after every championship. Won't we?"

I nod rapidly, pushing back, and he groans. Turning my head, I meet his lips and kiss him deeply, swallowing his groan as he yanks me all the way back on his dick and comes inside me.

Our kiss turns leisurely, and when we pull back, he's grinning. "Now let me clean up my boy."

We leave the locker room hand in hand, our hair wet. I have no doubt everyone knows what we were doing, but we don't care. We do, however, freeze when we round the corner by Noah's office and find him and Mackie kissing.

Sky's eyes widen, and I hear him gearing up to cheer, so I cover his mouth and drag him away. It isn't our place. Instead, I guide him over to celebrate with his friends and family. I let him feel the love and support so he knows where he belongs.

We dance, sing, and drink. The food flows, courtesy of Mama, and even Sanjay and some of Sky's other friends turn up. I can't help but laugh as he twerks on me and loudly declares to everyone that I'm his future husband.

Mackie appears sometime later, looking dazed and embarrassed. Noah follows shortly after, looking every inch rattled. Hopefully they will figure their shit out because it's worth it.

I find Skylar. His eyes are already on me despite everyone surrounding him.

It's so fucking worth it.

CHAPTER 54
SKYLAR

Two months later . . .

"Skylar Warren, what are you doing?" I wince as Bones's sharp voice fills the air.

I thought he was still sleeping. I freeze in the entryway of my apartment—not the one I bought to be close, but my actual apartment. He moved in here a few weeks after I won the race. We can't bear to be apart. We know we are in this together forever, so why wait and waste time?

"Uh, nothing?" I reply innocently, and his eyes narrow on my hands, so I shove the plant behind my back. He prowls my way, and I try to back up, but I hit the door. He feints right then left and grabs it.

I wince as he brings it into the light. "Sky, what is this?" he asks, holding up the plant.

"Uh, a new friend?" I say. "To go with your other one?" I bluff as I start to sweat.

"The one that's dead?" he snaps, annoyance flashing across his handsome face before it seems to click. "Don't tell me . . . Do you keep replacing it when I kill it?"

"Angel." I wrap my arms around him, ignoring his struggle. It isn't

365

his fault, he just doesn't have a green thumb, but he kept getting so sad when the flowers I got died after a few days. I made the mistake of buying him a plant, but when it started to die since he couldn't care for it, I panicked and replaced it.

This is the tenth time. Honestly, it's impressive how often he has killed them.

"You replaced it, didn't you? I knew it was dead!" He breaks from my arms and throws himself on the couch, covering his face. "Why? Why would you do that? I was so proud it was still alive."

Putting the plant down, I head over and crouch before him. "Angel."

He drops his hands, and tears swim in his eyes. "I know I'm being unreasonable." He sniffs as he cries. "But what does it say about me, huh?"

"What, angel?" I ask gently.

"I can't even keep a plant alive, Skylar. What does that say about me as a person?"

"It means you're not a plant person and I should have bought a fake one," I reply.

"No, it means I'm shit. I can't even look after a plant, Sky! I can't even keep that stupid cute plant alive. I suck at everything. I'm so stupid."

I see the fear in his gaze, and I know it's about more than the plant, so I wrap my arms around him. "You'll learn," I promise. "You aren't stupid. You are incredible. I will buy a thousand plants if it will make you happy, but this doesn't mean anything, angel. Some people aren't meant to have plants. It means nothing more. Hell, I can't even remember to change the toilet paper. It's just who we are, and I love you."

He drops his hands again, still looking far too sad. "Why does nature hate me?" he mutters.

"I don't know, but I love you," I reply, smiling sweetly.

He scoffs and wipes his face, and the glimpse of the scars on his hands makes my heart ache.

He pouts. "I wouldn't love me. I'm a plant killer."

God, I love this boy so much. I can't wait to put my ring on his finger and adopt a couple hundred babies . . . or maybe not, since he will cry if they get sick, and I hate seeing him cry.

"Come on." Tugging him to his feet, I remove my jacket as I turn on the radio. It's something we've started. Whenever we're sad or mad, we dance. We are both shit at it, but it's funny, and it reminds us why we keep fighting.

The beat flows through the room, and he rolls his eyes but starts to move, and when it switches to a faster song, I pull out the sprinkler move, and then the one-legged chicken.

His childlike laughter fills the apartment, and this is the most perfect moment—just the two of us with our futures spread in front of us and our pasts behind us. We are still so young with so much life to lead. I will cherish every moment so forty seconds become forty years, and I'll still be right here, dancing in our kitchen with him.

Everyone is always obsessed with happy endings, but me? I'm more interested in the story. I don't want to rush to my happily ever after. I want to live it.

EPILOGUE

BONES

"Sorry we're late," Alek says as he sits on the bench opposite me. The coffee shop is a cute, little place, located in the park where Alek and Evan like to hang. It's become a Sunday ritual for us to meet up. Sometimes Alice joins us, and today is one of those days. She smiles at me and accepts the iced coffee I push her way.

"Where's Sky?" Evan asks as he sips his drink.

I nod my head, and they follow my gaze. Sky is crouched in front of a bush, pointing at it. "How could you not love him? He's incredible. Why are you doing this to him?" he yells at the foliage.

I sip my coffee, and I feel the others staring. "Uh, Bones, what happened?"

"Sky bought me a plant. I somehow killed it and got a little upset about it. I jokingly said nature hated me, and now this is where we are."

"He's amazing, you green asshole!" Skylar yells as I sit with the others, completely unfazed.

"Okay . . ." Alek blinks and looks back at me. "How's moving in with crazy going? Are you sick of him yet?"

"Not really," I answer, and I'm not. I've never been so happy. I

369

have someone with me at all times, a life, and an apartment filled with warmth. He gave me things I never knew I was missing. "How's it going at the garage?" I ask.

"Good. We are prepping for the next championship. We all want the world title now," he replies.

"I have to ask, are we just ignoring what's happening over there?" Alice questions.

I glance over to see Skylar kicking and hitting the bush.

"Cool, just had to check," she mutters as she looks around and leans closer. "Are you sure you want to be in love with this guy? Blink twice if you need help."

Grinning, I glance back to see him pointing at the plant once more before turning and waving at me, wearing a smile so bright, I can't help but wave back. "Yes, yes I do."

"Okay, had to ask," she scoffs. "You're both crazy."

Sky sits next to me, draping his arm over my shoulders. "Hey, guys, when did you get here?"

"Right in the middle of you losing to a bush," Evan scoffs.

"Nah, I won." He winks at me and kisses my palm, something he's taken to doing all the time. They are scarred, but it's just another part of me. I was scared he wouldn't want me to touch him anymore, but if anything, he's obsessed with my scars. How could I ever hate anything he loves so much?

My phone vibrates, and I know it's my father again, so I ignore it. It seems like he's determined to be part of my life now. I don't know if I want him to be or not, so I'm taking time to figure out what I want before I make a decision. I'm happy, and that's all that matters. I spent years trying to please him, and now it's the other way around.

It isn't a bad feeling, but I know whatever I choose, my true family is right here.

Alek, Evan, and Sky are bent over his phone, looking over some sketches for their new campaign for Starfire, when Alice's phone rings. She grabs it, and I eye her as she answers it nervously.

"Tonight?" Alice meets my gaze, and I know why. "I'll be there."

"It's starting?" I ask, glancing at the others to make sure they aren't listening. I asked her to keep an eye out before everything went down.

"Yes, tonight. Don't worry. I've got this, Bones," she promises.

"Be safe, okay? I know we asked you as a part of Silent Rose, but don't put yourself in danger," I mutter.

"What are you talking about?" Evan asks curiously.

"Oh, nothing," Alice blurts out too fast, but then she distracts them by asking about Evan's internship.

Alek is watching her, though, with worried eyes. "How's Lally?" he asks.

She freezes, swinging her eyes to me and then Evan. "Uh, she's okay."

I know what she won't tell them.

Lally is not okay, not in the least, and Alice is determined to save her from the mess she got herself in.

I should tell Alek and the others, but these are Lally's and Alice's lives, and I have a feeling they need to break to be put back together.

ABOUT K.A. KNIGHT

K.A Knight is an USA Today bestselling indie author trying to get all of the stories and characters out of her head, writing the monsters that you love to hate. She loves reading and devours every book she can get her hands on, and she also has a worrying caffeine addiction.

She leads her double life in a sleepy English town, where she spends her days writing like a crazy person.

Read more at K.A Knight's website or join her Facebook Reader Group.
Sign up for exclusive content and my newsletter here
http://eepurl.com/drLLoj

OTHER BOOKS BY K.A. KNIGHT

CONTEMPORARY

LEGENDS AND LOVE *CONTEMPORARY RH*

Revolt

Rebel

Riot

PRETTY LIARS *CONTEMPORARY RH*

Unstoppable

Unbreakable

PINE VALLEY COLLEGE *CONTEMPORARY*

Racing Hearts

Crashing Hearts

DEN OF VIPERS UNIVERSE STANDALONES

Scarlett Limerence *CONTEMPORARY*

Nadia's Salvation *CONTEMPORARY*

Alena's Revenge *CONTEMPORARY*

Den of Vipers *CONTEMPORARY RH*

Gangsters and Guns (Co-Write with Loxley Savage) *CONTEMPORARY RH*

FORBIDDEN READS *(STANDALONES)*

Daddy's Angel *CONTEMPORARY*

Stepbrothers' Darling *CONTEMPORARY RH*

STANDALONES

The Standby *CONTEMPORARY*

Diver's Heart *CONTEMPORARY RH*

DYSTOPIAN

THEIR CHAMPION SERIES *Dystopian RH*

The Wasteland

The Summit

The Cities

The Nations

Their Champion Coloring Book

Their Champion - the omnibus

The Forgotten

The Lost

The Damned

Their Champion Companion - the omnibus

PARANORMAL

THE LOST COVEN SERIES *PNR RH*

Aurora's Coven

Aurora's Betrayal

Book 3 - *coming soon..*

HER MONSTERS SERIES *PNR RH*

Rage

Hate

Book 3 - *coming soon..*

COURTS AND KINGS *PNR RH*

Court of Nightmares

Court of Death

Court of Beasts

Court of Heathens

THE FALLEN GODS SERIES *PNR*

Pretty Painful

Pretty Bloody

Pretty Stormy

Pretty Wild

Pretty Hot

Pretty Faces

Pretty Spelled

Fallen Gods - the omnibus 1

Fallen Gods - the omnibus 2

FORGOTTEN CITY *PNR*

Monstrous Lies

Monstrous Truths

Monstrous Ends

SCIENCE FICTION

DAWNBREAKER SERIES *SCI FI RH*

Voyage to Ayama

Dreaming of Ayama

STANDALONES

Crown of Stars *SCI FI RH*

SHARED WORLD PROJECTS

Blade of Iris - Mafia Wars *CONTEMPORARY RH*

CO-WRITES

CO-AUTHOR PROJECTS - *Erin O'Kane*

HER FREAKS SERIES *PNR Dystopian RH*

Circus Save Me

Taming The Ringmaster

Walking the Tightrope

Her Freaks Series - the omnibus

THE WILD BOYS SERIES *CONTEMPORARY RH*

The Wild Interview

The Wild Tour

The Wild Finale

The Wild Boys - the omnibus

STANDALONES

Kingdom of Crowns and Daggers *Dark Fantasy RH*

The Hero Complex *PNR RH*

Dark Temptations *Collection of Short Stories, ft. One Night Only & Circus Saves Christmas*

CO-AUTHOR PROJECTS - *Ivy Fox*

Deadly Love Series *CONTEMPORARY*

Deadly Affair

Deadly Match

Deadly Encounter

CO-AUTHOR PROJECTS - *Kendra Moreno*

STANDALONES

Stolen Trophy *CONTEMPORARY RH*

Fractured Shadows *PNR RH*

Shadowed Heart

Burn Me *PNR*

Cirque Obscurum *PNR RH*

CO-AUTHOR PROJECTS - *Loxley Savage*

THE FORSAKEN SERIES *SCI FI RH*

Capturing Carmen

Stealing Shiloh

Harboring Harlow

STANDALONES

Gangsters and Guns *CONTEMPORARY*, IN DEN OF VIPERS' UNIVERSE

OTHER CO-WRITES

Shipwreck Souls *(with Kendra Moreno & Poppy Woods)*

The Horror Emporium *(with Kendra Moreno & Poppy Woods)*

AUDIOBOOKS

The Wasteland

The Summit

The Cities

The Nations

Rage

Hate

Den of Vipers *(From Podium Audio)*

Gangsters and Guns *(From Podium Audio)*

Daddy's Angel *(From Podium Audio)*

Stepbrothers' Darling *(From Podium Audio)*

Blade of Iris *(From Podium Audio)*

Deadly Affair *(From Podium Audio)*

Deadly Match *(From Podium Audio)*

Deadly Encounter *(From Podium Audio)*

Stolen Trophy *(From Podium Audio)*

Crown of Stars *(From Podium Audio)*

Monstrous Lies *(From Podium Audio)*

Monstrous Truth *(From Podium Audio)*

Monstrous Ends *(From Podium Audio)*

Court of Nightmares *(From Podium Audio)*

Court of Death *(From Podium Audio)*

Unstoppable *(From Podium Audio)*

Unbreakable *(From Podium Audio)*

Fractured Shadows *(From Podium Audio)*

Shadowed Heart *(From Podium Audio)*

Revolt *(From Podium Audio)*

Rebel *(From Podium Audio)*

Riot *(From Podium Audio)* Coming soon…

Cirque Obscurum *(From Podium Audio)* Coming soon…

Kingdom of Crowns and Daggers *(From Podium Audio)*

FIND AN ERROR?

Please email this information to thenuttyformatter1@gmail.com:

- *the author name*
- *title of the book*
- *screenshot of the error*
- *suggested correction*